Knowledge Quickening

Knowledge Quickening

The Nememiah Chronicles, Book II

D.S. WILLIAMS

Copyright (C) 2015 D.S. Williams
Layout Copyright (C) 2019 Next Chapter

Published 2019 by Sanguine – A Next Chapter Imprint
Cover art by Cover Mint
This book is a work of fiction. Names, characters, places, and incidents are the product of the author's imagination or are used fictitiously. Any resemblance to actual events, locales, or persons, living or dead, is purely coincidental.
All rights reserved. No part of this book may be reproduced or transmitted in any form or by any means, electronic or mechanical, including photocopying, recording, or by any information storage and retrieval system, without the author's permission.

CONTENTS

1	Peril	1
2	Deep Trouble	8
3	Knowledge Revealed	16
4	Conal	21
5	Allied	32
6	Entanglements	41
7	Transformation	48
8	Rescued	58
9	Desire	67
10	The Pack	75
11	The Tremaines	83
12	Tempers	90
13	Pacts	101

14	Home	113
15	Discussions	118
16	Complications of Love	128
17	Recovery	139
18	Defense	149
19	First Date	158
20	Strengthening	169
21	Holden	177
22	Running	185
23	Salvation	190
24	New Beginnings	198
25	Nonny	208
26	Talk of Angels	215
27	Epimetheus Vander	224
28	Confusion	234
29	Training	242
30	Demons	253
31	The Longest Night	261
32	Come Unto Me	267

33	Pain, Hurt & Agony	274
34	Enchantments	282
35	A Light Bulb Moment	292
36	Another	300
37	Reinforcements	306
38	Traitor	314
39	Plans	323
40	Confessions	331
41	Sfantu Drâghici	338
42	In the Devil's Lair	353
43	Recovery Operation	363
44	Blood	373

Chapter 1

Peril

It was patently obvious that I was in trouble. Serious trouble.

Regaining consciousness, I rolled over, blinking against the stark brightness in the room. I found myself lying on an old mattress, the dark cover stained and soiled. The room smelled musty, like worn socks that had lain in the bottom of the laundry basket for too long before washing. The last thing I could recall was being dragged away from Striker and Marianne's wedding celebrations by a group of men. What had happened between then and now, how much time had passed – I didn't know.

I pushed myself upright on the mattress and looked around. There wasn't much to see, the mattress lay on a concrete floor; the walls too, were made of solid cement. A tiny window, filmed by a thick coating of grime was situated in the top of one wall. It gave the impression this room must be positioned at least partially underground, to need the window so high. In the wall opposite the window, there was a door, made of metal and dead-locked. There was no handle. I raised my hands to my head, pressing my palms against my temples and squeezing my eyes shut as fear overwhelmed me. I had a funny taste in my mouth and felt groggy, slightly disorientated, which made me believe I'd been drugged. Shaking my head firmly, I tried to remove the last vestiges of fuzziness – I needed to be alert, knew I had to think logically about this situation if I was going to get out of here alive. My eyes were tired and dry, and I rubbed my fists against them.

With a quick glance, I confirmed I was still wearing the beautiful pewter dress and I sighed with relief. It gave the illusion nobody had touched me while I was unconscious and I clung to it, not wanting to consider the alternatives. Anything could have happened while I was out to it. My mouth throbbed and I touched it lightly, wincing when my fingers brushed across my lip. There was a deep split in the skin and it was swollen. Running my tongue across my lip, I discovered one of my teeth was a little loose. There didn't seem to be any other physical damage. It was satisfying to discover that the edge of the ankle cast was damaged, where I'd kicked the goon who'd touched me so intimately. He'd deserved it.

The biggest question to answer was what did these people want from me? My heart began to race as I pondered the question and I made a conscious effort not to hyperventilate. Panic was the last thing I could afford to do, not when I was in so much trouble. Breathing slowly and deeply, I tried to examine the situation logically, working my way through the moments before I was snatched away from the wedding.

I recalled Lucas and the others reacting in an identical fashion, mirroring one another's movements. They'd all raised their heads and sniffed the air, aware of something, or someone, approaching. Their sense of smell was acute, heightened beyond normal human ability and I suspected what they'd smelled was something supernatural, rather than human. It was the only logical explanation for their reaction, when they'd already been surrounded by dozens of human scents at the reception.

There was no doubt in my mind that the wedding planner had been vampire. When I'd met him and he shook my hand, his skin had been cool to touch, but I'd been fooled when he carried the bags of ice through the house to the marquee. No doubt, he'd done it deliberately to confuse me. I focused on his name, repeating it in my head, trying to think if I'd met him before, or heard his name mentioned in the past. I drew a blank. He meant nothing to me, yet he'd told the black-haired man I was the one they wanted. Why? What was it about me that they wanted so badly?

I got onto my knees and pushed up to a standing position, leaning against the concrete wall until the dizziness subsided. When I'd recovered my equilibrium, I began to pace backwards and forwards across the concrete floor, thinking through the situation incessantly. It was freezing in the small room and my dress wasn't suitable for low temperatures, so I wrapped my arms around my chest, rubbing my arms briskly to try to warm myself. The only viable motive for kidnapping me was my psychic ability. Without it, I was a normal human woman. But if they wanted my ability, what possible use could they have for it?

I was positive I'd met Gerard DuBonet for the first time this morning, but even that piece of information was open to conjecture – how long had I been held? How long was I drugged? Was it even the same day? The room was lit by a single fluorescent tube and it was impossible to know how long I'd been here, what time it was, what day it might be. The window was filthy, impossible to see through. I couldn't tell if it was day or night through the grime-caked glass. Stretching up against the wall, I tried to reach the window in the hope I could clear some of the grime, but it was too high. There wasn't a stick of furniture to help gain some height, only the mattress and its measly couple of inches wouldn't help. With a humph of frustration, I gave up the attempt and resumed pacing.

Another idea brought me to a standstill. Gerard DuBonet shook my hand when we met. Did he have some sort of ability, could he read me through touch? Was that possible? I almost disregarded the idea, but I was dealing with vampires –

anything was possible. In the past few months, I'd met Rowena, who could sense my emotions through contact, and Acenith and Striker, who could keep me calm with the touch of their hand on my shoulder. I knew some of the vampires could converse telepathically and Ripley could read other people's thoughts. It seemed plausible to think Gerard DuBonet might learn something about me through touch. I certainly couldn't disregard the notion. But I couldn't figure out how he could have met me in the morning and planned to kidnap me by evening. I couldn't force that part of the puzzle to make any sense.

There were still other questions to answer; for instance, why didn't Marianne foresee the strangers arriving at the wedding reception? The answer came almost immediately – her ability wasn't known for being faultless and with the excitement of her wedding day, maybe it had been misfiring more than usual. Although she seemed to be linked to me in some way with her ability – seeing many things involving me – perhaps this time it just hadn't worked.

Which led back to my first question. Even if Gerard DuBonet did recognize my ability, how did he find out about it in the first place?

I resumed pacing, thinking back uneasily through the day and beyond. My contacts were limited; my only friends outside of Lucas and the others were Lonnie, Hank, and Maude. Only Lucas and the vampires knew of my ability. I didn't think they'd even told Nick Lingard and his group of shape shifters. So where did the information come from?

Maybe I was on the wrong track altogether, although I couldn't think of anything that would single me out for kidnapping, other than my ability to speak with the dead. The black-haired man told Lucas I had something they wanted. The only logical option was the psychic gift. I had no idea why they thought it would be useful, nor what they could want to do with it. They didn't strike me as yearning to make contact with long-dead ancestors. Did they realize I only ever had contact with spirits who were important to me in some way? I doubted I could make contact with spirits, merely because someone tried to force me into doing it.

It was incredibly tempting to open the box in my mind and talk to Mom and the others. I was angry with myself for keeping them shut away so much, it had been a mistake. I'd been so smug about having the ability under control, only allowing contact when I wanted it. By doing so, I'd had no warning of the danger I faced. I clenched my fists in frustration and rolled my eyes at my own stupidity. I'd been so happy about gaining some control over the spirits, I hadn't thought about the possible repercussions of keeping them silent. If I'd kept the lines of communication open, they'd have given me warning about the impending danger I faced. Why hadn't Mom warned me though, at the wedding? Maybe she could only warn me if she was given enough contact to see danger approaching. By only releasing her for a few minutes, I hadn't given her a chance to recognize the imminent threat. It was the only logical explanation.

Now I wanted to talk to them desperately, but I was certain it would be reckless. If these people – whoever they were – wanted to use my ability, allowing the spirits out could be a mistake. I didn't know how or even if, they knew about my gift or what means they could employ to discover it. What if they had some way to recognize the spirits in my head? Could someone touch me and know about them if they were speaking with me? No. Releasing the spirits seemed like a bad proposition right now.

I circled the room with increasing frustration, knowing there was nothing to indicate where I was being held, but searching anyway. When they'd dragged me away, they'd taken off at a run through the woods. I'd been carried by the man who'd touched me so intimately and I shuddered at the memory. He'd smelled strongly of aftershave and when he'd thrown me over his shoulder, he'd taken great delight in holding his hand on my backside as he ran. I couldn't estimate how far we'd travelled through the darkened woods, before I was bundled unceremoniously into a car. A cloth held across my nose and mouth had been soaked in a sweet-smelling liquid, which knocked me unconscious. From there, I had no idea of where I'd been taken, how far we'd travelled, or where I was now.

Was Lucas searching for me? My heart lurched – would he be able to find me? The vampires might be able to track our path through the woods, but what happened when they reached where the car had been parked? Was there any hope of them tracking me from there? I assumed my scent would have disappeared into thin air from that point. I wasn't sure how their tracking ability worked, but I was certain they must need some scent, some trace of me to follow. When that was gone, there was probably no way of them following the direction in which we'd travelled. My already-shaken confidence took a further nose-dive at the thought of them being unable to find me. What if I was held here forever?

Shaking that thought from my mind, I mulled over my chances of rescue. The only thing I'd been able to do was attempt to get a message to Ripley about the wedding planner. The very same wedding planner, who *wasn't* a wedding planner. I cursed at myself – why hadn't I told Lucas about Gerard DuBonet? I should have mentioned how cold his hands were, even if I'd been stupid enough to believe his ruse with the ice. With everything going on in the lead-up to the wedding, the thought had completely slipped my mind. I'd been under the impression they knew him, and he'd seemed so confident and in control, I'd had no reason to think otherwise.

Breathing deeply, I tried to compose myself and keep the dread, which was bubbling away beneath the surface, under control. I *had* to keep it under control. Fear wasn't going to keep me alive.

Heavy footsteps approached and I stopped pacing, anxiously watching the door. The footfalls stopped outside and a key was slipped into the lock and turned.

Whatever they wanted, I was about to find out.

Chapter 2

Deep Trouble

To my utter disgust, the black-haired man stood in the doorway, his gaze lingering suggestively at my chest. "It's about time you woke up."

He strode across the room and captured my arm, dragging me out into a narrow hallway. He turned to the left, pulling me along beside him and tears welled in my eyes from his painful grip. There was no doubt; it was going to leave a bruise.

He hauled me up a flight of roughly hewn wooden stairs and I stumbled along beside him as he strode down another hallway. This one was lavishly decorated with flocked wallpaper, a claret leaf pattern on cream. The floor beneath my feet was polished and stained oak, the surface gleaming beneath the overhead lights. He stopped in front of a set of double doors, guarded by two heavyset men in dark suits. Neither of them glanced at us, their eyes focused on the opposite wall. The black-haired man rapped sharply on the door.

"Come."

One of the guards pushed the doors open and I was dragged unceremoniously into the room. It was a study, oval shaped with rows of leather-bound books adorning wooden shelves, flawlessly fitted into the curved walls. A man sat behind an enormous wooden desk in the centre of the room. A large window was open behind him, sunlight streaming into the room and the lace curtains wafted softly in the breeze. Carefully tended gardens were visible outside, planted with a selection of majestic palms and bright, tropical flowers. Vast swathes of lawn were richly green and meticulously mowed. We were nowhere near Montana – that much was obvious. The man who'd dragged me upstairs shoved me down onto a straight-backed chair before letting go of my arm.

"Leave us, Sebastian."

"Yes, Sir."

I glared at Sebastian as he strode past and left the room, shutting the doors soundlessly behind him.

"Miss Duncan."

I turned my attention to the man in the chair. He was tall and slim, with blonde shoulder length hair, which fell around his face in gentle waves. He was bearded, the hair clipped neatly around his jaw. The fine lines around his chocolate brown eyes suggested he was in his mid-forties and he was dressed casually in a white silk shirt, the neckline open to reveal a small 'V' of tanned skin.

"How do you know my name?"

He smiled. "Oh, I know quite a bit about you, Miss Duncan." He drew himself to his feet and strode around the desk, his movements curiously graceful given he was so lanky. Perching on the edge of the desk, he regarded me with a tight smile. "My name is Laurence Armstrong." He held out his hand and I shook it warily, not taking my eyes off him. His skin was warm, his hand smooth with long fingers and neatly manicured nails. With his eyes focused on me, I felt a whisper of power travel through his hand and into mine, an increase in warmth and a vibration, which made the hair on my arms stand on end. I pulled my hand away from his, rubbing it on my thigh. I didn't know what it was, or how he'd done it, but there was something strange about him, some sort of power I couldn't recognize.

"You're not a vampire?" I questioned warily.

He laughed dryly. "No, of course not. Tell me, what do you think I am?"

I shook my head. "I don't know."

"No matter. It's not important." He stared at me for a long moment, his eyes piercing and unemotional. "What is important is what you can do for me."

Playing dumb seemed like the best option. In fact, my only option, as I didn't have a clue why I was here. There was no valid reason to suspect this stranger knew about my ability, but it was still the only logical explanation I had for being kidnapped. Laurence Armstrong was trying to be charming and I didn't want him to know what I suspected. Better to hold the knowledge to my chest and see what I could learn from him. "I have no idea what you're talking about."

His gaze was piercing, as if he instinctively knew I was lying. "Oh, come now, Miss Duncan. We both know what I'm talking about." He leaned forward, so his face was inches from mine and spoke quietly. "You have a power. A unique power. I want it."

I shrugged, trying to keep my expression neutral. "I don't know what you're talking about. I'm an artist. I paint."

A long silence followed this statement. His brown eyes were calculating as he stared into my own, as if he could read the truth in my irises. I stared back, too frightened to blink, keeping my face as smooth, and relaxed as I could manage. When he spoke, his voice was hard, the polite composure gone. "You *will* tell me what I want to know. We can do this the easy way, or the hard way. It doesn't matter to me."

"What, like getting your cronies to feel me up?" I retorted angrily. "Are you going to let them rape me next?" The revulsion incited me to anger rapidly and I remembered Sebastian's fingers probing me, and shuddered at the strong memory.

Armstrong looked taken aback and caught more than slightly off-balance at my words. "What are you talking about?"

I glared at him defiantly, drawing myself up straighter in the chair. "That Sebastian. He touched me."

"Touched you?"

It was apparent I was going to have to spell it out. "He put his fingers... inside me." I fought against the rush of heat that rose across my cheeks, and failed miserably.

His eyes grew colder and he bellowed, making me jump. "SEBASTIAN!"

The door opened at once, giving the impression Sebastian had been loitering outside. He strode in; closing the doors and standing beside the chair where I sat. I could smell the stench of his potent aftershave and wrinkled my nose in distaste.

"Yes, Sir."

Armstrong stood up abruptly and he was a good couple of inches taller than Sebastian was. He was irate, tendons visible in his neck as he glowered at the shorter man. "What were your orders regarding Miss Duncan?" he snapped angrily.

"You told me to collect Miss Duncan from Montana and bring her here, Sir."

My assumption was correct; I was no longer in Montana.

"What were your *express* orders regarding contact with Miss Duncan?" Armstrong's face had reddened with anger, a vein pumping visibly in his temple.

Sebastian looked confused. "Sir?"

"I told you there was to be no sexual contact. Under *any* circumstances."

"But, Sir, the blood sucker told me he was her mate. I had no option but to check—"

I wasn't sure it was my imagination, or my own fear, but Sebastian appeared scared. His dark eyes had rounded owlishly and he was clenching and unclenching his fists.

Armstrong crowded the smaller man, fury clearly visible in his expression. "You were to leave her untouched! I made my orders exceedingly explicit in that regard!"

What happened next took only a split second, but I was subjected to every horrifying detail, as if time had deliberately slowed down so I couldn't miss it. I heard a quiet click; similar to the latch of a door being turned, and then Armstrong raised his left arm and slashed his hand across Sebastian's neck.

Sebastian dropped to his knees, clutching spasmodically at his ruined neck. I could see tendons, veins, muscle – even the glossy white bone of his spine through the shredded skin. Blood poured from the wound in a torrent, rapidly soaking his white shirt before he slumped face-forward onto the carpet.

I shrieked and screamed as Sebastian lay dying before me. Gurgling sounds emitted from his throat as blood pumped endlessly from his neck, a pool of scarlet forming on the carpet around him. I held my hands over my eyes, trying to block out the macabre spectacle. It stopped me from seeing his death throes, but didn't protect me from the mental image of seeing his throat reduced to so much meat and blood.

Now I was certain of what I was dealing with. Werewolves.

A hand gripped my arm, gentler than Sebastian's had been, but still firm. Armstrong hauled me to my feet as I continued to shriek. I struggled ineffectively against his grip as he pulled me from the room.

"Clean up the mess," he ordered the stunned guards. He drew me further down the hallway, pushing me before him into another room. He lowered me gently onto a leather armchair, crouching before me. "My apologies, Miss Duncan. I'm sorry you had to see that."

Inhaling deeply, I began to gain a little control, but I couldn't look him in the eye. He terrified me, more than any person I'd ever met before did.

"Would you like something to eat? Or perhaps a drink? Some coffee, perhaps?"

As if I could think about eating or drinking when I'd just witnessed a man getting his throat ripped out. *Stupid, Charlotte. Stupid. You need your strength. Accept the offer.* I nodded mutely.

Armstrong rang a bell near the doorway and I glanced away from him, concentrating on bringing my ragged breathing back under control. This room was large and luxurious, with couches and armchairs in sleek black leather. The walls were decorated with velvet-flocked wallpaper in pale gold and the floor was covered in plush white carpet. Antique lamps sat on elegantly carved wooden coffee tables. I stole a glance at the window, hoping for some clue to our whereabouts. Bright sunshine was casting shadows on the green lawn and the plants definitely seemed tropical. Where the hell was I?

A middle-aged woman appeared in the doorway, wearing a pale blue uniform with a white apron tied around her waist, sensible white shoes on her feet. She didn't look at me and seemed unperturbed by my presence. "You called, Mr. Armstrong?"

"Bring a plate of sandwiches and some coffee for our guest."

The woman curtseyed and closed the door quietly when she left the room. Armstrong walked back across to where I sat, lowering himself into an armchair opposite mine and resumed his unabashed study of my face.

"You really are a beautiful young woman."

I stared at him, waiting uneasily for whatever was coming next.

"Hmmm. The silent treatment. While I can understand your revulsion, I must warn you, I find the silent treatment very tiresome." He leaned forward, a frown creasing his tanned forehead. "Your blood-sucking friends weren't nearly as quiet when they were executed."

Startled by this admission, I blinked at him uncertainly. "He— Sebastian— he promised they wouldn't be killed."

"As you have just discovered, Sebastian isn't good at following orders. After you were removed from the Tine house, my men finished the job I'd ordered. The bloodsuckers, all their human friends. All dead. We couldn't take the risk of any of them trying to locate you."

For a few long seconds, I was numb – utterly devoid of conscious thought or feeling. Then pain rippled into my chest, as though my heart had been stabbed with a cold, sharp knife and it was all I could do to remain upright in the armchair, not fall to my knees with the pain.

"I don't want to hurt you." Armstrong's voice was gentler now, less harsh, and more persuasive. "All I want is information. When you have given it to me, you'll be free to leave."

I kept my gaze lowered, focusing on my hands and Lucas's gold ring on my finger. Could Lucas really be dead? Rowena and Marianne— everyone? Was this a trick, or was he telling the truth? I doubted his honesty and certainly didn't believe he would let me go if I told him what he wanted to know. More likely, he would kill me as soon as I gave up the knowledge.

I inhaled a deep breath and forced myself to look up into his cold eyes, speaking quietly and firmly. "I don't know what you want from me. I don't have a clue about what you're saying. I have nothing I could tell you."

Armstrong was furious as he launched himself from the armchair. I squeezed my eyes shut, convinced he was going to hit me, but instead he wrenched me up from the chair, his grip unyielding around my wrist.

He dragged me unceremoniously from the room, along the hallway and back down the stairs. He flung open the metal door and pushed me into the concrete cell. I stumbled and fell, hitting my shoulder and hip hard against the unforgiving floor.

"You will tell me everything you know. You can be absolutely sure of it," he shouted angrily.

The door slammed and I heard the key turn in the lock, the noise echoing throughout the empty room. I dragged myself to the mattress, sobbing with terror as I dropped down onto it. I curled up into a ball, my body trembling so violently I wrapped my arms around my legs to try to control the shakes. Tears flowed freely as I considered whether the only people I truly considered family in this world could possibly be dead.

Chapter 3

Knowledge Revealed

There was no telling how long I'd lain on the mattress, whether it was day or night, or how many hours had passed. Since Armstrong threw me back into the concrete room, I'd had nothing to eat or drink. My throat was parched and my stomach rumbled ominously, aching with hunger. The room was still freezing and I'd spent most of my time trying to retain what little body heat I could manage.

I'd dozed on and off and when I woke, a bucket, which hadn't been there before, was sitting in the corner of the room. I investigated and discovered it was empty, and with a sinking heart, I realized this was my bathroom. This was where I was to apparently deal with physical necessities during my imprisonment.

Before falling into a troubled sleep, I'd spent a lot of time considering if what Armstrong had said could be true. Could Lucas and his friends be dead? Not only them, but also all those guests at the wedding? Whether it was wishful thinking or not, I discounted the idea. I'd calculated the number of men who'd appeared so suddenly at the wedding and came up with fifteen. Even if they were all werewolves and vampires, I didn't believe fifteen people could take on over two hundred people and kill them all. Someone had to survive, I was certain of it. I needed to believe Armstrong was lying and stubbornly clung to hope.

In the meantime, I needed to stay alive and that was looking increasingly doubtful if I didn't get something to eat and drink soon. I huddled in the corner, legs tucked up to my chest and my arms wrapped around them. There was a good chance sustenance wouldn't be an issue soon, because in all likelihood I would freeze to death. This room was disorientating; trying to figure out whether it was day or night, or how much time had passed was hopeless. It was impossible to tell and the light over my head glowed constantly.

Like a mantra, I ran through the little information I'd managed to accumulate. As much as I loved Marianne, I knew her psychic power was haphazard at best and couldn't be relied on. Ripley might be able to hear my thoughts and it was the only hope I had. I didn't know the distance his mind reading could work across, but it was my only hope and I was clinging to it. For hours at a time, I repeated it in my head. *Gerard DuBonet, Laurence Armstrong, Gerard DuBonet, Laurence Armstrong.* I was certain if Ripley could pick up my thoughts, if they could track down Gerard DuBonet or find out about Laurence Armstrong, they might be able to find me. My rescue hopes relied on a lot of ifs and maybes, but it was all I had to cling to.

I heard footsteps approaching and listened intently. The door opened and one of the guards I'd seen upstairs came in, silently wrenching me to my feet and dragging me along the corridor. I was taken upstairs and into the living room I'd been taken to last time.

The guard shoved me down on a chair and I found Armstrong waiting for my arrival. He was seated opposite me, wearing black trousers and a sky blue shirt, his legs crossed at the ankle. On the coffee table was a plate filled with sandwiches and a pot of coffee; sugar and creamer neatly laid out beside it.

"You must be hungry," he remarked quietly.

I eyed him suspiciously, wondering if this was a ruse. Was he going to allow me to eat, or was this his idea of a sick joke?

"Please, help yourself," he said, waving his hand towards the food.

Snatching up a sandwich, I crammed it into my mouth, watching him cautiously as he poured coffee. He didn't speak again until I'd stuffed another half dozen sandwiches into my mouth, desperate to eat as much as I possibly could before he stopped me. The coffee was too hot to drink, but I grabbed the jug of creamer, gulping it down quickly.

Armstrong laughed; the sound cold and humorless in the room. "You are quite the little animal, aren't you?"

When I'd eaten every sandwich, I leaned back in the chair and eyed him suspiciously. "What do you want?"

"Now, Miss Duncan. You know exactly what I want. I want you to tell me how your gift works."

"What gift?"

He sighed heavily, rubbing a hand over his bearded chin. "I'd hoped you might have come to your senses by now. You've been here for three days and as you can see," he waved around the room expansively, "nobody is coming to your rescue."

I remained silent, watching him apprehensively. At least I knew now how long I'd been here, although it seemed much longer than three days.

"Alright, let me tell you what I already know." He paused, staring at me with those intense brown eyes. "You have a psychic ability. I am aware of it because your little band of bloodsuckers attacked some associates of mine. They released two of them, and one came to me with information. He told me about you and it was a very interesting conversation. This particular associate overheard the discussion you were having with your mother. Imagine his surprise, when he discovered your mother wasn't in the house, yet managed to warn you of their impending arrival. Although he was too stupid to consider the possibilities, I did, and a little investigation confirmed your mother has been dead for two years. So, I asked myself, how does this girl talk to a mother who is dead and buried already?" He leaned forward, tapping his forehead. "She obviously has some sort of psychic talent, a very powerful talent."

I continued to watch him, trying to keep my face neutral, wondering where this was going and how much he really knew.

"Still not going to talk? No matter. You will – one way or the other. For the moment, I will continue my little tale as you are listening with such rapt attention." He settled back on the couch, stretching his arm along the back of it. "Now, I think to myself, what use is a girl who can speak with her dead mother? There is nothing to be gained from such ability. What possible benefit could it be? But I admit, I was intrigued, wondering just how much psychic ability you had. You were having a complete conversation with your dead mother. A two-way dialogue. In the interests of conducting a full and complete investigation, I decided to send another blood-sucking colleague of mine to the Tine home."

"Gerard DuBonet?" The name slipped from my mouth unbidden and I wished I hadn't said anything. I didn't want to help him, no matter how close his conclusions were to the facts.

"Yes. Mr. DuBonet has a remarkable talent of his own. Through touch, he gets a snapshot of a person's history. Almost like flicking through hundreds of old photographs at once. And what do you think Mr. DuBonet discovered when he touched you?"

I didn't like where this was going. "I don't have a clue."

"He tells me you have a remarkable psychic aura. The only trouble is, Mr. DuBonet couldn't access the information I wanted. He tells me you have a shielding ability which he can't breach."

He stood up, walking slowly around the table to crouch beside me. I heard the odd clicking sound and enormous claws sprouted from the ends of his fingertips. He used one claw to stroke leisurely across my neck and I fought rising panic, struggling to remain seated and not give anything away in my expression. "That tells me you have something remarkable hidden in that pretty head of yours, but it seems I can't get to it. Which is why," he pushed the claw against my neck, where my jugular vein pulsed rapidly, "I want you to tell me about it."

My hands were shaking and I clutched them in my lap. I didn't know what he intended to do with any information I gave him, but I was certain no good would come from it. "I'm afraid you've been misinformed, Mr. Armstrong. I have no idea what you're talking about and I can only tell you what I've told you before. My name is Charlotte Duncan and I'm an artist. There is *nothing* unusual about me."

He didn't use the claws. His fist rushed towards my face and I shut my eyes, cringing from what was to come. His closed hand connected with my cheek, slamming me back against the chair with enough force to tip it over, spilling me to the floor. Pain registered only briefly, before I slipped into unconsciousness.

Chapter 4

Conal

Waking up in the concrete room after a beating became a regular event after that first punch, one I faced with increasing dread and despair.

Any information I came across was added to my mental S.O.S., although I was growing more convinced, nobody was coming to my aid. Despite the hopelessness, which was intensifying, I didn't want to give up. If I gave up, what else was there? So I continued to broadcast what I knew, uncertain if it would ever be heard by Ripley. Every time I was dragged up the stairs, I took mental note of anything that might be important. I'd begun estimating the number of guards, based on the area of the house to which I was escorted. I had a good eye for faces and could recognize new people as the shifts changed. Each time I saw someone new, I added him or her to my list. For hours on end, I ran through the information in my head. *Gerard DuBonet, Laurence Armstrong, fifteen guards, sunny and humid. Gerard DuBonet, Laurence Armstrong, fifteen guards, sunny and humid.*

Each time I was taken upstairs, I expected it to be the last time. Armstrong was becoming increasingly frustrated, the beatings he dished out more brutal with every day that passed. My face and arms were black and blue, my body aching almost constantly.

Once more, I heard footsteps approaching and I cringed, squeezing my eyes shut at the thought of another session with Armstrong. Eventually, he would tire of this game and kill me. I would be grateful when that time came. I wasn't sure how much longer I could do this, didn't know how long I could keep up the strength to deny him what he wanted. Even as I feared giving in, I knew I had to keep fighting against him. I still couldn't imagine what he intended to do if he found out about me, how my psychic ability could possibly be useful to him.

I was hauled back upstairs and taken into the study. I avoided looking at the patch of carpet where Sebastian had died. The blood had been cleaned up, but a faint stain remained and the vague notion occurred to me that Armstrong would have to replace the carpet. Why that particular thought crossed my mind, I didn't know, but it seemed better to think of practical things than what was about to happen. Maybe he was waiting until after he'd ripped my throat out, so he didn't have the expense of replacing it twice. I shook my head, knew I was surely losing my mind, and glanced up at Armstrong. I was surprised to discover there was a second man in the room with us. It made me instantly more wary – this was something different and I didn't trust it.

"Miss Duncan. How delightful of you to join us." Armstrong indicated a chair beside the stranger and the guard pushed me down onto it. I peeked cautiously at the stranger, not willing to make eye contact with him. He was a bear of a man, tall and muscular with broad shoulders and bronzed skin. He had a mop of unruly black hair, which curled across the collar of his shirt and his strong jaw was shadowed with the beginnings of a beard. He glanced down at me and before I could lower my gaze, I noticed his eyes were unusual. So dark, they seemed pitch black and they were animal-like in shape, something not completely human about them.

"This is Conal Tremaine, Miss Duncan. Conal, meet Charlotte Duncan." Armstrong introduced us, as though we were attending a formal dinner. I could sense the man studying me, his gaze flickering over the mass of purple bruises covering my face and neck.

"What the hell's going on, Armstrong?" The big man's voice was rumbling deep, deep enough that I could feel it in my chest when he spoke. "You kidnapped me and brought me here for this? Why the hell do I need to see your handiwork?"

"Yes, I brought you here for this," Armstrong agreed silkily. "I want you to find out exactly what is in her head. Miss Duncan is not being cooperative."

"You know I don't use my ability on humans, it's too dangerous."

"Tremaine, keep in mind your pack is currently being held by my men. I would hate to give them orders which could cause the unnecessary deaths of your people." Armstrong voiced his threat quietly, his voice calm. "But I will, if you don't provide me with what I want."

The big man's eyes flashed with rage, and I felt an energy building beside me, which seemed to come from him. It brushed over my skin, like a hot wind.

"Control yourself, Tremaine. Or those orders will be given sooner, rather than later," Armstrong warned.

The man swallowed deeply, seemingly controlling his anger and the heat dissipated as quickly as it had appeared. "I could damage her," he finally said.

Armstrong pursed his lips as if he was considering alternatives. "I really don't care. It doesn't matter what happens to her mind, that's not what I'm after. But I want what she's hiding in that brain, and you can get it."

Conal Tremaine scrutinized me, observing the bruises, the split lip, the cuts on my face and arms. "What exactly is this human pup meant to have in her mind that's so damn important?"

"Something I can use to my advantage, if I can get to it."

Conal Tremaine reflected on this statement for a moment or two, his forehead furrowed as if he were considering his options. "All right."

He turned his chair to face me and Armstrong grabbed the back of my chair, spinning it so I faced Conal Tremaine. He stared into my eyes for a second or two, before lifting his right hand as if to touch me. I reared backwards, terrified of what he intended to do, but Armstrong clutched me firmly around the throat with his arm, keeping me immobile.

Conal Tremaine raised his hand again, placing his fingertips to my forehead. Acute throbbing started up in my temples and I squeezed my eyes shut, whimpering softly. The throbbing escalated until I was sure I'd never felt such horrendous pain and I had a mental image of his fingers reaching into my brain, probing around the circuits and sections. His fingers moved slowly and vigilantly through my brain, looking this way and that, touching and feeling as he went. In a state of pure panic, I turned to my mental box, ensuring it was securely sealed. His fingers followed immediately to where it was hidden in the darkest recesses of my mind. It was agonizing, the seemingly real assault of his fingers inside my head and I began to tremble, sweat trickling down my back as I battled against him. I couldn't understand what was happening, but I wanted it to stop, needed him to take his fingers away from me and stop the relentless pain, which was making me nauseous.

I forced my eyes open and found him watching me, his black eyes staring into mine as he grappled for the lid of the box. With extreme effort, I focused all my attention on keeping the lid closed, battling against him, and shaking with the exertion it took. Against my will, he pushed harder and although I frantically tried to stop him, he pried open the lid of the box. I stared wide-eyed, mesmerized by the expression in his black eyes, as he saw my inner most secrets and the truth of what I was, what I could do. I knew he was seeing the people I spoke to often, could hear their voices swelling into my mind even as he probed.

And then he blinked.

He removed his hand from my forehead and I slumped in the chair, bile rising in my throat as my head pounded mercilessly. I couldn't stop the whimper that left my lips, or the fervent wish that he'd killed me. Death would be a better option, compared to this agony.

"She's powerful, considering she's human. There's something there, in her mind, but I can't reach it." He sat back in his chair, dropping his hand onto his thigh and turning his attention to Armstrong.

It was fortunate Armstrong stood behind me, unable to see my expression – there was no doubt he would have seen the startled look I failed to hide. Conal Tremaine glanced back at me for a second, his face showing no emotion whatsoever. His expression was completely neutral as he turned his attention back to Armstrong. "Whatever you think she has, it's extremely well hidden. I'll need more time to break through the barriers she's erected."

"Do it now," Armstrong demanded. "I want it; I want the power she holds."

"Okay." Conal Tremaine raised his hand again and I sobbed. "As long as you're happy for her to die here and now, that's fine by me."

"Wait!" There was silence for a few seconds, but I couldn't see Armstrong's face to see what he was thinking, what he was doing. All I could see was the man in front of me, his hand just inches from my forehead. "What's the problem?"

Conal Tremaine shrugged. "She's not like us, she's weak. There's a good reason I don't use the hand on humans, it reduces their minds to so much mush, kills the brain stem. Another attempt so soon after the first will see her die here in your study. Still," he said, leaning back in the chair and crossing his arms over his broad chest, "it makes no difference to me."

Armstrong was silent again and I could imagine him considering what the man had said. I couldn't see his face and I didn't dare to turn and find out what his facial expression would tell me. I was certain if I moved the pain in my head would only increase and I was having difficulty enough staying conscious. Black spots were dancing in and out of my vision, the nausea being held at bay only through sheer willpower. When Armstrong did speak, his voice was both angry and resigned. "Fine. I'll give you three days. Get the information from her in the next three days, or I'll kill you and have your pack annihilated."

"And if I get the information?"

"You'll be free to go and our blood feud is at an end. The debt will be forgotten."

"Agreed." Conal glanced fleetingly at me, before returning his gaze to Armstrong. "Keep in mind there's a full moon in two days."

"I'm aware of that," Armstrong snapped. He grasped my arm and wrenched me from the chair, dragging me towards the door. He shoved me unceremoniously out to the guards and screamed at them to return me to my prison. Once there, I promptly vomited into the bucket, retching repeatedly until I was dry heaving, my throat stinging, and my vision blurred by the intense headache. I dropped to the floor, lay my forehead against the cool concrete, and cried.

When I could, I crawled on my hands and knees to the mattress and lay staring up at the ceiling. Why had Conal Tremaine lied? He'd broken through whatever shields I had in place. Why hadn't he told Armstrong what he'd seen? I rolled onto my side, curling into a ball and trying to conserve some heat in my body.

For the millionth time I wondered why it was so cold down here, when it was so warm upstairs.

The familiar and unwelcome sound of footsteps came from the hall and I braced myself, unable to quell the frightened moan that escaped my lips. Not already, he couldn't expect me to go through that again already. I hadn't been back down here for long, it seemed only minutes had passed – I couldn't survive a second attempt so soon.

To my utter confusion, when the door opened Conal Tremaine was shoved into the room and fell to the floor in a crumpled heap. He'd been beaten, blood still pouring from a deep gash on his forehead.

The door slammed and I heard the key turn in the lock. I remained motionless for a minute, and then began to crawl towards the prostrate man on the floor. He remained utterly still, to all intents and purposes, he seemed unconscious, but I was wary. Having him imprisoned here made me nervous, I knew he wasn't a normal human, but I hadn't figured out exactly what he was. I sighed heavily. All I knew was that he hadn't given Armstrong my secret and for that, I owed him something.

I crawled to the second bucket I'd been supplied with a day or two ago, which held fresh drinking water. Armstrong had apparently figured out I couldn't survive forever without nutrients, so I now received a bucket of water and scraps of something inedible each day. I glanced down regretfully at my beautiful dress, which looked much the worse for wear after days of abuse. "Sorry, Acenith," I muttered, grabbing the edge of the train and tugging until I'd managed to tear a piece of material from it.

I dipped the material in the water, using it to dab gently at the wound on the huge man's forehead. Expending a lot of energy I could ill afford, I shoved and pushed until he lay on his back, only then realizing that the cut on his forehead was not the only injury he'd sustained. There were four deep scratches across his chest, visible beneath the torn shirt. After a few seconds of anxious deliberation, I undid the buttons of his shirt so I could clean the wounds, which looked like claw marks. I had no doubt who'd done this to him and why – because he'd kept my secret. The least I could do was to try to help him.

He was handsome, I mused, as I cleaned the wounds carefully. He wasn't classically handsome, but attractive in an earthy, outdoorsy way. Sooty black eyelashes framed his closed eyes, and there was a cleft in his chin, which was partially obscured by the stubble growing on his cheeks and jaw. I guessed he was somewhere between thirty and forty, exceptionally muscular with broad shoulders and an impressive six-pack. I wondered if he was married – did he have a family somewhere? A quick glance confirmed he didn't wear a wedding ring. The thought was comforting – although it didn't guarantee he was single, at least I could hope he didn't have a wife or girlfriend worrying about him somewhere. He did have a pack, which Armstrong was threatening. How many people were involved, how many would be hurt if I didn't tell Armstrong what he wanted to know?

I thought Conal Tremaine must be a werewolf, as I suspected Armstrong was. The assumption seemed to make sense with Armstrong talking about a pack. This meant I might be in a whole lot more trouble if he meant what he'd said about the full moon. I didn't know how much of what I'd read about werewolves was true, but I was positive the forthcoming full moon could only be bad. I continued my first aid efforts, fretting over the thought of this man turning into a werewolf in a few days' time. There was another smaller cut on his abdomen and I wiped it carefully, removing the blood that had spilled across his smooth olive skin. Satisfied that all the injuries I could see were clean, I was about to rinse out the cloth when he regained consciousness, gripping my wrist in a painful grasp.

I shrieked and tried to pull away, terrified when he growled deep in his chest. He opened his eyes and released his grip immediately, looking more carefully at me, his dark eyes taking in my disheveled appearance, the wet cloth still clutched in my fingers. Keeping his gaze on me, he touched his forehead, then his chest before pulling himself into a sitting position.

"You were cleaning my wounds?"

I nodded, terrified of this imposing man.

"You're in a great deal of trouble, Miss Duncan." His voice was deep, a rumbling growl which was strangely soothing.

"My name's Charlotte," I responded softly.

"Charlotte." He stood up abruptly, his movements fluid and graceful for such a tall and solidly built man. Walking slowly, he scanned the walls and ceiling, studying every square inch. I sat mutely, waiting while he finished his inspection, wondering what he was looking for in the bare room.

When he seemed satisfied, he walked back to where I was and sat cross-legged on the floor opposite me. "This room doesn't appear to have any hidden cameras or bugging devices. I don't think Armstrong thought it would take this long to get what he wants – I'm sure he didn't plan to keep two prisoners here. I think we're safe to speak freely."

Watching him cautiously, I was aware that my wrist still throbbed where he'd grabbed me. He could snap me like a twig and I wasn't convinced of whose side he was on. But he'd kept my secret, and I felt as if I should trust him, at least a little bit. What choice did I have? "Are you a werewolf? Like Armstrong?"

"I'm werewolf, Armstrong isn't. He's a shape shifter, a wolf wannabe." His black eyes flickered around the room again as if he wanted to confirm there was nothing here, which Armstrong could use to hear our conversation. "Shape shifters are scum, they're beneath us. They have no honor."

"He has your – people, Mr. Tremaine."

"If we're going to be on a first name basis, you can call me Conal," he responded. "Yeah, he's got my people. If I don't deliver what he wants, he'll kill them."

"And you?"

Conal inclined his head. "I'm a dead man already. No matter what he says, he's got no intentions of allowing me to leave." He gazed at me, his eyes searching my face. "I killed his brother a couple of months ago. I paid the required penalty, but that isn't enough for him. He wants an eye for an eye."

I wasn't up to trying to understand werewolf and shape shifter code of behavior. I shivered, freezing in the thin dress I'd been wearing for days. "You saw what was in my head," I stated, "why didn't you tell him?" There seemed little point in beating around the bush. Conal had seen my secrets and hiding anything from him now seemed pointless.

"What are you?" he questioned abruptly, ignoring my question.

"I'm just a human. I have some psychic ability."

Conal shook his head firmly. "I'm not so sure about you being just a human. How long have you been having corporeal visitations?"

"A month, maybe a little more. I heard their voices first, for years before I acted on them. Then the... visitations started."

"Your ability is unbelievably powerful. It surprised me, when I broke through your shield and discovered what you were hiding."

"It surprises me, too," I muttered and the thought was not an entirely happy one.

Conal stared at me for a full minute and I forced myself to return his gaze without looking away. It was like being studied under a microscope and I fought the urge to squirm. "You don't know why he wants that?" he finally asked.

I shook my head.

Conal inhaled deeply, letting the breath out with a sharp whoosh. "He wants to use what you have in your head as a weapon. To gain power over others around him."

I couldn't understand what he was suggesting. How could something in my head be used as a weapon?

Conal saw my confusion and enlightened me. "Those spirits in your head, you have a great deal of power over them. More so than I would imagine any human has ever had. Your ability is unusual in a mortal. Extremely unusual."

"I still don't get it," I admitted.

Conal's dark gaze fixed on mine. "You have corporeal visions, don't you? You see the spirits manifested physically before you?"

I nodded cautiously.

"I saw in your mind – you have the power to make those corporeal visions do your bidding."

I felt my eyes widening. "How do you know that?"

"I see things you've done when I'm probing your mind. My gift allows me to access your mind, comparable to searching a computer for files. You used one of the spirits to do your bidding."

I grimaced uncomfortably. "I got my Mom to trip up a waiter."

Conal shifted, folding his leg up and wrapping his arms round his knee. "Put that all together and you have the answer. You can use the spirits to do your bidding. Imagine being able to use an *army* of spirits to do your bidding."

The penny dropped.

Chapter 5

Allied

I drew myself to my feet clumsily, still struggling with the effects of Conal's probing. The headache was still pounding, exacerbated by what Conal had laid out for me. I paced backwards and forwards, digesting the implications. He continued to sit on the floor, seemingly content to wait for me to speak.

"I still don't get it. I'm not going to give him an army."

Conal stared at me, one eyebrow raised in unconcealed amusement. "You humans aren't real quick on the uptake. Remember what he said when I warned probing might damage you?"

I thought back over the conversation and realization dawned on me. "That's why he hits me around the face, the arms, upper body. Why he said he didn't care what happened to my mind." I shivered as understanding dawned. "He doesn't want my psychic ability. He wants my genetic makeup."

"Good girl. Maybe you're smarter than I gave you credit for." Conal chewed his lower lip thoughtfully. "He needs to know exactly how powerful you are. When he discovers the full extent of your abilities, I imagine he's going to harvest your eggs and fertilize them with shifter sperm. Probably his own. He'll create his own psychic children. Children who may be able to control and command an army of dead."

"But how will that help him?" I argued. "Even if they did carry the same psychic ability, it would be years before they're of any use to him."

Conal laughed harshly. "Back to thinking like a stupid human. Regardless of how long it takes, creating his own race of psychic shape shifters will give him tremendous power. More power than anyone could imagine. He's prepared to wait. With the correct training and encouragement, he could have them doing his bidding in eight years, maybe less. And in the meantime, he has you." He paused for a long moment, eyeing me impassively. "And if he tortures you for long enough, you'll give in to him."

"I won't," I stated resolutely, but my mind screamed doubts at me. The beatings were becoming increasingly brutal. How long could I hold out against that type of physical abuse? If he threatened to kill people, if I didn't do what he said, would I be able to stand up to him? I knew I couldn't.

My legs gave way under me and I slumped down onto the floor. My teeth were chattering and I wrapped my arms around my legs, trying to hug some warmth into my skin. This was more than physical coldness; the enormity of what Conal had explained was causing a chill that was more elemental, the result of shock and fear.

"You're cold," Conal stated mildly.

I nodded mutely, still trying to come to terms with what Conal had explained At last I could see why I was of value to Armstrong and I could understand, even more clearly, why it was imperative he didn't get the information he wanted. "I don't know why it's freezing in here, when it's warm upstairs."

"Armstrong is a master at torture. We're at least partially underground, which would keep the area colder than upstairs, but it's made of solid concrete and I imagine he has some way of keeping the temperature artificially cold. It's a very old torture method, the more discomfort you feel; the more likely you are to give him what he wants." He held his arms open. "I'll warm you up."

Wary of his intentions, I shook my head. How did I know he wouldn't attack me? I didn't even know him. He may appear to be on my side, but uncertainty still kept me wary.

"Please," Conal said gruffly. "You're cold and I'm a werewolf. My body is naturally much warmer than a human is. I won't harm you; I give you my word. I need you capable of talking to me so we can try to find a way out of here. It will help you to think more clearly if you're warm."

I crept towards him, watching him cautiously. He made no sudden moves, remaining perfectly still as I crawled between his legs in my own time. I stopped, uncertain of what to do next and Conal gently gripped my waist, turning me so my back was against his chest. He'd lifted me as though I was no heavier than a baby was and then dropped his arms around me, wrapping me in a cocoon of heat. I closed my eyes, relishing the warmth and relief drifted over me as I began to thaw out.

Conal permitted me a few minutes of peace as the heat spread through my body and I sagged further against his chest, feeling safer than I had in days.

"Now, I've told you what I've been able to work out. I need you to tell me everything you know, so I can try and figure out a way out of here," he announced, his voice rumbling through his chest against my back. It was both comforting and reassuring.

I told him the whole story, from beginning to end. I wasn't sure if I could trust him completely, but he was the only person in whom I could place any faith. He knew my secret, what point was there in hiding anything else from him? I worked through everything from when I first met Lucas, being attacked by the vampire, my recovery with Dr. Harding's help. I told him about the other vampires returning to take revenge with the werewolf

– and how my psychic abilities had sent the others to rescue Lucas and his friends. I worked my way through every psychic experience I'd had and continued through to the day of the wedding. When I'd finished, I lay expectantly against his hard chest, waiting for his response.

Conal took a long time to absorb what I'd told him, before he spoke. "You say he got Gerard DuBonet to infiltrate this Tine's place?"

I nodded. "He was there on the morning of the wedding. Told me he was the wedding planner. Do you know him?"

"I've come across him once or twice. He's a weasel. Always on the lookout for a way to make a fast buck."

"He could tell what I was by touching me?"

"Yeah. He's able to read people, through touch. He would have been able to tell you had a psychic ability, but that shield you have – it's incredibly strong. He wouldn't have gotten past it. He's not that talented." He lapsed into silence again, thinking. "These blood suckers – they've never attempted to create you?"

"No." I didn't like him calling them bloodsuckers, he said it with such contempt, and it was obvious he disliked vampires. "I don't want to be a vampire."

"That's usually doesn't stop the leeches. They don't feed on humans. You're sure about that?"

I nodded, aware of Conal's very warm skin against my back. "They have in the past, but they've all given up killing humans and survive on animal blood."

Conal was thoughtful, his huge hands rubbing over my arms subconsciously. "It's hard to believe there are leeches out there that don't attack humans. I've never heard of it before," he said doubtfully. "You're absolutely certain they don't kill humans?"

"Yes."

"And this... Ripley? You say he has the ability to read minds. What distance can he read from?"

"I don't know," I admitted. "But I've been trying to transmit information, hoping he might hear me."

"If he's still alive."

I pulled away from him, indignant at the suggestion they were dead. Despite what Armstrong had said, I wouldn't believe it. "I *have* to think they're okay."

Conal reached for me, picked me up, and deposited me back into the warm gap between his thighs. "You need to stay warm. They'll come back for us soon and you need your strength." His dark eyes were undecipherable as he gazed down at me. "I'm sorry I upset you. I even think you're possibly right. I can't imagine that fifteen shifters could kill two hundred and fifty people without someone having the opportunity to escape. The bloodsuckers are the obvious choice for survival; they would escape faster than the humans."

I bristled indignantly, prepared to leave the sanctuary of his warmth again, but Conal forestalled me, wrapping his arms more tightly around my body. It didn't stop me from voicing my anger. "They would never leave the humans to fend for themselves. You don't know them."

"Alright, alright," he responded soothingly, rubbing his hands across my arms as he tried to placate me. "I'll try and see things from your point of view, but you've got to remember, werewolves and vampires are enemies and have been for millennia. It's tough to believe there might be some good leeches out there."

"Stop calling them that! They *are* good people," I announced angrily. "It will help them to find us if you'll tell me what you know about Armstrong and where we are, so I can try and get the information to Ripley."

Conal rubbed my arms, pulling me closer to his chest. He didn't apologize for the leeches' comment, which annoyed me, but he was so warm and I relished the heat after being so cold, so I found myself willing to cut him some slack and didn't struggle to move away. His skin was smooth and firm against the exposed areas of my back and it was like lying against a sleek radiator. "Alright," he finally said. He seemed to have made up his mind to trust me. "I did a bit of reconnaissance when they brought me in here, I couldn't see anything because I was blindfolded, but my sense of smell is good. There are at least twenty guards in the grounds and the building. I can't be exact, because there were too many scent traces, some new and some old. It's a rough estimate."

"Okay." I wriggled in his arms, turning so I could see his face. "What do you know about Armstrong?"

Conal frowned heavily, as if the question bothered him. "That's the strange thing about all of this. He's usually a two-bit hustler, has a hand in some casinos in Vegas, and runs half a dozen strip joints. Enough to make him money, but anything bigger and he's usually working for someone else." Conal gazed down at me, his black eyes showing his puzzlement. "This is unusual for him. He's not gutsy enough to take on something like kidnapping."

"What day is it?"

"What does that have to do with anything?"

"Nothing. I just wondered how long I've been here. They took me on Saturday. I thought it might... give an indication of our chances." I didn't want to articulate what I was really thinking – if too much time had passed, Lucas was probably dead. They wouldn't be coming for me.

"It's Thursday. From the look of the sky when Armstrong removed the blindfold, I think it was late afternoon."

Thursday. It was five full days since I'd been kidnapped. It seemed much longer.

"Where were you when they took you?" I questioned.

Conal inhaled deeply. "With my Pack, in Natchez, Mississippi." He was rubbing my back and I shifted uncomfortably when his hand brushed across some of the bruising on my shoulder blades. "He's injured you badly," he snarled angrily.

"It's not so bad, mainly bruises. He hits me when he gets angry," I admitted quietly. I could see the deep cuts on his chest now I was lying across his lap, as he hadn't bothered to re-button his shirt. "He hasn't used his claws on me."

"I can see that." Conal gazed down at my face, lifting his hand to rub his thumb gently across the split in my lip and the cut on my cheek. "He doesn't want to do anything which would damage you enough to ruin his plans."

I shivered under the gentle caress, pulling away from his hand to look up at him. His expression was neutral, but I wasn't comfortable with the tender touch, it was too intimate between a man and a woman who barely knew one another. "Do you know how long it took to be brought here from Natchez?"

Conal dropped his hand to my back, resting it against the curve of my hip. "A couple of hours, maybe a little more."

"So where could we be?" My knowledge of geography was rudimentary at best; it had never been my favorite subject at school.

"I'm not sure which direction we headed in, I can only guess. Mississippi or Louisiana."

I couldn't hide my dismay. "That doesn't cut it down much. Do you know where Armstrong is usually based?"

Conal sighed. "I don't know that much about him. I think he might live in Louisiana, but I don't know where. New Orleans, maybe?"

Two states was a huge area to search – how could anybody possibly find us? Despite my doubts, I added these new details to the information I was collecting.

"Why did you kill his brother?" The question was voiced before I'd had time to consider whether it should be asked or not – but this man had killed someone. I was imprisoned with him; it seemed like a reasonable question.

Conal's eyes glittered black and hard. "His brother raped one of my pack members. She met him in a bar in Jackson and he followed her home to her apartment and attacked her. Beat the crap out of her. I hunted him down and killed him."

I shuddered, the visual picture he'd painted wasn't a comforting thought, although the reason he'd murdered could be justified. I wondered if I was being judgmental – I had a murder of my own in my background and couldn't throw stones.

We lapsed into silence; both deep in thought and my eyes began to close of their own accord while I mentally sent out my message to Ripley. *Gerard DuBonet, Laurence Armstrong, warm and humid, twenty guards, Mississippi or Louisiana, possibly New Orleans. Gerard DuBonet, Laurence Armstrong, warm and humid, twenty guards, Mississippi or Louisiana, possibly New Orleans.* A thought occurred to me, and I slightly amended the message. *Gerard DuBonet, Laurence Armstrong, warm and humid, twenty guards, Mississippi or Louisiana, possibly New Orleans, Conal Tremaine is a werewolf and he's helping me.*

Another question occurred to me and I voiced it. "Do you know why Lucas would tell them I was his mate?"

Conal was thoughtful for a minute before he answered. "Werewolves are dedicated to their partners. We mate for life. I imagine he assumed they were werewolves, not shifters. If I was kidnapping someone and I was told he or she was mated, I would have to reconsider my decision. I would never willingly part a couple who were mated. It's something we never do." He paused, rubbing his hand across my hip as he thought. "Your Lucas probably hoped they would reconsider if he told them you were mated to him. I imagine it was a last resort to try and save you from being taken, it sounds like he had few other viable options at the time." He dropped his gaze to mine, grimacing. "It was a risky move; he must have known they may... seek physical proof." He cursed harshly; his voice low and I cringed at his choice of words. "Werewolves would never dishonor a female like that. It was reprehensible behavior, something only scum like shifters would do."

We lapsed into silence for a few minutes and I wondered if he was partnered with someone. Although he wasn't married, perhaps he was already connected to someone in the special way he'd explained. "Do you have a mate?"

Conal smiled, shaking his head. "No, I don't. I'm the son of Lyell Tremaine, leader of the Tremaine Pack. I must choose another full blood werewolf to mate with, but I haven't yet found the one I would wish to mate with for life."

I thought about what he'd said, wondering about a race... did you call them a race, if they were werewolves? Wondering about selecting one person and committing to them for the rest of your life. Given my background, it was an alien concept to understand that kind of commitment to another person. I drifted off to sleep, feeling just a little safer with Conal Tremaine's arms around me.

Chapter 6

Entanglements

The dream was strange, almost realistic in its intensity. There was a dog licking me, its tongue both rough and soft against my skin. The moisture against my cheek was even cooling as the cold air hit it. How could there be a dog in the room? The dream began to distort as I woke, realizing where I was and what, or rather *who*, was licking me.

"What the hell are you *doing*?" I wrestled out of Conal's arms and got to my feet, knew my eyes were blazing with fury. I couldn't believe he'd been doing something so... *intimate*, without my permission or knowledge.

Conal leaned back against the wall, his face an emotionless mask. His black eyes were serious when he spoke. "You're wounded. My saliva will help to heal your wounds."

"You can't just go around... *licking* people!" I spluttered furiously. I was shaking from head to toe, infuriated by his calmness. "That's... well... it's rude, that's what it is! We don't even know one another!"

His eyes filled with amusement. "I think we probably know more about one another than most humans and werewolves ever do." He got to his feet and it was only then, standing near him, when I realized exactly how very tall and muscular he was. "And you weren't complaining until you woke up. Up until that point, you seemed to be enjoying it."

"I was not enjoying it!" Despite my denial, a hot blush rose over my cheeks.

"Alright," Conal said calmly. "I apologize."

For maybe a minute I glared up at him, trying to calm both my anger and ignore the fact that he was so handsome in a rugged, working class way and I was actually noticing it. I shook my head, trying to shake the thought from my mind and the anger dissipated rapidly as confusion took its place. How could I look at him and think handsome, when I was in love with Lucas? What was wrong with me?

He dropped down onto the mattress with his back against the wall and held his arms out, a silent invitation to return to the warmth he offered. I remained standing for a minute, trying to maintain the flicker of anger, but then my shoulders slumped in defeat. There was no point fighting with the one person who might be able to help me escape. I trudged across and sat down between his legs again, savoring the warmth, even as I tensed when my bare shoulder touched his chest. I thought about asking him to button his shirt, but decided not to bring the subject up.

"How long did I sleep?"

"An hour, maybe two." Conal arched his neck to stare up at the dirty window. "I think it might be nighttime."

I touched a finger to my cheek, brushing across the cut Conal had been licking. To my astonishment, it actually did feel better, certainly less painful than before I'd gone to sleep.

"I told you it would help," Conal said quietly.

"How?"

Conal shrugged his broad shoulders. "Our saliva has healing properties. When we're in battle, we sometimes get badly wounded. Licking the wounds makes them heal much faster.

Our saliva has anti-bacterial properties and an anesthetic quality."

My voice was rueful when I responded. "A couple of months ago that would have sounded crazy."

Conal smiled and I noticed the deep dimples in his cheeks. I found myself smiling back at him – the first time I'd smiled in days.

His smile disappeared too quickly, to be replaced by a deep frown. "I think they'll come for us soon. I've got no choice; I'll have to probe your mind again." He gripped my waist in his hands and turned me effortlessly, so I was facing him. "I don't want to do it, it's extremely dangerous."

"What could happen?" It was a question I didn't particularly want to hear the answer to, but I couldn't help but ask.

"You're the first human I've attempted it on. I've used it on others of my kind and shifters. It's killed some," he admitted softly. "Others have been left psychologically disabled."

I couldn't think of a single response. What could I say? What reply was there to make, knowing Conal was being forced to do something that could leave me disabled for life? "I don't suppose you can just pretend you're doing it?"

"Armstrong would sense it wasn't authentic." He sighed, rubbing his hands across my arms. "If I don't make this realistic, make him believe I'm making progress, he'll be pissed. We're going to have to give him a little information, make him think it's working and he's getting closer to his goal." His gaze flickered around the small room before he dropped his eyes to mine. "While you slept, I was thinking about getting us out of here. There are too many guards, I couldn't take them on by myself and protect you." He paused, studying me carefully. "I wondered if we could use the spirits; get them to unlock the door? It might give us a chance; provide us with the element of surprise."

"I don't think we can risk it. Armstrong can't learn about my power. It would be too dangerous if he understood what I could do. Besides, I've only made a spirit do something physical once. I can't guarantee it would work a second time."

Conal nodded thoughtfully. "I'm certain you can do it again, Charlotte. But you're right, it's a bad idea."

"Can't you just... turn into a wolf? Couldn't you fight him if you were a werewolf?" I asked hopefully.

He snorted derisively. "There you go, thinking like a human again. Werewolves are different to shifters. They change on a whim, or become half-man, half-animal. A true werewolf only transforms at full moon."

What he'd said to Armstrong came back to me and I shivered. "There's a full moon coming."

Conal nodded, his black eyes impassive. "In two nights."

"You'll become..." Full-on fear gripped my chest and I shut my eyes. He would become a wolf and I would be trapped inside this room with him. "Will it still happen, even if you're inside this building?"

"Regrettably, yeah. The myth says we have to be in moonlight to transform – that doesn't make a difference. I'll transform to wolf on the first night of the full moon and it happens for three nights in a row. In wolf form, I won't recognize you, won't know you. I'll kill you." His voice held no emotion; he stated it as a matter of cold, hard fact.

I rubbed my hands over my face and on through my tangled hair. "This situation just keeps getting better and better," I groaned.

"Let's worry about one thing at a time. We need to prepare for our next visit with Armstrong." He paused, gazing down at me and the expression on his face softened. "Charlotte, you need to concentrate."

It was a struggle to drag myself back from the terrifying thought of being ripped apart by a werewolf. When I looked up at him, I found it hard to believe this man was going to become a wild beast. It seemed incomprehensible. "Okay, I'm listening."

"I'm going to tell Armstrong I've broken though a shield, but you have a second shield in place. That will buy us some time. We have to let him think we're making progress. I'll probe your mind and it's going to be intensely painful, but I promise, I won't probe any deeper than I have to, to make it look authentic."

I nodded, swallowing nervously.

"In the meantime, we've got to find a way out of here. I thought about breaking that window and shunting you out of here before I transform. I figure you're tiny enough to fit through it. The only flaw with that plan is that there are shifters out there, guarding the grounds and they'll only take minutes to pick up your scent. Armstrong wants you kept intact – in which case, he'll be likely to kill me before the full moon. It's gonna be like walking a tightrope, trying to keep you alive, me alive and somehow convince Armstrong not to kill me before the full moon. If I can make it through until then and still be alive, we've got a fighting chance – but I still need to figure out how to get you out of harm's way."

My head was spinning and panic gripped my chest. I was certain I was going to die, no matter which way things eventuated. There wasn't a bright side to the mess in which we found ourselves. It was ironic to think I was looking for a way to kill myself a few months ago, but now I wanted to live. When I peeked up at Conal's face, I knew he would see the panic in my eyes. Tears brimmed against my eyelashes and rolled down my cheeks. I winced when the salty liquid stung the open cuts.

Conal leaned down and licked my skin gently, his tongue picking up the tears and brushing them away. His warm breath on my face was strangely comforting, his tongue flicking tenderly across the cut on my cheek. He captured me in his arms and turned me in his lap until I lay across his body, his arms encircling me. I lay still, closing my eyes as he gently worked his way down to the cut on my bottom lip. The tip of his tongue probed across the cut and the anesthetic effect of his saliva was soothing. The moment was broken when he stopped and I opened my eyes to stare up at him.

Conal was gazing at me, his pitch black eyes burning with emotion and tension visible in the ticking muscle of his jaw. I returned his gaze, a multitude of emotions assaulting me from all sides. The feelings I experienced were not just relief and comfort.

"I want to kiss you," he admitted huskily and there was tenderness in his expression, a softness I hadn't seen before. The look a man gives a woman when he wants her. He continued to gaze at me silently, my confused face reflecting back at me in his eyes as he waited for my response.

It was impossible to speak, to vocalize anything when I was choked by the emotions roiling through me. I was frightened, I was tired, and I was scared. In the midst of those emotions, there was something else, feelings for this man who held me so securely in his arms, who was doing everything he could, to try and keep me alive. This was a man who was willing to risk his own life to help me. Unable to find any words to express myself, I nodded hesitantly.

He dropped his head and his tongue pressed against my lower lip, pressing tiny licks against the split. When he was satisfied, he captured my mouth against his own in a smooth motion, his lips warm and soft. He kissed me gently, with exquisite tenderness and when he brushed his tongue across my lips, I opened instinctively for him.

I flicked my tongue across his teeth tentatively, desire flaring to life low in my groin as I explored his mouth with mine. Conal groaned and deepened the kiss, pulling me closer to him and his heat radiated through my thin dress. I wrapped my arms around his neck, aware of nothing that mattered, other than to have this man kiss me. His hand snaked upwards from my waist until he was cupping my breast in his palm, rubbing my nipple tenderly with his thumb as he kissed me over and over. I was aware of how much he desired me, knew I wanted him just as much. I trailed across his shoulder with my fingertips, drawing a path down to his chest, slipping my hand inside his open shirt. I found one hard nipple and rolled it between my thumb and forefinger, delighted by the way it made him react and he moaned into my mouth. His lips were so warm, so incredibly soft—

Reality hit me like a steam train and I wrenched away from him, crouching in the corner like a frightened rabbit. "I'm sorry, this is wrong, I shouldn't be..." My voice trailed off uncertainly and I cringed.

Conal smiled tenderly. The look in his eyes confirmed he was being subjected to the same rush of hormones as I had. "I should be apologizing, Charlotte. I shouldn't have done that. You're in love with the leech."

I nodded miserably. Shame and horror at what I'd done flooded over my psyche and I wrapped my arms around chest, trying to hold myself together. How could I have let that happen? What was I thinking? I loved Lucas, loved him with all my heart. *But Lucas might be dead,* my traitorous mind whispered. I shook myself physically, unwilling to believe Lucas could be gone forever and reprimanding myself for even considering the possibility. Even if he was gone, how could I kiss another man? Worse still – I'd enjoyed it. The guilt wrapped itself around my mind; like ivy, it strangled my soul.

And then, I heard the footsteps.

Chapter 7

Transformation

The pain was unbearable. I knew Conal was probing as lightly as he possibly could, but the pain was intolerable, excruciating. My head was going to explode, I thought my skull would split open at any moment and I wanted to die. I'd passed out before Conal removed his fingers from my temples and woke in the cold room that was our prison.

Conal lay on the floor, he was unconscious and had been badly beaten, one of his eyes swollen shut, visible skin black and blue. There were a multitude of claw marks across his back and shoulders and he groaned when I tried to drag him towards the mattress. It was physically impossible to move him, so I busied myself cleaning the multitude of cuts and grazes that had been inflicted on his body.

I hadn't come out of our session with Armstrong in much better shape. My shoulder ached from a punch Armstrong had meted out and there was another angry graze on my cheek. Armstrong had hit me across the head with his claws extended, resulting in a deep gash on my forehead. I had bruising on my throat where he'd gripped me tightly while Conal probed my mind. Tears rolled unchecked down my cheeks as I cleaned the bloody mess that was Conal's back, wondering how much more of this we could survive.

When Conal woke up, he drew me into his arms and held me close. There seemed no way out of this predicament, no way to survive what Armstrong was doing to us. Conal stood up, lifting me effortlessly in his arms, laying me gently onto the filthy mattress before lying beside me, enclosing me in the circle of his arms. I lay my head against his chest and moaned quietly. A headache was pulsing through my temples, with no way of relieving it. I would have given a million dollars for some Tylenol and wondered if Conal's probing had caused damage, whether the pain was a signal of some underlying injury deep within my brain.

Hours passed, hours spent cradled in one another's arms and waiting for the sound of approaching footsteps that would begin the next round of torture. Little was said between us, I was certain we would die here and suspected Conal would agree with me. Although I'd hoped and prayed for Lucas and the others to find us, it seemed increasingly likely they'd been killed by Armstrong's men back in Montana. My resolute determination to believe they were alive seemed more improbable as the hours wore on. Hope was fading, although a tiny corner of my mind kept reminding me that Lucas was strong, and if there was any way of him finding me, he would. But there seemed to be no hope of survival now. If Armstrong insisted on Conal probing my mind again, it would kill me.

Hours later, the footsteps did approach and the door was thrust open. It was Armstrong himself who stood in the doorway, staring at us lying on the mattress together. He laughed derisively and sauntered further into the room. "How cozy. The werewolf and his whore. It seems you've gotten very friendly with one another." Two guards stood behind him, guns drawn at the ready.

Conal remained quiet and I wondered what was behind this visit. Why was Armstrong down here, when normally we were dragged upstairs? Armstrong crouched beside us and leered at me. "Such a waste, you're such a pretty little thing. I would have been delighted to keep you." He glanced at the window, although I knew full well, there was nothing to be seen through it. "Full moon tonight, Tremaine. As you proud werewolves keep telling me, you only change at full moon. An hour or two from now, you'll have to transform, you'll feel the urge deep within your soul and be unable to avoid it." He stood up abruptly, gripping a handful of my hair and yanking me up with him.

I shrieked as a handful of my hair was ripped out by the roots, and he held me so his face was only inches from mine. "This is your last chance, you stubborn bitch!" Armstrong growled. "Tell me what I want to know! I know you have powers far greater than the wolf has let on; I know he's tried to keep the truth from me. Tell me the truth – right now – or I'll leave you in here while he transforms."

With my teeth gritted, I stared into his eyes defiantly and knew I was signing my own death sentence. "My name is Charlotte Duncan. I'm an artist. I don't know what you're talking about."

This time he didn't bother with any niceties when he hit me. He punched my stomach, knocking the wind out of my lungs and I slumped to the ground, stars flickering in my peripheral vision as I rolled into a protective ball. Armstrong kicked my back half a dozen times for good measure, uttering a tirade of expletives with each blow.

Conal roared gutturally and launched himself off the mattress, aiming for Armstrong's throat with his large hands. Armstrong was too quick for him, dodging to one side. The two guards joined Armstrong in beating Conal, kicking, and punching him until he lay motionless on the ground.

Seemingly satisfied with himself, Armstrong stepped back from Conal's battered body, wiping his hands against his trousers to remove Conal's blood from his skin. His attention turned to me and I whimpered. "I can see this is one situation where I'm not going to win, you dumb bitch." He knelt beside me, extending his claws and a frisson of fear trickled up my spine. "I could have given you anything you'd wanted, if you would have just cooperated. Now though, I'm going to leave you here with your buddy, Conal. He'll transform in an hour or two, won't be able to stop himself. Nothing will please me more, than to come in here tomorrow morning and see bits of you splattered all over the damn room. Then I'm going to kill Tremaine and every single member of his pack. And it will be your entire damn fault." In a movement I could barely distinguish, he brought his hand down and across my chest, ripping the skin with his extended claws. "There. That'll give your fuck buddy the scent of blood. He won't be able to resist it."

He stood up, grinning as he admired his macabre handiwork. Blood was spurting from where he'd ripped my skin open and I could feel it, warm as it trickled down over my breasts and ribs. In a last act of defiance, I continued to stare at him, refusing to be cowed by his bullying. He turned on his heel and stepped through the open door, the guards following behind and they slammed the door shut, turning the key in the lock.

When they'd left, I stared down at my chest in mounting horror. He'd torn my skin open from my left collarbone to my left breast. Sobbing wretchedly, I grabbed a handful of material from the bottom or my ruined dress and pulled it up, putting pressure on the wound to try and slow the flow of blood.

Clutching the material to my chest, I crawled across to where Conal lay, very still and worryingly silent. For one horrible moment I thought he was dead, but with relief, I saw the steady movement of his lungs moving up and down. I fell against him, wrapping an arm around him as I waited for death. Although it was obviously useless, I ran through the mantra in my mind, over and over again.

Conal regained consciousness sometime later and I could tell he was fast approaching the time when he would transform. His eyes were more animal-like and despite the beating he'd taken, he was filled with nervous energy, which radiated from his skin like a mild electrical current.

"What happened?" His voice was low, filled with pain.

"He's left me in here, so you'll kill me when you change into a werewolf," I explained dully. "Then he's going to kill you. And then he's going to kill your pack."

Conal gazed at me, eyes filled with disbelief. "Are you serious? After all this, he's willing to let you die because he didn't get what he wanted?"

"He's angry, I guess he figures he'll cut his losses and get rid of us." I was beyond caring. If this was the way it had to be, so be it.

Conal's attention moved to the clump of material I was still clasping to my chest and he sat up abruptly. With a groan, he held his head between his hands. "Fuck. I feel like I've been hit by an eighteen wheeler."

"You look like you've been hit by an eighteen wheeler," I agreed wearily. I painfully pulled myself into a sitting position beside him.

Conal reached for me, carefully moving my hand and peeling the blood-soaked cloth away from my skin. His eyes widened when he saw the shredded mess Armstrong had made of my chest. "That bastard. I'll kill him myself!"

"Great. You can get onto that, straight after you've eaten me." I giggled wildly, the sound bordering on hysterical as it echoed through the empty room.

"Charlotte." Conal pulled me onto his lap, cradling me tenderly in his arms. "Charlotte, listen to me. I'm going to try to remain human and keep myself from transforming. I'll have to use all my strength, every ounce of willpower to stop it from happening." He drew a deep breath and gasped with pain. "I need you to remind me of *who you are*. Do you understand me?" He captured my chin between his thumb and forefinger, drawing my face up until our eyes met. "I need you," he leaned forward and kissed my lips softly, "to remind me of why I can't transform. Remind me of who you are; how important you are to me and why it's imperative I stay human so I don't hurt you."

I stared at him, nodding tentatively. I understood what he meant, knew from the look in his black eyes that this was more than just him wanting to save me. This was an emotional bond, a depth of emotion that was beyond what he should be feeling for me. If I was honest with myself, I was experiencing the same emotions. The thought would have shocked me, made me consider my moral values, if I wasn't so terrified.

"Good girl. If we get through this, when that bastard opens the door in the morning I'm going to transform and rip his fucking throat out. And when I do, I want you to run, run, and find somewhere to hide from me until I can transform back. Find a cupboard, a wardrobe, preferably something that can be locked to try and keep you safe. When I revert to human form, I'll come and find you and I'm going to get you out of here."

I nodded, too traumatized to speak.

"Charlotte, I know you don't want to hear this. I know you love the bloodsucker. But I'm going to say it anyway. I love you. I think I've loved you from the moment I laid eyes on you. I don't want to kill you, but I need to think you love me back. Just for tonight. Just so, we can get through this. Okay?" He rubbed his fingers tenderly across my cheek, his dark eyes piercing. "Tell me you love me; remind me of why I love you, what I'm doing this for."

I reached towards him tentatively, rubbing my fingers across his bruised face. "I love you," I whispered huskily. "I love you, Conal."

And God help me, it was the truth.

He closed his eyes and took a deep breath, his whole body shuddering with the effort. "Good girl." With tremendous exertion, he maneuvered us both onto the mattress, then wrapped his arms around me, and held me firmly against his body. Lowering his head, he removed the material from my chest and stared at the shredded skin for a minute, before he began to lick near my collarbone hesitantly. He was cautious, as if he expected I would tell him to stop. I shut my eyes, forcing myself to talk to him as he helped heal the wound. "I love you, Conal. I want you to hold me and kiss me. I want you to remember my scent, remember the feel of me in your arms."

His arms tightened around me and he became more confident as he licked deep into the wounds, the movement of his tongue against the damaged skin making me wince. And still I continued to talk to him, my hands rubbing back and forth over warm skin that emitted a subtle energy as his need to transform grew.

Every minute seemed as if it lasted an hour, every passing second made it apparent how much of a struggle this was for Conal, how painful it was to try and halt something which didn't want to be stopped. He continued licking at my wounds and trembles emanated from deep within his body as he fought against becoming a werewolf. Occasionally, he moaned softly, stiffening as he battled against what was for him, a natural adaptation from human to beast. When it seemed it would become impossible for him to continue, I reached up and kissed him, probing his mouth soothingly with my own and he would calm again, breathing deeply against my skin as if it reminded him of what he was doing.

I was concentrating on Conal, using so much energy trying to keep him from losing control that it took a while to realize something out of the ordinary was happening outside our prison. At first, I heard unusual sounds from upstairs, as if furniture was being scraped across the floor and knocked over. Then I heard yelling, both from inside and outside the building. I didn't know what to make of it. I tried to listen whilst I talked to Conal, trying to help him concentrate. He'd given up licking my wounds and lay in my arms, panting with the supreme effort required to remain human. He was drenched in sweat, a fine sheen of perspiration across his forehead and he lay with his eyes closed, groaning almost continuously.

There was the sound of more shouting nearby and the resonance of footsteps running down the hall outside. And then I heard something I'd never thought to hear again.

"Charlotte! Where are you? Charlotte!" It was Ben's voice and I extricated myself from Conal's arms to sit up.

"Ben! We're in here, in this room!" I shouted hoarsely.

The door was smashed in with such power, it collapsed from its hinges, the heavy metal screaming in protest. Ben and Nick Lingard stood side by side in the doorway, Ripley at their backs.

"Where's Lucas?" Dread crept over me when I realized Lucas wasn't here – had he survived?

"He's safe," Ben reassured me quickly.

Conal hauled himself into a sitting position, his eyes wild and his breathing labored as he focused on Nick. "Shifter!" he growled harshly. His back arched and I could see he was almost beyond stopping himself from turning.

I placed a gentle hand on the centre of his chest. "Conal, Conal!" He looked ready to launch at Nick, his teeth bared, but the touch of my hand against his bare chest brought him back to himself and instead, he glanced down at me, his eyes animal-like and intense. "He's a friend, Conal. Don't hurt him."

With a nod, Conal turned his attention back to the men in the doorway. "Get her out of here. I can't stop the transformation any longer."

Ben glanced at Nick and inclined his head. "You take her. The blood..."

Nick was at my side instantaneously, before I could see him move and he scooped me into his arms. With Ben and Ripley running behind us, we were out the door and up the stairs in seconds, sprinting through the house I'd grown to despise. From behind us, there was a spine-tingling howl and I guessed Conal was transforming. I wrapped my arms tighter around Nick's neck, frightened to imagine what would happen if Conal caught up with us.

Everywhere I looked, there was carnage. Bodies littered the floor, some missing limbs, or worse, eviscerated and there was blood everywhere. I caught sight of William and Gwynn, fighting side by side, their clothes and skin covered with blood as they decapitated one of the guards. I squeezed my eyes shut and held Nick tightly, reluctant to see anything else.

Nick slowed his pace when we got outside and laid me on the grass. We were instantly surrounded by a guard of vampires and shifters, forming a circle around where I lay. Doctor Harding appeared, medical bag in hand and I smiled at him weakly.

Before I had a chance to speak, Lucas appeared in my peripheral vision, dropping to his knees. He was covered in blood, his blue jeans turned black with it and he was carrying a sword which he lay carefully on the ground before he caught my hand in his, drawing it to his lips to kiss my knuckles tenderly.

"Lucas, you came for me." In the distance I could hear screaming and yelling, the sickening noise of bodies being torn apart and yet, it didn't seem to matter so much now Lucas was by my side.

Lucas gazed at me, horror reflecting in his eyes when he cast a downward glance across my injuries. "Yes, my love. I came for you."

I suddenly remembered the state I was in and stared up at him, stricken with anxiety. "There's blood..."

Lucas squeezed my fingers, possibly the only part of my body that wasn't cut, scraped, or bruised. He kissed my fingers softly. "It's okay, Charlotte, I can handle it."

With Nick's assistance, Dr. Harding lowered himself to his knees and opened his bag, immediately operating in physician mode. "Charlotte, I'm going to give you something for the pain, and then we'll get you out of here."

I managed a faint smile. "I kept the cast on."

A ghost of a smile curved his lips. "I'm glad to hear it. Now stop talking and relax. You need to rest, you're safe now."

"Please, make sure no-one hurts Conal. He helped me, he saved me," I begged quietly.

"Charlotte, we got your messages. Ripley heard you. I will make sure Conal isn't hurt," Lucas said. "I give you my word of honor, no harm will come to him."

Dr. Harding injected something into my arm and I drifted away into a place that was peaceful and quiet, the worry, and stress floating away from me as though they no longer existed.

Chapter 8

Rescued

I drifted back into awareness with a television playing softly somewhere in the room. I was lying on my side, warm and comfortable under a pile of blankets. Memories began to seep into my consciousness; being rescued, the blood, the bodies. Relief was sweet as I relished being out of harm's way and knowing Lucas and my friends had survived. I rolled carefully onto my back, which was incredibly painful. I wasn't sure there was a square inch of my body that wasn't bruised and hurting. Badly.

I opened my eyes and glanced around slowly, in too much pain to move more than an inch at a time. It was dark outside and the room was illuminated by a couple of elegant table lamps. To my right, a large window revealed a view of the city, thousands of lights spreading out into the distance and twinkling brightly. I didn't recognize it and wondered where I was. I tried to raise myself on my elbows in the bed and groaned. Big mistake.

"Charlotte."

I breathed in deeply, inhaling the aroma of pine needles, ocean, and sunshine. Instantly I relaxed. Lucas was here, with me, and I was safe.

He sat on the bed cautiously, taking care not to jostle me. He smiled, but there was concern etched into his perfect features.

He reached forward and tucked my hair behind my ear, his cool fingers brushing across my skin.

"Hi," I croaked roughly, my throat sore and dry.

"Hi yourself," he breathed. The skin around his eyes was dark, confirming he hadn't fed recently. Lucas picked up a glass from the bedside table and held it for me so I could sip the cool water from the bendy straw.

"What day is it?"

"Saturday."

"How long have I been asleep?"

"About nine hours."

I tried a shrug and grimaced when pain rippled through my shoulders and back. "Seems like longer."

"It was a good, heavy sleep. Jerome said you needed rest before dealing with anything else."

"You didn't bite me," I stated seriously. "There was a lot of blood."

He smiled. "There was a lot of blood. Seeing you so badly beaten, the blood didn't seem to matter all that much. All I wanted to do was get you out of there and I knew I wouldn't be tempted. I knew I could control it."

"I hurt," I admitted.

"I know, my Charlotte." He leaned forward and kissed my forehead, his lips little more than a whisper against my skin. "You were wounded quite seriously." He motioned to a bag hanging on an IV stand, attached to a thin tube and needle inserted into the back of my hand. "Jerome is giving you saline to rehydrate you and he will give you something again soon for the pain."

"Where are we?"

"New Orleans. This is where you were being held, in a house to the north of the city."

I glanced around the room. "This isn't a hospital?"

"No. Once again, we were at a loss to explain your injuries. Those marks on your chest," his eyes flickered down to my chest, his eyes hardening visibly with fury, "were difficult to give explanation. We decided to bring you here to the hotel and when you are well enough, I'll take you home."

Home. What a wonderful thought. I wanted to go home, wanted to be held by Lucas, and made to feel safe. Tears welled unbidden in my eyes. This wasn't going to be as simple as I wanted it to be.

"Charlotte, what's wrong? Should I get Jerome?" Lucas leaned over me, his face inches from mine and I closed my eyes, frightened to tell him what I knew had to be admitted. It was only fair that I was honest and guilt filled my heart.

"Lucas – I'm ashamed of myself." Tears fell in earnest down my cheeks.

"Why, my love?"

"I— when we were being held, I did some things I'm ashamed of. Things that I shouldn't have done." I was struggling to put into words what needed to be said, things which needed to be brought out into the open.

"None of that matters now," Lucas responded soothingly. "You did what you needed to do to survive. We are amazed that you survived at all."

"No!" I paused, taking a deep breath. "I let Conal kiss me. And... I kissed him back." I looked away, squeezing my eyes shut – certain Lucas would be disgusted.

"I already knew, my Charlotte," Lucas said, his voice raw with emotion. He waited for a response and when nothing was forthcoming; he caught the tip of my chin with his thumb and drew me to face him. "Look at me, please," he commanded.

I bit my lip anxiously, but did as he requested. I searched his face for anger, but there was nothing to see.

"Charlotte, I know what happened. After Conal transformed back to human this morning, he and I talked. He explained that

Laurence Armstrong told you we were all dead. He told me what you'd been subjected to and what Armstrong was after." He sighed, the sound heavy in the quiet room. "And he told me that you kissed and how he feels about you. He assured me that he knew you were in love with me."

I wiped my palms across my cheeks, brushing away the tears. "You're not angry?"

"No, I'm not angry." Lucas's voice was reassuring, his expression neutral. "Jealous, definitely. But not angry, with you or Conal, not after everything you've been through." He leaned forward, his cool lips brushing fleetingly across my own. "I love you, Charlotte. I thought I'd lost you and I nearly went out of my mind, trying to find you."

"Is Conal okay?" I asked cautiously. The last time I'd seen him, he'd been badly beaten and struggling to maintain his human form.

"He's almost fully recovered. Werewolves are remarkably adept at recovering from serious injury. We assisted him to release his pack from Armstrong's men after you were retrieved safely."

"You hate one another," I pointed out. "Conal told me vampires and werewolves are enemies."

"That's true," he conceded. "But it doesn't mean we can't help one another if a situation arises. After what he did to keep you safe, I hold Conal in high regard. He did everything in his power to keep you alive. I owe him."

"Is everyone else okay?" I'd seen William, Gwynn, Ripley, and Ben. "Did you all come down to New Orleans?"

"Yes, and we are all fine. Of Nick's pack, young Marco has a broken arm, but Jerome has set it and he'll be fine in a couple of days. In fact, we have all come out of this relatively unscathed, in direct contrast to you."

"What happened to Armstrong?" I trembled violently, remembering him hitting me relentlessly in the past week.

"Dead. Conal tore him to pieces. So are all his men." Lucas's voice was cold, lacking any distinguishable emotion. "There was a mysterious fire at his compound. We have covered our tracks so the residents of New Orleans can rest easy in their beds at night."

The trembling morphed into full-blown shakes and Lucas gathered me into his arms, his movements slow and careful as he attempted to do it without hurting me. He held me against his chest and I savored being in the security of his arms.

I snuggled against his chest, feeling the hard muscle beneath my hands. "How did you know where I was?"

Lucas kissed my forehead. "It wasn't easy, Ripley heard your message about Gerard DuBonet, and that's all we had to begin with. We tracked your movements through the woods, but lost you when they switched to vehicles. We started with what we had, traced Gerard DuBonet and discovered he lived down here in Mississippi." His voice grew colder again. "It took some convincing before he would talk, but he eventually figured out it would be less painful for him if he told us who he worked for."

"Is he dead?"

Lucas nodded. "He deserved it. He was looking to make a fast buck and he didn't give a damn who got hurt while he was doing it. Armstrong apparently offered him a sizeable reward to visit us in Puckhaber and find out about you. Stupid fool, he didn't realize he was opening vampires up to a war with the shifters, if Armstrong had succeeded in getting what he wanted."

"I wish I'd told you about him. He introduced himself to me on the morning of the wedding. I thought he might be a vampire, his hand was cold when he touched mine, but then I saw him carting bags of ice around and I assumed that was why his hands were so cold."

"What I don't understand," Lucas said carefully, his gaze focused on mine, "is why you had no warning from the spirits."

I cringed, biting my lip anxiously. "I had them shut away."

Lucas sounded incredulous when he responded. "Why would you do that?"

"It was so peaceful, not having to listen to them all the time and I guess I got comfortable with the silence. It seemed easier to keep them shut in the box, once I'd learned how, than to deal with them constantly yammering at me."

Lucas sighed heavily and there was a note of frustration in his voice when he spoke. "Charlotte, that was a very dangerous thing to do. You have the ability to provide yourself with warnings of danger – you should be using it all the time."

"I know," I agreed miserably. He wasn't telling me anything I hadn't already beaten myself up about repetitively.

"You do realize, if you'd kept your lines of communication open, this might not have happened," he continued. I couldn't blame him for being annoyed, what'd I'd done was stupid and I knew it. The knowledge didn't make me feel any better and tears dripped down my cheeks silently.

Lucas was immediately remorseful. "Oh, Charlotte," he breathed against my hair as he held me close. "Don't cry. Please don't cry."

"You're angry with me," I sobbed.

"No, no. Not angry. I'm frustrated, because we may have been able to save you this pain if you'd used the incredible gift you've been given," he explained. He kissed my lips softly. "Please, promise me you won't shut them away again."

"I promise." Lucas rubbed his hands over my back as I composed myself, his touch tender against the bruising. "What happened after you got the information from DuBonet?"

"We had intelligence a few days ago, suggesting that Armstrong was holding you, but we couldn't find him. We split up into groups, working our way through every group of vampires and werewolves in the southern states, trying to figure out where you were being held. Nobody could tell us anything. Ripley, Thut, and I were in Mississippi, we'd been advised of the

Tremaine pack, but when we arrived there, we discovered the whole pack was missing."

"Thutmose is here?" I'd met Egyptian vampire, Thutmose Bustani just before the wedding, along with his Kiss, which comprised three beautiful young Egyptian women. Like Lucas and his Kiss, the Bustani group relied on animal blood to survive, and when I'd met them, I'd had an amusing mental picture of them hunting camels in the Egyptian desert, which, needless to say, I hadn't shared. Thut was officially the oldest vampire I'd met to date – he really *was* in Egypt during the time of the pharaohs. A man of regal bearing, he was tall and almost emaciated-looking, with dark curly hair cropped closely to his skull. He had a strong beak of a nose and black eyes lying beneath beetle-black eyebrows. Softly spoken, he had an accent that he'd no doubt retained since he was created in 3000BC. Yep, that's right, before Christ.

"The Bustani Kiss offered to help us search for you, as did Nick, and our friends from New York."

Lucas's friends from New York were another small Kiss of four members - Harley Fitzgerald and his partner, Ethan Underwood, their friend Alexander Ellis and his wife, Imogen Sparks. All four were young, in terms of vampires, with Harley being created in 1920 and he was the oldest of the group.

"You didn't want them to know about me."

Lucas smiled wryly. "After you were kidnapped, there wasn't much point in keeping anything from them. They were naturally curious as to why anyone would be interested in kidnapping you. Besides which, Amunet had been picking up traces of your spirit friends for days and she saw your mother trip the waiter, knew that she was a spirit and was wondering how she'd materialized in the middle of the wedding."

Amunet was one of the women in Thut's Kiss – with dark wavy hair and a quick smile; her pretty features were marred by copious scars from when she'd contracted smallpox, shortly before her creation. Lucas had explained it was unusual for a vampire to carry scars after they rose, but Amunet did and nobody appeared to know why. Amunet didn't let the disfiguration bother her, and with a voluptuous figure and a happy personality, you quickly forgot about it. Besides being a powerful telekinetic, able to lift furniture in the air and gently place it in another position, Amunet had been able to see the dead for many years, although she was unable to contact them. She used complicated herbal potions to help lay their spirits to rest and she and Acenith had spent many hours talking together about their shared interest in medicinal herbs. Of course, my particular talent had been kept secret by Lucas and the others but I'd found it fascinating to hear Amunet discuss her ability. "Traces of my spirits?"

"Apparently in the days before the wedding, Amunet could see traces of ghostly images, trailing around you. She thought they were spirits who had attached themselves to you for some reason and she was going to ask about it after the wedding, to see if I wanted her to remove them for you. When she discovered what you are able to do, she was very impressed and she can't wait to speak to you about the ability."

"They're still here?"

"No, they've returned to Montana along with some of the others. Ben, Striker, and Marianne have remained with me, along with Nick and his men. Harley and his Kiss have returned to New York."

"How did you find Conal's pack?"

We picked up the scent from where they'd been taken and found them being held here in Louisiana. Nick and his men managed to infiltrate the group, no easy task as werewolves and shifters hate one another. They got information about where you and Conal were being held. We headed straight to Armstrong's compound and Ripley started picking up your messages."

"He heard me?" I was dumbfounded, having believed he wouldn't hear me at all.

Lucas smiled. "Yes, he heard you. When we got within fifty miles of where you were held, he was picking you up loud and clear. It was remarkable, Ripley normally hears thoughts from a distance of perhaps a mile or two at the most, yet you managed to broadcast from a far greater distance. Thanks to you, we knew how many we were dealing with and importantly, that Conal was one of the good guys."

I closed my eyes, relief, and weariness washing over me in equal parts. It felt as if I'd been away from Lucas for months, not just days. I breathed deeply, filling my senses with his aroma and felt secure at last. Lucas snuggled beside me and traced his lips over my cheek, kissing me softly until I drifted back to sleep.

Chapter 9

Desire

When I woke again, Lucas was gone and Marianne was sitting on the edge of the bed, flicking through a magazine. Whilst her hair remained the rich-but-relatively-mundane black, she'd gelled it into half a dozen pointy spikes. She was wearing a black t-shirt decorated with skull and crossbones, black jeans with safety pins decorating the front of each leg and her feet were encased in Doc Martins with bright orange laces. What looked like a black leather dog collar graced her slender neck. She smiled brightly when she saw my eyes open, dropping the magazine onto the bedside table, and reaching forward to give me a careful hug.

"Where's Lucas?"

"He and Striker have driven out of town to hunt." She wrinkled her pert nose delicately. "The problems with a big city – too far away from a decent meal."

I decided to ignore that thought and attempted to sit up in bed, instead. It was no better – the aches and pains seemed to be increasing exponentially each time I regained my senses. A quick glance revealed I was still wearing the dress I'd worn to the wedding. Even my weak human senses could discern the need for a hot shower and a change of clothes.

Dr. Harding walked into the room and smiled warmly. "Charlotte, it's good to have you back."

"It's good to be back, Dr. Harding."

"For God's sake, Charlotte, call me Jerome. Dr. Harding makes me sound so old," he grumbled, limping across the carpet. He lowered himself onto the edge of the bed, his gaze flickering over my face. "You've had quite an ordeal, young lady."

I noticed the large window was wide open and a soft breeze was blowing the curtains. "Can I shower? I think I need one."

"You do smell of werewolf. Amongst other things. We've kept the windows open to clear the air a little," Marianne responded cheerily. She winked. "That's what happens when you hang out with werewolves and shifters."

"Marianne, for God's sake," Doctor Harding chided, "subtlety is not one of your strong points." He returned to his careful scrutiny of my expression. "How's the pain level?"

"Tolerable," I responded quietly. "What's the damage?"

"Surprisingly, nothing broken. Lots of cuts and bruising and this," he motioned towards my chest, "which is by far your worst injury. When I first saw it, I thought you'd need a multitude of sutures to pull it back together, but it seems to be healing on its own. Remarkably quickly, I might add." His gray eyes were inquisitive, as if he suspected there was some reason for the rapid recovery.

"Conal's saliva has healing properties. He—" There was no easy way to admit how Conal had done the healing and I flushed red with embarrassment. "He licked the wounds."

If Jerome was surprised by this frank admission, he was remarkably adept at keeping the sentiment from his face. I knew how it looked; the deep gouges had penetrated from my collarbone to the top of my left breast. He probed the skin near my collarbone gently, touching the jagged slashes that appeared to be sealing of their own accord. I was astounded when I glanced down and saw them – they'd been much worse when Armstrong had inflicted them, penetrating to the bone. "I'd heard that werewolves have amazing regenerative powers in their saliva. I've never seen the evidence until now. What Conal has managed to do has effectively sped up the healing process by at least a week or perhaps two."

"Can I get her into the bathroom and make her human again?" Marianne asked.

Jerome nodded. "I'll remove the cast."

"Isn't it too early?"

"Oh, I believe we can give you a little leeway. I had a glance at the cast before we brought you back to the hotel – after the kick you gave the shape shifter, the plaster isn't looking too stable." He winked, amusement clear in his expression.

"For future reference, Charlotte, as much as it was probably very satisfying to kick that creep, shape shifters are nearly as impenetrable as vampires." Marianne grinned wickedly. "But I did think it was very courageous of you."

"Thank you."

"I'll take the plaster off. Marianne, make yourself useful, run a bath, and get out of my way."

"Can't I have a shower?" I said, and there was just the tiniest note of a whine involved. I wanted to wash my hair, stand under a soaking hot spray, and get a week's worth of grime off my skin.

"No, you most certainly can't have a shower. You'd struggle to stand for long enough," Jerome grumbled. "You'll be weak and shaky for a few days yet, young lady."

"A bath it is, then." Marianne disappeared whilst I lay on the bed and Jerome cut the cast from my ankle. I wrinkled my nose at the revolting smell when he removed it – a bath was definitely a necessity, even if I would have preferred a shower.

"I'll leave you in peace," Jerome murmured gruffly. "I'm sure you don't need my assistance for a bath."

Marianne helped me up from the bed, supporting me as I walked slowly towards the bathroom. I was delighted to discover a roomy spa in the centre of the room, filled to the brim with fragrant smelling bubbles and steaming hot water.

Marianne pulled the zipper of the ruined dress down and I stepped out of it. "I'm so sorry, Marianne. I ruined your wedding day and the beautiful dress Acenith bought is destroyed."

Marianne glanced up at me from where she was crouching on the floor. "Don't worry about it, Charlotte. Striker and I have lived together for nearly forty years, missing our wedding night wasn't a crisis, I can assure you. That and the dress are the least of our problems. We can replace a dress; our honeymoon can be taken later. We couldn't replace you." She paused, her gaze roaming across my skin and she frowned sadly. "Oh, Charlotte, what a mess you are." I followed her line of sight and saw what she was seeing, the massive amount of bruising all over my body.

"Could have been worse," I suggested quietly. "He could have killed me."

Marianne inhaled deeply and recovered her composure. She deftly unclasped the bra I'd been wearing and dropped it on top of the ruined dress, followed quickly by the panties I'd been so embarrassed about a week ago. She helped me into the deep water and I lay back, relishing the warmth.

"Do you want the spa jets turned on?" Marianne asked, in the process of scooping up the ruined clothes.

I nodded, closing my eyes and resting my head against the edge of the tub. "I think I'd like that."

Pulsating jets of water began to blow the water around me, gently massaging my bruised and aching body and it felt wonderful.

"I'll be back shortly; I'm going to bag up all this stuff and get rid of it. You really do smell remarkably like a wet dog, Charlotte. Hanging around with werewolves will do that for you."

"Thanks, Marianne. You know how to make a girl feel good."

She laughed, the sound like a tinkle of bells in the room and I smiled to myself as she left. I began to scrub my skin (not vigorously, as it seemed the majority of me was bruised) and Marianne came back in and carefully washed my hair, which I was grateful for. I'd pulled the bobby pins holding my hair in the smooth chignon out days ago, but with the amount of hair products Gwynn had used, combined with not washing it for over a week, it was a real mess. After massaging shampoo through my scalp three times, then conditioning it twice, Marianne was satisfied and used a water jug to rinse the suds away. She sat on the edge of the spa and watched avidly as I began to shave all the areas that needed shaving after seven days of growth, particularly happy to shave the leg that had been encased in a cast.

When I was finally clean, fresh and smooth, I stepped out of the spa and Marianne wrapped me in a fluffy white towel. She slipped out of the room when I assured her I could dress myself, coming back with fresh underwear, jeans, and a pale blue t-shirt. Then she left me alone, closing the door quietly behind her.

I finished drying, standing in front of the mirror and frowning at the person staring back at me. Thanks to Conal's efforts, the cuts on my face were healing nicely, but most of my face was marred by bruising, some dark, some yellowing. There were massive plum-colored bruises over most of my body and a particularly large one on my stomach were Armstrong had punched me. I looked a mess and I was glad Conal had killed him, hoping he'd felt every minute of his death throes. It was a shock to find myself having such a thought, but I couldn't feel sorry about Armstrong being dead – not when I could see the evidence of his cruelty all over my body.

I dressed slowly, trying to ease the clothes over everything that hurt. The clothes were new, undoubtedly purchased by Marianne since they arrived in New Orleans. The jeans fit snugly and the t-shirt closely followed the contours of my chest and waist. It had a scooped neckline and the injuries were visible on my neck and chest. I couldn't believe how quickly they were healing – although I was positive, they were going to leave scars. The wounds were sealed now, angry red welts raised across my pale skin. I dried off my hair and ran my fingers through the curls, pulling them into some semblance of order.

There was a quiet knock at the bathroom door. "May I come in?"

"Sure. I'm decent."

Lucas stood in the doorway and I experienced a tug on my heart when I looked at him. He stepped into the bathroom and walked across to where I stood in front of the mirror, his skin showing the hint of color which confirmed he'd fed. I breathed in deeply, enjoying the aroma which made my heart soar. He was stunning, casually dressed in a grey V-neck t-shirt which skimmed his chest and blue jeans which accentuated his lean hips. "You look much better," he said approvingly.

"Being clean helps," I agreed.

"How is your ankle? Jerome tells me he's removed the plaster."

"Better than the rest of me." I glanced at my foot, where the mark from the incision was clearly visible against my ankle. "It feels stiff, otherwise it's okay."

When I glanced up, he was behind me, gazing at my eyes in the reflection of the mirror and I marveled again that this man, this vampire, loved me. I turned around slowly and he captured my waist between his hands, pulling me tenderly into his arms and taking infinite care not to hold too tightly. He lowered his head and caught my mouth with his own, the pressure of his lips cool against mine. I savored it, wrapping my arms around him and holding him close, losing myself in his kisses. The ropes of muscle in his back flexed beneath my fingers and he trailed a row of kisses down from my lips and over my neck, working his way across my shoulder. "Mmmm," he whispered huskily. "You smell glorious, love."

He scooped me up, depositing me on the top of the vanity and slipping between my legs. He captured my face in his hands and I slipped my own hands beneath his t-shirt, brushing my fingertips across the taut muscle in his stomach. I tugged at his t-shirt and he helped by ripping it off, throwing it to the floor. I marveled at the perfection of his physique. For a long moment we gazed at one another, Lucas breathing heavily and his eyes darkened to a blue which was almost black. He leaned towards me, capturing my mouth with his and I ran my fingers lightly across his skin, hard muscle contracting as I worked my way slowly lower over his chest. I rubbed my fingertips over his stomach and he inhaled sharply as I kissed my way down his neck, over his chest until I could capture one nipple against my lips. I'd never done this before and experimented, tentatively licking the tip of my tongue across the hard nub before I suckled at it gently. Lucas cried out, a tremor rippling through his muscles.

I heard a quiet snick and Lucas growled huskily. "Stop." I glanced up, dismayed to see his fangs extending down over his lower lip. "Charlotte, as much as this is... wonderful, I need you to stop."

I leaned back against the mirror obediently, aware he was struggling. I could see him wrestling with his desires and I waited silently, giving him time to regain control. Lucas ran his fingers through his hair, tousling the dark locks and then bent to pick up his t-shirt, pulling it roughly over his head and down over his chest. "Give me a minute," he commanded. He turned and leaned against the vanity, crossing his arms over his chest and I waited patiently, my own heart rate beginning to settle back to a more normal pace.

"Lucas." The complex feelings he struggled with were obvious when he turned to look at me, his fangs still clearly visible. I reached out to him and he stepped towards me reluctantly, allowing me to wrap my arms around his waist. "I love you."

"As I do you," he said quietly. "I'm so sorry."

I held his gaze with mine. "There's nothing to be sorry for. We knew this would take time and you haven't seen me for a week. You have to start with my scent all over again."

He sighed heavily and I was relieved when his fangs retracted. "I'm truly not sure what's worse," he admitted, his voice dismal.

I grinned. "What? Fighting the desire to bite me? Or the fact that you are probably the most sexually frustrated vampire on the planet right now?"

He stared at me for a long moment before a grin spread across his lips, and I knew I'd broken the awkward moment between us. He lifted me down from the vanity and took my hand in his, catching my lips in a brief kiss. "You're a minx, my love. Let's go and get you something to eat."

Chapter 10

The Pack

"Do you want the last slice, Charlotte?" Nick sat beside me on the couch and members of his pack – David, Toby, Rafe and Marco lounged around on the floor. Marco's arm was in a neat sling, which certainly wasn't slowing him down with regards to eating. He was younger than me, perhaps eighteen, with the long, lean look of a boy who was rapidly growing into a man. His sandy blonde hair hung in his eyes, his expression one of rapture as he devoured another slice of pepperoni pizza.

"Absolutely." I snatched up the last slice of the four super-sized pizzas Lucas had ordered and bit into it. I was savoring the opportunity to eat, it had been at least five days since I'd had anything substantial and I was making up for lost time.

Lucas sat beside me, his leg resting against mine, his hand resting possessively on my thigh. Ben sat in one of the two large armchairs and Marianne sat in the other. Striker stood by the window, watching the lights of downtown New Orleans, his arms crossed over his substantial chest whilst Jerome had settled at the small table, sitting on one of the dining chairs.

"I think if you eat much more, you may well explode," Lucas murmured indulgently.

"I'm thinking I could probably fit in a couple of those donuts," I replied, eyeing the box of Dunkin' Donuts sitting on the coffee table. "You have no idea how hungry I've been for the past week."

We were ensconced in the hotel in New Orleans, sharing three luxurious suites between us. The five members of Nick's Pack were sharing a two-room suite; Marianne and Striker were sharing with Jerome. Ben, Rowena and Lucas had been sharing the suite we were sitting in now. It was enormous and elegant, we were currently in the living area and the bedrooms were situated on either side of the room, providing each room with a stunning view of New Orleans below us. Bourbon Street was just around the corner and in the stillness of the evening; jazz music could be heard drifting up from the many popular bars and clubs.

"Perhaps one donut, Charlotte. You'll be sick if you overeat after having so little in your stomach," Jerome warned. "And from my count, you've already eaten eight slices of pizza."

"That's a good effort, Lottie, but maybe you have had enough," Rafe said with a broad grin. He was the tallest of the Lingard Pack members I'd met, a little over six feet five of powerful muscle. At twenty-four, he was generally quite serious, but had a wickedly sarcastic sense of humor. His brown eyes twinkled as he glanced at me, pulling open the lid of the donut box. "I'm getting in before you get started though, just in case."

"Whose side are you on?" I grumbled good-naturedly. I really liked the men in Nick's group and was grateful that they'd dropped everything to come and help rescue me. There was something very humbling about knowing so many people cared about me and were willing to risk their own lives to save mine.

Rafe held up his hands in surrender and grinned as he bit into the donut. "I'm not taking sides. I'm looking after my own interests, first and foremost."

The telephone rang and I saw everyone exchanging wary glances, before Ben picked up the receiver. I turned to look at

Lucas and he returned my gaze calmly. "Nobody has the room number. We've been using cell phones," he said cryptically.

I wanted to ask why, but before I could, Ben paused and handed me the receiver. "It's for you. Conal Tremaine."

I took the telephone from him, a blush working its way up my face in a rush of heat. "Hello?"

"Charlotte. How are you?" Conal's deep voice was friendly and filled with warmth.

"Much better. How are you?"

"Back to normal. I'm guessing you're still with the bloodsuckers, then?"

"Yes, of course." My eyes found Lucas and I saw he was watching me. I tried to guess what emotions he was feeling, but his face was utterly expressionless. "How did you find me?"

"Rang every hotel in New Orleans. You're a hard woman to track down. I'm in the lobby, with my father and some of our elders. My dad wants to meet you."

"Um, sure. That'll be fine."

"There you go, thinking like a human again. The leader of your Kiss needs to give us permission."

"Really?"

I could hear the smile in his voice. "Really."

I handed the phone to Lucas. "Conal, his father and some of their elders want to come up and see me. Apparently," I nearly rolled my eyes at the ridiculousness of it all, "they need permission from you." I wasn't even certain why I was explaining the conversation – when everyone in the room had no doubt heard every word I'd said and Conal's responses.

Lucas pressed his palm over the receiver and he and Ben exchanged a long look.

"What's going on?" I demanded. Something was off-kilter here, everyone in the room seemed apprehensive.

Marianne answered. "Charlotte, we have to be careful who we trust with regard to you."

"What?" I didn't understand what the big deal was. I turned to look at Lucas and he gazed into my eyes for a long moment before he spoke.

"Laurence Armstrong may not be the only person who will want to benefit from your psychic ability."

A frown creased my forehead as I struggled to comprehend what he was implying. I glanced from Lucas to Ben, across to Marianne, Jerome and scanned the Lingard men, all of whom seemed tense. Even Striker had turned from his position at the window, his face solemn. I returned my gaze to Lucas. "Are you saying... *what* are you saying?"

"I don't want you to worry, Charlotte. We will keep you safe."

"That's not an answer!" I turned to Ben, hoping for some reassurance. "Conal *saved* me. He risked his own life to try and stop Armstrong from getting what he wanted!"

"We know that," Ben responded patiently. "But his pack may want your psychic ability for themselves."

Anger bubbled up in my chest. "That's rubbish! I don't believe it for a minute." Conal had been there for me, when I'd thought there was no one else to help me and I couldn't – *wouldn't* believe he'd had an ulterior motive. I returned my gaze to Lucas and I knew he would see the determination in my eyes. "Either you let him come up here, or – I'm going down there."

Lucas met Ben's eyes and I saw Ben shrug. "It's up to you."

"No it's not! It's *my* decision whether I want to see Conal again!" I shouted angrily.

"Tell them we will allow them access," Striker announced, "but we will match them in numbers." His body was rigid with tension, his fangs already partially extended and I shivered.

Lucas lifted the phone to his ear and spoke. "Conal... yes, you have my permission to visit with Charlotte... no, I'm not happy about it..." He glanced down at me, his blue eyes hard. "She has the right to choose her friends, I accept that. How many people will you be bringing with you? We will have the same number here to protect Charlotte... no, I don't trust you... Yes. I understand." There was a long, protracted silence and Lucas looked across at Nick who was sitting stock-still on the couch. "Yes, Nick and his men are here, providing protection for Charlotte... no, I will not agree to that. If you are to bring six people with you, we will require at least two of the Lingard shifters to remain with us..." There was another, longer pause and I assumed Conal was conferring with the people he'd brought with him. "Agreed. We are in Suite 912... we look forward to meeting with you."

He disconnected the call and there was an instant flurry of action around the room. It seemed everyone was on edge, suffering apprehension about Conal's visit. Everybody except me.

"Rafe and I will remain here with you," Nick announced decisively. "Toby, David, Marco – take Jerome and go back to our room. David, Toby –shift in case we need you. Marco, you're injured, stay in human form and be prepared to escort Toby and David back here. They'll need someone to open the doors."

Marco looked ready to argue, but the look on Nick's face stopped him. They departed quickly, Jerome in tow, slipping out before Marianne shut the door carefully behind them and slipped the deadbolt. Lucas, Ben and Striker were huddled in the corner, their conversation so rapid that I couldn't begin to take it in and Nick and Rafe joined them. Marianne sat down beside me and took my hand, squeezing my fingers softly.

"I don't understand," I said quietly. "Conal wouldn't hurt me."

"I'd like to believe that he wouldn't," Marianne responded. "We didn't want to have this conversation until we got back to Puckhaber Falls. Jerome felt you needed some time to recover from this past week and honestly, we all believe you've had quite enough stress to endure. But the facts of the matter are that you have a truly unique psychic ability. Laurence Armstrong will not be the only one who sees that power and wants to take it for himself."

Anxiety began to gnaw at me with this latest development. "So what you're saying is that I'll never be safe? Someone is always going to be after me?"

"No, it won't be like that," Marianne responded soothingly. "We will keep you safe, Charlotte. But we have to take precautions to ensure your safety. Keeping your psychic ability secret is paramount. The Tremaines know about it, we need to take these precautions to ensure they haven't come here to collect it."

I honestly didn't know what to say. I didn't doubt for a minute that Conal wouldn't hurt me – there weren't any reservations in my mind about him. He'd protected me as much as was humanly possible during our imprisonment. But I didn't know his pack. Would they see this as an opportunity? Abruptly, I felt sick. Holding a hand over my mouth, I launched from the couch and ran for the bathroom. I made it to the toilet bowl and retched, kneeling on the cold white tiles.

"Charlotte." Lucas crouched beside me, one hand resting lightly on my back the other holding my hair back for me.

I retched into the bowl again, losing the rest of my dinner in the process. My face was covered in a fine sheen of perspiration and I wiped my hand across my mouth before slumping onto the floor next to him, my hands over my face.

"Charlotte," Lucas handed me a towel and I wiped it across my face. "You will be safe. We won't let them do anything to harm you."

I got to my feet, turning on the faucet and splashing water onto my face. The mirror confirmed I looked awful, my skin had lost all color and I could see the panic in my own eyes. I took a deep breath, and then turned to Lucas. "Is Marianne right? Do you think I'll be in danger all the time?"

Lucas rose gracefully from the floor and captured my shoulders. "You will be protected with me, my Charlotte."

"That's not what I asked!" I shrieked. "Am I in danger? How many others will come after me? How can I ask you and the others to be watching out for me constantly?"

"You don't have to ask us, love. We will do whatever it takes, to keep you safe. I don't expect that you will be in constant danger. The only people alive who know about your ability are Nick and his group, the Tremaine pack and Thut and Harley and their people. We will endeavor to keep it that way."

"I'm not your responsibility. We're not family. You'll get sick of constantly coming to my rescue," I said dully. The thought of being relentlessly on the run, continuously looking over my shoulder – it was inconceivable. Had I only escaped from the nightmare of my family's death to enter immediately into another one?

"Charlotte," Lucas breathed softly. "Look at me."

I forced my eyes up to meet his and he cupped my face in his hands. "I will protect you for the rest of your life. I love you. More than anything else in this world. You mean everything to me. You are my responsibility, because I have chosen that duty and I accept it fully. I cannot go on with this existence without you being in it with me. Being apart from you, it's something I cannot endure."

"I accept that responsibility also."

Ben was standing in the doorway and he stepped into the bathroom. "Charlotte, you're like a daughter to Rowena and I. We love you and want you to be a part of our lives. We will protect you from harm."

"And Marianne and I accept that duty also." Striker appeared in the doorway, his hand interlinked with Marianne's smaller one, his demeanor somber. "It is my honor to protect you and I will do so to the best of my ability."

I looked from Ben to Striker and Marianne, then back to Lucas, shaking my head. "How can you be accountable for me? You'd have been better off if I'd never crossed your path."

"On the contrary. Our existence is incomplete without you in it," Lucas murmured as he drew me into a comforting embrace. "You provide light and dark, shade and substance to what is otherwise a mundane journey through decades. You are providing us with as much, if not more, than we are providing you. And you are giving me the greatest gift of all – happiness and love. I can assure you, I will not give up that gift."

I looked into his dark blue eyes, my own filling with tears at the show of unity they'd provided for me. I nodded hesitantly and Lucas kissed me, a brief brush of his lips over mine. "They will be here very soon. Are you ready to meet with them?"

"Can I have a couple of minutes? I want to brush my teeth and tidy up a little."

"Of course." He kissed my forehead before releasing me and Ben gave my shoulder a gentle squeeze as they left the bathroom. I flushed the toilet and dropped the seat lid down, slumping onto it wearily. Closing my eyes, I reached into the recesses of my mind, opening the box. Lucas had been right. I wouldn't make the mistake of shutting the spirits away again – from now on, I would be prepared for anything.

Chapter 11

The Tremaines

The tension was tangible when I stepped back into the living room, the very air filled with something akin to static electricity, strong enough for me to feel it on my bare skin. On one side, Lucas and his Kiss, Rafe and Nick. Opposite them was Conal and five of his pack members. Nobody spoke. Everyone watched the opposing group suspiciously. Lucas and our group had their backs to me and Conal was the first to see me, smiling warmly, his black eyes lighting up with obvious delight. "Here she is."

Lucas turned and nodded imperceptibly, but the stance of his body and that of the others showed they were prepared for a fight. Lucas's fangs had extended which I found both mildly disturbing and very worrying. This situation could turn into a bloodbath and I hurried to stand between the two lines of combatants.

Someone obviously had to keep the peace in this meeting. From the looks on the faces of Conal's werewolves, they were just as ready for battle as my little cluster of vampires and shape shifters. This looked like a meeting between Israelis and Palestinians. Except *they* didn't generally rip each other apart with claws, fangs and superhuman strength.

"Conal, thank you for coming to visit me." I stepped in front of him and hugged him, feeling the tension release from his shoulders a little when he wrapped his arms around me. He looked much improved on the last time we'd seen one another, the bruising on his face virtually healed. He was dressed in faded denim jeans and a black shirt, well-worn boots on his feet. His dark hair framed his face like a halo as he grinned down at me, his black eyes twinkling.

"You look well, Charlotte. Except for a ton of bruises." His eyes travelled down my neck and chest. "That looks better. It could have done with some more... uh... treatment."

Behind us, Lucas growled from low in his chest and Conal glanced at him. "I'm not suggesting anything, bloodsucker."

"Keep your eyes to yourself, dog," Lucas snarled, anger vibrating in his voice.

"Will you both stop this, right *now*!" I ordered, forcing myself to sound firm. "I won't tolerate you being rude to one another." Both Conal and Lucas looked at me with unconcealed surprise and I put my hands on my hips. "The least you can do is speak to one another with some respect. After all, you were both on the same side, unless you've already forgotten that tiny detail?"

"Charlotte is correct," Ben agreed in his usual calm manner.

"Alright, alright. I won't call him a bloodsucker," Conal agreed begrudgingly, his voice a husky growl.

"Or a leech," I reminded him tartly.

Conal crossed his arms over his chest and glared down at me, but I could see the flicker of amusement in his eyes. "Okay. No calling him a leech, either."

I turned and stared at Lucas, giving him cool eyes. After a few seconds, he nodded. "I will refrain from rudeness," he agreed, the silver highlights in his eyes swirling like a mini-tornado.

I turned back to Conal; found his attention was focused on my hair. "I didn't realize it was so curly."

I touched my hair self-consciously. "Yeah, well, you didn't get my best look."

"I can see that," he said quietly, his dark eyes soft and appreciative. I heard another deep growl from behind me, and hurried things along, glancing at the man standing nearest to Conal. "Are you going to introduce me?"

"Yeah. Charlotte Duncan, this is my father and head of the Tremaine pack, Lyell Tremaine."

He was tall with shoulders as broad as his son, and there were obvious similarities in the shape of the brow and nose. But Lyell Tremaine's dark hair held a considerable amount of grey, his face lined and weathered as though he'd spent many years working outside. His eyes were also grey, the color of pewter and coldly impassionate as he watched me. I glanced back at Conal, puzzled by his father's reaction.

Conal shrugged and threw me a sheepish smile. "Dad's convinced you're a witch. Thinks you put me under some kind of spell while we were being held by Armstrong."

My lips twitched and I fought the urge to smile. "A witch, huh?"

"I've tried to tell him that's not what you are, but he's not buying it," Conal said apologetically.

I stepped in front of Lyell Tremaine, waiting until he met my gaze before I spoke. "Mr. Tremaine, I've been called a few things in my time, but never a witch. May I shake your hand?"

He looked down at me suspiciously, but the man beside him spoke. This man was lean and wiry, probably mid to late fifties, with thick black hair and piercing blue eyes that scrutinized me cautiously. "You cannot touch the hand of our Alpha, until we have ensured you will not bewitch him also."

"Alpha?"

Conal emitted a deep sigh. "It's what werewolves call their leader, Charlotte. This is Ralph Torres, Dad's Beta. He's the second-in-command in our pack."

"Mr. Torres. May I shake *your* hand?"

He studied me intently, his gaze calculating, before holding out his hand. I took his hand and he shook mine firmly, almost hard enough to hurt. I wondered if he was doing it deliberately. "It's a pleasure to meet you, Mr. Torres."

He nodded, still eying me suspiciously and I decided to take matters into my own hands. Now I'd made physical contact with him, I scanned my mind and located the new voice, one I hadn't heard before. I listened for a few seconds, closing my eyes to study the new spirit. When I opened my eyes again, I focused on Ralph Torres and smiled warmly. "As I said, I'm not a witch. I have a psychic ability, which allows me to speak to those who have died. May I share some information with you?"

Ralph Torres glanced to Lyell Tremaine for guidance and he nodded his assent.

"I have your father, Rudi Torres with me. He passed over about twelve months ago; he had cancer of the stomach, which spread to his liver. You and the pack did everything you could to save him, but in the end, the cancer could not be treated, by conventional treatments or with your traditional medicines. You and your Dad spent a lot of time fishing together; he particularly liked trawling for catfish where you live in Natchez." I listened intently for a minute and smiled. "Your dad wants to admit to a guilty secret – you thought he'd given up smoking the pipe after he was diagnosed with cancer, but he wants to own up. He did still sneak a few puffs. He had a spot where the river forks, there's a group of three boulders and he would go out there in the afternoon and have a quiet smoke when you thought he was napping. He wants you to know he has no more pain now and he's spending a lot of time with your Aunt Ada."

The information I'd imparted was clearly accurate, there was a tear trailing slowly down Ralph Torres's cheek and he shook his head slowly, as if he had trouble believing what I'd done. "How do you— Is *this* what your ability is?" He turned to Lyell

Tremaine. "Conal's right. She's not a witch; she has the ability to speak with our dead."

"She sees them, too," Conal added. "I've seen them in her mind, as clearly as if they were still here amongst us."

I stole a glance at Lucas and was relieved to see the approval in his eyes. He nodded imperceptibly and his rigid stance had loosened slightly, as though he thought some of the danger had passed.

I turned my attention to the next person in the row. "As a gesture of goodwill and to give your pack further proof that I'm not a witch, will you allow me to shake your hand?" He was easily the shortest of the six men, with a stocky build. His head was balding, his features sharp, his skin the color of milk chocolate. Conal introduced him as Kenyon Douglas, the pack's Gamma, or third in command. I took his hand in mine and he offered me a gentler handshake than Mr. Torres' did, his dark brown eyes watching me with curiosity.

"Your Grandmother Lope is speaking with me. She died when you were seventeen and wishes she'd lived long enough to see you graduate from high school. She was happy you decided to study law and she's very proud of the work you do for your people. Your grandmother remembers how much you loved her pecan pie; you used to tell people for miles around that Grandmother Lope made the best pecan pie in Mississippi." Another voice joined Lope and I listened for another few minutes. "Your twin brother, Adolph has joined your Grandmother. He wants to remind you of the fun you two had playing little league together and how you would confuse Mr. Trimble in second grade by swapping seats and pretending to be one another. Adolph is sorry he had to leave you so soon, he... he knows how foolish it was to drink and drive. He says the accident was nobody's fault but his own. He knows you had a lot of trouble believing that at the time, but he takes full responsibility for the amount he drank before he got in the car. He's thankful it was only him who was killed and Gracie survived."

"Remarkable," Kenyon breathed. "Incredibly accurate. You can tell all that from shaking my hand? You can see them?"

I nodded and smiled, the tension in my shoulders relaxing a little. Closing my eyes, I mentally called Lope forward and gave Kenyon a description of her. "Your Grandmother Lope has dark skin, weathered from spending so many years picking cotton on the family farm. She has very green eyes and her hair is white, she has it braided and it lies against her back. She's wearing gold hoop earrings, a brightly colored shirt and her favorite shawl is draped over her shoulders. It's black with fringing and has a pattern on it; flowers I think. I think it's roses, in pink and yellow. And she's wearing a gold St. Christopher medallion on a necklace, says she never takes it off."

Kenyon was nodding when I opened my eyes. "Absolutely correct. Grandma Lope wore that St. Christopher medal every day – she never took it off. She was buried with it around her neck. Whenever any of our family travelled, she would hold the medallion in our hands and make us rub it for luck."

"See, Dad?" Conal stated calmly. "I told you she wasn't a witch."

Lyell Tremaine exchanged a lengthy glance with Ralph Torres and Kenyon Douglas and I saw them both nod. He turned back to me and for the first time since their arrival, he seemed more relaxed and even smiled. "It seems I've misjudged you, Miss Duncan. I apologize. I will complete the introductions myself." He waved towards the man standing next to Kenyon Douglas. "This is my Delta and head security officer, Phelan Walker."

Phelan Walker was roughly six feet tall and slender, his dark eyes almost bordering on black. He gripped my hand firmly, his eyes intent on mine and I stumbled back from him as I heard a swell of urgent voices. I looked at Lyell Tremaine and my voice was shaky when I spoke. "It seems Mr. Walker doesn't agree with your opinion. I can't read his ancestors, but I'm receiving a warning from the other spirits. Mr. Walker has a knife concealed in a hidden recess in the bottom of his boot."

Chapter 12

Tempers

I was yanked backwards with vampire speed as Striker grabbed me, pulling me back to our group without my feet ever touching the ground. Lucas wrapped his arms around me, with Striker and Nick adopting a protective stance in front of us, their backs to me. I could just make out Phelan Walker through a narrow gap between their arms.

"She's a liar!" Phelan Walker yelled. He took one menacing step towards us, but Conal and Ralph Torres grasped him firmly by the arms as he continued to vent his anger. "She's a whore, a witch-whore who will destroy our pack! She lives with bloodsuckers! She consorts with shifters! She can't be trusted!"

"Be *quiet, Phelan*!" The elder Tremaine commanded in a booming growl of a voice, which would tolerate no argument. Phelan Walker stopped yelling instantly, bowing his head to the ground in what seemed to be a submissive gesture.

"My apologies, Lyell. I am merely attempting to warn you and ensure no more of us are tricked by the witch-whore." His voice was quieter, more subdued.

"We will see." Lyell turned to Lucas. "My people were ordered to bring no weapons to this meeting. With your permission, I'll have Conal check to confirm who is telling the truth."

Lucas nodded his agreement, his anger showing in the swirling silver in his eyes. His body was tightly wound, all the tension that had started to dissipate was back and I could feel it in the muscle of his body as I leaned against him.

Displaying open condemnation, Conal shoved Phelan Walker firmly in the chest, pushing him back onto the couch. Conal kneeled down, pulling the boots from the more subdued Walker's feet and carefully examined the bottom of each. He shook his head, and then looked up at his father. "Your Delta has failed to obey your orders. He's armed."

Conal stood up, holding a small thin blade in his left hand, which he displayed to everyone in the room. He held it between his hands and snapped it into two pieces, stepping forward to offer it to Lucas.

Lucas took the pieces from Conal and the two men eyed one another warily before Lucas spoke. "Thank you."

Lyell Tremaine stared at his security officer, his grey eyes frigid. "You have failed me, Phelan. You allowed your prejudices to get in the way of the truth we have witnessed here tonight. You will leave this room immediately. Your punishment will be decided by the pack Elders tomorrow evening."

Phelan Walker blanched, his head sinking low against his chest. "I was doing what I thought best for our safety."

"Too often you jump to conclusions, Phelan. You prejudged these people, as we all did, but you are unwilling to respect the truth of what Conal told us, when we have been given clear evidence. You have greatly offended both Miss Duncan and her friends with your blatant disrespect. Leave. Now. You will wait downstairs for us."

Conal strode to the door and held it open, whilst Phelan Walker nodded to his pack leader, bowing his head. He trudged slowly towards the door; his shoulders slumped, and carrying his boots in his hand. When he'd left the room, Conal shut the door and locked it behind him.

I realized I was trembling, my teeth beginning to chatter with the shock of what had just happened. Lucas held me close, rubbing his hands up and down my back. He kissed my forehead softly and looked down into my eyes, his thoughts not requiring words. He was proud of me and he loved me. I knew in that instant that he would do anything necessary to keep me protected from danger. When he loosened his grip, Striker and Nick relaxed their stance, stepping to either side so I had a clearer view of Conal and his pack.

"Miss Duncan," Lyell began. "My Delta has brought shame on our pack by bringing a weapon with him to this meeting. I ask for forgiveness."

I nodded, still not composed enough to speak.

"We outnumber you now. Will I remove one from our group?" Lucas questioned.

Lyell shook his head decisively. "No, that won't be necessary." He looked across to me, his grey eyes softening. "Miss Duncan looks somewhat shaken. Might I suggest she sits down?" He glanced back at his group. "Perhaps we could all sit down to finish the meeting."

For the first time since they'd arrived, Lucas permitted himself a tiny smile. "That would be agreeable." I noticed though, that all the vampires' fangs were still run out. Clearly, they hadn't relaxed completely either.

I found the courage to speak. "I'd prefer you to call me Charlotte."

"Alright. Charlotte it is, then." Lyell Tremaine settled on the couch while Nick and Rafe busied themselves locating extra chairs for everyone. I wasn't sure if only I noticed, but we were all maintaining exactly the same positions as before, only now everyone was sitting, rather than standing. Lucas guided me to an armchair and settled me before he sat on the arm, his hand gripping mine possessively.

The last of the Tremaine Pack remained standing; he was American Indian, of average height but solidly built. "Lyell, I believe it would be wise to allow Charlotte to shake my hand, so she can confirm for herself that I can be trusted."

Lyell nodded his agreement. "Of course, and I think it's high time you shook my hand, also." He crossed the room and allowed me to shake his hand, then introduced the American Indian man as Zeff Brooks. In both instances, I was immediately in contact with their ancestors and received no troublesome messages.

When everyone was settled again, Lyell Tremaine crossed his legs and scrutinized me with undisguised interest, making me squirm a little in my seat. "From what I understand, you didn't make contact with Phelan's ancestors?"

"I've come to the realization tonight that I don't receive messages from anyone who poses a threat to me," I explained carefully. I looked up at Lucas, knowing he would be interested in this revelation. "While I was in the bathroom, I opened my mind to the spirits. I have no spirits related to Laurence Armstrong, or Gerard DuBonet in my head. But I could hear Conal's ancestors. I talked to them and they helped me understand why. I'm... protected, or I guess, warned might be a better word – about people who intend to harm me. If their ancestors don't come to me, they pose a danger."

"Fascinating," Ben seemed pleased with my announcement, turning to Lyell to explain. "Charlotte has only embraced her abilities in the past few months. The capability has always been there, but as is often the case with humans, she feared the gift. Since she's been living with us, she has actively encouraged the relationships between herself and her spiritual contacts, to the point where her ability is increasing exponentially. Knowing that she can identify people who intend to endanger her will be a valuable aspect of her gift, a way of protecting herself from harm."

"Conal tells me you can make the spirits appear corporeally and do your bidding. Is that right?" Lyell questioned. He was leaning forward on the couch, hands clasped between his legs.

"I think so. I've only attempted it once and it was my mom who helped me, I haven't attempted it again." I exchanged a look with Lucas, remembering how annoyed he'd been when I'd asked Mom to trip a waiter at the wedding. It had worked, and the waiter had tipped his tray of drinks over the girl who'd been shamelessly flirting with Lucas. I'd known it was childish, and silly to be jealous, but you can't help how you react sometimes and I'd honestly been amazed to discover it would even work.

Lucas smiled softly at me, apparently recalling the same event. "Go ahead, Charlotte. Show them."

I closed my eyes, deciding to ask one of the new spirits who'd joined me to help. I located Conal's Uncle Felix, one of the spirits I'd spoken to earlier. Like Conal, he had a mass of unruly black hair and the same canine-like black eyes. He listened as explained what I wanted him to do and nodded eagerly, suggesting his own improvements to my presentation.

I found Conal when I opened my eyes and smiled warmly. "I have your Uncle Felix; he's going to do something harmless to each of you in turn." I laughed aloud, enjoying Uncle Felix's whispered asides in my ear. "He has a wicked sense of humor."

Uncle Felix had appeared corporeally and he moved along the row of werewolves. He tapped Conal on his right shoulder and Conal instinctively turned, to see who'd done it. Uncle Felix had already moved along the row, gently tugging on Lyle's earlobe and Lyle swatted at his ear, turning as Conal had, to try and see the invisible troublemaker. Before he could turn back, Uncle Felix had tweaked Ralph Torres on the nose, making him let out a startled yelp. Moving on to Kenyon, the playful spirit tapped out a drumbeat on Kenyon's knees and everyone could see the material of his pants moving, although I was the only one who could see Uncle Felix. Lastly, he caught Zeff's hand in his own and shook it vigorously. Uncle Felix gave me a little salute and a grin, and then dissipated into a white mist that disappeared within seconds.

"Damn," Conal said, "that was exactly the sort of mischief Uncle Felix always loved. I saw this ability when I probed your mind, but to experience it in real life is unbelievable."

"And leaves us with a predicament," Lyell said heavily.

"I know Charlotte will never use this to harm us. She went above and beyond what could be expected of her to stop Armstrong learning her secret," Conal reminded his father.

"I can see the clear evidence of her denying Laurence Armstrong what he wanted," Lyell responded, his eyes grazing across the mass of bruises and cuts on my face. "You've handled your enforced imprisonment with honor, Charlotte. Many men, physically stronger than you, would have broken under such duress and given away the secrets they held." He sighed heavily, rubbing a hand over his chin. "However, there are others who would covet what Laurence Armstrong failed to take. I have to wonder, although it gives me no pleasure to do so, what will happen if your vampire friends decide the power you hold is too tempting? It would be a powerful weapon indeed, against not only our pack, but also many others. What happens if the vampires decide to create you to their kind?"

"That won't happen," I stated firmly, letting him hear my determination.

"You have the innocence and trust of the young, child," Ralph Torres responded. "Vampires have attacked and killed, created new vampires for thousands of years. They are dangerous and don't hesitate to use something if it will give them an advantage."

"Werewolves have killed and maimed for a millennia, also. You are not any more innocent than the vampire," Striker stated coldly.

"How can you be trusted with her, when her blood pumps so perfectly through her veins? The scent of her must be enough to drive you wild," Conal said, his eyes cold and firmly fixed on Lucas. "You could create her and call it an accident."

"As you could be trusted, wolf? Knowing that at the full moon, you could attack her and turn her to your kind?" Lucas retorted with a growl.

I squeezed Lucas's fingers, uncertain how to stop this and worried that both Lucas and Conal were lurching towards a fight that would become far more personal – less about the werewolves fears and more about two men fighting over one woman.

"You leeches can't be trusted with her safety," Kenyon argued, his voice relatively calm. "You consort with shifters, which can only increase the danger she's in."

The power in the room was increasing with every new retort and accusation. I could feel it from both sides - the heat and almost electric static from the werewolves and something similar from the shifters, but alongside that was a cooler, less biting form of energy. I'd never felt it before, but knew instinctively it was coming from the vampires and it was a slow-moving but powerful force of its own, travelling across my body like thick liquid spreading across my skin. The feeling was so intense; I almost looked down to see if my arm was damp. Everywhere the energy touched began to feel cooler, tingling in a different way to the werewolves and shifters power and the combination of the two was disconcerting to say the least.

"We'll protect Charlotte with more honor than you dogs ever would," Nick growled, as he and Rafe got to their feet, their bodies rigid with anger. There was an increase of the tingling hot energy across my skin, it rolled over me like a small wave at the beach, seemingly innocuous but with a strength hidden beneath the surface.

"What sort of life is it for her, with you? You're all dead, leeches. Every minute with her must be a temptation for all of you. Her blood must smell sweet to those who constantly crave it," Conal snarled. It was becoming apparent that I was right and Conal was about to make this very, very personal.

"I love her. I would never hurt her," Lucas stated coldly. His fangs were fully run out, his eyes a swirling maelstrom of fury, so much silver that the dark blue of his eyes was almost drowned out.

"You? A bloodsucker with a stone cold heart? You'll never be able to love her, as she deserves to be loved. You can't even give her children. *I* can and I would love her and cherish her, as she deserves to be loved. By someone with a heartbeat."

"Not that it's any of your business, wolf, but Charlotte understands why we can't have a child. She accepts it because she loves me unconditionally. She only kissed you because she was frightened and alone. She feels nothing for you!" Lucas had also gotten to his feet, his posture stiff and his eyes flashing. He let go of my hand and I rubbed my arms, trying to get rid of the cold trickling and warm sparking power that was still washing over me.

"I'll bet you haven't bedded her. You can't fuck her without killing her! She provides too great a temptation for you! It would be impossible for you to keep from draining her!" The veins in Conal's neck were clearly visible, pumping with tension as his neck muscles corded.

"Stop! Stop! STOP!" I shrieked loudly, jumping to my feet, my heart hammering wildly in my chest. "You're driving me crazy with all this energy! It's crawling all over my skin!"

That got their attention and Lucas looked down at me, his eyes wide. "What did you say?"

The room descended into a deathly silence with both sides showing the signs of increased tension. The vampires were crouched in obvious battle stance, along with the shape shifters. On the other side, the werewolf pack was standing in readiness for a fight.

"I said, your energy is leaking all over the place – all over me. I don't like the sensation and I can't get rid of it."

"You felt our power?" Ben questioned and he sounded shocked.

"Yes, yes. I feel your power, cold and liquid running across my skin, it feels like it's burning but it's not, not really." It was a struggle to explain exactly how it felt, but Ben seemed satisfied with my answer.

"And ours?" Lyell asked.

"Yes. You and the shifters feel hot, like a mild electrical shock tingling through my arms."

Conal glanced at his father, at almost the exact same moment that Ben and Lucas were exchanging a bewildered glance. Lyell was the first to speak. "She cannot be human, not completely. There's something other about her."

I looked from face to face, tears running down my cheeks. "I don't care about any of that right now. What I care about is that you're all fighting and you're all saying you're on my side, but you're energy is overwhelming me." I took a deep breath, willing myself to calm down. "There is an old proverb. 'The enemy of my enemy is my friend'. It seems that saying is tailor-made for this situation." I turned to Lyell Tremaine. "Mr. Tremaine, it seems we have to come to some agreement in this situation, but I'm not willing to do it with all these people here. I *won't* be treated like some possession to be fought over." I glared angrily at first Lucas, then Conal, sending them a clear warning about their behavior. "Would you agree to reduce the numbers, now you know I'm not a threat to you?"

Lyell Tremaine stared at me for a full minute, his grey eyes considering. "What do you propose?"

I turned to Nick and Rafe. "Can you guys go back to your room? And if you leave, Zeff and Kenyon should leave too."

"Agreed." Lyell and Lucas said simultaneously.

I watched the four men leave, closing the door quietly behind them.

"Does this meet your requirements?" Ben murmured.

"No." I smiled at Marianne, who was watching me with concern apparent in her features. "Marianne, I know you had nothing to do with this bun fight, but I also need less people in here. Why don't you and Striker go back to your room and I'll see you after this is over."

Marianne grinned. "Sure you don't want my stupendous fortune telling ability?"

"Yep, I'm sure."

Marianne laughed and grabbed Striker's hand, skipping daintily past the werewolves and out the door. I turned to Lyell. "Can Ralph leave now, please."

Lyell nodded to Ralph Torres and Ralph looked over at me with a pleasant smile. "Charlotte, it's been a pleasure to meet you. Thank you for what you've shared with me about my father." He departed the room.

I rubbed at my temples, closing my eyes as I contemplated the situation I found myself in. My head was thumping, my body ached and I was sick to death of people pulling at me as if I was some sort of human piñata. I looked across to Conal and he returned the look, his black eyes heated with some strong emotion, which wasn't anger, but I didn't want to give him any false hope for anything else.

"Conal, you and I have shared some intense moments in the past week and I'd like to think we will always be good friends. But I don't love you the way you want and what you just said was completely unfair and uncalled for. I'd like you to leave."

"I will not leave my father alone here with two vampires," Conal responded solemnly.

"Your father will be perfectly safe." I turned to Lucas and he regarded me seriously. "Lucas, I need some space. I love you, but you can't protect me from every little thing. I need to fight my own battles sometimes. What you were saying a few minutes ago made me feel more like a possession than the woman you love. Please leave."

"I'm not leaving, Charlotte. I am leader of my Kiss and will negotiate with the Tremaine Pack."

"Not while you're acting like a possessive fool, you're not. Ben can handle it, he's not as emotionally involved as you are and I know you trust him." I sighed, brushing my fingers through my hair. "I kissed Conal. I know it was wrong and I'm so sorry I hurt you. But I can't change what happened and you can't look at this situation logically because you're jealous of him. It would be better for me if you and Conal both left."

For a long moment, I thought he would refuse, then he stepped towards me and squeezed my shoulder. "I apologize, my love. I let my temper and my emotions get the better of me." He dropped his hand and strode towards the door and a second later, Conal followed him.

I waited until the door quietly clicked shut and then turned to Lyell and Ben, my shoulder slumping with fatigue. "Now I'm satisfied. Can I please have some coffee and perhaps we could sit down and talk this through rationally, without all the anger and resentment and mistrust?"

Chapter 13

Pacts

Ben ordered coffee from room service and it arrived hot, steaming and strong. I sipped from my cup, feeling better immediately. Lyell had joined me for coffee and he sat opposite me in one of the armchairs, the cup gripped between his hands.

Ben sat in the other armchair and he and Lyell both faced me. Ben's fangs had finally retracted, which made me feel better. I'd curled up on the couch, needing to rest. I was still reeling from the events of the past hour – the name-calling, the screaming, the stress – it was more than I was ready to deal with after a week of captivity. Ben had given me Tylenol to counteract the headache and in conjunction with caffeine, I was beginning to feel more human.

The two men spoke quietly together, getting to know one another. They traded questions and answers, giving me time to settle after my angry outburst. Lyell seemed to be gaining confidence in Ben's integrity; Ben had spoken at length about the Tine Kiss' lifestyle and his employment as a social worker, which had impressed Lyell. Ben had explained their desire to abstain from drinking human blood and Lyell had questioned him extensively about their decision. In turn, Lyell had explained the intricacies of his pack, how they were gradually declining in numbers due to a lack of full-blooded werewolves mating with each other. This explained Conal needing to marry another purebred werewolf, rather than choosing a human or half-breed werewolf mate.

More ground had been gained in the fifteen minutes that they'd spoken together, than in the hour when everyone had been here.

I took a deep breath when there was a lull in the conversation and spoke. "It seems to me we need some sort of agreement between the vampires and the werewolves."

"Yes," Lyell agreed. "I know this world is strange and new to you, but I imagine you can see why it's difficult for us to trust each other. We have been enemies…"

"For a millennia." I sighed heavily. "Yeah, I got that."

Ben smiled indulgently. "Charlotte sees things in black and white, Lyell. She feels there must be a simple solution to this."

"We can't trust the vampires, Charlotte," Lyell said slowly. "If they create you into vampire, the power you have now could multiply tenfold. You could be used to create a spirit army, to do their bidding."

"I'm not going to be created," I repeated stubbornly.

"You may not have a choice," Lyell argued, though his voice remained calm. "What if you're created against your will?"

I turned to Ben. "What does happen? Would I automatically do your bidding?" As much as I hated the idea, I'd never asked these questions.

Ben shook his head. "Ultimately, your existence as vampire is dictated by how you lived your human life. Creation takes three days, after which you rise. For the first twelve to twenty four months, you are classified as a newborn. During that time, you are driven by your thirst for blood and little else. At no time could you be forced to do another vampire's bidding. Your decision making process is still your own." He smiled warmly.

"Ripley created Acenith, as you well know, to save her life. Have you noticed Acenith doing exactly what Ripley tells her?"

I smiled back, thinking over his statement. It was true, Acenith was gentle and quiet, but she certainly had a mind of her own and I'd seen her and Ripley together many times – she had her own opinions and wouldn't let Ripley; or anyone else for that matter, sway her when her mind was made up.

"What about the mind abilities?" Lyell argued. "What about if a vampire controls her with his mind?"

"Charlotte is not susceptible to our abilities. Something to do with her gift, I believe."

I was surprised by this admission and looked at Ben accusingly. "You've tried to use your mind-tricks on me?"

He had the good grace to look bashful. "Tried, but failed. About the only thing we can do is hide our natural eye color from you. Even that, Lucas can't do."

"Why would you do that?"

"An experiment, Charlotte. We've all found your ability to be truly remarkable. Ripley suggested a few little experiments to see if we could use the power of suggestion with you, plant ideas in your mind."

"And?" I demanded.

"A complete failure. You are immune to us."

Pushing the thought of murdering Ripley to one side, I turned to Lyell. "Do you believe him?"

Lyell shrugged, leaning forward to place his cup on the coffee table before he spoke. "I'd like to believe him, but I have generations of history affecting my judgment. I need proof you won't use your ability against my pack."

My attention was caught by a voice in my head, shouting for attention. It was Lyell's great-grandfather and I listened to what he had to say. "Lyell, your great-grandfather is suggesting a blood pact between you and me. It's a special ceremony you haven't used in decades, but it will bind us and make me a Sister of the Pack. Even if I was created, which I can assure you will never happen, I'd be duty bound to protect the members of the Tremaine pack."

"No, Charlotte," Ben protested. "You have shed enough blood, more than enough in the past couple of months."

I glanced at the scars on my chest, touched the bruises on my cheek. "Do you honestly think a little more blood and another scar will make much difference?"

Lyell thought about my suggestion, his forehead furrowed. "I think it would work. Normally it would be done between the leaders of the respective packs." He turned to Ben. "In this case, is that possible?"

"I don't believe it would be considered a true blood sharing. The blood in our bodies is not our own, it comes from our feeding and dissipates quickly," Ben responded quietly. "Does this pact continue from father to son? If something happened to you as pack leader, would the pack be required to honor the agreement made here tonight, if we were to agree?"

Lyell nodded. "The blood pact is a permanent commitment between my pack and your Kiss. No matter who leads us, he and Charlotte are considered blood relatives and it's completely binding unless the parties involved mutually agree to disband the pact. Only then, with agreement from both, can the pact be dissolved. May I go downstairs and speak with my people? They need to witness it. You will require witnesses also. At least two."

"Blood— as you can imagine, it's an issue for us. I will need to talk with Lucas before our witnesses can be named."

"Agreed."

I nodded brusquely. "Okay, let's do this."

Lyell stood and left the room, closing the door silently behind him and Ben regarded me gravely. "Charlotte, there must be another solution. I don't like to see you hurt more than you already have been."

"Ben, I want to go home. I'm tired and I'm frightened. I have to make this right, so I won't have to worry constantly about the Tremaine werewolves coming after me. This way, they can't hurt me." I paused, choosing my words carefully. "Phelan Walker could be an enemy – he wanted me killed to keep their pack safe. If he accepts me being a Sister of the Pack, well, that's one less person I need to watch my back with."

Ben nodded, much to my relief. "If you insist, Charlotte. But Lucas isn't going to like it."

"This is the best solution for all of us," I responded, my voice calmer than my nerves. "Lucas has to accept it, whether he likes it or not."

"I'll go and speak with him and the others. Stay in the room, don't open the door."

After he left, I stood for a moment in the silence, relishing the peace. I wandered out onto the balcony to view the lights. Now seemed as good a time as any to contemplate what I'd just volunteered to do.

Leaning on the balcony railing, I enjoyed the balmy breeze, which lifted my hair as I watched the traffic on the street far below. I didn't relish the idea of being a blood sister, but what choice was there? Even if I started running now, I was too deep into this bizarre world. I couldn't hide from them and would never be safe without their assistance. My psychic ability was known now and couldn't be hidden any longer. Lucas was right; the only people who knew of my ability were congregated in this hotel and back in Montana. Everyone else who'd discovered it was dead. With the pact in place, I would be safe. Safe to continue my life with Lucas and that's where I wanted to be. Despite the dangers living with him and the others might entail, I couldn't imagine life without them.

"Charlotte, you aren't honestly going to do this?" Lucas stood in the doorway, his eyes filled with fury. "I can't allow it."

"It's not your decision to make. It's mine," I stated, lifting my chin defiantly. "I'm going to go through with the blood pact with Lyell Tremaine. It will keep us safe."

He blinked, his eyes widening. His lips twitched. "Now it's you, keeping us safe?"

"Someone's got to do it," I said heavily. "And as I'm the only one on our side who can provide her own blood..."

Lucas crossed his arms over his chest. "You aren't doing this because you are angry with me, are you?"

"I'm not angry with you."

"You seemed angry. When you kicked me out, you seemed very angry."

I grinned. "I didn't kick you out, I asked you to leave. That's different. There was too much testosterone pumping in that room, between you and Conal."

"He is absolutely in love with you," Lucas stated quietly. "His feelings for you are almost as strong as my own."

I walked across and touched his cheek. "He may be in love with me, but I'm *completely* in love with you."

Lucas pulled me into his arms. "I know that, yet I still find myself insanely jealous every single time he looks in your direction." He lowered his head, capturing my lips against his in a breathtaking kiss. When he pulled away, he spoke again, his voice low. "He can give you what I can't."

"I don't want what he can give me. I want you," I said obstinately. "All I want is you."

"Are you sure?" Lucas searched my eyes, his own troubled. "It seems you are constantly in trouble since you've been with me."

"Did you hear what I told you about my life before I met you?" I asked incredulously. "I killed my stepfather; saw my mother and siblings murdered. That hardly rates as keeping out of trouble."

Lucas sighed. "No, I suppose it doesn't. But I don't like the idea of your blood being spilled. Enough has been spilled to last a lifetime."

"It's a little cut, it's nothing," I stated confidently.

"Still," Lucas said doubtfully. His eyes grazed across the visible scars on my chest. "I don't want you to be hurt anymore."

"I'll be fine." The others had begun appearing in the room behind him. "You'd better go."

"I'm staying with you."

I bit my lip anxiously. "I'd like you to be here with me. But blood... my blood – I don't think we should push our luck."

"I can hear your heart racing – you're frightened," he stated quietly. "If I were a proper boyfriend, I would stay to offer you strength and support."

I caught his hand in mine and started tugging him inside. "You are a proper boyfriend. You just happen to be a vampire. Vampires and blood – not a good combination. Go. It'll be over soon and I expect you to offer me sympathy and lots of kisses and cuddles to make me feel better."

Lucas came to a standstill and his eyes hardened. I followed his gaze to where Conal stood near his father. The two men glowered at one another, antagonism clear in their eyes. "If he's staying, I'm staying," Lucas said resolutely.

"Lucas, this is ridiculous," I muttered, tugging on his arm. It was the equivalent of trying to move a block of solid granite - completely impossible, yet I had to try. The thought of him being here when my blood was being spilled was nerve-racking, enough to cause my anxiety to worsen. "Go and wait with Nick's boys."

"No." He stood immobile, his eyes focused on Conal.

Ben overheard our hushed discussion and came to join us. "What's the matter?"

"Lucas is insisting on staying." I sighed heavily, wondering what I could say to convince him I'd be okay without him. The look on his face was determined, his eyes darkened with anger.

"You should not be here," Ben said.

"I am leader of the Tine Kiss. My place is here."

"Lucas..." Ben began quietly.

Lucas turned on him. "I choose to stay." His tone made it obvious he wouldn't be changing his mind.

"There'll be blood, Lucas. It isn't wise, not when you're struggling with your reaction to Charlotte already."

"I'm staying."

Ben put a cautioning hand on Lucas's shoulder. "You can keep control?"

Lucas glanced down at me and put his arm around my waist protectively. "I will. I can control this."

Marianne sidled up to us. "Lucas..."

"Marianne, I love you like a sister. But don't tell me what to do," Lucas snapped.

With a sigh, Marianne turned to me, her anxiety written in her eyes. "Are you okay with this?"

I could see the tension in Lucas's features, the stubborn set to his jaw. I knew he was determined to do this, to prove himself to me. "I'm okay."

Lucas pulled me close against his side, pressing a brief kiss against my mouth. "I promise you, my Charlotte. I will do nothing to harm you."

"We're ready," Lyell announced.

He stood at one side of the coffee table, his pack spread around him in a half circle. All the men had come back, including Phelan Walker. He greeted me solemnly, keeping his eyes downcast. "I will perform the ceremony. It was last performed by my ancestor and I will perform it now with honor befitting my pack."

Too terrified to speak, I nodded my agreement instead. A huge bowie knife, its handle intricately carved with symbols sat on the coffee table. A small bowl sat beside it, which I assumed was to collect the blood. Looking at it a second time, I swallowed nervously – despite its size, I imagined it could hold a whole lot of blood. I glanced at Jerome, who'd joined us and he nodded encouragingly, although his face belied his apprehension. His medical bag was sitting beside the coffee table in preparation, which did nothing to reduce my nerves.

Ben, Marianne, Lucas and Nick, along with the Tremaine pack, gathered around the table and I took my place beside Lyell. Phelan Walker picked up the huge knife and began chanting, his words foreign to me. He pointed the knife towards Lyell Tremaine, resting the blade against his forehead then turned to me, repeating the process. My heart thumped nervously – it was only an hour or so ago that this man had wanted to use a knife to kill me – and it took all my reserves of willpower to remain motionless. Relief swamped me as Phelan pulled the knife away and held it in both hands. Raising it above his head, his intonation continued.

Now he spoke in English and I watched, mesmerized, as he performed an elaborate maneuver with the blade, passing it towards the four cardinal points. He gripped Lyell's right hand and Lyell stared steadfastly into my eyes as the blade cut deeply into the fleshy skin below his thumb. Blood flowed freely and Phelan held Lyell's hand over the bowl until it was half-full. He released his grip on Lyell's hand and Jerome handed Lyell some cotton gauze to stem the flow of blood. I risked a peek at Lucas and Marianne who both watched the blood in the bowl with steely determination. Marianne caught my eye and managed a faint smile. Nick and Ben had positioned themselves on either side of Lucas and they were focused on him, not on the ceremony being performed.

Phelan turned to me and with the same incantation, gripped my hand firmly. I squeezed my eyes shut, the pain sharp as the knife cut deeply into my skin. I was shaking, my knees quivering and my skin clammy, but I managed to stay upright, taking the cotton gauze from Jerome gratefully and pressing it to my palm.

Phelan mixed the blood together with the blade of the knife, and then lifted the dripping blade into the air. "The Tremaine Pack recognized Lyell Tremaine as blood brother to the Tine Kiss. Their blood is combined and the blood bond will forever leave them indebted to one another." He touched the bloody blade to Lyell's forehead, touching the right, the left and the center of his tanned and lined skin.

He turned to me. "The Tine Kiss recognizes Charlotte Duncan as blood sister to the Tremaine Pack. Their blood is combined and their blood bond will forever leave them indebted to one another." He touched the blade against my forehead, performing the same precise movements and I felt the sticky blood running warmly down my skin.

Phelan turned his attention to the assembled group. "Let all here bear witness to the joining of Lyell Tremaine and Charlotte Duncan as blood brother and sister. They will serve one another, protect each other and the pact will result in death for anyone breaking their promise given here tonight in blood."

He placed the knife on top of the bowl and Lyell spoke. "I thank you, Charlotte, for performing the blood pact with me. I consider you now my sister, pack member, friend of the pack. We will protect you, fight with you, and recognize you as a member of the Tremaine pack."

"Thank you."

Lyell turned to Lucas. "The pact is complete. We are friends of the Tine Kiss and will assist you if the need arises."

Lucas nodded, visibly struggling to draw his gaze away from the blood in the bowl. "I welcome your offer of assistance, and recognize you as friends of the Tine Kiss. You will be given help and assistance whenever you require it."

Lyell relaxed his solemn stance and turned to me. "I would suggest you sit down and have that hand attended to. Charlotte, it's been a pleasure to meet you and we'll come to your aid if you are in need of our help." He pulled me into a hug and when he released me, Jerome caught my arm and guided me to a chair. I sank into it gratefully and Nick began to wipe my forehead with a damp towel to remove the blood.

Lucas was at my side in an instant, kneeling beside me to hug me against him.

"Lucas, the blood..." I said tiredly. Despite the gauze against my palm, the coppery scent of blood was prevalent in the room and even I could smell it.

"It's alright, Charlotte," Lucas promised softly, releasing me to let Nick continue wiping at my forehead. "I've coped with it." The effort it had taken was obvious however, his forehead was creased with exertion and his fangs extended over his bottom lip.

"Will you require stitches, Lyell?" Jerome asked gruffly as he rummaged through his bag.

"No, I'll be fine. We will take our leave."

One by one, the Tremaine Pack said their goodbyes and Conal leaned over to gather me in a tender hug. "I'll be in touch," he whispered against my ear and Lucas stiffened with unconcealed fury. Conal handed me a small brown bottle. "Use this on your injuries, it will reduce the scarring."

I stared at him suspiciously. "You're giving me a jar of... *saliva*?"

Conal grinned wickedly. "There you go, thinking like a human again. This is a secret herbal remedy, given to members of the Tremaine Pack to heal wounds. Rub it on twice a day. It will help those bruises too. And this is my number – call me, anytime." He handed me a business card.

"Thank you. For... everything."

"No probs." He held his hand out to Lucas, and after a moment's hesitation, Lucas took it. "Look after her, bloodsucker."

"I will," Lucas agreed solemnly.

The Tremaine werewolves left the room and I leaned back against the chair, while Jerome treated the cut on my hand. When he lifted the gauze, blood poured from the cut and Lucas recoiled, stepping back from the sight.

"Go," I urged him.

"I can control it," Lucas said determinedly, his mouth set in a grim line.

"Lucas, I don't have the strength to argue with you. And after everything I've been through, I don't think I can face a bite," I said tiredly.

Lucas pressed a kiss to my forehead and left the room quickly, with an apologetic backwards glance from the door. Marianne murmured an apology and left, Ben on her heels.

"Nick, could you get rid of the blood and the bowl? I have some cleaning spirits here." He handed a bottle to Nick and turned back to me. "Now, let's look at this hand. Don't know why the hell I have a job at the hospital, it seems you keep me busy enough as your full time medical practitioner nowadays..."

Chapter 14

Home

We flew back to Montana the following day. Although Jerome grumbled about wanting me to rest for another day or two, I longed to get back to Puckhaber, wanted to leave New Orleans behind. It held no happy memories and I wanted to return to the safety and security I knew in Puckhaber Falls.

Ben booked flights back to Billings and I settled onto the first flight available with Lucas sitting on one side of me, Ben on the other. Lucas kept his arms around me and I slept against his chest for the entire flight home.

We disembarked in Billings and I was aware of the curious glances from the other passengers. With a badly bruised face, the heavy bandage around my hand where Jerome had stitched up the knife wound, and the bruises and healing injuries on my arms and chest, I looked as if I'd been in a car accident.

William and Gwynn met us in the terminal and Gwynn held me in her arms for a long hug.

"I'm so pleased you're safe," Gwynn said softly. She looked into my eyes; her own filled with warmth and affection. "We were so worried."

Ben and Jerome's car had been left in the long-term park at the airport when they'd flown to New Orleans and William and Gwynn had driven up to Billings in their cars, giving us plenty of room for the trip back to Puckhaber Falls. Ben, Marianne, Striker, Nick and Rafe piled into Ben's car, while William and Gwynn would be driving home with the rest of Nick's Pack. Jerome had set off on his own, preferring his own company on the long drive. Lucas and I would be travelling home in Gwynn's beautiful white sports car and Lucas unlocked the doors, helping me settle into the luxurious leather passenger seat before he slipped in the other side.

"We could have taken a couple of people in here," I suggested wearily.

Lucas reversed smoothly from the parking spot and steered the car into the thoroughfare of the high-rise car park. "I think they believe you and I might like some time alone."

"Oh."

Lucas reached across and laid his hand on my thigh, squeezing gently. "Have I told you today how much I love you?"

"No, I don't think so."

"I love you," he said tenderly, glancing across to smile. He rubbed the back of his fingers across my bruised cheek, his actions exquisitely gentle.

"I love you, too."

Lucas stopped to pay the parking fee and I watched with amusement as the female attendant nearly fell of her stool when she caught sight of him. She fumbled with the cash Lucas handed her, stumbling over her tongue as she counted out change and handed it back.

I leaned back against the headrest, a tiny smile playing on my lips. "You really aren't fair."

Lucas looked at me in confusion. "What?"

"You are so handsome; women can't help but get tongue-tied around you."

Lucas shook his head in disbelief. "I haven't noticed you being tongue-tied, love."

"I was, when I first met you," I admitted, my eyes heavy again as Lucas pulled into the freeway traffic. "You overwhelmed me."

"As you did me, my love," Lucas responded softly. "You overwhelmed me with your magic. Maybe Lyell Tremaine was correct, perhaps you are a witch and you have me under your spell."

"Oh, ha, ha." I laid my hand on Lucas's thigh and he looked mildly surprised. "Is that okay?" I asked.

"More than okay," he agreed huskily. He laid his hand over mine and I slept.

I woke again as Lucas slowed down to enter a small town, the sky was beginning to darken and he'd turned on the headlights. I straightened up, looking around with interest.

"Are we getting close to home?" I questioned, rubbing my eyes.

"About forty minutes to go. Actually, now that you're awake, probably closer to an hour and a half. Obviously I will have to slow down," Lucas admitted wryly.

"That's because you drive too fast," I grumbled.

"I am a very safe driver," Lucas reassured me, his tone reproachful.

"Unless you crash. And in case you haven't noticed, I'm breakable."

"Remarkably breakable," he agreed. "And I never crash."

I rolled my eyes at him. "Overconfidence is not a good thing."

"I've lived for more than one hundred and sixty years. I've earned my confidence."

I giggled. "That's the problem with you vampires, you think you've got everything under control, but what about all the other lunatics on the road? You hit me, remember?"

"Vampire reflexes. I can allow for anything. Except a beautiful young woman stepping out onto the road without looking to see whether it's safe. Despite the fact that I hit you, you're still hanging around."

"Of course," I stated confidently. "You can't get rid of me that easily."

"I must admit," Lucas said, glancing at the rearview mirror. "I'm impressed. You have incredible staying power. Besides hitting you with my car, you've been attacked by a vampire, kidnapped by shape shifters, made a blood pact with werewolves. Most normal people would have run a mile by now."

"I'm not most normal people."

"Apparently not," Lucas murmured with a tiny smile.

We left the town behind and Lucas accelerated smoothly on the quiet road. I peeked at the speedometer and was reasonably satisfied that he wasn't tearing along at a ridiculous pace.

"I worry about you, you know," Lucas announced abruptly.

"Me? Why?"

He sighed. "What I said in New Orleans was true – I'm not a proper boyfriend."

"You're everything I want," I responded simply. I wondered where this was coming from, he was obviously worried about something and I had no idea what it was.

"But I am not like other boyfriends you could have chosen. Our relationship is not what would be classified as normal for a young woman to experience at twenty."

I turned to look at him, saw the small frown creasing his forehead. "Lucas, what are you trying to say?"

"I think I should be courting you."

I knew my eyes widened and a smile stretched my lips. "Courting me?"

"Yes. Like real boyfriends do. We should go out to movies, or I should take you dancing. We should have dinner dates."

That last suggestion made me giggle. "Dinner dates? That would be thoroughly entertaining. You don't eat."

"Alright, perhaps the wrong example," he admitted with a grin. "I believe I should be giving you all the experiences a young woman of your age should have."

"Lucas, I really don't need to be... courted. You already have me forever," I responded softly.

He turned to me, squeezing my fingers. "I don't want you to miss out on anything, just because you've chosen to love me. Humor me, my love."

I shrugged. "Okay. I will agree to be courted."

Chapter 15

Discussions

I hobbled slowly downstairs, Gwynn's etching tucked under one arm, the ointment from Conal in my other hand. I was rapidly discovering that the longer I sat still, the more painful my body became, with aches and pains developing everywhere from the beatings I'd taken.

Lucas appeared at my side in a blur, Rowena following closely behind. Rowena reached out to take the painting and the ointment. "Here, let me take that," she offered.

"Let me carry you, my love. You look like you're in pain."

I shook my head. "I'm better off walking. The movement helps loosen everything up."

"I swear," Lucas said grimly, taking a gentle grip on my arm to help me down the stairs, "if Conal hadn't killed Armstrong, I would have torn him apart with my bare hands."

When we reached the bottom of the stairs, Rowena handed me the painting and I limped slowly into the living room. I'd spent the past couple of hours upstairs, enjoying a hot shower and trying to make sense of the mountains of clothing Marianne and Acenith kept purchasing for me. After sleeping for most of the day, I was wide-awake, even though it was late in the evening. Another reason to enjoy living with vampires, I'd mused, as I prepared to come downstairs – no problem finding company in the middle of the night.

"I'm sorry it's late, Gwynn," I said, handing her the wrapped parcel, "I wanted to give it to you on your birthday, to express my thanks for your accepting me staying here."

Gwynn ripped the paper from the gift and for the longest time, stared at the charcoal portrait of her mother. So long, in fact, that I began to feel nervous, wondering if she liked it at all. When she looked up, the expression on her face spoke volumes. "Charlotte... I honestly don't know what to say. Thank you isn't enough to express how wonderful this is."

"When did you draw it, Lott?" Striker questioned, taking the charcoal from Gwynn to study it himself. "I didn't see you working on it."

"I wanted to keep it secret," I admitted. "I did a few minutes here and there while everyone was preparing for the wedding. I got it framed when I had Marianne's portrait done." I grinned wryly at Marianne and she smiled happily back at me. "Of course, Marianne chose that particular moment for her psychic ability to work, so she knew about it, but she kept it secret."

"I absolutely adore it," Gwynn announced, standing up gracefully to wrap me in a hug.

"I'm so pleased," I responded happily.

"Did you need some ointment rubbed on?" Rowena questioned when everybody finished admiring the sketch.

I made a face. "I can't reach my back. Would you mind?"

"Of course not. Let's slip into the kitchen for some privacy."

I followed Rowena through to the kitchen and drew my t-shirt up over my head so Rowena could rub the ointment into my skin.

There was a heavy silence for a few moments. "Oh, Charlotte, how terrible," Rowena said quietly.

"What?" Confused for a moment, I suddenly recalled the dark, plum-colored bruises I'd noticed when I stepped from the shower. Two days after my rescue, the bruises were really coming out, the majority of the skin on my back discolored. "Oh, the bruising."

"What's wrong?" Ben appeared in the doorway, followed closely by Lucas.

"Have you seen her back?" Rowena demanded, her hazel eyes flashing angrily. "Did you see exactly what that creature did to her?"

I flushed crimson as Ben and Lucas examined my back. This was the closest to naked Lucas had ever seen me and I was embarrassed. To his credit, Lucas took it calmly enough, although I could see the fury in his eyes as he surveyed the discolored skin.

"They are certainly very pronounced," Ben agreed mildly. "There appears to be more bruising on your left side than your right, Charlotte."

I thought about it for a second before realizing why. "The night you rescued me, Armstrong had lost his temper when I wouldn't tell him what he wanted to know. He punched me in the stomach and when I fell, he kicked me. They'll be worse on the left side; because that was the side I was laying on."

Lucas growled ferociously. The sound was definitely not human. Ben touched my skin delicately, probing the dark bruises. "I am amazed nothing is broken, but Jerome assures me there isn't."

"Can't anything be done to heal them?"

"I'm afraid not, Rowena. The medical profession has no cure for bruising. I'm sure the ointment Conal gave Charlotte will do far more good than anything else," Ben murmured.

"I'll apply it for Charlotte," Lucas offered quietly.

"We'll leave you to it," Ben agreed. I saw him place his hand on Lucas's shoulder reassuringly. "She'll be fine, Lucas. Charlotte will recover from this." He took Rowena's hand and drew her through to the living room.

"Come over here in the light," Lucas commanded. He put the ointment on the counter and I turned so my back was towards him. I was anxious about him seeing so much of me naked and there was a charged tension in the air, as if we were both holding our breath.

He ran his cool hand over the bruising on my back, following the marks with the tips of his fingers before he reached for my bra. "May I undo this?" he asked softly.

I nodded, certain the need for ointment had moved us into new, far more dangerous territory. Lucas gripped the slip of material around my back and deftly undid the clasps.

He reached for the ointment, lightly rubbing it onto my skin, following the contours of my back to ensure it was evenly covered. His touch was delicate, his fingers rubbing the ointment into my skin tenderly. "Tell me if I'm hurting you."

"It's okay, you're doing a great job," I reassured him. The feel of his hands against my skin was soothing... and extremely erotic. The familiar tendrils of desire began to swirl through my body and I could hear my own breathing grow quicker.

He finished up with the ointment and did up the bra, before pulling the t-shirt back down over my skin. I turned to face him and saw the look in his eyes when he returned my gaze. It was clear he was feeling the same heady desires as I did. "That was... interesting," he said with a half-smile. And then he pulled me into his arms and kissed me deeply, his cool hands resting on my hips as I snaked my arms up around his neck.

Too soon, he pushed me away a little and smiled down at me. "It's a while since I've had the opportunity to undo a bra," he admitted.

"You apparently haven't lost the knack," I responded, tamping down the surge of jealousy that rose at the thought.

"You have no idea… just how much more I would like to do with you," he whispered huskily and his sweet aroma assaulted me, so close to my face. He closed his eyes, breathing deeply against my hair.

"I think I've got a pretty good idea," I whispered back and kissed his cheek, holding him tightly against me. "They're probably the same ideas that cross my mind constantly."

With a low growl, he pulled me into a close hug and I relished the scent of his skin against me. "I swear, love. I will never hurt you, as you have been hurt this past week. No matter what it takes, I'll keep you safe."

He released me; catching my hand in his and leading me back through to the living room. We sat together on the couch, Lucas keeping my hand firmly clasped within his own.

"I can't believe how rapidly those claw marks are healing," Acenith announced, eyeing the skin under my collarbone.

"Conal's ointment is making a huge difference," I agreed.

"Jerome would very much like to discover what goes into that ointment," Ben admitted. "Whatever it is, it has almost miraculous healing properties."

"I guess he could analyze it," I suggested.

Lucas shook his head. "You might be a sister of the Tremaine pack, but I doubt they'd be happy if we discovered what's in that ointment. I imagine they keep it a closely guarded secret."

"I agree," Thut announced. "Werewolves would not want us to know their business." He was sitting on one of the couches with Amunet and the other two women who made up his small Kiss. Nephthys was the youngest physically of all the vampires – transformed at sixteen; she barely hit five feet tall. Her eyes were deep set and the color of turquoise, her chestnut hair hung straight to her shoulders. With skin the color of milk chocolate, she was a dazzling beauty. Preferring to be called Nellie, she was vivacious and funny, retaining a childlike innocence despite having been created more than eight hundred years before.

Tadinanefer sat beside Amunet, her legs crossed elegantly and showing off a great deal of stunning, coffee-colored skin beneath the short leather skirt she wore. Her rich brown eyes were heavily defined with black kohl and she wore her hair in a multitude of beaded plaits, which clicked as she turned her head from side to side. She preferred to be known as Jennifer in the modern age and was friendly and outgoing, and according to Acenith, an unrepentant flirt with any man who took notice of her. I imagined that would be a lot of men, as she was truly stunning.

"Did Armstrong hit you from the very beginning?" Jennifer asked quietly. She was appraising the yellowing bruises on my arm. It was clear she was curious, but worried about bringing up a subject I might not be comfortable with discussing.

"No, that came later. When he figured out I wasn't going to tell him what he wanted to know, he got angry. Initially he was pretending to be nice; he said if I told him about my ability, I could go home. But he got progressively angrier when I played dumb."

"Did you know what he wanted from the beginning?" Ripley questioned. He was lounging on the other couch, an open book lying on his lap.

"I didn't. Not a clue," I admitted. "I only guessed he was after my psychic ability. I was sure he wouldn't have gone to the trouble of kidnapping me for anything else, but I couldn't figure out why he would want it, or what he was going to do with it."

"Conal said you were kept in that room we found you in, for most of the time," Lucas added, squeezing my fingers.

A shiver rippled up my spine as I remembered that room. "It was freezing in there. Armstrong brought me upstairs when he wanted to talk to me. The first time, he had me brought up by that guy, Sebastian, the one who took me from here. I think that was the day after the wedding." The image of what he'd done flashed through my mind and I shook my head, trying to block the image. It wasn't something I wanted to recall.

"What happened to that bastard?" Striker asked, his voice hard. "I wanted to kill him for what he did, but he wasn't at the compound."

"Armstrong killed him. He'd been assuring me I wouldn't be harmed and I told him what Sebastian did. Armstrong called him into the room and ripped his throat out," I explained. "I didn't understand at the time, but it was because of what he wanted from me. He didn't want me – touched in that way, because of what he was planning."

There was silence for a few seconds and Lucas released his grip on my hand, pulling me into his arms for a reassuring hug. "You were very brave, Charlotte. Amazingly resilient. Conal told us you refused to give Armstrong what he wanted, no matter what he did to you."

"I didn't understand initially, what he had planned to do. It was only when Conal was thrown into the room with me – he'd figured out what Armstrong was after. That he wanted to use my genetic makeup to try and create an army of shape shifters. Shape shifters who could summons spirits to do his bidding." I shook my head in disbelief. "I knew he couldn't be given the information he wanted, it was too dangerous."

"How much did Armstrong know?" Thut asked.

"I don't think he knew much." I thought back over my conversations with the shifter. "He said he'd found out about me from one of those vampires who came here looking for Ambrose – they heard me talking to my Mom, but couldn't work out where she was, why she wasn't in the house when I took off into town. Armstrong had put two and two together, realized I had some sort of ability, but he sent Gerard DuBonet here to find out what it was. I guess he read something from me through physical contact, because he shook my hand on the morning of the wedding.

But... he couldn't see exactly what it was; Armstrong told me that it was because I had it shielded."

Lucas and Ben exchanged a look. "We think when you put the spirits in that mental box of yours, it's actually a shielding ability you have," Lucas explained. "You seem to have the power to keep other people out of areas of your mind that you wish to keep private."

"He got increasingly frustrated because I wasn't telling him anything about how it works. I wouldn't admit to him that I had the ability, because I figured he didn't know what he was looking for. And I was certain he didn't want to access it for any positive reasons."

"And he told you we were all dead?" Acenith asked.

Remembering the shock and numbness I'd felt when Armstrong told me everyone I cared for was dead, was still intensely painful. "He did. He told me his men had come back after they'd taken me and killed all of you, all of the wedding guests."

"But you didn't believe him?" Striker questioned. He was beside Marianne, his arm intertwined through hers.

"Initially, I was devastated. But after I'd had a little time to think about it, I decided what he'd told me was impossible."

"Why's that, Lottie?" William was sitting on the floor in front of Gwynn, his long legs crossed casually at the ankles.

I thought about his question before answering. "I guess, because I know that you're so strong. I counted in my head, figuring out rough numbers of how many men Sebastian had with him. Logic dictated that his fifteen men, even if they were shape shifters, couldn't possibly take on fifteen vampires, seven shape shifters and two hundred odd wedding guests. Somebody had to have survived."

"Good thinking, my Charlotte," Lucas kissed my cheek. "I'm so very proud of you."

"So Conal was brought in because you wouldn't give up the information?" Ben questioned gently.

"Conal has a unique ability of his own," I said, trembling a little at the memory. "He probed my mind, I don't understand how it works, but he could put his hand on my temples and I felt his fingers, as though they were really inside my head."

"Conal felt dreadful about what he had to do, he told me it's an intensely painful procedure and he worried about what it would do to you," Ben responded quietly.

I nodded. "It was awful. It literally felt as if his fingers – were *probing* inside my brain. He got into my box straight away, the first time he did it. But he didn't let on to Armstrong that he'd broken through my defenses. It cost him dearly; Armstrong beat him up, and then threw him in with me."

"He said he probed you a second time," Lucas added quietly.

"He didn't have any choice. Armstrong was determined to get what he wanted and Conal told him he'd broken through one defense, but I had another one in place and he couldn't see what my ability was. It was a lie of course, Conal said it to buy time, but it meant he had to probe my mind again."

"Did you consider using the spirits, to see if they would help you get out of there?" Gwynn asked.

"The thought crossed my mind, but I couldn't let Armstrong know about them. Once he'd confirmed what he thought I could do, he would have gone ahead with his plan to produce his psychic shape shifters. If I'd opened my mind to the spirits, tried to escape and failed, he would have known exactly what he had. It seemed smarter to keep the spirits shut away, try to find some other way of escaping." I found myself shaking; reliving the memories of the past week was taking its toll.

"Pretty gutsy, Lott, for a human girl," Striker remarked smugly. "I'm proud of you, kiddo." He winked at me, his eyes gleaming with pride.

"And I am impressed," Thut said in his heavily accented English. "I was very surprised by what Lucas revealed after your kidnapping. You have indeed been gifted with a powerful psychic ability."

I cringed inwardly. "I'm not likely to be kidnapped by you guys in the near future, am I?"

Thut threw his head back and laughed uproariously. "You are indeed an amazing human, Charlotte." His humor disappeared and he gazed at me solemnly, his almost-black eyes serious. "We will protect your secret. We are... how you say... allies with the Tine Kiss. However, I would like the opportunity to experience your abilities, if you would agree."

I nodded thoughtfully. Safety was now high on my list of concerns but Lucas had reassured me of Thut's loyalty and I believed him. "I think I might have thought of some ways to keep myself safe, ways I can use my... gift."

"What sort of ways?" Lucas questioned.

I glanced towards the windows, where the darkness was impenetrable. "Let's wait until tomorrow and I'll show you," I suggested with a tight smile.

Chapter 16

Complications of Love

When I woke the following morning, I was in far too much pain to do anything, my plans to show everyone my strategy delayed until I recovered. Every square inch of skin ached and I spent more time in bed than out of it, under express orders from Jerome, who'd been called to visit and confined me to bed until further notice with a gruff order and threats about what he'd do to me if I didn't follow those orders.

Lucas spent hours with me, content to lay by my side while I slept, or quietly talking with me during my waking hours. For a girl who'd struggled with insomnia for so long, sleep was now a constant companion as I recovered from the traumas of recent times. Jerome was concerned about my constant exhaustion and thought I might be suffering from mild anemia after losing so much blood. Rowena was given instructions on the iron-rich foods I was to consume at mealtimes and Jerome provided iron supplements along with protein and calcium-rich shakes, which were delivered on a regular basis.

Usually when I woke, Lucas was beside me, his fingers twisting softly through my hair, so it was a surprise when I opened my eyes to find him gone and Acenith in his place one afternoon. She was leaning against the headboard, and smiled warmly.

"Lucas has gone to feed."

"It's about time," I announced, rubbing my eyes. "I've been trying to convince him to go since yesterday."

"He can be very stubborn. Men are all the same." There was an edge of annoyance in her voice, unusual for the usually peaceful Acenith.

I edged up in bed slowly, allowing bruised muscles plenty of warning before I settled gently against the pillows Acenith had plumped. "Wanna talk about it?"

She sighed heavily, her gaze flickering towards the window. "Ripley is an ass."

I raised my eyebrows, taken aback by her abrupt admission. Since moving into Lucas's home, I'd sensed the dynamics between Ripley and Acenith, long before I'd spoken to Ripley's mother. Ripley treated Acenith as if she were his younger sister. While his attention was caring and loving, it was strictly platonic between them, at least, from his point of view. Watching Acenith quietly from the sidelines, those stunning green eyes told a completely different story. "Are you in love with him?" I questioned.

She turned back towards me, her eyes wide. "Is it that obvious?"

"Not to everyone," I hurried to reassure her. "But I've seen how you look at him, when you think no one is watching."

Acenith slumped – unusual for a vampire, they just weren't the slumping types and normally sat with excellent posture – but there was no other word for it. She looked so utterly defeated, sadness visible in her green eyes as she clasped her hands in her lap. "Do you think he's noticed?"

"No, I don't think so. I've never seen any sign of it," I reassured her. Then I had a thought. "But can't he read your mind?"

Acenith swore, suddenly and viciously, in her native French. I couldn't understand the words, but they were definitely in a foreign language and definitely sounded like cussing. It was so unlike Acenith that I ended up staring at her, at a loss.

She inhaled deeply and slumped even further into the pillows. "It is true, I have loved that man for three hundred and fifty years, but no more. I will not allow myself to continue wanting him, when he so obviously doesn't want me."

"You can't stop yourself from loving someone, even if you want to. We can't help how we feel, Acenith," I said carefully.

She lowered her gaze, pressing her hands together in tight fists. "For someone so young, you are so very smart," she admitted with a sigh.

I brushed my fingers over her hand and she released the fierce grip she had on her clasped fingers, to wrap one of her hands around mine. "What has happened, to make you so angry today?" I questioned softly. I wasn't sure what to do with this angry and fragile Acenith, but I wanted to try and help her. She was my friend and I loved her.

"Ripley has taken Jennifer down to the stables, to his little hideaway. I saw them together, earlier today. He was kissing her, and when he drew her into the stables, I knew he intended to make love to her. Whilst Jennifer is my friend, our friend..." Her usually American-sounding voice had a distinct French accent to it, as though she couldn't moderate her voice when she was so upset emotionally. "...she is a lover of men, vivacious and attractive. It is not her fault she wants Ripley, it is just what she does. It means nothing to her, nor to him."

"You mean... it's just fun?" I was way out of my depth here and wondering how much help I could possibly be.

"Oui. The American term is 'friends with benefits'. They see each other occasionally; they make love. Nothing more, nothing less."

"Have you ever told Ripley how you feel about him?"

For a long time she remained silent, and I was certain she wasn't going to answer, but then she spoke. "Yes, I have told Ripley," she confirmed with a heavy sigh. "But he considers me off-limits."

"Why?"

She laughed, but it was a hollow sound, with no happy emotion behind it. "You know Ripley created me?"

I nodded, rubbing my thumb across the back of her hand.

She sighed, turning her focus back towards the window before she began to speak again. "When I was human, living in Montsegur, I was a healer amongst the villagers. I was practiced in the use of herbs for medicinal purposes and of course in those times, that was all the medicine we had. Whilst many used the barbaric practice of bloodletting to treat patients, I was using my herbs to treat people with fevers or other maladies such as infected wounds, with some success. I was also the village midwife and my potions helped the women with the difficulties of delivering their babies." She frowned, her pretty features showing distress she'd held close for centuries. "Whilst I was fortunate enough to help heal some people, others succumbed to their injuries. Some of the babies died during childbirth, it was an era in which things could go wrong, swiftly, and we knew nothing of the mechanics of helping to deliver the child, outside of receiving it when the mère pushed it out. The villagers were suspicious of what I did and some of them believed I was practicing witchcraft. When people I tried to help died, the rumors began to spread and our local priest, Father Jaquille, was one of the most vocal."

"I imagine in the seventeenth century, that was a bad thing." I knew it was a time when the witch trials had been at their peak - our own persecution of supposed witches in Salem, Massachusetts had been nothing compared to what happened in some countries in Europe.

She nodded, squeezing my fingers gently. "My sister Marguerite was very pious, devoted to God and the Church. When Father Jaquille made his suspicions known to Marguerite, she prayed for me, every single day." Her voice grew softer as her eyes grew more distant and I was certain she was seeing the images from a time so far in the past. "Marguerite was easily swayed by the Father and his accusations; she was so very young and a true believer. When Father Jaquille swore to her he'd seen me practicing witchcraft and that my eyes had burned red, Marguerite thought her only choice was to turn me over to the authorities, to help save my soul from eternal damnation."

I was shocked by this pronouncement. "He couldn't possibly have seen what he said, that's just ridiculous."

Acenith turned to me, her face a mask of anguish. "It is true; it's what he said, in an era when people were terrified of the unknown and deeply suspicious of what they perceived to be witchcraft. What Marguerite couldn't know was that Father Jaquille had attempted to rape me a few weeks beforehand. He was a member of the Catholic Church, the highest authority in our small village and had taken a vow of celibacy. After what he did, he needed to get rid of me, for fear of what I would tell his flock." She lowered her eyes, as if ashamed of what she'd admitted and I wrapped my arm around her thin shoulders, trying to offer the only comfort I could give.

"Acenith... I'm so very sorry. None of this was your fault, not any of it."

"Father Jaquille told me what happened between us was my fault, I was pretty and tempted him with the sins of the flesh and he could not help but succumb to my temptations. Even as he attempted to rape me, he was muttering about it being my sinful nature, my witchcraft, which made him unable to resist the temptation to fornicate."

"Bastard."

Acenith's lips formed a weak smile. "Oui. He was indeed, a petit bâtard." She grew solemn again. "But he was the leader of the community in our small village and his word was gospel. When the authorities came to arrest me, it was Father Jaquille who condemned me as a practicing witch and it was he who judged at these trials and handed down the verdict."

"Couldn't you tell your family and friends what he'd done?"

"I did," she responded simply. "They didn't believe me."

I was too dumbfounded to speak, didn't know how to respond to her answer. How could everyone have believed the priest and forsaken the young girl? She'd only been caring and good-natured, trying to help those around her.

As if reading my thoughts, Acenith spoke again. "Even then I had the ability to help calm through touch, what I can do now is stronger, but it is an extension of my own human ability. People were so suspicious in those years, and hysteria grew daily over anything unusual or different. The church had proclaimed witches to be the work of the devil and they had so many ways of twisting the truth to their advantage. Nobody who was accused could truly protect themselves once the authorities had made the charges known. I was not the only innocent who was proven guilty, only to save the loss of face of someone who was respected in their community."

"But that's so wrong."

She shrugged, the movement offhand, as if to say there was nothing anyone could do to change the wrongness of the event. "Times have changed, my friend. People are more open-minded, far less superstitious than they were three centuries ago."

I thought about this response for a minute or two before I spoke again, uncertain whether I should ask anything more or not. I wasn't sure how Acenith would take my questions, or if she would want it dredged up again. We seemed to have gotten off the track of her and Ripley, but this was the first time she'd ever spoken about herself with me and I wondered if she wanted to talk about it – and if it would eventually lead back to Ripley. She was usually very polite, so very restrained and I realized I knew very little about her that she'd willingly shared. Most of what I knew had come from talking to Lucas and Marianne and even then, it had been generalities. "I've read a little about what was done to the witches in Salem," I finally said.

Acenith shuddered and her eyes took on that faraway look again, even as she squeezed my fingers a little tighter. Her other hand played with the braided length of her hair, which was lying across her breast, a nervous gesture.

"I'm sorry, I shouldn't have said anything."

She smiled at me; her eyes stunningly green as she studied my face. "It happened a very long time ago, Charlotte. In the modern world, I'm sure I would be told it was therapeutic to speak of what happened, but I've never found it easy to do. With you though," and she squeezed my fingers again, "I find myself wanting to talk and let it out. I intended to only explain Ripley's reluctance to be involved with me, but somehow I find it comforting to tell you about my past."

I lapsed into silence, not sure how to respond and Acenith smiled gently, wrapping her arm around my shoulder. "You need not say anything, Charlotte. Just listening is enough."

"I'm honored that you feel that way."

"After I was arrested, I was taken to be interrogated by the authorities, which was a pseudonym for what they were really going to do. They wanted me to admit to witchcraft, which of course, I would not do. I had done nothing wrong; all I'd tried to do was help those around me. I wouldn't, and couldn't admit to witchcraft when it was a lie." She sighed, brushing her fingers across her braid in a gesture that seemed to represent her anxiety. "They kept me in a cell and the first thing they did was have the Bishop check me for the witches' mark. I was stripped naked and he checked all over my body for a third nipple, which would denote that I was a witch. It was humiliating and horrifying for a young woman who had never lain naked with a man. Of course, they would use any mark on the body as evidence and I had a mole under my right breast. Once they found it, they were convinced I was a witch and then they resorted to torture to make me confess."

I wrapped my arm around her slim waist, wanting to offer her comfort and winced with the effort, but I needed Acenith to know I was there to support her, to listen. If she could be brave enough to live through it, I could be brave enough to listen.

"They began what was known as the trial by ordeal by pricking; using a long, sharp knife to penetrate the skin. If you had an area that was pricked and it didn't bleed, you were a witch. Even if you bled from every place on your body, the accusations didn't go away. The next step was to burn my skin with red-hot pokers. If the injuries healed within three days, you were a witch. If it didn't heal, you were innocent. Of course, in my situation, I didn't heal, but Father Jaquille needed me to die, so each time I passed one of their so-called tests, he would find other reasons to keep the accusations alive." She shuddered delicately, as if the memory was too much to recall and I hugged her closer.

"You don't have to explain any more, Acenith. Not if you don't want to."

She took a deep breath and seemed to settle herself. "I will make it brief, for both our sakes. The trials continued for nearly two weeks, at which stage I was so close to death that I welcomed its embrace and prayed for it both day and night. When I still would not confess to my supposed crimes, they decided to move on to trial by water."

"I've heard of that. You were thrown into a body of water; if you floated, you were guilty. If you sank, you were innocent. And unfortunately, you were dead anyway, in most cases."

Acenith rubbed her hand against my shoulder. "You do know some of the history and you're right. I couldn't swim, most people couldn't. I was close to death, sinking to the bottom of the lake when Ripley rescued me."

"How did he know about you?"

"I had met him once or twice in the village I lived in, on market days when I visited the stalls to buy our supplies. Of course, I didn't know he was a vampire."

"Why was he in your village?"

Acenith smiled warmly. "He has never told me."

My curiosity was piqued. "Maybe he was watching a certain pretty girl with very lovely green eyes?"

She laughed out loud at that response, startling me. "I think non, my friend. I think he just found it interesting to travel to different countries, meet new people. He never showed an overt interest in me, but he learned of my abilities with herbs and we discussed my efforts at healing. And besides, there were much prettier girls in the village. He could have had his choice."

I didn't agree with her, but remained silent on the subject, hoping to discover why Ripley kept himself distant from Acenith. "So I guess Ripley could swim?"

"Oui. He knew I was being tried for witchcraft and seemed intent on rescuing me. He couldn't reach my cell, but waited until I was brought out for the ordeal by water. When I was thrown in, he swam out and retrieved me. Of course, when he had brought me back to land, he realized how very close to dying I was."

"So he created you?"

"Oui. Three days later, he helped dig me from my grave and taught me everything I needed to know in this strange new life I found myself in."

"You weren't angry about what he did?"

"Non. I wanted to live. Of course, I had to leave my family behind, my friends and move away from Montsegur; but I have never regretted his choice."

"Did you stay with Ripley?"

"For five years, oui." The more relaxed countenance disappeared and she frowned again. "I realized almost immediately that I loved Ripley, but he kept me at a distance, preferring to treat me as a sister. After five years of such treatment, I grew tired of pretending and left him to forge my own life." She sighed, twisting the braid around in her fingers. "I've spent the next three hundred and fifty years running away from him, only to convince myself we could have something more if I tried again, and returning to his side."

"Why do you think he won't take that step?"

She gazed down at me. "He does not love me, Charlotte." She shook her head, as though she was disagreeing with herself. "Non, that is not true. He does love me, but it is a brother's love for a sister. Nothing more."

"Is that what he says?"

She smiled sadly. "Oui... yes. He told me we could not have anything more, because he is my creator."

I frowned thoughtfully. "Maybe he wants something more, but doesn't think it's possible. What is it about him being your creator that makes it different?"

It was Acenith's turn to frown. "The relationship between a vampire and their sire is unique. I am Ripley's creation, but he feels guilty about it. He created me when I was twenty-three in human years. I am the first and only vampire he created. He had already been vampire for fifty years and he was thirty-one when he was created, so he feels he stole much from me. Not only my humanity, but I was still a virgin, I had never lain with a man. By creating me, he took away my chances for human love and children."

"But you were happy with the choice, with him?"

"Oui."

"So there's no... rule about a vampire dating his... creation?"

Acenith smiled at my abysmal effort to voice a question about vampire protocol. "Non. There is no rule."

I considered the problem some more, thinking about Acenith's reaction to Ripley and in turn, his reactions to her. He was always protective of her, but she was right, it was innocent, nothing romantic in his manner or actions. "Have you dated anyone else?"

Acenith chuckled. "Charlotte, I've been on this earth for a very long time. I have dated others, yes."

"How did Ripley react?"

There was silence for a few moments, before Acenith looked at me and I could see the surprise in her expression. "I've never dated when we've been living under the same roof. It does not make me comfortable."

An idea was formulating in my mind and I let it simmer slowly, while Acenith went and got a snack from the kitchen. By the time she came back, with a plate of fresh fruits and more importantly, coffee, I'd come up with a plan.

"Acenith," I announced, biting into a ripe red strawberry. "You need to date."

"Is that not what I told you? That I need to forget about Ripley and go on with my life?"

"No," I announced smugly. "You need to date so Ripley is aware of it. Let him see what he's missing. I think it will prove if he's truly not interested."

Acenith considered the idea for a few minutes, her mind working as I continued to pick at the fruit on the plate. "You believe it will make him jealous?"

"I don't know. But you need to decide what you want. Either you hang around waiting for Ripley, or you prove to him that you're willing to move on without him. Then it's up to him to make a decision. I can't promise what he'll decide, but I think it will allow you to know, once and for all if you have a chance."

Chapter 17

Recovery

Much recovered by the following Saturday, I was happy to be up and about for the first time in three days. Now that spring had arrived, the weather was quite glorious with brilliant sunshine and the hint of growth in the garden was evident as I came downstairs.

Lucas waited expectantly at the foot of the stairs and he glanced at my chest, visible in a low-cut turquoise t-shirt. "If I hadn't seen it for myself, I would not have believed those scars would heal so completely," he commented as he drew me into his arms for a long kiss. He released his grip and ran his fingers over the rapidly healing scars, which were fading to a soft pink from the deep red welts they'd been a few days ago. His touch made me tremble a little with expectation, his fingers grazing the top of my breast.

Lucas had been teaching himself to cook and this morning he prepared bacon, scrambled eggs and toast as I watched on from the table. For a man who didn't eat, he was becoming adept in the kitchen and was proud of his increasing abilities. As he explained, although he couldn't eat, he could enjoy the aromas the food created as it cooked. He put the plate in front of me, along with a steaming cup of coffee and sat down to watch me eat.

I scooped some of the hot eggs into my mouth and savored the flavor, while he waited expectantly for a reaction. "Yum. I think you're a better cook than I am."

Lucas grinned and rested his elbows on the table, clasping his hands together. "Considering you told me you ate out of cans for the past two years, I imagine that isn't as greater compliment as I might hope."

"No, really," I assured him, "I think you are better than me. Cooking isn't one of my best abilities."

"After you finish breakfast, would you like to come out for a hike?" He glanced towards the kitchen window, surveying the weather. "It's a glorious day. I think if we hike up the mountain we'll quickly be above the cloud cover."

I nodded, swallowing down a mouth full of bacon. "Is it far?"

Lucas shook his head. "A couple of miles. I won't tire you out. If you like, I can carry you."

I grinned. "Sounds great." I remembered the last time Lucas carried me, running faster than I could imagine through the forest.

He stood up, his eyes warm. "It's still cool; I'll go upstairs and get you a jacket. We can set off as soon as you're ready."

I finished up, drinking down the last of the coffee quickly, as I was keen to get out and spend some time outdoors. Having been cooped up for days on end, the thought of fresh air and sunshine filled me with delight and I shrugged on my jacket before we headed towards the front door. "Where is everyone?"

"They're around. Ben is at work, he'll be home around three o'clock. We'll see them later." He stopped on the gravel drive and turned to me. "Would you like to walk for a while, or will I carry you?" Amusement was readily apparent in his blue eyes.

"Hmmm. Think I could walk for a while," I agreed, although I was looking forward to my ride.

Lucas caught my hand in his and we headed out past the garage, walking hand in hand through the short grass and on towards the river. Lucas kept his pace steady, matching the tempo of his footsteps to mine. I was a little apprehensive as we approached the river, wondering if we had to cross it, but Lucas led us along the rough pathway, turning left to follow the riverbank.

After a few minutes, he paused and put his finger to his lips, warning me to be quiet. Lucas pointed to a spot in the distance and following his line of sight, I discovered what he was showing me. A mother deer and two fawns, stood high on the ledge to our left. He smiled at me, enjoying the delight in my eyes at discovering the local fauna.

"You aren't thirsty, are you?" I questioned anxiously.

Lucas tipped his head back, laughing loudly. The mother deer and her fawns disappeared in the blink of an eye as the sound of Lucas's voice echoed up the hill. "No, my love. And I would never hunt a new mother and her babies. We try and keep our hunting ecologically sustainable, we're aware of endangered species and only hunt creatures that are not in danger of extinction."

"A vampire environmentalist," I commented with a smile.

"Yes, I guess that's what you would call us," Lucas agreed.

"What do you hunt?" I asked curiously, as we continued our gentle meander through the forest. "Do you have a favorite... meal? Do different bloods taste different to you, like I have favorite foods?"

Lucas continued to guide me along the forest floor, considering my question before he answered. "There are subtle differences in tastes. For instance, I prefer to hunt bear over deer, as an example."

I shuddered at the idea of Lucas being attacked by a bear and then pushed the errant thought from my mind – I sometimes forgot the bear was in far greater danger than Lucas would ever be.

"I've frightened you, haven't I?" Lucas stopped walking and looked at me, a small frown creasing his perfect forehead as he gazed down into my eyes.

I shook my head briskly. "I'm okay. I think I'm coming to terms with the fact that hunting is as natural for you as eating a donut is to me. But I still think like a human – I'm more concerned for your safety – until I remember that you're far more dangerous to the animals you hunt, than they are to you."

"That's true," Lucas commented mildly. We walked on again, my hand clasped in Lucas's cool one and I enjoyed the milder weather of early spring as we strode through the forest.

"It is truly beautiful here," I commented as we made a steady upwards climb through the heavy woodland.

"It is. I will miss living in Puckhaber Falls when we move again."

"Will that be soon?" I questioned curiously. There'd been mention of relocation, though it hadn't been discussed at any great length.

"We will start making preparations soon. I will need to enroll in college in our new area."

"You're going back to college?"

Lucas nodded. "I'm going to do a degree in genetics."

"I thought you'd already studied genetics?"

"I do have a degree in genetics. As time passes however, and knowledge improves, new things are discovered. And I figure with our situation, a refresher might be helpful." He smiled down at me, his eyes hooded with desire. "I haven't forgotten we have a physical inconsistency to overcome."

The gradient had begun to increase considerably and I stopped, catching my breath for a moment. I was beginning to tire and needed a few minutes to rein in my thoughts. Did Lucas intend for me to travel with them? Or would I be left behind in Puckhaber when they left?

"That's enough walking for you, my Charlotte." He swung me up onto his back in a lightning-fast movement. When he was confident that I was secure and comfortable, he took off at a run and again I was exhilarated as he ran rapidly up the mountain. His movements were fluid, the trees passing us by in a blur. It had taken almost half an hour to walk along the riverbank, covering no more than a mile and a half. It took Lucas less than five minutes to reach the top of the mountain and I laughed aloud as we passed through the cloud cover. He came to a standstill within the shadow of the trees.

Lucas dropped me lightly onto my feet and I marveled again at the ability he had to run at such an immense speed, yet not even raise a sweat. There was no sign of exertion from him as he held me until I was steady on the rough ground.

"That is... incredible," I announced, smiling up at him with a gleeful look. I felt like a child who'd just experienced a roller-coaster ride.

"I'm glad you enjoyed it." He gazed down at me and I saw a troubled look appear in his eyes as he gazed at me. "What's wrong?"

I shook my head, glancing away. "Nothing."

He wrapped his arms around my waist and drew me close enough so we stood body to body. "Charlotte, tell me."

"When you leave... what happens to me?" I blurted out.

Lucas frowned deeply, his blue eyes sparkling with silver. "You come with us, of course." His frown deepened. "You don't think I'd leave you behind?"

"I wasn't sure," I admitted quietly. "Our situation is... difficult."

"You silly girl. I don't care how difficult it is. Yes, I want to make love to you, but I'm not going to lose you over an inability to do so." Lucas drew a deep, shuddering breath as he kissed me. He caught me by the waist and we dropped to our knees on the mossy ground, entwined in one another's arms. Lucas drew me down with him until we lay in the grass clearing, kissing each other repeatedly.

"This is dangerous," Lucas murmured against my mouth, even as he tugged at the hem of my shirt, pulling it out of my jeans so he could touch the bare skin beneath.

"We should stop," I agreed unenthusiastically, unsnapping the buttons on his shirt. Once the buttons were dealt with, I traced a line from Lucas's collarbone with my fingers, following the smooth skin to his chest and rubbed one fingertip lazily around his pale nipple, delighted when he arched against my fingers and groaned. I admired the muscular development of his chest, the smattering of dark hair that grew below his belly button and disappeared below the waistband of his jeans.

"I don't want to stop, Charlotte," Lucas whispered huskily against my ear. "I'll control it; I swear to God, I'll control it—" He captured my mouth against his, brushing his hand across my waist and tentatively reaching upwards until he reached my breast and cupped it in his hand.

Longing clenched things low in my body and I moaned softly.

Lucas lifted his hand immediately, concern etched on his features. "Am I hurting you?"

I caught his fingers, gently replacing them against my breast. "No, you aren't hurting me."

"Tell me, if anything I do causes you pain," he demanded quietly.

"I think it's going to cause more pain if you stop," I whispered, trying to encourage him. I raised my head to capture his mouth against mine and he returned the kiss, his fingers caressing my breast through my soft cotton bra.

I continued my exploration, shoving the shirt down Lucas's arms relentlessly until he pulled it off and threw it to one side. I rubbed across his muscled bicep, on past his elbow and the soft dark hair on his forearm. Then I returned to his chest, exploring the sheer exquisiteness of his physique as I traced down his chest, over his washboard-flat stomach, trailing a path towards the button on his jeans.

I heard the quiet snick of his fangs before he groaned and let go of my breast to capture my hands in his. When I glanced up, his eyes were wild, silver swirling wildly in his irises. "Stop, my love. Please."

Drawing up into a sitting position, I waited quietly. Lucas lay back against the grass; his eyes closed and raised his arms over his face while he endeavored to compose himself. He took a deep breath, then a second, before he opened his eyes to gaze at me. He cursed softly. "My apologies, my love. As much as I yearn for this, I still struggle with control when I'm so close to you."

I smiled, hoping to offer him some encouragement. "You're getting better."

Lucas sighed. "Not enough to risk going further with you."

"It will happen, in time. You just have to be patient."

He laughed harshly, the sound echoing around the clearing. "You do realize I've been celibate for decades? My patience is stretched, to say the very least."

A change of subject was in order. "Tell me more about your life." We talked often about Lucas's life, both before and after his transformation. I found it endlessly fascinating to hear about a life that had stretched over a century and a half. Things that I could only learn about from history books, he'd lived through – the Civil War, the Titanic sinking, World War One and Two, the Civil Rights movement – literally dozens of historical periods were remembered with perfect recall by Lucas.

"What would you like to know?" he asked. He still lay on the ground, his hands clasped behind his head and from the expression on his face, he was still struggling with both his frustrations and his fangs.

"What did you do in the nineteen twenties?" I was prone to asking about decades I'd only read about, and Lucas had perfect recollection of his past – unlike the human memory that faded with time, he could recall every single day, every single minute of his life since his creation. His memories were fascinating to me, full of interesting information about an era I could only imagine.

"I spent most of the twenties in Chicago, my home town," he began, closing his eyes, "I spent some of the previous decade living overseas, learning more about the history of Europe and meeting other vampires on the continent. By the twenties, I knew everyone I'd known would be dead and gone, so I felt safe returning to Chicago, knowing that nobody would recognize me."

I was filled with sympathy. "That's so sad, Lucas."

"It's merely a fact of this existence," Lucas responded quietly. "After a few decades, everyone you know dies. You come to terms with it."

Taking his mind off things wasn't working as well as I'd hoped. "What did you do? Were you working or studying?" Lucas had followed a pattern of working for a number of years, followed by studying for most of his vampire life.

"I worked during the Chicago years. It was an amazing decade, after the end of the First World War, people wanted to celebrate and they lived life to the fullest. I worked in construction during those days, helping to build some of the first skyscrapers in the United States. Owned my first car during the twenties, too – a Model T Ford." He grinned. "Actually, that's probably a car you would have liked – it was exceedingly slow."

Sitting cross-legged on the grass, I listened in rapt attention as Lucas described the beginning of prohibition, and the speakeasies that sprang up all over Chicago for people to drink in secret. He told me about the bootlegging industry, and how gangsters like Al Capone made their fortune by securing alcohol from across the border in Canada, spiriting it illegally into the United States. The sun rose higher in the sky above us as Lucas described the music of the era, the jazz with Louis Armstrong, the first silent movies which you could see on a Saturday evening for a nickel. He described dance halls where the Charleston and the Lindy Hop were popular, and how women cast off the repressiveness of the previous decade, taking up jobs, raising their skirts, cutting their hair into short bobs and taking up smoking – a scandalous situation at the time.

I didn't know how much time had passed as Lucas talked, lying on the grass with his hands tucked beneath his head. The stories he told were so interesting, I almost forgot about him being bare-chested – almost. I still found myself staring mesmerized at his chest from time to time, before I managed to drag my eyes back to his face. He caught me once or twice, and grinned.

A cool wind began to blow and Lucas sat up, checking his watch. "We should head back." He stood in one lithe movement, reaching down to pick up the shirt he'd dropped so carelessly. He slipped on the shirt, leaving it unbuttoned as he caught my hand in his own and pulled me up from the ground. He leaned forward to kiss me, his lips lingering against mine. "Thank you, Charlotte."

"What for?"

"For taking my mind off things. And being incredibly patient with me." He caught hold of my arm and swung me in a swift movement onto his back again, giving me a minute to settle and wrap my arms around his neck. "Ready?"

I nodded happily and he set off at the same unbelievable pace, flashing through the forest without taking a split second to work up speed. He ran smoothly, his footsteps sure and steady, his ability to navigate through the trees at such tremendous speed mind-blowing. The look on his face was pure, unadulterated enjoyment – the wind rushing through his hair, the glint of delight in his eyes and I realized how much he loved this element of being a vampire. The complete freedom of choosing his speed, enjoying himself, it was amazing to see the emotions in his face as he ran headlong down the hill, along the river and back through the garden to his home.

I was more breathless than Lucas was when he dropped me carefully onto the gravel driveway, steadying me as I gulped down a lungful of air. "You enjoyed that, I can hear your heart pounding," he remarked.

I took his hand. "Would you like to feel it?"

He nodded tentatively and I lifted his hand in my own. Pulling the edge of my t-shirt away from my skin, I slipped his hand under the top of the material, and guided him to where my heart pounded beneath my left breast. Lucas closed his eyes and inhaled sharply, a small smile playing against his lips. "The warmth of your skin, it continuously amazes me, Charlotte," he murmured softly. He removed his hand from my t-shirt and captured the back of my neck, his fingers still warm where they'd been pressed against my skin. "I love you."

"And I love you," I agreed with a small smile. I reached on tiptoes to capture his lips against my own. We were interrupted by the grumbling of my stomach, complaining about the lateness of lunch. Lucas casually released me and rolled his eyes.

"Come on, my love, let's get you some food."

Chapter 18

Defense

After satisfying my appetite, we joined everyone on the patio, overlooking the formal gardens. Ben had arrived home about fifteen minutes earlier, but Acenith was missing, visiting with friends. Thut and his group had left the previous day, heading back to Connecticut where they were based.

"So, Lottie? What's the secret plan?" Striker questioned. As usual, he was a bundle of energy, bouncing from foot to foot as he waited for me to reveal my idea.

"I'll need a volunteer," I stated quietly. Somehow, this didn't seem like such a good idea in the cold light of day. I was uneasy, wondering if I really could get the spirits to do what I asked and uncertain how to go about it. Although I'd talked at length with Mom and the others about what I needed to do, they had the most infuriating way of running me around in circles, not giving specific answers and leaving me with the impression that using their presence in my mind was something I had to master by myself.

"Sure, I'll do it," Striker agreed easily, his handsome features enhanced by a wide grin. "What do I have to do?"

"I'm not entirely certain," I muttered doubtfully. "I don't want to hurt you."

Striker's look was scornful. "Lott, look at me. Do I look like I'm gonna get hurt?"

I glanced up at him, eyeing the strongly muscled torso, the heavyset arms, thick with muscle. "Striker, I'm not sure how this will work," I admitted. "And I'm sure – if something powerful enough attacked you – more powerful than a vampire, you could be hurt."

Striker set off down the stairs at a jog, bouncing with vitality. "Give it your best shot, Lott. I'm feeling pretty secure."

Lucas squeezed my shoulder. "He'll be fine, Charlotte. He's the strongest of all of us."

"Hey guys." Nick and Marco walked around from the side of the house and Nick greeted me with a wave. "Looking much better, Charlotte. Guess the werewolf knew what he was talking about with that ointment." He turned his attention to Lucas. "Thought we might come and see what the secret weapon is." He threw me a casual wink and my nerves increased exponentially. I hadn't allowed for causing such interest amongst the vampires and shape shifters.

Moments later, Acenith walked around the corner of the house, hand in hand with Rafe Munoz, Nick's second-in-command. They were smiling and laughing together and Rafe bumped his shoulder gently against Acenith's, as she smiled at something he'd said. I sought out Ripley instinctively and found him staring at them, but his face was a blank smoothness, any emotion carefully hidden.

"Okay, Lott. What do you want me to do?" Striker called from halfway down the grassed area.

"Just stand there," I called back. I closed my eyes, summoning the spirits and automatically selected Mom. She was the obvious choice; the one I'd already established would do what I requested. The problem being, what exactly did I need her to do? Physical combat was an area I knew nothing about. When I opened my eyes, Mom stood on the grass by Striker, watching me with interest. Tripping Striker wouldn't have the desired effect and I struggled with a decision. It was important to prove I could defend myself, but the thought of hurting someone was making me jittery.

The assembled group was silent, waiting with open curiosity. I sent a request to Mom and she nodded her agreement. To my absolute astonishment, she immediately did my bidding. She turned to Striker and punched him squarely in the abdomen.

Striker looked shocked for a second, but didn't move from where he stood, didn't give any indication he might be hurt. "Well, that was freaky, Lott. I felt something, but unless you're trying to tickle me to death, it's not gonna be real effective," he announced with a cheerful grin.

The Lingard men guffawed and I blushed, even more convinced this wouldn't work. Maybe I couldn't protect myself – if I didn't have any combat experience, how was I possibly going to teach the spirits to use fighting techniques?

"Let me try something else," I called back, flustered. I drew another spirit forward, one of Lucas's brothers and he appeared besides Striker as Mom faded away. I gave him commands and he turned and punched Striker in the stomach.

"Nup. Can feel it, but it's not powerful," Striker announced cheerfully. "Looks like I'll be protecting you for the rest of eternity, Lott."

I pinched the bridge of my nose, angry at Striker's casual cheeriness and Nick's snide amusement. I had to be able to do this; I couldn't bear the thought of constantly looking over my shoulder for the rest of my life.

Lucas spoke sharply to Nick and placed a steadying hand on my shoulder. "You can do this, Charlotte, I have faith in you."

Striker was bouncing around, punching the air like a crazed boxer. "C'mon, Lott. Gimme something to work with here."

I inhaled deeply, searching amongst the spirits to locate Conal's grandfather. A heavyset werewolf with grey hair and slate grey eyes, he appeared on the grass and I gave him instructions. He nodded his understanding and rolled up his shirtsleeves. Rage and frustration were bringing me close to tears and I hoped this time it might work.

What happened next astounded me and everyone else. Conal's grandfather turned to Striker, drew his arm back, and swiftly punched forward. I watched in horror as the blow caught Striker in the sternum, lifting him off his feet and throwing him fifteen feet away where he landed heavily.

Marianne shrieked, running swiftly down the stairs and across the grass, Ben and Ripley following behind. There was a stunned silence on the patio and I burst into tears, covering my face with my hands. Lucas took me in his arms as I sobbed against his chest, convinced I'd killed Striker.

"Shhh, my love, he's fine. Shhh. Don't cry, Charlotte. Here – see? He's coming up to the patio now." I twisted in his arms to find Striker jogging towards me an enormous smile on his face. Lucas released me so Striker could enfold me in a bear-like embrace.

"Now that was more like it, Lott. Let's do it again."

"No, I can't." I shook my head vehemently, backing away from him. It was horrifying to see Striker thrown through the air and although he appeared to be perfectly okay, it wasn't something I wanted to repeat.

"Striker's in good health, Charlotte," Ben said, his brown eyes sincere. "Just had the wind knocked out of him. It would be pertinent to continue this experiment, see how much you can handle."

"No! What if I manage to hurt someone?" I protested.

Marianne joined Striker and smiled reassuringly. "I think you should continue, Charlotte. We want you able to defend yourself. Striker is okay and we know you wouldn't intentionally hurt us. But you must keep trying, it's important for us and you, to know you can defend yourself."

Gwynn spoke up. "You're part of our family, now. We want to be sure you can protect yourself if the need arises."

"They're right, my friend. You must continue and learn to use your ability as protection," Acenith added. She was standing with Rafe at her side, his hand still linked with hers.

"We're all pretty tough, Lottie," Rafe agreed. "It takes a lot to injure us."

"Some more than others," Ripley added snidely. I glanced at him and saw him staring grimly at Rafe. Perhaps he did feel more for Acenith than he'd let on?

"What's that supposed to mean?" Rafe asked.

Lucas glanced from Rafe to Ripley, his expression questioning. Ripley shrugged and smoothed his face back into a neutral expression. "Nothing. My apologies, Rafe."

Rowena breached the awkward silence that ensued. "I think you must try again, Charlotte. We're vampire; we'll heal from any injury quickly."

"Okay." As soon as I agreed, Striker bounced back down the stairs, certainly looking no worse for wear after his meeting with Conal's grandfather.

"Why don't we try something different?" Ben suggested. "See if you can ask the spirits to restrain Striker."

I appreciated him giving me something less violent to attempt and I drew Conal's grandfather back to the fore.

On the first attempt, he captured Striker's arms, pinning them behind the powerful man's back. Striker did his utmost to fight against Conal's grandfather, but to no avail – he could not release his arms from the tight grip in which they were being held.

"Remarkable," Lucas breathed. "And quite bizarre."

I asked Conal's grandfather to release Striker and he did so, fading away before I turned to Lucas. "What's bizarre?"

"You can see the spirits, Charlotte. We can't. To our eyes, Striker is struggling against some invisible force."

Striker ran towards us, his eyes bright with approval, still rubbing his wrists where Conal's grandfather had grabbed them. "That was awesome, Lott." He turned to Lucas. "It was immensely powerful. Didn't matter how hard I struggled, I couldn't get free."

Lucas smiled warmly, his expression filled with pride. "It seems Charlotte has found a way to protect herself."

"I wasn't really my idea," I admitted. "Armstrong put the thought in my head. If he could use the spirits to attack people, why couldn't I use them to protect myself?"

"How about we try something else?" Ripley suggested smoothly, apparently over his snit about Acenith and Rafe. "Do you think you can attempt two of us at once?"

"I guess so." Confidence in my own ability had increased after two successful attempts.

William stepped forward from beside Gwynn. "I'll volunteer."

"Perhaps Rafe should be the one to volunteer?" Ripley announced and this time there was no questioning the emotion in his voice – it was clearly animosity.

Rafe didn't seem bothered and ignored him, whilst Acenith stared at Ripley as if he'd done something surprising. I wondered if she was shielding her thoughts, stopping him from reading her and if she was genuinely interested in Rafe. Or was she baiting Ripley? If it was the latter, I hoped she could shield enough so Ripley wouldn't see through the ruse.

Lucas glanced from Ripley to Acenith and a flicker of some emotion appeared in his expression but I couldn't decide what it was. It had disappeared before he spoke. "William offered first. Let him go."

"Good," Ben agreed. "William has a lot of experience with hand-to-hand combat; it'll be interesting to see how he fares against your spirits."

Striker and William ran down into the garden and I decided to experiment, using one of the vampire spirits and a werewolf spirit. It took a little extra focus to deal with them both simultaneously and I frowned, working to bring them into the grassed area of the garden. Once again, I instructed them, the werewolf attacking Striker, the vampire taking on William. Striker was knocked halfway down the garden and William stayed exactly where he'd been standing.

"What happened, Charlotte?" Ben asked curiously.

"It was an experiment." I watched as Striker flipped himself back onto his feet and he looked across to me with an encouraging smile. "I need to try it once more before I can give you a firm answer. Can I try that again?" I called to the two men.

"Sure, that one was easy," William called back.

This time, I selected two werewolf spirits. To my intense satisfaction, it was more successful and both Striker and William found themselves airborne and soaring backwards across the grass, landing in messy heaps on the ground.

"This is fun," Marianne announced with a grin. "It's not often Striker and William find something that's a challenge to them."

The two men ran back across the grass, arriving before my naked eye could distinguish their movements.

"What was the difference between the first attempt and the second?" Striker asked. He ran his fingers through his long hair, neatening it after the wild flights across the garden.

"I asked a werewolf to attack you and a vampire to attack William the first time. The second time, I used two werewolf spirits."

Ben nodded thoughtfully. "So vampire spirits won't attack other vampires? Is that the conclusion?"

"I think so. At least, that's how it seems to me."

Nick stepped forward. "Well, let's give that theory a test. I'll give it a go."

"Do you want to take on three of us?" Striker asked. He was a bundle of enthusiasm, obviously geared up for another round.

"Okay." Again, I called to the spirits and as suspected, my theory was proven correct. The trick was to choose the right... species. Vampires would attack shape shifters and presumably werewolves. Werewolves would attack vampires and shape shifters. And shape shifters would attack vampires and in all probability werewolves, although there was no way to prove it as we were fresh out of werewolves. It seemed a creature would not attack one of its own kind and after a number of attempts; I clarified this to Lucas and Ben.

We continued the trial through the afternoon, Lucas and Ben making a number of suggestions of configurations they wanted me to attempt. The session was very successful, but I had increasing difficulty with more than three people. Anymore and it became problematic as I struggled to divert my attention and the spirits to different combatants. When Rafe joined the group on the lawn, my head ached severely with the effort of trying to bring four spirits into being and Lucas insisted I focus on three. Lucas, Ben and even an apparently sulking Ripley all seemed greatly impressed with the progress I'd made and Lucas called a halt to the proceedings after another half dozen attacks. Striker, William and Nick ran back to the patio, covered in dirt and grass stains, but otherwise unharmed.

"Would you like to stay for dinner?" Rowena offered to Nick and his friends as the skies began to darken. "I can order pizza."

"Not for me, thanks. I'm taking Acenith to the movies," Rafe announced.

I peeked at Ripley and he'd apparently lost the battle to hide his emotions behind vampire calm. He was positively seething as he stared at Rafe and Acenith, as though he would bore a hole through them if he concentrated hard enough.

"Sure, thanks Rowena," Nick agreed after conferring with Marco.

I'd sunk onto a chair with Lucas, my head still aching mildly after the mental exertions of the afternoon.

"Are you okay?" Lucas asked softly, playing with the curls on my shoulders.

"Fine," I agreed.

"Would you like to go out?" he questioned casually.

"Okay." Lucas's desire to 'court' me was fresh in my mind and it didn't seem a good idea to decline his first invitation. Curiosity got the better of me. "Where are we going?"

He smiled teasingly. "It's a surprise." Standing up, he drew me to my feet. "You'll want to shower and change."

Lucas turned to Rowena. "We'll make our excuses, Rowena. I'm taking Charlotte out on a date."

Chapter 19

First Date

Lucas drove into a parking space off Main Street, striding around the car to open my door. It was a chivalrous action, which I found charming. We'd driven to Puckhaber in his Jeep, rather than the fancy blue car and I realized why when we entered town. Puckhaber Falls was celebrating the commencement of spring with its annual Festival and the town was literally bursting at the seams with visitors attending the event.

Lucas took my hand and we walked towards Main Street, following other visitors towards Puckhaber Park, a large recreational area, which lay near the center of town in a large square. From this distance, I could pick up the sounds, sights and smells of the fair-like atmosphere and I squeezed Lucas's fingers eagerly.

"This was a great idea," I announced happily.

"I thought you might like it." Lucas released my hand and draped his arm around my waist as a group of people walked by on the narrow pavement. "What would you like to do first?"

"Eat."

Lucas rolled his eyes heavenward and smiled sardonically. "And yet again, you fail to surprise me."

We strolled across Main Street and entered the park, where delicious smells assaulted my senses as we wandered amongst the brightly colored stalls. Vendors were selling roasted turkey legs, corn dogs, hamburgers, and steaming hot bowls of chili. I decided on a turkey leg and Lucas purchased it, handing it over doubtfully. "That looks hideous."

I took a big bite and swallowed blissfully. "Very tasty."

He shook his head and caught my hand in his, leading me through the crowds as we wandered amongst the stalls and exhibits. I marveled at how comfortable Lucas was; in amongst a veritable smorgasbord of scents, he was relaxed and happy, not showing the slightest sign of discomfort.

"Do you know what was up with Ripley and Acenith this afternoon?"

I swallowed the mouthful of turkey I'd been enjoying and glanced up at Lucas. "Acenith is in love with Ripley and he doesn't want her. She's decided to date and it seems that she's dating Rafe."

"And how do you know all these details, my love?" Lucas questioned with a tiny smile of amusement playing on his lips.

"When you went out a few days ago and Acenith was sitting with me, she kind of blurted out the whole history of her life. She was angry because Ripley had taken Jennifer down to the stables and she told me how she's loved him for a long time."

"She told you of her past?" Lucas queried, his gaze holding mine.

"Yes. Some of it she kind of glossed over, but most of it she explained."

Lucas stopped walking and stared down at me. "Acenith never tells anyone of her past, never speaks of it."

I shrugged, picking a piece of turkey from the leg and chewing it thoughtfully. "She said something like that, but she must have felt comfortable because we talked for a long time. She was trying to decide what to do about the Ripley situation."

Lucas raised an eyebrow. "The Ripley situation?"

"Yeah. He doesn't want her, and it was driving her nuts. So she's decided to start dating other people."

"She's dated before."

"She told me that, but she says she's never dated when she's been living with Ripley in the same house. Now she is."

"Did you have anything to do with this change in strategy?"

I chewed my lip, looking up at Lucas cautiously. "Would it be bad if I did?"

Lucas chuckled. "Not at all. I've been trying to convince Ripley to act on his feelings for years."

I was my turn to raise a surprised eyebrow. "Excuse me?"

Lucas shook his head. "Ripley has loved Acenith from the moment he saw her. He's denied it to himself for years, convinced himself it would be wrong for him to begin a relationship with her, when she was so young and he was... responsible for her condition," he finished cautiously, throwing a watchful glance towards the crowds milling around us.

"Considering how long she's had this... condition, I would have thought he could have gotten around to doing something well before now," I retorted softly. "So if this forces him to make a move, surely that would be a good thing."

Lucas grinned. "Yes, it would be a good thing. But no more matchmaking from you, my love. Ripley and Acenith have danced around one another for a very long time. I believe they must sort this out for themselves, without any help from you, my little cupid."

"But I want to help Acenith," I protested.

"You've done enough, Charlotte. You have let Acenith see that perhaps going about this in another way could be beneficial. Now they must sort it out for themselves—"

"But..."

Lucas leaned down, pressing a mind-numbing kiss against my lips. "No more, my love. Please, let Ripley and Acenith sort out their issues for themselves. Do not pressure them into making a rash decision."

"Is that even possible after this length of time?"

Lucas brushed another kiss against my ear, whispering to me. "I am the leader of their Kiss, Charlotte. Whilst I can give advice and encouragement, I cannot pressure them into something that I have no way of knowing will be of benefit to them both. Love is something we cannot guarantee and I would ask that you leave them to their own devices, to decide for themselves how this pans out. It would be a bad thing if they are pushed into something and it doesn't work out. Disruptive both to themselves and the other members of our group."

I sighed heavily, knowing he was right. "Okay. I promise I'll leave them to it."

He rewarded me with a glorious smile and another tender kiss and we returned to wandering through the exhibits.

Finishing up the turkey leg, I wiped my face with a napkin and threw the rubbish into a nearby trashcan. "What next?"

"How about some rides?" Lucas suggested.

I agreed and Lucas led us towards the rides, which were located in a semicircle at the rear of the park. He bought a mountain of tickets and for the next hour or so, we delighted in ride after ride. Lucas took me on the Ferris wheel and we spun slowly around with a glorious view of Puckhaber Falls below us in the darkness. He'd had a quiet word with the operator before we got on and I'd caught sight of him handing over something, though I couldn't see what it was. I caught on when we reached the top of the ride and came to a gentle standstill, the carriage rocking gently in the breeze.

"What did you do?" I questioned accusingly, catching sight of the tiny smile playing on Lucas's lips.

"I wanted some time with you in privacy up here. I slipped him a fifty and he agreed to give us five minutes at the top," Lucas admitted.

"Wow. Ten bucks a minute. We'd better make the most of it," I responded with a grin.

Lucas slipped his arms around my waist and as he kissed me, I felt the familiar butterflies in my stomach as his aroma surrounded me. His kisses were insistent, his lips cool and firm against mine and I ran my fingers through his dark hair, wanting to hold onto this moment forever. Five minutes later, the ride slowly began to turn again and Lucas released me reluctantly, pressing a last, lingering kiss against my cheek. "Should have given him a hundred," he grumbled quietly.

I was still laughing as we stepped off the ride and Lucas slipped his arm around my waist, holding me close as we went in search of a drink. We found a stand near the dance floor and Lucas ushered me to a seat before he went to purchase a soda.

It was entertaining to sit and watch the dancing couples enjoying the music. The live music was being played by what I presumed was a local band and they were very good, playing songs which made you tap your feet. It was crowded, with dozens of people milling around in the mild spring evening. I smiled indulgently as I watched couples, both young and old, on the dance floor, with kids mingling around between them, slipping across the wooden dance floor in their socks. I caught a whisper of a voice in my head and listened to the message.

Lucas slipped onto the wooden bench beside me a few minutes later, handing me a bottle of soda. "Would you like to dance after you've had a drink?"

"I'd love to." I twisted the cap off the soda and drank a little before replacing the cap. "I guess we need to fill in some more time before we head home, it will give Ben and the others longer to finish their discussion."

Lucas looked startled for a moment, one eyebrow rising sardonically as he gazed down at me. "Now what makes you think they're discussing anything? And what do you think they're talking about?"

I twisted the cap off the soda and took another sip. "Galen told me." I glanced around cautiously, but the people around us were busy with their own conversations. Other than a few young women eyeing Lucas with that predatory gleam in their eyes, I was certain our conversation was private. "Since we got back from New Orleans, I've done what you suggested and kept my – lines of communication open. The spirits pop in and tell me anything they think is important. Galen spoke to me while you were getting the soda, told me the others have some concerns about what happened this afternoon. He says they're discussing safety issues involved with having me around." I lifted my gaze to Lucas's and found him staring at me wordlessly. "But I guess you already knew that."

Lucas leaned forward, resting his elbows on his knees. Clasping his hands together, he thought for a minute before he spoke. "I can see it's going to be nearly impossible to keep things from you, Charlotte."

"So it's true," I stated quietly. I didn't know how I felt. Hurt? Angry? I couldn't blame them for wondering if it was safe to have me around, but I'd thought they'd all accepted me. From what Galen told me, I wondered now it that was true.

Lucas sighed, lowering his gaze to the ground below his feet. "Yes, I'm aware they are discussing you whilst we are out. I spoke with Ripley and Ben while you were in the shower. It isn't what you believe, though. They are one hundred percent behind you, and want you to live with us. That hasn't changed." He glanced around the crowd and lowered his voice, leaning towards me so he was mere inches from my face. "What they – and myself for that matter – are worried about, is whether it's safe for you to continue living with us. It isn't our safety we are concerned about. It's yours."

"I don't understand."

Lucas caught my hand, holding it between his palms. "You know more about us now than anyone. Remember those – other people? The ones we spoke about?"

I nodded. "The ones who live in Europe."

"Yes. One of the reasons I couldn't tell you what I am was because of the rules we are governed by. Those people," he glanced around, ensuring our conversation remained private, "live in Romania and are, to all intents and purposes, like a government to people like me."

"You have... a *government*?" This wasn't the type of conversation we should be having in a public forum, but I was impatient to understand the information Galen had provided and its context to what Lucas was explaining.

"Of sorts," Lucas responded guardedly. "They are called the Consiliului Suprem de Drâghici Vampiri. Do you recall I told you how powerful those people are?"

"Yes."

"One of our rules is not telling people... like you... about people... like us."

"And you told me."

"Technically, I didn't. Ambrose told you. But he is dead and if the Consiliului find out about you, they'll assume the information was passed on by myself and the others."

"And that would be... bad?" It was difficult following this guarded conversation and it would be better to conduct it in privacy. But I had to know, wanted to know what this meant for me, for us. And whether I was going to have to make a decision to leave Lucas and his Kiss.

"Not as bad as if they find out about your particular – talent. They are very keen on collecting – interesting items." He gazed at me, his blue eyes relaying the significance of what he was saying.

"And... they would find me interesting."

"Very, very interesting."

"Lottie! Lucas!" I turned and saw Hank standing nearby, dressed in a blue check shirt and jeans. He was holding hands with a woman of about his age and I guessed she was his wife.

Hank closed the distance between us and kissed my cheek. "Good to see you, kid. See you've got the plaster off."

"Hi, Hank." I hugged him briefly before he turned to shake hands with Lucas.

"This is my wife, Mary. Mary, this is Charlotte Duncan and you know Lucas."

She was a small woman, petite with graying hair and an open friendly face dominated by piercing blue eyes. Wearing a pair of faded blue jeans and a red shirt, she looked down to earth and wholesomely attractive. "Hi Lottie, it's a pleasure to meet you. Hank has told me so much about you."

"Hi Mary," Lucas said with a charming smile.

"Lucas, we haven't seen you for ages. How have you been?"

"Fine, Mary. Just fine."

Hank held his hand out. "Now, Miss Charlotte, how about you and I go and trip the light fantastic. Will you honor an old man and let me take you for a whirl?"

I glanced at Lucas and he nodded his agreement. "Go ahead, Charlotte." I handed him the soda and Hank drew me towards the dance floor, putting one hand at my waist and taking my hand in his. The song was an older one and Hank whirled me around the dance floor, leading me expertly after I'd admitted I wasn't a good dancer.

"You and Lucas look mighty happy together."

My gaze automatically sought out Lucas where he was talking to Mary and nodded. "Yeah, we're very happy."

"Still planning on moving?"

"Yeah, it should be in the next couple of months."

"Gee, I'll miss having you drop in when you're gone. You look so much better now, as if you've discovered living again. You're looking really content."

I drew my attention from Lucas and smiled up at Hank. "Yes, I am happy." And yet, worry gnawed at me. What if Lucas's friends decided it was too dangerous for me to live with them? Where would I go? What would I do? Lucas had said it might be too dangerous for me to live with vampires. Did that include him?

The music changed and Lucas strode across the dance floor. "May I cut in?"

"Of course." Hank kissed my cheek. "Catch you later, Lottie. Better see if Mary wants another whirl before we head home."

Lucas drew me into his arms, his arm around my waist and capturing my hand in his. He tugged me until I was standing close against him and expertly guided me through the steps. "I need to give you dancing lessons, my love," he murmured when I stumbled.

"It's not fair, you lived through all the good dancing decades," I grumbled under my breath.

"Ballroom dancing has made a resurgence in the past few years, we could go to classes if you would like."

I lifted my head, momentarily forgetting to watch my feet. I stumbled and Lucas held me firmly whilst I regained my footing. "Don't you mean we can go to classes if you and the others don't leave without me?"

Lucas stopped dancing, his expression serious. "Charlotte, we need to talk about this more thoroughly and not here. But I can assure you, I have absolutely no intentions of leaving you behind. We may separate from the others, but I will remain with you."

I eyed him suspiciously. "Even if it's safer for me not to be with... *your* people?" It was maddening to keep talking in code like this, but with the dance floor crowded, there was little choice.

Lucas effortlessly picked up the rhythm again and murmured against my ear. "No matter what the others decide, I will remain with you. If anything should happen that is untoward – and I very much doubt we need to worry about it in the immediate future – you and I will still be together. I promise you, my Charlotte. I will never leave you."

Relief flooded my psyche, the intensity in his voice confirmed he was telling the truth.

Another interruption came in the form of my cell phone ringing and I fished it from the pocket of my jeans. I knew it would be Marianne without checking caller ID and answered it, holding my hand to my other ear so I could hear her. "Hi Marianne."

"For God's sake, will you please stop stressing," Marianne scolded firmly. "Yes, we have talked about you staying with us and the general consensus is that we're all very happy with the status quo. The chances of the Consiliului finding out about you are slim and I can't see anything in the future to cause us any concern."

I giggled. "Marianne, perhaps you can't be relied on completely."

"I can be relied on regularly enough with your future," Marianne responded with a trace of irony in her voice. "I may not see everything, but I seem to see more of your future than anyone else's. For now, we're safe. The problem with you, Charlotte, is that you think in human terms with regards to immediacy. We vampires, who have lived for a heck of a lot longer than you have, know things can take decades to happen. Or a millennium. Besides," she continued, "we have all agreed you're safer with us watching over you and we will continue to do so."

The last of the stress dissipated from my shoulders and I smiled up at Lucas, who was watching me calmly. "Okay."

"And Charlotte?"

"Yes?"

"We will never ask you to leave us. Is that clear? So stop fretting and enjoy yourself."

"Okay." I disconnected the call and looked up at Lucas. "I guess you got the gist of that?"

He pulled me back into his arms. "Yes. I heard the conversation. Now, can we please relax and enjoy our first official date?" He kissed my forehead and I relaxed against him, knowing that whatever was in my future, Lucas and his Kiss would be at my side.

Chapter 20

Strengthening

"Damn it!" Striker had beaten me once again, playing Mario Karts on the Nintendo Wii.

"I told you – it's impossible to beat me. I've got vamp reflexes, Lott. Superior to yours in every single way," Striker boasted with a triumphant smile.

"Children," Rowena commented mildly. She was sitting at the computer desk, trawling eBay.

"Do you want a rematch?" Striker offered. "I'll even give you a five second head start."

"Okay, but no head start. If I can't win on my own merits, I don't want to win at all," I announced, taking the moral high ground.

"Your funeral," Striker shrugged nonchalantly.

The past few weeks had been idyllic; enjoying the company of people I was coming to love had given me a new lease on life. My days were continuously filled with happiness and it showed in my overall well-being. Looking in the mirror now, the girl who looked back at me was happy and healthy, with bright eyes, skin that glowed with good health, shining hair. The scars from my kidnapping ordeal had faded to almost nothing, although if I looked closely I could see the faint marks on my chest.

With a constant diet of nourishing food, my weight had stabilized and I'd gained the pounds I'd lost. Lucas found my curvaceous figure even more desirable and the smoldering heat in his eyes showed just how much he enjoyed watching those curves when I walked past him, or we were alone together.

After much contemplation, I'd begun taking tentative steps towards establishing a relationship with my father. Our contact consisted of emails, sending regular messages and getting to know one another gradually. It was something I didn't want to rush and Ben and Rowena in particular were supporting me through the first uncertain steps towards establishing a connection. It was nice to know more about my father and his family. I doubted we could establish a normal relationship, but it was a positive start.

My relationships within Lucas's Kiss went from strength to strength. The more time I spent with them, the more I liked them. I found conversations with Ripley stimulating, when he wasn't writing he was happy to sit and talk with me. His history spread across four hundred years and I enjoyed nothing better than visiting him in the stables and perusing the many photographs and paintings that hung on the walls. In accordance with Lucas's wishes, I'd steered clear of Acenith and Ripley's complicated relationship and Ripley never brought the subject up.

Rowena became more like a mother to me as time passed – although she couldn't replace Mom, she was a brilliant substitute. Calm and assured; she provided a sensitive and caring shoulder to lean on when the need arose. She offered guidance when I needed it, and a shoulder to cry on when I had a bad day.

And I was still having difficult days. Despite my happiness and the anti-depressants Jerome had prescribed, I suffered through days where I woke in a funk and struggled to recover. The loss of my family weighed heavily and Jerome maintained the depression might continue for some time. Everyone insisted

I was doing well, considering everything I'd experienced in the past few years. When I contemplated my existence before I met Lucas, I had to admit my recovery was above and beyond what I'd considered possible.

"Okay, are you ready Lott?" Striker's voice interrupted my musings and I picked up the controller, ready to try and win again. This had been a pattern with Striker and myself for a few days now – a late afternoon game of Mario Karts had become a competition of mammoth proportions. Of course, the contest was ridiculously one-sided – Striker naturally excelled at everything and even though I'd played the Wii and Mario Karts in the past, he creamed me in every race. It bugged me that he always won, but I was determined to find a way to beat him, one way or the other.

"Are you two ever going to give up on this?" Lucas questioned placidly, dropping down onto the couch beside me.

"Nope." I was concentrating on the race and from the corner of my eye; I caught the subtle shake of Lucas's head. Whilst he was a thoroughly modern man in so many ways, he hadn't embraced video games and didn't understand why Striker and I made such a competition out of it. To Lucas, it was something unreal, a pretend world that he didn't understand and couldn't see the fun in.

As far as I was concerned, it was escapism at its finest. When I was playing a game, I didn't have to think about the more mundane things in life. *Huh,* I thought to myself, *mundane things. That's a hoot. I live with vampires, life certainly couldn't be considered mundane.*

Striker's vehicle was drawing away from mine, his reflexes superior when negotiating the corners. This time I had a plan, however, and I bided my time, keeping up with him as much as possible, but not doing anything stupid, such as falling off a cliff which would put me too far behind him.

At the end of the second lap, I put my plan into action, shifting some of my focus to the spirits. I was aware of Lucas eyeing me curiously and I smiled.

Striker was already hooting about imminent victory when the controller was snatched from his hands. I laughed out loud, steering my car carefully around the track whilst from the corner of my eye I could see Mom running around the room with Striker's controller clutched in her hand triumphantly.

Striker roared his surprise and leapt from the couch. I was hunched over, shaking with uncontrolled laughter as I guided my car across the finish line.

"No fair, Lott," Striker grumbled as he chased the floating controller around the room. I could imagine what the others were seeing – a controller moving by itself and Striker trying in vain to catch it. Although he was much quicker than Mom was, she had the advantage of being invisible to him – consequently she twisted and turned around the room, keeping just out of Striker's reach.

Continuing to bellow like a wounded bull, Striker persisted in chasing Mom and we were soon joined by everyone in the house, curious to learn what the ruckus was. By the time I drew Mom back into the recesses of my mind, everyone was laughing and Striker cuffed me softly across the head. "Cheater."

"I'm not a cheater," I protested. "You keep telling me you use your superior vamp reflexes – I guess in this case, I used my superior psychic skills."

"She's got you there, Striker," Ripley agreed. "That was quite the funniest thing I've seen in many years."

"So let me get this straight," William said with a bemused smile, "now you can call the spirits without having to fully concentrate on them?"

I stretched my legs out, considering his observation. "Yeah, I guess so." It came as a surprise when I realized it was true. Whilst Ben and Lucas actively encouraged my defense practice with the men, I usually needed to concentrate intensely to get the spirits to do what I wanted. I hadn't noticed that it was becoming easier; I always assumed I needed to focus deeply and acted accordingly. It seemed after the controller incident, that perhaps I didn't need to work quite so hard on reaching out for help now.

"Astonishing," Ben commented mildly.

"There's no doubt her skills are increasing at a remarkable rate," Lucas agreed. He caught my hand in his and leaned over to kiss me. "How was your morning? Did you spend the entire time playing this game with Striker?" Lucas and William had driven to Billings early this morning, to begin preparations for our departure from Puckhaber.

"No!" I retorted indignantly. "I've been painting all morning; we've only been playing for about an hour."

Lucas squeezed my fingers. "You know I'm only teasing you."

I leaned across to kiss his cheek. "Yep, I know."

He patted my thigh. "Right now, you need to do some practice."

"Really?" I groaned.

Lucas grinned. "Yes, really. You're doing so well with your lessons; we need to keep you practicing. Given the prowess you've just displayed, I'm expecting big things this afternoon."

We headed out into the garden - Striker, William, Ripley, Lucas and I. Ben was at work and Marianne and Acenith were visiting the library in Puckhaber. Gwynn came out to watch and Rowena appeared a few minutes later with a glass and a jug of juice in preparation for when I needed it. Lucas insisted on working with my abilities each day, and wouldn't be dissuaded – no matter how much I moaned. Rowena had taken to preparing drinks and snacks to keep me motivated, which was an uphill slog. I would never be a fighter, hated using the men as guinea pigs. It was one instance where Lucas and I disagreed – he insisted I needed to do this to protect myself – I insisted I'd learned enough and didn't want to become any more combative. I'd done what I hoped to do – I could use my ability to buy myself some time if I was attacked. I didn't want to hurt anyone and worried for my friends' safety.

We started out as we usually did, with Lucas directing the practice and gradually increasing what he asked of me. First, I worked with Striker, adding William, then Ripley. We worked on a combination of the spirits attacking and restraining the vampires and Lucas joined the group out on the lawn after I'd successfully restrained and attacked the three men a multitude of times. This was the most difficult part, I still struggled with more than three, but Lucas kept assuring me that coping with more was imperative. As they kept reminding me, Laurence Armstrong had sent fifteen shape shifters – we couldn't guarantee it would be less the next time. The suggestion of a next time was the most disquieting aspect – a possibility that bothered me more than I was willing to admit.

"You're doing fine, Charlotte," Rowena called from the patio. She and Gwynn were sitting together on the patio chairs, elegant and calm with sunglasses shielding their eyes from the brilliant sunshine.

I smiled faintly at her, walking towards the patio for a glass of juice before I tried again. "I wish it wasn't necessary."

"Hopefully it isn't necessary," Gwynn offered. "We can't always be with you, Charlotte, so even though it might not be required, it's reassuring for us to know you can protect yourself."

With a tiny grumble under my breath, I headed back out onto the grass to continue working. Lucas and Ripley were standing together and Lucas glanced up as I walked across, smiling tenderly. "Ready, my love?"

I huffed out a sigh. "Yep."

"I think we should try something new, Charlotte," Ripley began. "We've been working on passive maneuvers up until now, but I believe we should also prepare you for enemies being less compliant."

I raised an eyebrow in question.

"What Ripley is trying to say, in an entirely convoluted way, is that anyone who's coming after you might not stand around and wait for you to restrain them or attack them," Striker explained, joining our small group. "You need to learn to attack a moving target, Lott."

"I don't think I can do that," I admitted. "You guys move really fast."

"Your mind can move faster," Lucas reassured me softly. He wrapped his arm around my waist, pressing a kiss to my forehead. "I wouldn't ask this of you, if I didn't think it was necessary."

"So what do I have to do?"

"We'll start with William trying to attack you. He's going to run towards you and I want you to try and get your spirits to capture him, or attack him. Whatever you think will work best for the situation," Lucas explained.

William offered me a tiny smile. "You need to remember that I won't just run at you, we can jump and leap at rapid speeds also."

I nodded, already troubled about this new idea. I'd seen how fast they could move and didn't think I could possibly do anything to stop them. They'd be on me before I had a chance to ask for the spirits aid.

As I'd suspected, it was disastrous - I was struggling to call a spirit before William was on me. He didn't physically attack, veering off at the last minute but more than once, I shrieked as he rushed past in a blur, making my hair blow in the breeze he created.

Lucas stood at the edge of the lawn, offering encouragement and guidance and as time wore on, I made modest progress but my attacks were too little and too late.

I heard the telephone ringing and from the corner of my eye, I saw Rowena slip inside to answer it, then my attention was captured by a vampire standing near the side of the house. He was tall and blond, his clothing dirty and disheveled. He dropped a backpack onto the ground and surveyed the garden, settling on me, the only little human. I was terrified but William had rushed towards me in the same split second and I had no opportunity to shout a warning.

Chapter 24

Several things happened at once. The mysterious vampire leaped from the patio and I heard Gwynn shriek. Lucas launched into motion from across the garden in a burst of superhuman movement. From the corner of my eye, I saw the stranger racing towards me and I tumbled backwards, hitting the ground. Striker snatched for the stranger but he was much too fast, escaping Striker's clutching hands as he ran like a cheetah towards me. I scrambled in reverse, saw Lucas launch himself towards the strange vampire even as Ripley leapt forward. It seemed as though all the men were going to reach a pivotal point – me – in the same instant. Despite this all happening in milliseconds, to my eyes, it was happening in slow motion. In tiny split second increments of time, I watched them coming towards me, knew they couldn't be stopped. The stranger was going to attack me before the others could reach him.

I cringed, certain I was going to be attacked. My mind went utterly, peacefully blank, cleared in that infinitesimal split second and I instinctively reached my hand forwards and up.

A flash of luminous white light erupted from my fingertips and billowed out towards the men. Lucas and the stranger were caught within the main body of the light, which wrenched them backwards through the air like rag dolls. Their bodies folded over on themselves as if they'd been hit by a giant, invisible fist. The stranger smashed into the house, crashing through the patio doors. Lucas was slammed into the wall of the house, the stones smashing and a flow of dust and small rock erupting as his body hit, then slumped to the patio floor. William and Striker were caught in the peripheral edges of the white glow, with William thrown into the trees beyond the grass, where he crashed into the trunk of a large tree that bordered the riverbank. Striker had been leaping towards the stranger and he was blown back across the grass, his body digging a trench through the grass to reveal the damp brown earth below. Only Ripley escaped unharmed, far enough from the center of the blast to escape being caught up in it.

Gwynn shrieked and bounded nimbly from the patio, running to William and lifting him in her arms. Ripley hurried to Lucas, where he lay surrounded by broken wood and stone and covered in a dusty white layer of cement dust.

Gasping for breath, I tore my eyes away from Lucas and shifted my focus back to the others, wary of another attack. Striker had gotten up and, limping heavily, was making his way towards the house. Rowena ran outside and knelt next to Lucas, helping Ripley to straighten out his legs. When I turned back to Gwynn and William, Gwynn was gaping at me, apprehension etched into her pretty features. She looked as if she didn't recognize me and was obviously frightened by what I'd done.

There was an incessant buzzing in my ears and my skin felt chilly, icy cold. I heard the screeching of tires and car doors banging, then Acenith appeared in my peripheral vision, approaching slowly, her movements calm and deliberate. "Charlotte?"

Wide eyed and horrified, I tried to explain. "Acenith, I didn't mean it..."

"Of course you didn't," Acenith said soothingly, holding her hand out to me. "Why don't I take you upstairs? We'll get your hand cleaned up and bandaged."

I didn't understand what she was saying. I touched my hand and as if it had required a touch to create sensation, it began to throb. Looking down, I saw that I'd grazed my palm when I fell, spots of blood welling to the surface of the skin. My attention flickered back to where William lay, Gwynn cradling his head in her lap. Marianne rushed across the patio, following the path Striker had taken. I looked into Acenith's eyes, tears beginning to fall from mine. "The stranger, he was going to attack me."

"He's not a stranger, Charlotte. He's Striker's brother, Holden. He normally lives with us, but he's been travelling for months. We didn't know he was coming back today."

"He was going to attack me," I repeated blankly.

"Come inside with me, Charlotte," Acenith insisted quietly.

"Have I— are they—"

"I'm sure they'll be just fine," Acenith reassured. "Right now, I need to get you out of here – the blood…"

I was abruptly aware of my hand again, noticing the small beads of blood.

"I'll go. The blood – I can clean it up myself."

"I think I should come with you," Acenith insisted. "I fed this morning; I'm okay with the blood. You should have someone with you; you've had a terrible shock."

"No!" I shrieked, shaking my head vehemently. She might insist she was okay with blood, but the tips of her incisors pressed against her lower lip. They were vampires. It was dangerous to bleed around vampires. I jerked onto my feet. Edging nervously away from Acenith, I tried not to look at Lucas and William, tried not to see the horrified expression in Gwynn's eyes. I stumbled around the side of the house, sobs bursting from my throat as I ran upstairs, taking two at a time. I ran down the hall and into my bedroom, dropping to my knees and gasping with horror at what I'd observed. What had I done? How had it happened?

I knelt on the floor for a while, trying to piece together exactly what had occurred. How had they all been picked up like that? I hadn't done anything – there'd been no time to call for the spirits, so what caused the events I'd witnessed? I knew, without a doubt I had done it - but what *exactly* had I done? Striker's brother was going to attack me. Wasn't he? Why else would he have suddenly sprinted towards me? Why had they all ran towards me? Had I made a mistake? A devastating thought bubbled to the surface. Had I *killed* them?

Pulling tissues from the box on the bedside table, I blew my nose and wiped away the tears. My breathing calmed as I analyzed what had happened, trying to make sense of it.

I'd been startled by the sudden appearance of Holden, but why had he started running towards me? Was his intent to attack me? I'd thought he was like Lucas and the others, which meant he didn't feed on humans, but now I wasn't certain of anything. It had been a mistake to use my ability, I'd worried that I would hurt someone and now I had. Maybe I'd even killed them.

I didn't understand how, but when I'd thought Holden was attacking me – by some unknown means and with devastating results – I'd *attacked* back. I couldn't comprehend how it was feasible. If I'd had time to reach for the spirits, maybe – but in those few seconds, the thought hadn't entered my mind. Whatever happened outside had been a mechanical and calamitous reaction, completely out of my control. But there was no doubt – it had come from me. That... white light had been produced from my body; had sprung from my fingertips. I'd seen it for myself. There was no disputing – it was something I'd created.

"Charlotte? May I come in?" Rowena peeked around the doorframe, her pretty face pinched with concern.

I twisted around so I was sitting on the carpet with my back against the bed. I was still clutching the tissues. "Are they— will they be alright?"

"Yes."

Relief surged through me and I began to cry again. Rowena slipped into the room and dropped gracefully onto the carpet beside me. She drew me into her arms and let me cry against her shoulder, whispering soothing words of comfort.

"Charlotte." Ben walked into the room, his expression somber as he knelt in front of me. "Lucas, William and Holden are going to be fine."

"I didn't mean to do it, Ben! I don't know what happened. I didn't do it consciously, I swear I didn't." My words came out in a rush, panic filling me again at the idea of hurting Lucas and his friends.

"Nobody is blaming you, Charlotte," Ben said soothingly. "You thought Holden was attacking you."

I looked up at him, my eyes widening. "He was attacking me! He was running across the garden, everyone was trying to stop him!"

Rowena cuddled me closer. "It was a combination of awful misunderstandings, Charlotte. Holden had just arrived home and found you surrounded by vampires. He's been away for a long time and misunderstood the situation. He thought they were intent on attacking you. Then William rushed towards you, not realizing Holden had arrived and it seems to have convinced Holden you truly were in danger."

Ben continued the explanation. "I believe Holden thought he could stop them. Unfortunately, with vampire speed there's little time to resolve questions. Holden raced towards you, William raced towards you, Striker, Ripley and Lucas realized what was happening and were trying to protect you. All you did was protect yourself. Undoubtedly they will understand that when they wake up."

I was certain I'd misheard him. "When they wake up? What do you mean, when they wake up?" I heard the edge of hysteria in my voice. What he was saying made no sense – vampires didn't sleep. Why would they need to wake up?

Ben touched my shoulder, his contact reassuring. "They're unconscious. Jerome is with them now. Holden has a severe concussion and both his arms are broken. William has a concussion and his knee is dislocated. Lucas has a fractured skull, his right leg is broken and he has a couple of broken ribs."

It didn't make sense. Vampires were indestructible. The only way to kill them was to behead them. How was this possible? How could they have broken bones and concussions? "I don't understand," I finally admitted. "Vampires can't suffer broken bones, concussion."

"They can, when something is powerful enough to do it," Ben responded quietly. "And it seems you have that power."

I looked from Ben's calm face to Rowena's pinched features. "I have to leave," I announced decisively. I stood up, wrenching open the wardrobe to pull my old duffel bag from the floor.

"Charlotte, that's not necessary," Ben responded softly. "You didn't mean to hurt them."

"You're right. I didn't mean to hurt them and I *did*!" I wrenched drawers open, pulling things out and shoving them haphazardly into the bag. "Who's to say I won't hurt someone again?"

"Charlotte, you were protecting yourself – it was a misunderstanding," Rowena protested.

"Yeah, a misunderstanding. You're right. This happened because you're vampires and I'm not and it's insane to think I can live here with you. I was an idiot to think it could work, to have a person like me living with vampires. No matter how wonderful you all are, I'm still thinking the worst. I meet a strange vampire and automatically assume he's going to harm me. It's too dangerous when I don't even understand this ability and it was foolish to think I could use it and not hurt anyone. Lucas was trying to protect me and—" I sobbed brokenly, "I've hurt him and I don't even know how I did it." I turned to the wardrobe, wrenching jeans and shirts from hangers and shoving them into the bag.

"Let me get Jerome, he can give you a sedative to help you calm down. I think you should sleep on it and make this decision in the morning," Ben suggested.

"No! I'm not staying – I can't stay! I could do that to any one of you! Or maybe I'm capable of doing worse? Who knows?" Anguish was clear in every syllable I spoke. "It could be you next, or Rowena! Hell, I could even hurt Katie, without even meaning to! I *can't* take that risk. I *won't* take that risk." I wrenched my jacket from the back of the chair and shrugged it on. "The best thing for your protection is for me to leave. Now."

"I don't believe you would ever hurt us intentionally," Rowena protested.

"No, maybe not. But apparently, I'm just as capable of doing it unintentionally. I can't take the risk of that happening," I responded quietly.

I hitched the bag onto my shoulder and picked up my purse from the bed. Turning back at the door, I gazed at Rowena and Ben for a long moment, tears running down my cheeks. "Thank you, for everything you've done for me. Tell the others I said goodbye."

Before either of them could protest again, I ran down the hallway, stopping in the bathroom briefly to throw my toothbrush, hairbrush and deodorant into my purse. The glint of gold on my finger captured my attention. I stared at Lucas's ring for a long moment, before I wrenched it roughly from my finger. I laid it carefully on the bench top, rubbing my finger across it one last time. Then I ran downstairs to the living room, yanked open the drawer where the keys were kept. The living room was empty and I wondered where everybody was. *Probably hiding from me,* I thought irrationally.

I snatched up my keys and ran downstairs, throwing my stuff into the trunk. Yanking open the garage door, I started the car and careered down the drive as rapidly as I could, wanting only to get away from this house and what had happened.

Chapter 22

Running

I stepped out of the tiny bathroom, my hair wrapped in a towel, and wearing fresh clothes. The motel room was tiny and old-fashioned, but spotless, with worn cotton sheets on the bed and faded curtains at the window.

My cell phone was vibrating again, as it had done every ten minutes since I'd left Puckhaber last night. Despite my complete lack of technical ability, I'd pulled to the side of the road about two hours out of Puckhaber Falls and furiously pressed buttons until I discovered a way to stop it ringing. Now it vibrated silently, but at least it wasn't so noticeable and it wasn't driving me to distraction.

I slumped onto the side of the bed and glanced at the illuminated display on the phone. It was Rowena and I ignored it as I towel dried my hair, running my fingers through the curls to push them into order.

I'd driven throughout the night, putting as much distance between Lucas and myself as possible. The tears stopped falling about three hours into the trip, when it seemed impossible to have any tears left. The rest of the long night had passed in a numbing blur as I left Montana and headed southward. I had no plan, no thought of where to go, what I was going to do next. All I could recognize was the need to escape, I needed somewhere on my own, some place where I could think – work through what had happened.

Dawn lightened the heavens as I drove steadily onwards, watching the sky turning the magnificent shades of pink and purple that herald a new day. I felt a pang of sadness, knowing that in the rush to leave I'd left behind my art supplies, the only means I had of providing myself with an income. I straightened my shoulders resolutely, knowing I wouldn't go back. What I'd done to Lucas, William, and their friend, Holden – it was impossible to consider returning now.

I had no idea where I was going, no plan on what the final destination would be. I chose roads at random, following wherever they took me. The day passed in an endless blur of highways and byways, with stops intermittently to refuel and pick up takeaway coffee. The heavy forests of Montana were replaced by the flat plains of Wyoming, which under any other circumstances I would have found breathtaking. In my current state of mind, I barely noticed the beauty of my surroundings.

Weariness overcame me as darkness fell again, and I pulled off the road when I spied another small motel situated off the highway. The neon sign flashing outside offered rooms for forty dollars and I accepted it, prepared to deal with anything if it meant I could shower. I dumped my duffel bag on the floor, collapsed onto the bed and surprised myself by falling into a deep sleep. It was a sleep filled with strange and disturbing nightmares, with Lucas lying broken and injured on the floor, his friends staring at me accusingly.

When I woke, my hair was sweaty, my skin covered in a fine sheen of perspiration. Taking in the cheap room and realizing where I was, my heart plummeted. After a shower, I was ready to hit the road. I threw the last of my things into the duffel bag, slung it in the car and turned onto the highway again.

I knew I couldn't continue like this, my financial situation was tenuous at best and staying in motels, even cheap ratty ones, was going to eat a rapid hole in the cash I did have. But I had absolutely no idea where I intended on going, no plan for what I would do. My initial tears were replaced by a profound numbness, mind blank, heart empty. I was alone again. Worse still, I felt more alone than ever, after spending the past few months learning to love again, enjoying other people's company. Now I had absolutely nothing.

The day followed the same pattern – driving, buying gas, drinking coffee. I took little notice of my surroundings, barely considering which direction I was heading. The cell phone continued to buzz persistently.

It was after midnight when I pulled into another small motel, the neon sign out front missing half the letters of the motel's name. I paid for a room and fell onto the bed, not even bothering to remove my shoes.

I slept until dawn bathed the room in light, my nightmares filled with Lucas, the same horrifying realization of what had happened hitting me when I woke. Over forty-eight hours after the event, I still had no suggestion of how it had eventuated. I got up and began preparing for another day on the road. Slipping off my sneakers, pulling off my socks, I padded through to the small bathroom to shower.

My cell phone was buzzing angrily when I stepped back into the room, nearly vibrating itself onto the floor. I glanced at the illuminated display, saw it was Conal. Since the kidnapping, he'd kept in regular contact with me, always starting his conversation with the same sentence – *"Still with the bloodsucker?"* He'd proven to be a good and loyal friend. Although he insisted he kept in touch because of the blood pact, I knew he was interested in more. Lucas didn't like my continued contact with Conal, but he'd accepted it without complaint, saying only that I had the right to choose my own friends. I wavered for a minute, trying to decide whether to answer or ignore it. With a sigh, I flipped open the phone. "Hello."

"Thank Christ. Where the hell are you?" Conal demanded, relief tangible in his voice. "I've been trying your number for hours."

I swallowed nervously. "I've been ignoring it."

"That much was obvious," Conal stated, his deep voice husky across the line. "Where are you, Charlotte?"

I glanced around the room, viewing the faded wallpaper, the worn carpet covering the floor. "To be honest, I don't have a clue."

"Acenith telephoned yesterday, told me you'd run off. Said something happened with your blood-sucking boyfriend, although she wasn't big on details. Did he hurt you?" Conal questioned. I could hear the barely-concealed antagonism in his voice.

"No. He didn't hurt me." I stared down at my hands, wondering for the millionth time how I'd created such destruction. "I hurt him," I admitted quietly.

There was a long silence at the other end of the line and I waited for Conal to speak. "What the hell does that *mean*?" he finally asked.

"I don't know. I don't know what I did, or how I did it." I paused, trying to put together a reasonable explanation for what had occurred. "All I know is something I did injured Lucas, William and Striker's brother. William's knee is dislocated and he's got concussion. Striker's brother, Holden, has a severe concussion and his arms are both broken. Lucas has a fractured skull, his right leg is broken and he's got some broken ribs."

Once again, there was a protracted silence at the other end of the line. "And you think... *you* did that?" Conal queried incredulously.

"I know I did that," I stated dully.

There was another minute of drawn out silence before Conal spoke again. "Where are you? There must be something around to tell you where you are."

I glanced around the room, spying the room service menu sitting on the scarred wooden desk. "I'm at the Paddlers Motel, Steamboat Springs."

"Colorado?" Conal said disbelievingly.

"Yeah, apparently." I'd driven further than I'd imagined, not even realizing the distance I'd travelled.

"Okay. Don't move. I'm heading out to the airport and I'll catch a flight to Denver. I'll hire a car and meet you in Steamboat Springs."

"Conal, that isn't a good idea. You don't know what happened; you don't know how strong this power is. I could hurt you."

"This isn't up for discussion."

"I'm serious, Conal. I'm too dangerous to be around anyone until I figure out how to control this."

"I'll take my chances. You won't hurt me," Conal responded firmly. "And I won't take no for an answer."

"Conal… you don't have to do this," I protested softly. Deep in my heart, I was grateful. I was completely directionless, with no idea of where I was going, what I was doing. It would be nice to have someone take control, stop me from spinning uncontrollably as I was doing now.

"Yeah, I do. Promise me, you'll stay right there until I come and get you." His voice was unyielding, filled with determination.

I took a deep breath. "I promise."

Chapter 23

Salvation

It was late in the evening when I heard the soft knock at the door and went to pull it open.

Conal stood in the doorway, as tall and muscular as I remembered, wearing jeans and a black t-shirt, his dark hair a wild mane around his attractive face. He looked down at me, his dark eyes softening. "Charlotte."

For a long moment, I stared at him, until my eyes welled with tears again. He pulled me into his arms and hugged me as I cried, whispering comforting words against my hair until I got my emotions under control. I pulled back, wiping the tears away with my fingers. "Come in."

Conal released his grip and followed me into the tiny motel room. When I turned back, he was dwarfing the place with sheer size. "You really know how to pick a classy place, don't you?" he announced dryly.

"It's got a bed and a shower. It met my needs." A ghost of a smile played on my lips, disappearing as quickly as it came.

Conal gazed down at me and I could see the questions in his black eyes. He surprised me though. "When did you last eat?"

"I— I don't know." The past forty-eight hours had seen me drinking plenty of coffee, but I couldn't recall eating anything since I'd left Puckhaber.

"You look like hell, Charlotte. I saw a diner a couple of miles down the road. Let's go and get something to eat and some coffee."

We sat in a booth at the roadside diner, this late at night there were only a couple of other patrons, truckers on their way through a long haul, stopping to eat and drink. The waitress took our orders and Conal leaned back against the brown vinyl seat, eyeing me curiously. I'd poured out the whole story of what happened, not leaving out anything and even stumbling over the fact that I'd thought Holden was attacking me. When I finished, I felt the nervous energy seep from my shoulders as I waited for his response.

"I warned you about the bloodsuckers, didn't I? They can't be trusted, Charlotte." Conal's voice was low in the quiet diner. "It might have been a misunderstanding this time, but you're right to be frightened. Ultimately, they can't fight the desire for human blood." The waitress stood at the counter, the other patrons far enough from us that it was unlikely they'd overhear our conversation.

"I'm sure they wouldn't have hurt me," I protested quietly. "It really was a misunderstanding."

Conal shook his head, his dark hair sweeping against his shoulders. "They are what they are. There's no denying that they only live— exist, for one thing. Blood. The Tine Kiss might be subsisting on human blood, but I can't believe they can control it perfectly. Sooner or later, Charlotte, it was gonna go pear-shaped." He was sitting cross-armed, but now he reached one hand across the table, touching a curl that hung against my cheek. "And what happened, when you think you attacked them. You're absolutely certain it came from you?"

"My abilities have been steadily increasing." I explained the events of the past weeks, how I was refining the control I had over the spirits and increasing my mental abilities. "But it's never been like that before. Conal, I broke their bones... that shouldn't be possible."

"It's not impossible," Conal replied slowly. "But improbable. Vamps are virtually indestructible. It would take a tremendous amount of power to break one of their bones. More power than any human has. Or any werewolf, for that matter."

"Well, apparently I managed it. And I didn't break one bone; I broke a whole lot of them." I bit my lip, forcing control over my tightly strung emotions.

The waitress appeared with our orders – espresso for Conal, soda for me and a huge hamburger for each of us. I picked at the lettuce peeking out from the bun, popping it into my mouth.

"Was Acenith worried about me?"

Conal sipped his coffee, eyeing me thoughtfully. "I like that girl, Marianne too. Despite them being leeches. Yeah, she was worried about you. Practically begged me to find you, because you wouldn't pick up your cell phone."

I shut my eyes, a wave of misery swamping me. "I like them, too."

Conal bit into his hamburger, chewing before he spoke again. "She wanted me to tell you the men are okay." His black eyes were scrutinizing me carefully as though he was seeing into my soul. "They want you to go back."

"I can't go back."

"Why? Because you're frightened of them? You *should* be."

I shook my head, picking at the sesame seed on the top of the bun. "Because I might hurt them." I saw the cynical look cross Conal's handsome features and hurried to explain. "You didn't see it, Conal. You didn't see how much damage I did. I threw Lucas – through a wall – without *physically* touching him. Hard enough to break the stone and wood behind it. I can't risk doing that again. And William has a little sister, Katie. I couldn't bear to think I might hurt her."

"A bloodsucker with a sister?" His voice was heavy with cynicism. "She a vamp, too?"

"No, she's just a little girl. She's not really his sister... more of a descendant. But he and Gwynn love her like a daughter."

"The bloodsuckers risk having a human kid living with them?"

"Not all the time. She lives with a carer."

"Convenient. Probably saves her from being eaten by them. What did they do? Kill the parents to take the kid?"

"It wasn't like that," I flashed angrily. "Her mother was a drug addict; Katie was put into foster care."

"Probably better off," Conal said mulishly.

"How can you say that?"

For a long moment, we glared at one another, before Conal backed down. "Okay. Let's agree not to fight over this. You know them better than I do." He finished the last mouthful of his burger. "Now eat, Charlotte. You haven't touched your food."

I bit into the burger and had to admit, it was good. Conal sat quietly opposite me, allowing me to eat in peace and I surprised myself by finishing a good portion.

"So," Conal clasped his hands together on the table as he watched me. "You aren't going back."

I shook my head. "I can't."

"What about you and Lucas? I thought you were pretty happy together." He was studying me, his eyes devoid of any decipherable emotion.

Tears welled in my eyes. "I can't put him at risk. It's better for him if we don't see one another again."

Conal watched me for a long moment, his black eyes like endless pools of night. "I think you should come back to Mississippi with me. Stay at my apartment, take a bit of time to figure out what you want to do. I've got a spare bedroom you can use." He pushed my phone towards me. "But the bloodsuckers should hear it from you. I don't want them getting the impression I'm coercing you in any way."

I shook my head frantically. "I can't."

"Charlotte, we have a blood pact with you as part of the Tine Kiss. By having you come across to our side, it could make the pact... messy. I have to think of my own pack. Lucas and his friends need to know you're coming with me willingly. I don't want them thinking they need to come and rescue you."

"I'm not sure it's a good idea, Conal, it could be dangerous for you."

Conal smiled. "I'll take my chances. Now call them."

I stared at the phone, picking it up with fingers that trembled. I flipped it open and dialed Acenith's number. The coward in me hoped she wouldn't answer, that maybe she would be out hunting. Typical of my luck, she answered on the second ring.

"Charlotte! Thank goodness! Are you okay?" Her voice was filled with anxiety.

"I'm fine," I responded quietly. "Conal's with me."

"Lottie, what happened wasn't your fault; you weren't to know your ability had increased so dramatically. We all completely understand, you thought Holden was going to attack you. Lucas is devastated that it happened and you felt so threatened." Acenith spoke in a rush, as if she needed to say everything quickly in case I hung up.

"Is— are they okay?"

"Yes, of course. The bones have mended and no one is worse for wear. Holden is sorry for appearing so abruptly and frightening you, he hadn't got our messages about you coming to live with us, so he was shocked to discover a human at the house. He misread the situation, thought William had lost control of his thirst and was attacking you. He wouldn't have hurt you; he was trying to save you." Acenith's tone changed, almost begging. "Please come home. This is nothing that we can't work out."

"I'm not coming back, Acenith. I'm—" I inhaled heavily. "I'm going to stay with Conal for a while. I need to work out some things."

There was silence at the other end of the line and I imagined Acenith's face, knew she would be crying if she were capable of doing so. "Please, Charlotte. Don't do this," she pleaded softly.

"I'm terrified of hurting someone else. What I did – it could happen again. I can't take that risk. Next time it could be you, or Marianne, or Rowena. Worse still, I could hurt Katie. I can't let that happen." I paused, trying to get my errant thoughts into order. "I need time to work out what happened, why it happened. How to control it."

There was a lengthy silence. "Charlotte."

It was Lucas and my heart plunged, tears running unhindered down my cheeks.

"I am so sorry, my love. I failed you. I swear it will never happen again."

I struggled to stop the tears, drawing a ragged breath as I glanced at Conal. His strong features were emotionless, his eyes impassive. "I'm not coming back."

"Can't we talk this through?" I heard the wretchedness in his voice, could imagine his expression and tears dripped onto the table.

"No, there's nothing to say."

"On the contrary, I think there's a lot to say," Lucas responded resolutely. "Charlotte, what happened was a debacle. Holden picked the worst possible moment to return to the Kiss. We all know William worries about his self-control and for Holden to arrive and see him racing towards you, a human – he honestly believed you were in danger. To add to the fiasco, Marianne got a warning, but by the time she'd deciphered it and called Rowena, it was already too late. Can you not forgive us for one mistake?"

"I'm not blaming you or the others. But it... it frightened me, I can't explain what happened, how I managed to— hurt you. And I can't take the risk of being around you in case it happens again." I inhaled sharply, fighting for courage to say the next words. "I think it's best for everyone if we don't see one another again."

"But you can take the risk of being with Conal," he stated harshly.

I winced at the bitterness in his voice. "Conal isn't a risk to me, Lucas. He doesn't have the same issues with his... condition, as you have."

"I have never threatened you, Charlotte. Never lost control."

"But one of you might." I hated saying it, didn't want to hurt his feelings, but I had to. Deep in my heart, I had to admit I'd been terrified when Holden ran towards me, had been convinced he would attack me. If it happened again and this power I held flared – would I kill one of them? "Please, Lucas. Please accept that I have to leave."

The silence at the other end of the line seemed endless. Even before Lucas spoke, I knew what he would say, knew he wouldn't force me into anything I didn't want to do. He had promised he never would and when he spoke, his words confirmed it. "If that's what you have decided, I'm bound to accept it, my Charlotte. I promised you I would never make you do anything you didn't want to do. And I promised myself I would never hurt you. I have failed on both accounts."

I was crying in earnest now, great sobs that left my chest aching. I couldn't bear this, couldn't tolerate never seeing him again and yet, there was no alternative. "Promise me you won't do anything stupid. Promise you'll take care of yourself," I begged. I couldn't live with myself if he chose to do something drastic because of me.

Another long pause before he spoke again, his voice desolate. "I will make that promise, as long as you promise the same thing."

"I promise," I agreed softly. "Goodbye, Lucas." I shut the phone and stared at it for a long moment, before I buried my face in my hands.

Conal slipped from his side of the booth and into mine, wordlessly drawing me into his arms and letting me sob against his shirt.

Chapter 24

New Beginnings

It had been a little over two months since Conal rescued me from the motel room in Colorado. He'd taken control, arranging transportation of my car to Mississippi and driving us to Denver so we could catch a flight to Louisiana.

I'd learned Conal had two homes – one on the outskirts of Natchez, in a group of houses where members of his pack lived in a close community, and an apartment in the heart of Jackson where he lived during the week. His elegant apartment was spacious and comfortable with two bedrooms, two bathrooms, a large living area and a small balcony that looked out over the city.

Conal was an engineer and worked at his father's construction company, designing high-rise structures to be erected around the United States. He was away from Jackson frequently and insisted I was welcome to live in the apartment while I pulled my life together. He was absent for two or three nights most weeks and I spent the time coming to terms with my new circumstances.

For the first few weeks, I was in a continual funk, deeply depressed and struggling to comprehend a life without Lucas. I sat around the apartment, drinking coffee and watching reruns on cable. Most days I didn't bother changing out of pajamas. To his credit, Conal was amazingly patient, letting me work through my feelings in my own time. I'm certain that some days I must have driven him to distraction and made him wonder why on earth he'd invited this wretched woman into his home. If I'd been him, I would have kicked me out on my ass.

He was a perfect gentleman. The first night at the apartment, Conal insisted on giving me the master bedroom and he moved to the second, smaller bedroom. He made no mention of anything more than friendship, though I was aware of the way he gazed at me when he thought I wasn't looking. I sometimes caught the smoldering desire in his eyes when I glanced up unexpectedly and he'd turn away until he'd recovered his composure. We both studiously ignored mentioning it.

The finality of my break with Lucas came a week or so after my arrival in Mississippi, when a delivery truck arrived at the apartment with the rest of my belongings from Puckhaber Falls. My art supplies, clothes, books – every single one of my belonging had been carefully packed into cardboard packing crates and were delivered to Conal's doorstep. My heart shattered all over again as I unpacked and found a letter from Lucas in the top of one crate. For the rest of the day I'd stared at the sealed envelope, wavering between the desperate desire to open it and complete terror regarding what he might have written. For the sake of my own sanity, I chose not to read it. I was wavering on the wings of depression, as it was – nothing Lucas said would make it better. When Conal arrived home from work, I handed him the envelope, requesting he get rid of it. I couldn't bear to do it myself.

As the weeks passed I began to crawl out of the doldrums I'd wallowed in, although I didn't recognize the change until Conal heard me laughing at an episode of 'The Big Bang Theory' and commented on it. Although my heart was still wounded and I missed Lucas desperately, I was coming to terms with my new life. Little by little, I returned to the living.

We went out frequently, to dinner, the movies and Conal played tour guide on Sunday afternoons, showing me the sights of Jackson and the surrounding area. To all intents and purposes we were very good friends and I liked it that way. I didn't think I would become involved with another man, couldn't imagine loving someone else. My love for Lucas had been... *was*, all-encompassing. He could never be replaced in my heart.

The Tremaine Pack had been informed of my arrival in Mississippi and Lyell Tremaine and his wife, Amoux had visited us for dinner one night, soon after my appearance. Amoux Tremaine was an attractive woman in her fifties, her black hair highlighted with silver streaks and her olive skin unlined. She greeted me with southern graciousness and didn't seem concerned about our living arrangements; although I was sure she must be curious as to the true nature of our relationship.

Conal had explained the circumstances of my abrupt departure from Puckhaber Falls and the older Tremaines treated me sympathetically. They mutually agreed to keep the exact circumstances leading to my arrival in Mississippi from the pack. Lyell said they were naturally mistrustful and superstitious and would be fearful of my radically enhanced abilities.

Lyell drew me to one side after dinner to ask about the pact with Lucas's Kiss. Whilst Conal and his mother cleared the dishes, Lyell explained I had the right to break the pact between the two groups, asking if I wished to do so. I shook my head, assuring him that despite breaking up with Lucas, I still considered them my friends. Lyell used his cell phone and contacted Lucas, telling him the pact between the werewolves and vampires remained in place. My heart plunged, knowing he was doing what I couldn't – contacting the people I loved most and considered family.

"Ready to go?" Conal appeared in the doorway, striking in a white open-necked shirt and dark blue jeans, his feet encased in sturdy boots. The white shirt accentuated the olive tone of his skin, his toned arms darkened by the sun.

I pulled a brush through my hair, flicking it up into a ponytail high on the back of my head before grabbing up my purse. "Yep."

Conal caught my hand in his. "You look beautiful," he said softly.

"Thank you." We left the apartment to catch the elevator downstairs. Conal had invited me to a pack cookout and we were driving the hour and a half to Natchez, where the Tremaine pack lived in a community a little outside the city limits. It was my first visit and I'd dressed with care to meet the pack. I didn't want to embarrass either Conal or his parents.

Conal drove his black pickup smoothly through the mid-afternoon traffic, keeping up a pleasant flow of conversation about work and our plans for the weekend. Conal had mastered the art of selecting entertainment for us, which didn't imply 'dating' – something he knew I'd shy away from doing. No intimate dinners in romantic restaurants, no events which smacked of anything other than two friends enjoying one another's company. I worried constantly that I wasn't being fair to him, but I couldn't bear the thought of not having him around. In these early days of my breakup, I clung to him like a lifeline. He was the one certain anchor in my life right now.

My interest in our surroundings peaked as we reached the outskirts of Natchez and Conal pointed out various points of interest. I'd never visited Mississippi before and was gradually getting to know the area. I wasn't sure I could get used to the heat. In the early days of summer, it was humid and oppressive and without the air conditioning blowing in the cab, I imagined my clothes would be sticking to my skin.

We drove through the heart of Natchez, before leaving behind the historical buildings and following a narrow road, which followed the edge of the Mississippi River. We drew into a small community and Conal pulled up outside a compact white house, its gardens planted smartly with a bright array of flowers, the lawn neatly mowed.

"This is Mom and Dad's place," he announced, coming around the truck to help me get out. I slipped down onto the ground, glad I'd chosen a white cotton shirt and apricot linen skirt, teamed with strappy flat sandals for the cook out. The natural materials were perfect for such humid weather and I felt reasonably comfortable, albeit somewhat nervous. Conal pointed out other houses in the wide street, naming who lived in them. It seemed every house in the area belonged to a member of the pack and I mentioned this to him.

"It's convenient to live close together for the full moon, when we need to be able to access the woods. They're directly behind us, down beyond the river."

I smiled softly, shaking my head, and Conal squeezed my fingers. "What's amusing you?"

"I sometimes forget you're a werewolf."

"That's because I don't constantly think about eating you. Only happens for three days a month," he grinned wickedly. "And then I get out of the way, so it won't happen."

We walked around the side of the house and I could hear the steady murmur of voices from the garden beyond. As we turned into the yard, I was assaulted by a wave of sound and color, with people everywhere. Some were standing in groups, others sitting in clusters under the shade of spreading trees. There was a big pool with dozens of kids jumping and splashing in the water.

Conal drew me through the crowd, introducing members of the pack and reacquainting me with some I'd met in New Orleans after our rescue. Kenyon greeted me with a warm hug, whilst in contrast; Phelan Walker voiced an icy hello and walked away. He was noticeably uncomfortable in my presence, but at least he'd said hello. I'd take what I could get.

Conal led me further through the crowd and I lifted my fingers to my head, rubbing at the slight pounding of a headache behind my eyes. "Charlotte? You okay?" When I looked up, Conal was eyeing me with concern.

I nodded. "Touching people lets new spirits into my head; I haven't managed to control that part yet. It gives me a headache until I've had time to process them all."

He squeezed my fingers softly. "I'll introduce you to my grandmother and get you a drink." He scanned the crowd and drew me towards an elderly woman holding court amongst a group of other older ladies.

"Conal, come and give me some sugar!" She eyed me with undisguised interest. "Who is this lovely young lady?"

Conal leaned over, kissing her cheek affectionately. "Hey Nonny. This is my friend, Charlotte Duncan. Charlotte, this is my grandmother, Juanita Tremaine."

The elderly woman held her hands to her cheeks, her mouth opening with delight. "Come sit by me, child. We have a lot to talk about." She turned to the woman sitting next to her. "Move on over, Bonnie. The pack made a treaty with vampires for this girl. I want to learn some more about her."

"Now Nonny, don't you go frightening her," Conal warned mildly, but he winked at me as Juanita drew me down onto the chair beside her. "I'll be back in a minute, Charlotte."

I watched helplessly as he disappeared into the crowd then turned back to Juanita Tremaine with a nervous smile. I guessed by the fine wrinkles etched into her skin and the whiteness of her hair that she must be in her eighties. Her face showed signs of faded beauty, suggesting she'd been a stunner in her youth. She had piercing black eyes, the same color and shape as Conal's and she studied my face carefully, appraising every detail. "You're a beautiful young woman, Charlotte. I can see why my grandson likes you so much."

My cheeks reddened, the heat rushing up my face. "I like him, too."

"Not the way he wants you to, I hear." I searched her face for some sign of judgment, but found nothing. Her expression was smooth and calm as she watched me astutely. "But we can't choose who we love."

"No, we can't," I admitted shyly.

"My son Lyell tells me you have very a special gift." She offered her hand and I took it, knowing what she sought. Around us, the other women watched keenly as I heard the voices spilling into my head like a slow trickle of water.

I listened until I detected the strongest voice, typically an indication of someone important. "Your husband, Rafael, is with me. He's a very handsome man. He says he loves you and misses you. He remembers the dances you went to and how much you loved to waltz." I caught sight of the necklace she wore, a gold chain with a little bird-shaped charm, its wings outspread. "Rafael gave you that necklace on your fiftieth birthday. He says you reminded him of a bird, free and soaring through life with honesty and love. It was his favorite thing about you, the way you accepted everyone and the love you demonstrate for your family and friends."

She squeezed my fingers tenderly, eyes shining with unshed tears and her hand soft and warm in mine. "You are indeed very special, Charlotte."

Conal appeared, handing me a plastic cup and I sipped from it gratefully. It was icy cold and the welcome sweet coolness trickled down the back of my throat as I swallowed.

"Sweet tea. You're in the south, now," he explained with a grin.

"It's yummy," I announced, sipping from the cup again.

Conal held out his hand. "C'mon, let's get something to eat." I took his hand and let him draw me to my feet.

"It was a pleasure to meet you, Mrs. Tremaine."

"Call me Nonny, everybody does," she said with a sweet smile. "And Conal, you bring her back to talk with me later, you hear?"

"Yes, Ma'am," Conal said, winking at the older woman.

I held the drinks whilst Conal piled plates high with food from the vast tables sitting in the center of the lawn. Conal led me through the crowd, finding a quiet area near the banks of the Mississippi, which ran along the rear of Lyell Tremaine's property. I sat down on the warm grass, enjoying the tranquility of gazing out over the water, after the hustle and bustle of the Tremaine cookout.

"Enjoying yourself?" Conal asked quietly. He was sitting cross-legged, his plate sitting on his lap, a bottle of Corona in his hand.

"I am, actually." I pulled some of the marinated meat from a barbecued chicken drumstick, popping it into my mouth.

"You sound surprised," he commented, sipping his beer.

"I guess I am." I glanced across at him, dropping the drumstick back onto my plate. "I wasn't certain I could feel happy again," I confessed.

"It's my charming personality that's making the difference."

"Sure it is." I laughed, picking up the drumstick and throwing it at him.

With instinctual reflexes, he caught the drumstick between his thumb and forefinger and immediately put it in his mouth, chewing some meat off it. "My grandmother likes you," he commented when he'd finished eating, throwing the remains back onto his empty plate.

"She's wonderful," I said. "I enjoyed talking with her."

He eyed the crowds around us, their noise creating a hubbub in the still June evening. "Do you want to go for a walk?"

"Sure." I got to my feet and Conal disposed of the rubbish before catching my hand in his and leading me along the edge of the river. We walked in silence for a few minutes, moving closer to the woods, which cut away at the curve of the river. "It's not full moon tonight, is it?"

He shook his head. "No, it's not a full moon tonight. Besides, it won't be full dark for a while yet. You would still be safe."

I giggled nervously and Conal moved closer, his fingers warm against mine. "You don't mind leaving the party for a bit? All those voices give me a headache after a while."

"No, I don't mind. All those voices give me a headache too, and I'm dealing with the ones outside my head *and* inside."

We walked in silence along the riverside and a fresh gentle breeze blew up from the river, cooling the dampness of my skin. Crickets began to chirrup as Conal led me along the path that entered the woods. The light faded a little, as the trees grew thicker around us.

"Sure it's not a full moon tonight?"

Conal stopped walking and turned to face me. "Of course it's not a full moon. You know," he moved closer to me, fingers brushing a tendril of hair back from my face, "I would never put you in any danger, Charlotte."

"I know," I whispered.

For a long moment he gazed down at me, his eyes filled with affection, his breathing slow and steady as he watched me. "Charlotte. Do you think..." he paused, inhaling sharply. "Is there any chance you could love me? Even a little bit?"

I didn't know what to say and wished I could escape the longing in his black eyes. What did I feel? I cared for him, but I wasn't sure I could ever love him. Not the way he wanted. "I can't tell you what you want to hear," I finally admitted sadly, lowering my gaze.

He caught my chin and lifted my face so he could look into my eyes, his fingertips warm against my skin. "Don't be sorry. I think I have enough love for both of us." He paused, studying me intently. "What would you say if I wanted to kiss you?" he said huskily, his voice only just above a whisper.

I swallowed anxiously. "I think I would say… yes."

He captured my face in his hands and leaned in, his lips brushing against mine. His lips were soft and pliant, the warmth of his mouth causing a tendril of desire to ignite and flare low in my body. I wrapped my arms around his waist and he dropped one arm around my back, his other hand holding the back of my head and angling my face the way he wanted. His lips grew more insistent against mine, teeth nibbling gently across my lower lip until I opened my mouth to him. He deepened the kiss, firm and unrelenting as he explored the bare skin of my back under his hand. He pulled me closer until our bodies were aligned and my knees went weak at the thought of his muscular body pressed against mine, only thin layers of clothing between us. His heart pounded rapidly, matching the rhythm of my own as he released my lips and trailed a row of kisses down my cheek, across my neck and over my shoulder.

Conal breathed heavily when he released me, a broad smile deepening the dimples in his cheeks. "I think we should go back."

"Did I do something wrong?"

"No. Hell no," he reassured me huskily. "But if we stay here any longer, I'm gonna want to do so much more than just kiss you."

"Oh." I was startled by his honesty and blushed furiously.

With a delighted grin, he captured my hand in his and we headed back to the party.

Chapter 25

Nonny

The party was quieter by the time we walked back to the Tremaines yard; many of the younger couples with children had headed home.

Nonny Tremaine spied us walking back and waved us over to where she sat, her eyes twinkling with delight.

"What have you been up to, Conal Tremaine?" she demanded when we reached her side.

"Nothing, Nonny." I saw Conal wink at his grandmother. "I took Charlotte for a walk by the river."

"Nice night for a moonlit walk," Nonny said with a knowing grin.

I blushed furiously and Conal grinned sheepishly at his grandmother. "What's up, Nonny?"

The elderly woman looked at me pointedly. "Sit down, child. I would like to talk to you some more, now those old busybodies have gone on home to their beds."

I met Conal's eyes and he shrugged, pulling a chair over so I could sit beside his grandmother. He sat alongside me, clasping my hand in his. "What do you want to talk about?"

"I've been thinking about Charlotte's gift and I know from what an old lady hears when she's supposed to be sleeping, that there are some other things going on, things the pack haven't been told," Nonny began.

"Nonny, have you been eavesdropping?" Conal asked good-naturedly. He squeezed my fingers. "Don't worry, Nonny isn't big on superstitions."

"Not all superstitions, young man, have any foundation in truth," Nonny scolded him. "But sometimes, superstitions and stories from the history of our pack should be remembered and recognized. I think young Charlotte is one of them."

Conal looked mystified, his eyes narrowing as he watched his grandmother. "What are you talking about, Nonny?"

Nonny glanced around the still-crowded yard. "Not something we should discuss here. Too many people. Can you pick me up tomorrow and take me for a drive? I'll tell you more then. And we need to visit someone for more information."

For a long moment, Conal stared at his grandmother, watching her shrewdly as if he was silently appraising what she'd said. "Alright, Nonny. We'll come by and pick you up. What time?"

"About ten." She reached across and squeezed my fingers gently. "I think I can help to explain your abilities, Charlotte. I'll see you tomorrow morning." Patting my arm, she turned to Conal. "It's about time this old lady was in her bed. Conal, you can have the honor of helping me into the house."

Conal stood up, helping his grandmother to her feet. "I'll be right back," he promised and I watched him help the tiny old woman across the lawn and into the house.

On the drive back to Jackson, Conal and I discussed what Nonny had hinted. "Do you think she really does know what's going on with me?"

Conal shrugged. "With Nonny, anything's possible. She's the keeper of the pack's history, knows a lot she doesn't tell. The stories from our pack have been handed down, from generation to generation. Of course, the younger ones don't put too much store on the old stories; think a lot of them are superstitious mumbo jumbo. But Nonny's family has been the healers and secret keepers of our pack for thousands of years past. If anyone knows anything, it's likely to be Nonny."

I yawned tiredly, watching headlights coming towards us on the steamy road. Even at close to midnight, the temperature was warm, the night air humid and sticky.

"You're tired," Conal commented softly.

"I don't sleep well," I admitted. There seemed to be no way of escaping Lucas in my sleep – every night he reached me in nightmares and it was always the same – Lucas running towards me, bloodlust clear in his eyes and I would attack him, a bright light erupting from my fingers and forcing him away. In my nightmares, he never survived and I woke at least two or three times each night, seeing him lying with his eyes wide open and lifeless.

"It's not surprising; the nightmares are keeping you from sleeping properly." He reached across in the darkness and rubbed my thigh softly. "I hear you moaning and crying. Sometimes you scream."

"I'm sorry. I didn't realize. I must be disturbing you."

"It's okay, I wasn't complaining. But I worry about you." He stopped rubbing my leg and held his arm up across the back of the seat. "Come over here," he demanded quietly.

I slid across the bench seat until I nestled against his hip and he held me close as he drove along the quiet interstate. "You still miss him, don't you?"

Tears welled in my eyes and I brushed them away. "I'm trying, Conal, I really am."

"I know, Sugar. What I don't get is the hold he has over you. It's like... I guess it's like a piece of you died when you broke up with him. You're here, you're living, but you still seem... tied to him. Like your happiness is dependent on him being part of your life."

I squeezed my eyes shut, thinking over his words. "I guess – I don't know. I feel like I am tied to him. My heart, my soul – everything inside me feels as though it's a part of him."

Conal's arm stiffened on my shoulder and I peeked at him. His jaw was clenched, his eyes hard. "I'm sorry. I know this isn't what you want to hear."

"You know he's dead?" he said abruptly. Seeing my startled look, he swore under his breath. "I know, I know. He walks and talks and pretends to breathe and all, but he's dead," he said, bitterness in his tone. "And I'm alive, and breathing, and wanting you so badly that I ache when I hear you crying during the night."

I blinked back tears, trying to find the right words to say. I wanted to make him feel better, but didn't know if I had the power to do it. "Conal—" I paused, trying to figure out what to say. "I do like you. I think a part of me loves you, a little bit. I'm just not sure there's enough of my heart left to give you. I don't think I can love you as much as you want me to. As much as you deserve. And I wish it were different. Maybe, with time, it will be."

"That's all I want," Conal responded huskily. "To think there might be a chance for you and me. I'm prepared to wait for it to happen, as long as I think there's a chance." He kissed my forehead and squeezed my shoulder softly.

We continued the journey in companionable silence and I thought over a myriad of things. The silence in the truck gave me the opportunity to compartmentalize the new voices of spirits who'd joined me, allowing them to introduce themselves.

"Do you still hear their voices?" Conal queried in the darkness. "The spirits of Lucas's ancestors and the others?"

I nodded. "I hear all the voices, although I try to box theirs up." I cringed at hearing Lucas's name spoken aloud; it was something I avoided because of the painful ripple it caused in my heart. "But sometimes when I'm tired, or not concentrating, they manage to reach me."

There was silence for a moment before Conal spoke again. "What do they say?"

"I'd rather not talk about it," I admitted carefully. I'd already hurt Conal tonight, I didn't want to hurt him more by letting him know Lucas's ancestors, along with Marianne's, Striker's, Ripley's – in fact all of them – were doing their level best to get me to return to Puckhaber Falls.

Conal seemed content to let the subject drop and lifted his arm from my shoulder as we reached the city. We pulled into the underground car park at his apartment block and made our way upstairs. At my bedroom door, Conal paused. "Goodnight, Charlotte."

"Goodnight." I was torn between a desire to have Conal kiss me again and an urge to flee into the bedroom. We stood there gazing at one another until Conal leaned forward and brushed a fleeting kiss over my cheek. I watched him walk away, down the hallway to his bedroom before I turned to enter my room. I was more confused than ever, disappointed that he didn't kiss me, relieved that he hadn't. Perhaps I was losing my mind.

I changed into a tank top and cotton pajama bottoms, throwing my clothes into the hamper in the bathroom. After brushing my teeth and washing my face, I fell into bed and lay on my back, staring at the pattern on the ceiling thrown by the bedside lamp. When sleep came, it was filled with the recurring nightmares I'd suffered for weeks. Lucas could be kept from my mind during the day, but couldn't be escaped at night. Repeatedly, I saw him leaping at me, teeth bared, eyes wild as I tried to run from him. Every time, the nightmare would suddenly shift and I'd be lifting my hand towards Lucas, white light erupting from my fingertips and he would be flung away from me. When I looked down, he was laying at my feet, his eyes staring and lifeless…

I woke to the sound of screaming, realized it was my own and sobbed, clutching my head in my hands. Clammy and breathing heavily, I felt the bed shift and turned to find Conal beside me. His upper torso was bare, he wore only pajama bottoms and in the lamplight, I could see the firm muscle in his chest and abdomen. Without a word, he pulled the covers back and climbed into bed beside me, holding me in his arms as I sobbed.

Conal lay silently until my crying jag subsided and I had calmed. His fingers traced endless patterns against my shoulder, his touch warm and comforting.

"Thank you."

"For what?"

"For being here." I pulled myself up so I could lean against my fist and look down at him. His black eyes were fathomless in the dim lamplight, his face more boyish, less rugged. I reached up to touch his dark hair and my fingers brushed across his cheek. He captured my wrist, encircling it with his big hand.

"Charlotte – don't," he said gruffly. "Don't do this, unless you really want to follow through."

I stared at him, my thoughts confused, wondering what I really wanted. "I don't know," I finally admitted.

He sighed and released my wrist, capturing my hand in his and intertwining our fingers. "I've dreamed of you being in my bed for so many nights, dreamed of all the things I want to do with you. I know in my heart that you aren't ready for my dreams. But..." he looked up into my eyes, his own a pool of swiftly whirling emotions, "let me stay tonight. Just share this bed with me, nothing else. Let me sleep with you in my arms, holding you close and I'll keep the bad dreams away. Please." The last word was soft, almost pleading and I closed my eyes, unable to bear the fact that this man loved me so much and I wasn't capable of returning the love he deserved. But I could give him this, could stay with him, and let him hold me close, feel his heart beating beneath my cheek.

I nodded and dropped down into his waiting arms. He encircled me with his strength and love and I felt safe.

Chapter 26

Talk of Angels

Nonny Tremaine was waiting when we arrived the following morning, sitting out on the porch in a wicker chair. She was dressed in a bright red skirt and a colorful floral blouse, her feet encased in flat sandals. Her white hair was plaited and hung down across her right shoulder. She saw the car arrive and picked up a straw hat, shoving it firmly onto her head whilst she waited for Conal to help her down the steps.

"Slide over, young woman," she commanded with a grin when Conal assisted her into the truck. "Conal, why can't you have a normal car that's easy for an old lady like me to get into?"

Conal smiled tenderly at his grandmother. "Come on, Nonny. You know you love going out in my truck." He helped her with the seatbelt, and then shut the door gently before striding around and easing back into the driver's seat. He glanced past me at his grandmother. "So where are we going?"

"Merryweather Street in Jackson. The old Episcopalian church."

Conal frowned as he started the ignition. "I thought that church closed years ago."

A small smiled played across Nonny's lips. "It did."

"So why are we going there?" Conal pressed.

"Because I know someone lives there. Someone who remembers a lot of our past, along with the history of other supernatural beings. I think he may have answer for young Charlotte."

"Mrs. Tremaine?" I saw her disapproving frown and adjusted accordingly. "Nonny, do you really think you can tell me why I have this ability?"

"I have my suspicions of what you are, my dear. But the gentleman we're going to visit is the one with the true knowledge. I think we should wait to talk with him. But why don't you tell me a little bit about yourself? Conal tells me you're an artist..."

The drive to Merryweather Street took us back into the heart of Jackson. Where Conal's apartment was southwest of the city, he drove further east, through an area which seemed older and dilapidated. There were a lot of brownstones, peeling paint on their stoops, windows cracked and filmed with dirt. This area was quiet; very few people venturing out on what was shaping up to be a beautiful Saturday morning. It felt a little creepy and I shivered, goose bumps rising on my skin. Conal, who'd been resting his hand against my thigh (much to Nonny's delight), squeezed my leg gently. "This area of Jackson is where most of the supernatural live. There's another pack of werewolves, smaller than ours. Some shape shifters, a Kiss of vamps and a few warlocks."

I was Alice and I'd stepped through the looking glass. Not so long ago, the mythical beings he'd mentioned had belonged in books, legends to be screamed at in the movies. It still seemed somewhat unreal to know they really existed. Not only did they exist, but also, I was sitting sandwiched between two of them right now. A smile played on my lips as I considered Nonny Tremaine turning into a wolf. The image was somehow incompatible with the little older lady sitting beside me in a bright red skirt.

Conal pulled the truck to a halt in front of a big old church, the grey stone aged and pockmarked. In my estimations, it must have been built more than a hundred years ago. Tall arched windows nestled at either side of wooden double doors and gargoyles with sightless eyes watched over the hodgepodge of old headstones that littered the grounds. It was like no Episcopalian church I'd ever seen before – this church seemed more suited to medieval England than southern America. The grounds surrounding the church were enclosed by an antiquated fence built of stone and mounted with wrought iron spikes in a regular formation. Any traces of paint had worn off years ago and the metal spikes were the rich red-orange of rust. There was an air of decay about the building, a sensation of abandonment that made me shiver in the warm June air. The hairs on my arms rose and I felt a trickle of something, some power floating around us. I couldn't begin to figure out what it might be, but it made me nervous.

Nonny was marching towards a rusty gate, which was fixed into the imposing fence. She was remarkably sprightly and I wondered how old she was. I asked Conal as we walked to the gate, trailing behind Nonny.

"She's one hundred and twenty seven next month," he responded, holding the gate open.

"One hundred and twenty seven," I repeated vacantly.

"Werewolves live longer than humans."

"I see." We walked up the weed-covered path towards the church and I stopped abruptly, looking at Conal and Nonny curiously. "Can you go in there?"

Conal grinned, the dimples in his cheeks deepening. "We're werewolves, Charlotte, not bloodsuckers. They can't enter consecrated ground, but it doesn't make any difference to us."

Nonny pounded on the heavy wooden door and we waited in the sultry heat for a long while.

"Maybe they aren't home?" I suggested after another minute. I was hoping they weren't – the spine-tingling chill hadn't gone away and I wanted to leave.

"Of course he's home," Nonny announced. She banged on the door again with surprising strength. "He's expecting us."

"Who's expecting us?" Conal asked.

There was the sound of locks being turned from the other side of the heavy door and it eased open slowly, allowing a glimpse into the darkened interior. A head suddenly popped around the door, beady blue eyes staring at us from behind enormous round spectacles. "Nonny Tremaine, a pleasure to see you again. Come in, come in!"

We entered the cool sanctuary of the church and I looked around with interest. The inside of the church was as *unChurch-like* as it could possibly be. Where there should be pews, an altar and the vestments of an Episcopalian church, instead it had been converted into an apartment. A remarkably full apartment. Every wall was covered with bookcases, spreading from the floor right through to the highest level of the vaulted ceiling. There was a long wooden table where the altar should be, piled high with books and masses of paper and a variety of artifacts, all of which looked both interesting and slightly alarming. An aroma of old paper, leather and tobacco smoke hung heavily in the air. To one side, a fire burned in a hearth, an enormous iron kettle hanging near it on a sturdy hook. In the middle of the room was an overstuffed couch, resting on spindly legs. It too was piled high with books, some resting open and others piled precariously one upon the other.

"Epimetheus, I'd like to introduce you to my grandson, Conal Tremaine and his friend, Charlotte Duncan," Nonny announced. "Charlotte, Conal; this is Epimetheus Vander."

He was short, probably only a smidgen over five feet tall. His face was dominated by huge round glasses, held upon a bulbous nose. He looked ancient – his face lined with wrinkles which were deep and gave him the appearance of a tiny elephant. His head was almost bald, just a tuft of white hair created a halo around his skull.

He wore strange clothes - old-fashioned brown pants with a dull red tunic, leather boots on his feet. The tunic had been hand sewn with leather cord, the stitches large. He held out his hand, shaking ours with a firm grip that belied his apparent age. "And what brings you here on this fine Saturday morning, I wonder?" he asked.

"You know why we're here," Nonny responded impatiently. "I rang you to talk about this young lady."

I doubted this was a good idea – the man's appearance and attitude were so bizarre, he might have lost his mental faculties, or been gripped by dementia. He couldn't possibly help us.

Conal was obviously having similar doubts, wrapping his arm around my waist protectively. "Nonny, what is this about?"

Nonny turned her attention to me, a soft smile on her lips and curiosity in her eyes. "Did you read anything from him, Charlotte?"

I shook my head wordlessly. I hadn't realized there were no new voices until Nonny mentioned it. I'd been so stunned by the strange little man standing before me; he was all I could think about. I searched a second time, but found nothing and shook my head again.

"As I suspected," Nonny grinned triumphantly. "Epimetheus is a warlock."

"I don't understand." I was completely nonplussed by this announcement and nervous because I couldn't hear voices from this tiny man. It meant I could be in danger.

Epimetheus was suddenly all business and seemed clearer-minded. "What you told me might be true, Nonny." He smiled broadly at Conal and I, the wide beam showing a distinct lack of teeth. "Let's sit down and chat, shall we?" He waved his arm politely towards the overstuffed couch and I wondered how we were expected to sit on it, when it was covered with books. The couch faded and disappeared, replaced by a rather rickety table with four chairs around it. I blinked, and not for the first time, I thought I was losing my mind.

Conal led me over to the table and pulled out a chair. I sat down gingerly, wondering if something which had just... *appeared* could possibly be solid. Conal pulled a second chair out and sat by my side. Nonny sat to our right and Epimetheus took the chair opposite.

"Now, let me explain what that was all about, my dear." He spoke in a clear voice, unexpected from someone so elderly. His voice was strong with a trace of an accent, possibly English. "When Nonny telephoned and told me about you, I was convinced you were just an excellent psychic, perhaps even a fraud. I wanted to see if you professed to being able to read my mind, or whether there was the remotest possibility of you being what Nonny suspects."

I glanced from the old man to Conal and back, frowning in confusion. "I'm sorry. I don't have a clue what you're talking about."

Epimetheus spoke to Nonny. "You haven't told them anything, I take it?"

"Of course not. We need to be certain," Nonny responded.

Conal stood up abruptly, his eyes blazing with annoyance. "Nonny, I didn't bring Charlotte here to listen to you two talking in riddles."

"Sit down." Nonny's voice was firm, her words echoing around the interior of the church.

Conal sat down slowly, staring at his grandmother as though he was wondering about *her* mental faculties.

Epimetheus studied me for a long time, his eyes magnified enormously behind the glasses. 'Charlotte, if you had come in here and been able to contact my ancestors, I would have chosen one of two options. You were a remarkably good psychic – and that was all – or you were a fraud. You went down neither of those paths. Which proved to Nonny and myself that you may be what I've studied and searched for, nearly all of my life." He saw the puzzlement in my eyes and shook his head. "I need to start from the beginning, I can see."

"That might be helpful," Conal said, with a heavy edge of sarcasm.

Epimetheus ignored him. "There is a legend, as old as time itself. Thousands of years ago, the Angel Nememiah mixed his blood with the blood of men and created a superior race of humans. They were created to rid the world of demons, to provide the supernatural creatures of this world with rules and conventions, which would keep the peace and prevent them from destroying themselves. The humans that Nememiah created kept the world peaceful and demon free for hundreds of years. But as time went on, Nememiah's Angels destroyed themselves through infighting and excessive pride. They began to believe they were the most important men on earth and grew arrogant. It's a long story, but ultimately, the Angel's children destroyed themselves through their loss of humility. Where once there had been unity, now there was discord. Where once they worked together in harmony, now brother fought brother and many abandoned the group, disenchanted with the changes. The blood of the Angel Nememiah was diluted and weakened, until there was nothing left of the powers bestowed upon Nememiah's race. They disappeared, more than a thousand years ago."

"While I'm sure that's a very interesting story, I don't see what it has to do with Charlotte," Conal stated mulishly.

"If you would let me finish." Epimetheus glared at Conal, his eyes blazing. "I would have told you that for many years, I have been studying the history of Nememiah's Angel children. There is a further legend, which suggests if one of the supernatural groups gains too much supremacy; the children of Nememiah will re-emerge to return the world to balance." He turned to me, his expression sincere. "Nonny seems to think you may be one of those children of Nememiah."

"Me? Why would you think that?"

"Because you have a very extraordinary gift. A gift that has grown in strength and power in recent months. A gift which allowed you to singlehandedly beat back vampires, giving them injuries such as we never thought possible." He leaned forward, his eyes boring into mine. "And because you couldn't reach my ancestors. The history of Nememiah's children states that traditionally, they couldn't reach a warlock's spirits. You couldn't read mine."

"I still don't get it," I responded. In fact, I had no idea what the point of the story was. Was this strange old man suggesting I had something to do with these Angel children? The idea was completely ludicrous.

"Warlock's have demon blood. In fact, out of all supernatural creatures, our blood is more than fifty percent demon. Not being able to contact the spirits was one way in which Nememiah's children could detect demons. Demons took many shapes and forms and could hide behind the façade of normality, especially as demons learned to take on human characteristics. But with the touch of a shoulder, a hand, the demon blood could be recognized. So could other enemies." Epimetheus tapped on the table with his fingers, staring at me for another long moment. "I presume there have been some that you couldn't read?"

"I... yes, there are some. Usually people who are trying to... hurt me." Eyeing him curiously, I asked the question uppermost in my mind. "You think I'm somehow linked to these Angel children?"

"Let's not be hasty," the old man said, waffling his hand carelessly through the air in front of him. "We have merely revealed there is a possibility. There are many other things to discuss and establish before that conclusion could be made."

"What sort of things?" Conal asked. He seemed more relaxed now, squeezing my fingers gently as he watched the old man attentively.

"I want Charlotte to tell me exactly when this ability presented itself and how it manifested." Epimetheus waved his hand towards the kettle, which immediately started boiling with steam pouring from the spout. "But first, let me offer you a hot drink. Where are my manners?"

Chapter 27

Epimetheus Vander

Epimetheus questioned me for hours, wanting to know every little facet of my abilities, when they had presented themselves, how they had manifested, what changes were occurring. He asked about my family history, any psychic ability within the family, and spent a considerable period drawing a timeline on a sheet of paper. From time to time, he would leap from his chair, running back and forth around the room, selecting volumes from the bookcases seemingly at random. Bringing them back to the table, we sat in silence whilst he looked up various passages. There was a great deal of grunting, humming and haaing, as he pored over the books, his glasses perched on the very end of his bulbous nose and his bony fingers following lines of archaic writing on the parchment.

My stomach rumbled alarmingly during this interrogation and Epimetheus glanced up from his books. "My dear, I keep forgetting about the human need to eat."

"Not to mention a werewolf's," Conal muttered.

Epimetheus idly waved his hand and a plate appeared in the center of the table, piled high with sandwiches. Another plate appeared with cakes and cookies and I tentatively reached forward to pick up a sandwich, hardly believing they were real until I touched the soft bread and smelled the delicious aroma of chicken and mayonnaise. I took a bite of one and found it delightfully tasty.

On through the afternoon we talked, with the stack of books piled on the table beginning to rise alarmingly. The sky outside was darkening when Epimetheus pushed back his chair, standing up agilely to walk to the long table where an altar had once stood. He shuffled things, searching for something - eventually he came back carrying a small box as though it was the most important item he owned.

"My dear, I believe you may be one of Nememiah's Angel children. All the signs are there. However, I think this artifact – which came into my possession many, many years ago – will prove this, one way or the other. He placed the simple wooden box on the table and opened it with a flourish. I looked inside, disappointed by what I saw. Laying in the bottom of the box lay a small piece of driftwood. On closer examination, I realized it wasn't driftwood, it was much darker, the wood shiny and smooth as if it had been touch and rubbed over a long period of time. It was about five inches long and perhaps two inches around. It was twisted and curled, with one end tapered to a point, rather like a pen. I stared at it for a long time before I returned my attention to the old man.

"What is it?"

"One of the wonders of the Angel children's world. I wonder, very much, if you would pick it up?"

I reached forward to take hold of it, but Conal gripped my wrist firmly. "What is it, old man? And how do I know it's not going to hurt her?"

"It will not hurt her if she is merely a normal human with psychic powers. Nor will it hurt her if she is one of the Angel children. But the difference will be whether it operates, or not." He gazed at the object with a certain amount of adoration in his eyes. "But if you are worried, I will allow you to touch it first. I warn you though; the effects will not be pleasant."

Before Nonny or I could object, Conal reached into the box, gripping his hand around the object. I shrieked when he was flung away from the table, soaring through the air and landing in a heap on the floor beside a bookcase. It was much too similar to what I'd done in Puckhaber, and I threw my chair back, running to him. When I reached Conal's side, he had pulled himself upright and was rubbing the back of his head cautiously. "Shit," he growled. "What the hell was that?"

"The power of the Hjördis. It was the item used by the Angel children to mark their skin, protecting them from demons and enhancing their powers. It is designed specifically to be used by Angel children. It cannot be used," he grinned a little maliciously, "or touched, by the supernatural or demons."

Conal hauled himself to his feet and we walked back to the table, where he slumped onto the chair, still rubbing his head gingerly. He eyed the Hjördis warily. "That thing. It threw me across the room."

"Because you are not meant to use it, wolf."

"You should have warned him," Nonny grumbled at Epimetheus.

"I did." Epi was nonchalant about the events of the last few minutes and smiled smugly. "It is not my fault he didn't ask further questions before he acted."

"Try picking it up," Nonny suggested softly to me. "You're human. It won't hurt you."

I glanced at Conal uneasily and saw his almost imperceptible nod. My hand trembled as I reached towards the nondescript piece of wood. I took a deep breath, forcing myself to wrap my fingers around it. Nothing happened. I lifted it carefully from the box and it started to vibrate against my fingers. The wood grew warm, hotter than it should have been and I dropped it to the table, staring at it suspiciously.

"What did you feel, child?" Epimetheus sounded breathless and excited. Leaning forward in his chair, his eyes focused on the object lying harmlessly on the table.

"I don't know." I'd been unnerved when I touched it and chills crawled up and down my spine.

"Pick it up again."

"No."

"Pick it up again, child." Epimetheus's voice was firm, filled with determination.

"No!"

Conal stood up, his eyes flashing with anger. "Leave her alone, Vander. I don't know what you're playing at, but it's over. I've had enough." I could feel the tension roiling of his body in waves, felt his power washing over me. It wasn't making me feel any better.

Nonny stood up, rubbing her hands across my shoulders and back before she leaned forward and snuggled her face against mine. "You're both frightening Charlotte. Stop it now." The two men continued to glare at one another, while Nonny kept rubbing her cheek against mine and I began to calm again. I'd seen some of Conal's pack doing something similar at the party, almost as if they were marking one another with their scent. Whatever it was, it helped to settle my nervous outburst and I found the touch of her soft skin calming. "What happened, Charlotte, when you held the Hjördis?" she asked quietly.

"It vibrated," I admitted slowly. "And it felt, kind of warm, almost hot. Hotter than it should have been."

Nonny's hand flew to her mouth, her eyes wide with disbelief. "It's true! You are one of the Angel children! I knew it!"

"Now, Nonny, not so fast. It is true she can hold the Hjördis. That is not proof that she is strong enough to be an Angel child," Epimetheus said sternly. He pushed the piles of books and papers away, leaving a bare patch on the table in front of me. "Draw something, child."

I met his eyes, completely bewildered. "Excuse me?"

"Draw something. Place the Hjördis in your hand; let your thoughts focus on it. Use it like a pen, a paintbrush. Don't over think. Draw something, using the Hjördis as a tool."

I stared at him for a minute, seeing the exhilaration in his eyes. I picked up the Hjördis tentatively, less startled this time when it began to vibrate softly. The wood heated, not hot enough to burn, but certainly warmer than should be normal. I had no idea what he meant by drawing something. I could draw people, places, and things. What did he want me to draw? And how could I draw something with an old fragment of wood?

"I said, *don't over think*!"

I scowled at the old man, before turning my attention to the battered table. Closing my eyes, I inhaled deeply and let the breath escape slowly through my lips, trying to release everything from my mind, concentrating on the wood in my hand. It buzzed louder against my palm, warming ever so slightly and I held it as I would a pencil or a brush. An image formed in the recesses of my mind and I drew it, aware of the smell of burning wood reaching my nostrils as I worked. When I opened my eyes, I found Nonny, Conal and Epimetheus staring at the table. An intricate symbol was burnt into the wood, but the lines weren't blackened and charred as I had assumed they would be – they were luminous, the color of indigo.

"What the hell is that?" Conal breathed quietly. He was staring with undisguised surprise at the symbol I'd drawn.

"Let's see if Charlotte knows," Epimetheus suggested smugly. "It has a meaning. And watch your language, wolf. You are in church."

I ignored their bickering and stared at the carved symbol. Deep in the recesses of my mind, there was a familiarity – a feeling that somehow, I did know what it meant. I closed my eyes, seeing the symbol emblazoned against my eyelids.

"Courage," I murmured. "It means courage." I knew this was the meaning, without doubt. There was no reasoning for the knowledge – I just *knew*.

Epimetheus leapt to his feet, running towards the long table on the altar. He scrambled around the many books, until he found a small one, bringing it back to the table with him. This book was ancient; the leather cover faded so its original color couldn't be distinguished. He laid the book reverently on the table and began carefully turning the fragile pages. He stopped all of a sudden and pushed the book towards me, pointing at a drawing.

It was identical to what I'd drawn.

"She is an Angel Child," Nonny breathed in awe.

"There is one more test. Charlotte, do you have any scars, birthmarks? Anything unusual?" Epimetheus asked eagerly. "It may be something incongruous, something you've never given thought to, but has been there since childhood."

I stared at him, wondering how he knew all this information, wondering whether I could believe what he was saying. I lifted my hair from my shoulders and pointed to a spot behind my left ear.

Conal, Epimetheus and Nonny congregated behind me to examine the spot I'd pointed out. It was a mark I'd had since childhood; my mom had said it was caused by the forceps when I was born. I'd never thought anything of it until now. Mom called it my lucky mark, telling me it was special as no one else had one. It was a small pale blemish on my neck, in the shape of a wing.

"An Angel wing," Epimetheus announced, sounding somewhat breathless. "She is one of Nememiah's Children."

≈†◊◊†◊◊†◊◊†≈

"So you're suggesting everything that's happened in the past few months – Ambrose's attack, his Kiss returning to the house, the kidnapping— they were all tied to this Angel child thing?" I questioned skeptically.

It was late in the evening and the sole topic of conversation throughout the long day and into the night had been me. Epimetheus Vander had grilled me like an FBI interrogator, asking a myriad of questions. As time wore on, even Conal seemed to agree with him and Nonny – that I was indeed one of Nememiah's Children. What perturbed Epimetheus greatly was the amount of contact I'd had with supernatural beings in the past few months, and the number of disasters that had befallen me. He had suggested someone – who knew about Nememiah's Children – wanted me and the events of the past few months were linked.

"I believe so," Epimetheus agreed. "Whilst the initial vampire attack was probably an unfortunate coincidence – I believe the other incidents are related to your role as Nememiah's Child."

"If that's so," Conal asked slowly, "Why has it happened now? Why not when Charlotte was younger?"

Epimetheus responded to Conal, as though he were speaking to a small child. "Because you said so yourself – Charlotte had not embraced the ability. She had, to all intents and purposes, some psychic ability – which she admits herself she ignored as much as possible. But for those of us seeking the return of Nememiah's Children, her true nature would not be revealed until she began to accept it herself. And use it."

"Which means," Nonny added, "that someone else knows about Nememiah's Children and is searching for her."

"Yes," Epimetheus agreed. "We need to teach her how to use her powers and we need to instruct her on how to defend herself. We must keep her safe. The history of Nememiah's Children says they reach full maturity at twenty-one. Once past the age of twenty-one, they cannot be turned to any other supernatural force. Before that time, she is capable of being turned. Her powers could be harnessed by someone wanting to gain power for themselves."

I felt sick. I was only just beginning to comprehend what they were suggesting and hardly believed it. And now I was going to have to learn how to defend myself? Needed to be protected?

"Charlotte, when do you turn twenty one?" Conal asked.

"September second."

"That doesn't give us much time," Nonny calculated. "Less than three months."

"The pack will protect her," Conal announced.

"But they must be told what they are protecting, what's at stake," Nonny responded. "Conal, the pack must be advised of what has gone on here this day." Her dark eyes were firm, the set of her jaw determined.

They exchanged an uneasy glance, Conal frowning. "Nonny, do you think that's wise? You more than anyone know how suspicious some of the pack members are."

"We have no choice, Conal. This is much too big to keep secret. We must go back to the pack, call a meeting with your father and the elders. It must be tonight."

Conal sighed. "You're right. But I'm taking Charlotte back to my apartment first. I don't want her anywhere near the pack until we know how much support we're going to get."

"You think the pack won't like this?" I questioned.

Conal squeezed my fingers softly. "If this is all true—"

"Which it is," Epimetheus interrupted, glancing up from the book he'd been flicking through.

Conal glared at him. "As I said, *if* this is true, it means there's trouble in the wind. If Vander's right, Nememiah's Children are being resurrected because of some imminent danger. We don't know what it is and the pack might not believe an ancient warlock and my elderly grandmother. No offense, Nonny," he finished with a weak smile for Nonny.

"None taken," she responded cheerfully.

Conal continued. "The pack is exceedingly superstitious. They may think your emergence is a bad omen. They might believe it's the ramblings of two senile old people..."

Epimetheus harrumphed loudly.

Conal ignored him and continued. "They might decide it's a nonsense. I can't predict how they'll react. You know what Dad was like when he met you. He was freaked out, thought you were a witch."

I nodded wordlessly.

Conal was frowning, his black eyes solemn. "Until I'm certain of their support, I want to keep you separated from the pack. I'm not sure who we can trust. We have to think this through, make some plans."

"You think someone from your pack is behind this?"

He shook his head. "No, I don't. But someone is. And the less people who know where you are, the better. At least until we work through this. Have you got your phone?"

I dipped my head in acknowledgement, feeling more than a little overwhelmed.

"Call Lucas, tell him what's going on. They need to be kept in the loop."

Nonny lifted her head from the book she'd been studying. "Is that wise? How do we know they're not behind this?"

Conal heaved a sigh. "As much as I don't like to trust a bloodsucker... they seem like they're okay. They aren't behind it." He looked down at me expectantly.

"I don't want to ring them. They'll be safer if they aren't involved," I announced after thinking for a few minutes. "They don't need to know. Whoever is after me, has known where I am. If anything, I'm more concerned about you."

Conal's harsh features softened; his eyes like liquid licorice when he gazed at me. "You're staying with me, Sugar. I'm not leaving you to deal with this on your own."

A random thought occurred to me, plucked from the never ending and growing list of things rampaging through my mind and I looked at Epimetheus. "How can you be in a church? If you have so much demon blood, surely you've been damned? Isn't this consecrated ground?"

Epimetheus beamed. "I am different. Yes, I have demons blood. Far more demons blood than Conal and Nonny here." He pulled at the neck of his tunic, dragging it down to reveal a tattoo on his shoulder. "But I fought on the side of good in the final war which destroyed Nememiah's Children. The leader of the Angel children was a brave man, who valued the truth and integrity of Nememiah's teachings. He gave me this mark."

It was a wing, similar to the one on my neck, but starkly black against the old man's wrinkled white skin.

Chapter 28

Confusion

Three in the morning came and went as I paced in Conal's apartment. He'd dropped me off shortly after midnight, checking the apartment thoroughly before he left with Nonny to convene an emergency meeting with his pack.

A pile of books lay on the coffee table, but I was too agitated even to glance at them. The old man insisted I take them, wanting me to start learning about my 'prodigious gift' as he called it. My first task was to study the meaning of numerous pictures he called 'sigils'. I needed to memorize them and Epimetheus would be visiting the apartment later to commence my tuition.

I was still reeling from the revelations I'd been swamped with, and I was distracted and edgy. For the hundredth time, I questioned if what I'd been told could be true. It explained a number of episodes that had occurred in the past few months and how I'd managed to hurt Lucas and the others. But Nememiah's Child? Could I really have the blood of an Angel coursing through my veins?

The thought of this being some sort of... *destiny* weighed heavily. Epimetheus had insisted Nememiah's Children were warriors, fighters – slayers of demons and protectors of the weak. A description that sounded as far from *me* as it was possible to get. I'd backed away from fights my whole life, taking a pacifist approach to everything. Why would I be marked as a child of Nememiah? It didn't make sense. Besides, I'd killed someone – murdered my stepfather in cold blood. That didn't make me a likely candidate for having Angel blood.

I heard a key turn in the lock and relief flooded me when Conal walked into the hallway, shutting and bolting the door behind him. From the slump of his shoulders and the dejected look in his eyes, I could tell what the pack's answer had been.

"They didn't believe you."

Conal dropped his keys onto the bench top, noticing me for the first time. "I thought you'd be in bed." He drew me into his arms, holding me tightly against his chest.

"I didn't think I would sleep." I searched his eyes for confirmation of what I'd deduced. "Guess they don't believe it, huh?"

Conal inhaled deeply, his black eyes ringed with tired shadows. "It's not so much that they don't believe it," he said, rubbing my shoulders soothingly, "it's that they don't *want* to believe it."

"So I'm on my own," I said evenly, turning away to continue pacing.

"No, you aren't on your own. Nonny and I believe in you. Some of the others, they believe it deep down. But the pack follows its leaders and they voted against making preparations." He caught my hand, drawing me to the couch and sinking onto it, pulling me down on his lap. I nestled against his chest, immediately calmer.

"Did they all vote against it?" I queried dully.

"No, it was close. My father voted with you, if that's any consolation."

"So what do I do now?"

Conal snuggled me tighter against him. "*We* are going to bed. It's been a long day and a longer night. We'll start our own preparations tomorrow. Someone or something is trying to get you. I'm going to make sure that doesn't happen. Vander is going to teach you the Angel shit – I'm going to teach you how to protect yourself."

I eyed him doubtfully. "How can you do that? You're away for at least three days a week and you've got to work."

Conal rubbed my back reassuringly. "I'm taking leave. Immediately. I've got about three months' worth of holidays owing to me."

"How is your Dad going to feel about that? Won't he guess you're going behind his back?"

"I'm not going behind his back," Conal reassured me quietly. "It was Dad who suggested it. Like I told you, he voted *with* you. He can't be seen to be going against the pack's vote – but he can support you if he keeps it quiet." Conal yawned and patted my leg. "Come on, Sugar. We can talk about this later. Time for bed."

Utilizing his immense strength, which continually amazed me, Conal lifted me from the waist, setting me gently onto my feet before he stood up behind me. He escorted me down the hallway, stopping outside the bedroom to kiss my cheek softly. "Goodnight, Sugar." He turned to walk down the hall but I caught his hand, drawing him back.

"Wait."

Conal turned back, his dark eyes smoldering. "What's up?"

Swallowing nervously, I stumbled over the words. "Will you... can you—" I inhaled deeply. "Conal, stay with me. Please?"

Conal leaned one hand against the wall, dropping his gaze to the ground. "I can't, Charlotte. I want to; Christ knows I want that more than anything in the world. But I don't think I could share your bed and not touch you, not want to do more than I think you're capable of dealing with right now," he admitted huskily. "I don't think—" he paused, clenching his hand into a fist. "I don't have the strength to lie beside you and not make love to you."

"What if— what if that's what I want you to do?" I responded quietly.

Conal was silent for a long moment, his eyes betraying the internal battle he fought. "Why? Why now? Because you're frightened and think that what we heard today means you're in danger? Or because you genuinely want to make love to me?" He rubbed his hand across his chin tiredly as he watched me. "I want you to be making love to *me*, Charlotte. I don't want you to be thinking of the bloodsucker and I don't want to agree to this, then wake up in the morning and find a look of regret in those beautiful green eyes."

I knew he was right. The thought of imminent danger, the fact that I might be attacked by some hidden enemy, that someone might want to harm me before I had a chance to make my twenty-first birthday – all those thoughts were influencing my decision-making process.

"Forget it," I stated numbly. "You're right. Bad idea." I slipped through the bedroom door, closing it soundlessly behind me. Tearing off my clothes, I slipped into the shower, angry at making myself look foolish and embarrassed by my behavior. The hot water was soothing, pouring across my aching shoulders and neck but as the anger and embarrassment began to fade, it was replaced by fear. The tears began to flow again and I sank onto my haunches, holding my face in my hands as I tried to pull myself together. Falling apart was not going to change the situation. Deep in my heart, I believed Epimetheus and Nonny. It explained so many things. But I was absolutely, utterly and totally terrified.

I scrubbed clean and stepped from the shower, toweling dry and throwing on pajamas. I brushed my teeth and took a minute to stare at myself in the mirror. I looked like the same girl I'd always been, but one way or another, I wasn't that person any more. I was one of Nememiah's Children, put on this earth for entirely different reasons than I'd imagined. A trickle of fear rolled through my chest again and I shook my head vehemently. I wasn't going to let this scare me. Poking my tongue out at the mirror, I turned off the bathroom light and walked into the bedroom.

I came to a standstill, staring at the bed in surprise. Conal was lying there, the sheets pulled up to his waist and his dark hair still damp.

"I thought we decided this was a bad idea," I stated quietly.

"It is a bad idea. I'm not here for that," he responded, just as quietly. "You need me to help keep the bad dreams away." He held out his arms and I slid into the bed, letting him hold me close.

"Thank you," I was laying against the hard muscle of his chest, listening to his heart beneath my ear.

"You're welcome," he responded huskily, rubbing his fingers idly through my hair.

"You don't have to do this."

He inhaled deeply, the movement making my head rise and fall against his chest. "I think I do. Given the current situation, I think I'm more comfortable in here with you, making sure you stay safe."

"Do you think someone could find me here?"

He shook his head a little. "I'm not sure. But I feel a hell of a lot better being with you, rather than down the hallway."

I retreated into silence for a few minutes, absorbed in thought. Wondering how my life could possibly have become so bizarre. "Conal?"

"Mmmm?"

"Had you ever heard of Nememiah's Children?"

"I've been thinking about that myself. I remember hearing stories of Angels, demon hunters and the like." He shrugged. "Can't say it's a legend that I ever really believed. But now, I guess it might be possible."

"Six months ago, I didn't even know *you* were possible," I said ruefully. "Vampires, werewolves, shape shifters – they were all myths. There's a whole world I didn't know about. And then today, meeting a real live warlock. It's stuff I thought only existed in fairytales." I tilted my head to see Conal's face. "Do you think this is happening because of any of them? Or are demons really out there and I just haven't come across them yet?"

"Demons are Otherworld creatures. According to the myths, they invaded this world thousands of years ago. Our legends say all of the werewolves and vampires were created by combining human and demon blood. The demons were supposedly eradicated from this world, centuries ago."

"Myths?" I questioned quietly.

Conal smiled and it was just a little weary, a little more tired than his usual bright smile. "I'm a myth, Charlotte. Us, the bloodsuckers – we're all myths." He laid his hand over mine, where it lay on the smooth expanse of his chest. "Do I feel like a myth?"

"No," I admitted softly.

"How do we know, Charlotte? I'm real, yet I'm relegated to a myth because we need to keep our true nature a secret. What makes me real, but the Yeti, the Loch Ness Monster, Bigfoot – they're all disregarded as mythical creatures? Vander might be right; the demons may not be a myth either. Just because we haven't seen them, doesn't mean they don't exist."

"If being one of these Angel children means I can sense the presence of demons – how can I contact your ancestors?" I asked. "If you have demon blood, doesn't that mean I shouldn't be able to hear them?"

"I don't mean you any harm, Sugar. From what Vander was prattling on about, I'm guessing people who mean you harm personally, whether they have demon blood or not, are the ones that you can't read," Conal responded, after a moment's thought. "Epi said warlocks have more demon blood than anyone else, something about being more than fifty percent. The rest of us, presumably, have less."

But you can go into a church." I continued my train of thought, working through the points that I was sure would add up to a conclusion, if I followed each one. "If you've got demon blood, doesn't that stop you entering consecrated ground?"

Conal shrugged. "Maybe it's the amount of demon blood. All I know is I've gone to church since I was a little kid. Nothing horrible ever happened to me – well, I guess I did get a whipping once for trying to look up one of the Nuns' habits. But I don't think that had anything to do with demon blood," he admitted with a wry grin.

"So why did some become vampires and others become werewolves?"

"Demons came in many shapes and forms. I guess it depended on which demons blood got into the mix."

"Well, that all sounds very scientific."

Conal sighed. "Charlotte, I don't have all the answers. I just know that I'm a werewolf and I was born a werewolf. Others become werewolves through being bitten. Vampires are humans who've been bitten by another vampire. Shape shifters, from what I understand, they happen because of genetic mutation. No demon blood required."

"Really?" I questioned sharply.

"Really."

I considered for a moment. "What would happen if you and I... well, you know? Do we have werewolf babies?" I held my breath, wondering if this line of questioning would make him angry. I didn't want to say anything that would put any ideas in his mind, or make him unhappy.

"That sounds like an offer I wouldn't refuse," he admitted with a smile. "If you and I had babies, they'd have a fifty-fifty chance of being werewolf. There's a higher rate of miscarriage in mixed blood babies though, as high as seventy percent."

"What happens if I don't have human blood? What if I have Angel blood?"

Conal took a deep breath and allowed it to escape slowly between his lips. "I don't know. If you're going to keep propositioning me like this, you should ask Vander – he might have the answers." He caught my chin with his fingertips and lifted my face to his. "Right now, you need to go to sleep. And so do I. Goodnight, Sugar." He kissed my lips softly, and then hunkered down until he was under the covers, settling me against his chest with his arms encircling my back.

I lay for a long time, listening to the sound of his steady breathing before I fell into a deep, dreamless sleep.

Chapter 29

Training

The following days flew by, as Epimetheus and Conal taught me everything they could. Evenings were filled with studying the books Epimetheus continued to give me at an alarming rate. I found memorizing the sigil's comparatively easy, almost as if they were being rediscovered from somewhere deep in the recesses of my mind and had always been there. I had no idea what they were used for yet, Epimetheus was giving no clues, only urging me to remember each and every one of them.

Learning the history of Nememiah's Children was a fascinating experience. There was no single history book dedicated to their memory, but Epimetheus had amassed a massive collection of archaic works dedicated to their legend, power and demise. He insisted I learn as much as I could and I was enjoying the process.

Nonny joined us whenever she found opportunity. Conal insisted the pack mustn't know what we were doing, so she couldn't spend as much time with us as she'd have liked. I'd wondered aloud what might happen if the pack found out, and Conal's response was blunt – anyone acting against the pack vote would be cast out, disowned by family and friends.

As Conal had predicted, some members of the pack believed our story and our numbers were swelled by those who swore to help us if the need arose. Kenyon appeared at Conal's apartment a couple of days after the meeting, introducing us to his wife Marissa, and son Javier. A few days later, we were visited by Ralph Torres, along with his brother Rudolph. Ralph greeted me with respect, asking to unite with our group.

They were followed by other pack members in a steady trickle, younger men and women who believed what was happening must be prepared for. Conal was keeping them up to date with our planning and Ralph took up the role of Beta to Conal's Alpha. He worked with our small group to train for whatever was coming our way. Conal insisted I be kept separate from them, so we continued working with Epimetheus alone.

The spirits were more forthcoming with information and in long conversations; I gained a deeper understanding of my task. Whilst all this was a new discovery to me, they'd always been aware I was a child of Nememiah. They just hadn't enlightened me, until after I discovered it for myself. Which annoyed the heck out of me, but they'd argued it was another rule they were bound to follow. Now they were offering both advice and information. It didn't mean I was completely in the loop, but they would help me where and when they could. I passed on information to Conal and Epimetheus and learned how to work with the spirits' assistance. They could protect me from many attacks, but warned again and again that I wasn't immortal, and could easily be killed. This declaration only increased my apprehension. They refused to give information about what we faced, despite asking them a multitude of times.

June melted into July and the full heat of summer was upon us. I sweated through lessons with Epimetheus at the church when Conal was with the pack. Epimetheus had no air-conditioning and seemed blissfully impervious to the shimmering heat of Mississippi's summer.

I'd memorized many of the sigils, which were designed to provide extra strengths and powers during battle. Courage, agility, and speed were but a few. There were an amazing array and Epi was intent on teaching me every single one of them. How they were used remained a mystery, Epimetheus assuring me that knowledge would come in time.

Conal and I arrived at the church on a simmering Sunday morning, to be greeted at the door by an excited and exuberant Epi. He opened the doors to us and stepping inside, I came to a sudden halt.

"Epi – where's the furniture?"

The church's interior had been transformed and I glanced at Epi, becoming aware of his clothes. Gone were the old-fashioned tunics and rough worsted trousers. Today he wore a navy blue tracksuit, which seemed incongruous on his tiny frame. I noticed he was wearing Nikes and stifled a smile.

The church was completely devoid of furniture and every single inch of the floor, the walls – even the high ceiling had been covered in thick foam padding.

"Today we begin practicing what you've learned," Epi announced, his voice tinged with excitement. "You have learned the theory. We know you have Angel blood pulsing through your veins. Now we get to see how much power you really have."

"What's that going to entail, exactly?" Conal asked. He pushed the doors shut and locked them securely.

"It is time to put the sigils to practice." Epi handed the box containing the Hjördis to me. "Until now, you have only practiced the marks on paper. You are ready for the next phase and you must learn to draw the sigils on yourself."

Images of the scorched table immediately flew to mind and I gaped at him.

"You're not serious?" Conal was aghast, staring at Epi as though the old man had finally lost his mind.

Epi glared back at him, his eyes enormous behind the thick glasses. "Drawing the sigils on paper will not give Charlotte any powers. Marking them on her skin will."

"Did you see what this thing did to the table?" I questioned frantically. "It burnt the wood!"

"The Hjördis is designed for this task, Charlotte," Epi stated matter-of-factly. "That is what it was used for in times past." He touched my shoulder, patting it gently. "You must trust me, child."

"No. No way." I backed away from him, deeply disturbed by what he was suggesting.

Epi turned away from me, gesturing to a group of pictures he'd pinned to the wall. Each one depicted people with their bodies painted in swirling blue symbols. I walked closer to study them and realized some of the symbols were familiar. I moved closer again and knew I'd learned them from the books Epi insisted I read. "What is this?"

"They are a race of people known as the Picts. They existed in Scotland from about 7000BC through to 845AD."

I moved from one picture to the next, studying the designs they'd painted on their bodies, recognizing more sigils I knew. "They were Nememiah's Children?"

"The first of Nememiah's Children. Their name – 'Picts', comes from the word 'Picti' in Latin, which is what the Romans called them. It means 'the painted ones'." His eyes roamed over the pictures, a faraway look in his expression. "They were the very first of Nememiah's Children, given the task of protecting the world from the evils which were, even then, prepared to destroy and maim. Nememiah begat of his own blood to create the first of the Children. He provided them with weapons and abilities to protect the world from danger. The influx of demons from the Otherworld had spawned vampires, werewolves and other creatures. Nememiah gave the Picts the task of both monitoring these supernatural beings, and returning all demons to the

Otherworld. This Hjördis," he said, pointing to the box, "is the last one in existence. There are no more." He lapsed into silence, studying the pictures almost reverently.

I turned to Conal, asking a question silently with my eyes. The box with the Hjördis safely concealed inside it felt heavy, as if the knowledge of what it was, what it could do was weighing me down.

"I can't tell you what to do, Sugar. It's up to you," Conal admitted quietly.

"Give me a second." I called to the spirits and asked for their advice, gaining their reassurance. With trembling fingers, I withdrew the Hjördis from its box and it heated and vibrated in my hand. I glanced up at Conal. "Can you hold my arm?" Conal caught my wrist in his hand and I put the Hjördis close to my forearm. "What do you want me to use?" I asked Epi.

"Let's start with agility."

I inched the Hjördis towards my skin, closing my eyes as it made contact and expecting to feel an excruciating burn. The sensation was uncomfortable, but to my surprise, there was little pain. It created more of a sharp, stinging sensation against my arm. I drew the sigil carefully, watching the skin beneath the tip of the Hjördis turn a rich, indigo blue. When I'd finished, it looked as if I'd inked an intricate tattoo into my skin.

"Is that gonna stay there forever?" Conal asked, eyeing my arm with a frown.

"No. The power of the sigil fades. Each one will last for a period, dependent on how much of that specific ability has been expended during battle. The sigil drawn on the skin will fade away to nothing."

I flexed my arm and rubbed at the mark, discovering it had sunk into the skin, exactly as a tattoo would. I had my doubts about Epi's assertion that it would fade to nothing, but it was too late now. I wondered what should happen next. "Am I meant to feel any different?"

"The test of the sigil will be in the use of it," Epi explained. "Hence the redecoration of my home." He waved his hand expansively around the large room. "Today, we begin to train in earnest. Conal and I will be attacking you, and you must learn to fight us off."

I fought an urge to laugh. "Conal I can understand, but Epi..." I paused, choosing my words carefully because I didn't want to hurt the old man's feelings. "I think I could fight you off, even without the marks."

"Don't be so certain, young lady. I have been on this earth for fifteen hundred years and I still know a thing or two. As I keep telling you, physical attacks are not the only thing you must expect. There will be other forms of attack. Warlocks have many different powers, which we shall be trying to prepare you for."

"You think my enemy is a warlock?" I paused, my eyes widening. "Wait - you're *fifteen hundred years old?*"

"Yes I am, and I should think that would mean I deserve a little more respect from you both," Epi grumbled. "As to the idea your enemy may be a warlock – I do not know, child. But we need to be certain you are prepared for anything and warlocks are amongst the most powerful of all the supernatural."

Epi meant what he said. For an elderly man, even an *ancient* man, he had a strength I'd never expected and threw himself at me with abandon, overwhelming me with attacks both physical and magical. I was convinced the sigil wasn't doing a damn thing as I was repeatedly pummeled.

"You aren't concentrating," Epi said crossly, when I landed on the padded floor in a crumpled heap for the fourth time in a row.

"It's so hot in here!" I complained, wiping the sweat from my forehead with the back of my arm. The t-shirt I was wearing was dripping, and clung to my skin, while the unpleasant trickle of perspiration was running down the back of my thighs.

"The field of battle isn't going to be air-conditioned, you foolish girl! If you think the worst you will deal with is being a bit sweaty and uncomfortable, you are sadly misinformed! Battles are ugly, they're violent; your combatant isn't going to stand around waiting for you to cool off!" Epi was almost apoplectic with anger. "Now, try again! And believe in yourself!"

He raised his hand and a wave of shimmering air raced across the room towards me. I knew it would throw me into the wall with substantial force as it had done repeatedly. I lifted my hand angrily and watched in surprise as the wave suddenly turned on itself and flowed swiftly towards Epi. The old man was launched into the air, hitting the high ceiling before he fell to the ground in a little heap of navy blue. I was horrified and began to run towards him but Conal had already reached his side and was helping him stand up.

"Now that was more like it!" Epi announced cheerfully, smiling his toothless grin and appearing no worse for wear. "Conal, try a physical attack again."

Conal had stripped down to jeans during the workout, his t-shirt lying in a crumpled heap on the floor. We moved towards the center of the room and Epi watched as Conal prepared to attack me. He moved quickly, more rapidly than any human could and had managed to pounce on me every single time. I took a deep calming breath, trying to concentrate on the sigil as I watched Conal for the first sign of movement. He launched himself at me with a wolfish growl. In the split-second when he reached me, I lurched gracelessly to one side; with speed I didn't know I was capable of. I turned to watch him fall harmlessly onto the floor, rolling catlike until he was on his feet again. He looked at me with admiration and grinned. "Nice one, Charlotte."

"Yes, yes! Wonderful! Now a little more practice like that, and we will add another sigil to the mix," Epi agreed delightedly.

With practice, I was able to hold off each man individually. As the day wore on, I could actively deal with them together. The progress came at a cost, my head ached and being slammed backwards continually was having an adverse effect on my muscles, making them ache with fatigue. Despite Conal wanting to stop when my head began to pound, I begged him to continue. I knew I was running out of time, although where the certainty came from, I couldn't tell. But there was a sense of urgency in my efforts, a feeling that I was going to need this and the time was rapidly approaching.

"Excellent!" Epi shouted happily, when I again defeated the two of them with little effort. My arms were covered in sigils – Epi insisted I must overcome my predominantly right-handedness and learn to mark both arms. With practice, it was becoming easier – although my artistic side felt the marks on my left arm were far superior to my right.

"So can we quit for tonight?" Conal asked. He was breathing heavily, his hair slicked back and the top of his denim jeans were darkened with perspiration, which poured from his torso.

"Of course not. There isn't time to 'quit' as you put it. Charlotte has managed to defeat us, but we are not a true test of her abilities," Epi snapped. "Although you appear to be attacking her with force, the truth is, you hold something back in yourself so you won't hurt her." Epi looked from my face to Conal's, his blue eyes owl-like behind his glasses. "Charlotte cannot rely on the spirits alone. Nor the sigils. She must learn to handle weapons."

"Not tonight—" Conal began tiredly.

"Yes! Tonight!" Epi shouted. "She must do this!"

Conal and I glanced at one another and Conal saw determination in my eyes. "Okay, okay. What's next, old man?"

Epi motioned for us to follow him and we walked to the other end of the long room. He waved his hand and the foam covering the wall disappeared, leaving the stone visible. I wistfully considered laying my face against the cool stone to cool down my overheated skin, but forced myself to concentrate on what Epi was saying. He pointed to a place on the wall. "See that stone?"

They all looked identical to me and I stared at them for a moment, and then turned my attention back to Epi. "What?"

"Look closely, young lady. Allow the stones to talk to you. Whilst this is a warlock's magic, you should be capable of seeing it."

Breathing deeply, I stared at the wall again, allowing other thoughts to drift from my mind like leaves scattering in the wind. As I concentrated, the most central stone shimmered a little. I turned to Conal. "Can you see that?"

Conal was watching the stones, but I could see from his neutral expression that he couldn't make out what I was seeing.

"He cannot see it because he does not have the ability," Epi said quietly. "Only you and I can." He motioned me forward. "Go, child and take what you find."

I slowly walked across to the wall, touching the shimmering stone. As my fingertips reached it, the stone block disappeared, leaving a neat open square.

"How did you do that?" Conal asked.

I shrugged. How did I do it? There was no explanation for my actions, only a knowledge of what needed to be done. I reached into the dark recesses of the square opening. My fingers closed over a neat package, bound with a leather strap and I pulled it from the hole.

"What is it?" I asked Epi.

"Weapons of the Angels. Like the Hjördis, these are the last ones left."

I pulled the leather strap holding the bundle and carefully unrolled it. Inside, I found two sharp daggers, their hilts encrusted with sigils and the shafts glowed brilliantly. They looked like silver, but I realized it wasn't silver; this was a different material – almost luminescent – and a glow seemed to come from inside the daggers themselves. I stared at them for a long moment before putting them aside and picking up the other two items.

These were round and flat, covered with similar sigils and with five razor sharp blades spaced evenly around the edges.

"They are the *Katchet* and *Philaris*," Epi explained. "The weapons of Nememiah's Children. The daggers are used in hand-to-hand combat; the Philaris are useful for throwing from a distance. They can also be used in close combat, to strike down the enemy."

Conal reached for one of the daggers, but Epi gripped his arm firmly. "You cannot touch them. They will create the same effect as the Hjördis did when you touched it."

"Thanks for the warning, old man," Conal muttered. He withdrew his hand.

"I— I don't think I can use these," I said quietly, staring at the weapons. I'd only ever used a weapon once in my life, when I'd been filled with the rage created by my family's murder.

"You will learn to use them, child. You must," Epi said.

"What's she going to use them on?" Conal asked. "Us?"

"Of course not," Epi responded, his tone abruptly businesslike. "Now you have to work together against a common enemy. Charlotte, there will be a belt with the weapons. Put it on and place the weapons in it. And then you have to mark Conal."

"Excuse me?"

Epi shook his head impatiently. "I keep forgetting there are gaps in your knowledge. I truly wish you could read faster," he muttered. "Charlotte, as one of Nememiah's Children, you can use the sigils on other supernatural beings. They cannot use the Hjördis or the weapons, but they can be marked, be given some of Nememiah's shielding. You are going to give Conal markings, to give him added protection."

"Is that going to hurt him?" I demanded. Instinct told me marking his skin might be more painful than marking my own.

"Yes, yes, he will feel some discomfort," Epi agreed, waving his hand to re-cover the wall with padding. He saw the skepticism in my eyes and shrugged. "All right. It will be painful. But it will give him extra strength to deal with the foe."

"Don't worry, Charlotte. I'll be okay," Conal said gruffly. He held his arm out and I drew the Hjördis from my pocket, gripping his wrist in my left hand. I began a mark and saw the muscle tighten in his forearm as the Hjördis burnt the sigil onto his skin. I was dismayed when the smell of burning flesh wafted into my nostrils and stared into Conal's eyes, my own filled with tears. "Just do it," he commanded roughly, his black eyes flashing with determination. He turned his attention to Epi as I worked. "So what foe are we talking about, old man? What have you got in mind?"

I finished the sigil for agility and began the one for endurance.

Epi was busy drawing something of his own on the padded floor. "Your foe is going to be a demon," he stated.

Chapter 30

Demons

Conal and I gaped at Epi with remarkably similar expressions. Complete disbelief.

"What did you say?" Conal growled.

"A demon." Epi looked up from what he was doing and pushed his glasses further up his bulbous nose. "Nothing too difficult to begin with. Perhaps a simple Valafar. Something that is difficult for you to kill, but easy for me to return to its Otherworld origins if it should get out of control."

"Well, that's certainly comforting," Conal groaned, gritting his teeth against the burn of the Hjördis on his skin. "Are you nearly finished, Charlotte?"

"Yes." I drew the Hjördis away and blinked away the tears that brimmed against my eyelashes. "I'm so sorry."

Conal hugged me. "It's not your fault, Sugar." The dirty look he threw at Epi left no doubt, who Conal blamed. "So, Vander – how can you bring one of these demons through from the Otherworld, if it's a no-no?"

Epi looked ever so slightly chagrined. "It is for the greater good."

"You mean, nobody knows you're doing it," Conal stated.

"That is correct."

"Won't you get in trouble from the... Warlock's Union or something?" I asked.

"No. I am only bringing through a small demon, virtually harmless. But highly necessary if you are to learn how to defeat them." He stood up; studying the lines he'd marked on the stone floor. "And there is no Warlock's Union, you foolish child."

"What is that?" I walked across to the markings he'd made on the floor.

"It is a pentagram," Epi announced, studying his work with some satisfaction. There were sigils in four of the five triangular corners; the fifth was empty. "Traditionally used to call demons from the Otherworld." The old man turned to Conal, watching him with interest. "You will need to transform into your wolf."

Conal sneered. "Werewolves only transform at full moon. We're not shifters."

"Oh, don't be so ridiculous," Epi retorted mildly. "You're only repeating what you've been taught since childhood. Werewolves are not so different to shape shifters and they can transform whenever there is a requirement."

"I can't," Conal growled angrily and for a brief second I saw the wolf-like curl to his lip. "We only transform during the full moon. Three nights. I can't transform with Charlotte nearby, I could kill her."

"That's because you *think* that's the only time you can transform," Epi responded cheerfully. "And, might I ask, who is the smarter race? The shifters, who can change form whenever it is required, or the werewolves, who stick to their antiquated beliefs and only transform during the full moon?"

The first waves of Conal's power began to roll from his body and goose bumps rose on my bare skin. "Don't anger me, old man," he growled.

Epi continued, completely ignoring the warning signs of Conal's anger. "You've just forgotten you can transform whenever you want to. Or need to. And you won't hurt Charlotte; your wolf form will recognize her as Nememiah's Child, just as easily as your human form does."

Conal cursed loudly. "You're crazy, old man. It's been this way for as long as I can remember—"

"Which isn't nearly as long as I can remember," Epi retorted mildly. "No matter. We will continue with the training and see what happens. Of course, you need to keep in mind you would fight harder and stronger as a werewolf, but if you want to attempt defeating a Valafar in human form..." he reached down and completed a fifth sigil in the pentagram and the ground beneath the church trembled "... that is completely up to you."

I staggered backwards, falling to my knees as the pentagram swirled with thick red and black mist. From the center of the mist, a creature began to form and it climbed out through the pentagram to face me.

It was hideous, with the head of a bear and the body of a man. A man who was at least seven feet tall, and built like a fanatical weightlifter. The entirety of its body was black, a shiny, wet looking black, as if it had stepped through an oil slick. Its fangs were long and it had substantial claws at the ends of each limb. It roared, the sound like a steam train echoing through a tunnel and took a step towards me. I shrieked, dragging myself to my feet and searching for an escape.

"Use your abilities, Charlotte!" Epi yelled from across the room.

Conal ran past me, attempting to grab the creature's neck. The Valafar gripped his arm and threw Conal, its reaction instinctive. It turned back to me and with an unearthly scream, began to pace forward. I summoned the spirits, watching the Valafar get hit with a blocking wave of energy. It was thrown backwards, falling with enough force that the ground trembled beneath me. The Valafar flipped onto its feet and raced towards me, clearly angered. I pulled one of the Katchet from my belt, gripping it in my right hand. I jabbed nervously at the Valafar, but the attempt was ineffective and razor-sharp claws glanced across my right arm.

"Concentrate, Charlotte!" Epi yelled urgently. Ignoring the searing pain in my forearm, I turned to watch the Valafar approaching again.

From the corner of my eye, I caught a blur and heard a deep snarl, recalling it from the night I'd been rescued in New Orleans and Conal had turned into a werewolf. As the Valafar lunged again, a streak of black fur flew past. I stared open-mouthed as Conal, in werewolf form, launched himself at the Valafar, forcing it to the ground and biting fiercely at its neck. The Valafar and Conal rolled around the floor, biting and snapping at one another and I watched in horror when the demon lashed one heavy arm up, slashing it towards Conal's hindquarters. The Valafar howled, splitting Conal's fur and skin with its claws. Conal yelped and the terrible sound spurred me into action. I grasped the Katchet more firmly in my right hand, hurtling towards the Valafar with anger and rage feeding my movements. My head cleared, my body calmed – and I knew exactly what I needed to do. I caught the Valafar around its thick neck and plunged the dagger unswervingly into its chest. It collapsed to its knees – bear-like mouth open and howling. Sticky black liquid sprayed from its chest, splattering against my face and clothes. It began to fold in on itself, becoming smaller and smaller, until it disappeared, leaving only a blackened scorch mark on the padded floor.

Dropping the Katchet, I ran to Conal. He'd reverted to human form, naked and breathing rapidly, angry slashes oozing blood from his calf and thigh. "Conal!"

"See. I told you – you can transform whenever you want to," Epi announced smugly.

"Epi! What do I do? How can I help him?" I shrieked angrily.

"Use a healing sigil, of course."

I pulled the Hjördis from my pocket and reached for Conal's arm. His face was haggard, his breathing uneven as he looked up at me bashfully. "Charlotte, I'm naked..."

"That doesn't matter," I breathed. And it didn't. All that mattered was helping him.

"Shit, that thing tastes terrible," Conal growled and spat black liquid on the floor beside him.

"Not on his arm, Charlotte. The healing sigils must be drawn close to the injury," Epi explained, kneeling to show me where I should place the marks. "You need to use the one for blood and the one for poison."

"Poison?" I repeated blankly, marking the blood sigil against Conal's thigh.

"Yes, of course. Most demons are poisonous. Not to worry, this one isn't life threatening but its poison will cause a significant amount of pain."

"Epi," I muttered through gritted teeth, "you don't think you might have mentioned all this *before* we had to fight it?"

"Of course not," he said dismissively. "Charlotte, the demons won't stop and give you instructions. This little exercise has proven exactly what I anticipated. You can fight in battle against the demons. And more importantly, you can win. Not only has it been proven to me, but it has also proven this fact to *you*."

I finished the second sigil and slumped onto the floor, anxiously watching the wounds on Conal's leg. The sigils suddenly erupted with an iridescent glow and the torn skin began to knit together, leaving newly healed scars behind, the skin glossy and smooth. The blood and poison sigils receded simultaneously, fading away to nothing. It probably took less than three minutes and I glanced at Conal's face anxiously. "Are you okay?"

Conal stretched out his leg, staring at the scars skeptically. "Yeah. It feels better." He caught sight of my arm, which was seeping blood and stung like crazy. "Do the marks on yourself, Charlotte," he reminded gently.

I nodded and drew the blood and poison sigils against the cuts on my arm, watching the same procedure repeat on the wounds.

"How did you know I wouldn't hurt her, old man?"

"She is Nememiah's Child. One of the Angels. You will never hurt her. Part of Charlotte's allure is to make people protective. That is the Angel blood, heightening your desire to care for her. It will happen with all supernatural beings who don't wish her harm. She will draw from the people around her a desire to love and protect her."

"What are you saying? That people might— *think* they love me, but it's just an illusion?" I felt ill, thinking what this would mean for Conal's feelings – and Lucas's.

"I never said that, child. I truly wish you would listen correctly. But of course, you are very young. There are many forms of love. The love I speak of is affectionate love, the desire to keep someone safe, an overwhelming feeling of caring and protection. You will draw that feeling from many people, purely because of the blood running through your veins. The love you speak of is something entirely different. And yes," he admitted with a sigh, "that is possible for you too. Someone, or perhaps more than one, will love you in both ways."

Conal asked the question we'd discussed a few weeks ago. "What happens if Charlotte fell in love with a supernatural? If she was to fall pregnant?"

Epi eyed Conal solemnly for a long moment, his blue eyes piercing. "The Angel blood will always dominate. No matter whom Charlotte loves, if she produces a child, its genetic makeup will follow the mother. Never the father."

I greeted this information with silence, exhaustion and stress mixing with... profound relief. And another emotion. *Regret.* What Lucas had spent so long trying to save me from, was something that could never happen. His child wouldn't have killed me. His child – *our* child, would have been safe and healthy. I swayed a little and my vision swam, but Conal's strong arms caught me, holding me close.

"Alright. I think that is enough practice for today," Epi announced, as though we'd survived nothing more dangerous than a brisk walk through a park. "Go home, get some rest. You might like to shower. Demon blood smells like corpses, it's not particularly appealing. I will see you here again tomorrow morning."

"You've forgotten one thing, Vander," Conal stated in a low growl. "I can't drive through Jackson like this."

I peeked down and blushed. Now that the drama was over, it seemed weird to see Conal naked and I tried to keep my eyes averted from certain areas of his anatomy. And failed. He was powerfully built in *all* areas. I turned away, trying to recover my shattered composure.

Epi flourished his hand and when I turned back, Conal was wearing a pair of jeans. He got to his feet and then helped me up, hugging me close.

"Let's go home, Sugar," he whispered against my hair.

I took the Hjördis from my pocket to place it back in the wooden box, but Epi shook his head. "It is yours now, Charlotte. Keep it with you. You are the true owner of the Hjördis and the weapons. You are Nememiah's Child."

Despite everything he'd put me through, I was grateful for having met Epimetheus Vander. He'd provided answers to so many questions and was helping us. Even if he was a pain in the ass. I slipped from Conal's arms to give Epi an impetuous hug.

"What was that for?" he asked and I was certain he blushed.

"For helping me to get through this."

"You're welcome my child. And you have given me more than I ever dreamed. Finding an Angel child has been my life's work. I thought it would never happen and yet, here you are. I'm proud of you, Charlotte. You have proven yourself, far beyond my wildest dreams. I imagined when Nonny brought you here, you may have a little of Nememiah's blood. You have proven today that you are truly one of the Angel children. You will protect our world, I'm certain of it."

Conal caught my hand in his and we walked toward the doors. I stopped in the open doorway and looked back to find Epi watching me, his blue eyes bright with tears.

Chapter 31

The Longest Night

I stared at the girl in the mirror, not certain I recognized her anymore. Epi had been right – demon blood did smell like death. It was a sickly, nauseating smell, a combination of rotting meat and feces, which clung to my skin and coated the back of my throat. I'd scrubbed with strawberry shower gel until I was sure the odor was gone then washed my hair three times, ensuring the sticky black gunk had been completely eradicated.

I studied my reflection. Many of the sigils had disappeared completely and those that were left had faded from brilliant indigo to the palest shade of blue. The scar from the Valafar's claws had grown fainter between stepping into the shower and now, little more than a silvery mark against my fair skin.

There were physical differences – weeks of intense activity had strengthened muscles, providing definition in the shape of my arms and legs. My stomach was washboard flat and there was muscle in my abdomen that I'd never had before. My hair was longer – we'd been so busy, I hadn't bothered to get it cut and now I could pull it back easily into a braid, which was convenient if Epi insisted on fighting more demons.

I knew there were other differences – not physical but psychological. I was tougher than I could ever remember being, more focused, more in control of my emotions. It sounded ludicrous, but I felt what was happening to me – it was destiny. This was what I was meant to do. This is who I was. There was no doubt in my mind; nothing would make me believe otherwise.

Subtle differences presented themselves in the mirror. My eyes seemed greener, my hair darker and my cheeks held a hint of color. My lips were redder, as if I perpetually wore lipstick. I'd considered myself ordinary but now, with the knowledge of my heritage, I felt – if not beautiful, certainly more attractive. The girl before me felt in control of herself and confident. She was able to tackle whatever the future held.

I slipped into jeans and a cotton t-shirt, padding barefoot down the hall to the living room. Conal was already out of the shower, sitting on the couch with a beer cradled between his hands. He looked up as I approached and smiled warmly. "Thought you were never coming out. I've ordered pizza, should be here soon."

"Demon blood is pretty revolting," I grimaced. "Took me ages to wash it out of my hair."

"Want a drink? A beer?" he offered.

"No thanks. Still under twenty one, remember?"

Conal shook his head, a smile playing on his lips. "Hard to believe you're only twenty – in some ways you seem much older. Did you know I'm almost twice your age?"

I selected a can of soda from the refrigerator and sunk onto the couch beside Conal, flicking open the ring pull. "I've never asked how old you are."

"Thirty eight."

"And you still haven't found the right girl?" I teased, sipping the soda. "You're leaving it a bit late."

Conal put his beer on the table and wrapped his arm around my shoulder. "Oh, I think I've found the right girl. Problem is, she's an Angel and not a werewolf." He kissed my forehead. "Yum, strawberries. Much better than demon blood." I could see my reflection in his black eyes and saw the familiar look of yearning in his handsome face.

Thoughts flitted thought my mind as rapidly as a hummingbird flaps its wings. Being here with Conal – knowing the way he felt about me – it all seemed so natural and right. He desired me – and I desired him. He loved me – and I felt love for him. There was no way of knowing what I faced and my future was uncertain. In a tumultuous rush of thoughts, I made a decision.

I leaned forward to touch his lips with mine, placing my hand against his cheek as I brushed my lips over his. He growled; a deep throaty rumble and captured me against him, deepening the kiss as his tongue probed my mouth with a ferocity and longing that overwhelmed me. I ran my fingers through his hair, drawing him closer and his hand slipped beneath my t-shirt, nimble fingers undoing the lacy bra underneath. His hand slipped beneath the lace and captured my breast, his warm fingers gentle on my skin. I gasped and released my hold on his hair. Fumbling with nerves, I undid the buttons on his shirt and rubbed my hands across his chest. He was warm, his body temperature higher than mine and I moaned as he bent to replace his hand against my breast with his mouth. I inhaled sharply, pleasant butterflies roiling through my stomach and lower regions.

Conal returned his attention to my mouth before his lips trailed languorous kisses across my neck and shoulder. "If you want to stop this, say so now," he growled huskily.

I tugged him towards me in response. Conal gently laid me back against the couch, holding his body above mine without touching. Our eyes met and he understood what I wasn't capable of vocalizing. Conal shuddered with desire and dropped his body over mine, kissing me repeatedly until our breathing was ragged.

Four things happened within seconds of one another. My head swiftly filled with voices, dozens of them yelling at once and clamoring for attention. I shrieked, lifting my hands to my head to try and quell the pain that erupted in my temples. Conal's cell phone and mine both began ringing shrilly and the apartment phone rang a second later. Conal sat up, his eyes filled with alarm as he tried to help me. "Charlotte! Charlotte, what's wrong?"

"I— I don't know!" I tried to stand and fell forward, my knees hitting the ground sharply and I bent over double, squeezing my head between my hands. "Will you answer one of those damn calls?"

Conal snatched up his cell, answering it brusquely. He knelt beside me, rubbing my back as I struggled to regain control. I called to the spirits, asking them to relay their messages slowly, pulling strands towards me to collect information. The voices were so loud I could barely hear Conal's voice over the ruckus. With painstaking effort, I started to build a picture of what had happened. What I heard from them was horrifying, chilling my body down to the marrow. I didn't need to hear Conal's words when he disconnected the call – I already knew the worst.

"The pack has been attacked," he announced bleakly, his eyes filled with panic. "By vampires."

It took only minutes to prepare; while Conal collected his car keys I ran to the bedroom, to pull on shoes and snatch up the Hjördis, then strapped the weapons belt around my hips. Conal stared when I returned to the living room and he saw the weapons belt. "You should stay here, Charlotte."

"I'm coming with you," I announced. "If the pack were attacked, I'm no safer here. I'd rather be with you."

To my relief, Conal didn't argue. "Come on."

The drive to the outskirts of Natchez seemed interminable, broken only by the telephone call I returned on my cell phone. It was a number I didn't recognize, but I knew the voice when he answered.

"Nick? It's Charlotte. What's wrong?" I asked the question, despite already knowing a good percentage of the answer. The spirits were still bombarding me with information, but so many of them were attempting to contact me, it was hard to piece together everything at once.

"Charlotte— Lucas and Ben, all of them – they're gone." His voice was filled with anger.

"Who took them?"

"The house is a fucking mess, stuff broken up, windows smashed—"

"Who, Nick? Who took them?" I repeated impatiently, needing confirmation.

There was a long silence on the line. "I don't know, but the whole house reeks of vampires. Scents I don't recognize."

"They're all gone?" My heart raced with panic and as much as I denied it, I knew my heart still belonged to Lucas.

"All of them," Nick confirmed. I could hear his ragged breathing, knew he was struggling to control his rage and frustration.

"What about Katie?"

"She's safe. She's with my pack." He paused and I caught the murmur of voices in the background. "Do you have any idea who could have done this? I didn't know who else to call, and I thought you'd want to know."

It was my turn to pause, hot tears splashing down my cheeks when I squeezed my eyes shut, wishing the truth could be denied. "It's my fault, Nick."

"What?"

"It's me," I confirmed. "They want me."

"Who?"

"The vampire council… I don't remember what they're called. The vampires that govern all the others."

"I knew you were fucking trouble, from the minute I met you," Nick snapped angrily. There was another round of hushed discussions before Nick spoke again. "Jerome insists I'm being too hard on you, but I'll withhold judgment on that one. What the hell is going on, Charlotte?"

"Look, Nick, things are pretty chaotic right now. Give me an hour or so to try and figure some stuff out. I'll ring you back. In the meantime, keep Katie safe."

"What's going on?"

"Too much to explain right now." I took a deep breath and glanced at Conal, catching the wild look in his eyes. "The Tremaine pack has been attacked. By vampires."

Nick cussed fiercely. "This is linked to Lucas being taken, isn't it? The two attacks can't be isolated events," he announced.

"I think so."

"And you're right in the middle of it." The disgust in his voice was enough to shake me, even with the distance between us.

"I'm sorry, Nick. I have to go now, but I promise I'll ring you back as soon as I can."

"Don't bother; we'll work out how to rescue them ourselves."

He hung up before I could say anything else and I was left staring at the cell phone in dismay.

Chapter 32

Come Unto Me

It looked like hell. The neat houses, the manicured yards – all had been damaged or destroyed. Houses burned, some of the pack valiantly spraying them with garden hoses, a useless gesture against the ferocity of the flames. Bodies lay at odd angles everywhere, loved ones looking on in silent desperation. Others were being tended to by members of the pack and as Conal screeched to a halt outside his parents' home, all I could see was the dead and dying, the wounded and bereaved. It was horrifying and I jumped from the cab, watching Conal as he sprinted towards his parents' house. Amoux and Nonny knelt by the porch, staring at a body laid in front of them. Conal dropped to his knees, pulling his mother close and clutching Nonny's hand. I turned away, sick to the pit of my stomach.

I bent over with my hands on my knees, gasping breath into my lungs to try and still the nausea that threatened to overwhelm me. The smells were horrifying, a combination of blood and smoke and burning flesh – I closed my eyes, willing myself to find the strength to deal with this. And absolutely, incontrovertibly convinced this attack was my fault.

"Charlotte." Kenyon laid a comforting hand on my shoulder. "Are you alright?"

I forced myself to straighten up, ignoring the nausea churning in my stomach. "Kenyon. I'm so sorry." What else was there to say, what else could I do? There was death and destruction everywhere I looked.

"We've lost nearly half the pack," he stated, his voice as desolate as his eyes. "Many others are injured." His eyes flickered to where Conal knelt beside his mother and grandmother. "Lyell Tremaine is dead."

"I know," I whispered. I'd known before we arrived that Lyell was dead. I'd heard his spirit in the car and it had chilled me to the bone. It hadn't seemed right to tell Conal during the drive here and I'd kept the knowledge to myself, silently agonizing over what Conal would discover when we got here. Had I done the right thing? I didn't know – I just didn't know. It was a question I would deal with later – not now, when there was so much agony and terror all around us.

I reached for the belt that hung low on my hips, grasping the Hjördis in my fingers. With sudden clarity I knew what I needed to do, the only thing I could do right now. "Kenyon, I can help the injured. Show me where they are."

He considered my words for a long moment, thoughts swirling in his eyes, including a healthy dose of indecision and worry. He glanced at the Hjördis in my hand, the weapons strapped to my hip. Then he nodded his silent assent. He led me to another house, which had sustained less damage than most. People were carrying the wounded to this house and the yard was littered with frantic people and their injured loved ones.

There was a tall man moving amongst them and Kenyon introduced him as Quinn Saunders, a paramedic. The man regarded me grimly as Kenyon explained who I was, his blue eyes impassive. Kenyon asked Quinn to help by selecting the wounded in order of urgency and left us, patting me on the shoulder. Quinn immediately led me to a couple, their small son held in his mother's arms. He had sustained a brutal slash to his chest and blood soaked into his Barney pajamas, staining the material with a dark blemish. He was whimpering softly, tears trickling silently from his dark eyes.

Quinn shook the father's arm gently. "Rafe, Ayame – this is Charlotte. She says she can help Caleb."

Rafe glanced from Quinn to me, uncertainty in his expression. "This is the Angel?" he asked hoarsely, his voice rough with grief.

"Yes. She reckons she can help your son, if you'll let her."

Husband and wife exchanged glances and I could almost hear the unvoiced discussion between them. The chest injury their son had sustained would kill him, of that I had no doubt, but superstition and doubt made them fear what I would do to him.

"I promise, I will do no harm," I said softly.

The husband hesitated uncertainly, but his wife nodded. "Please," she begged. "He is all we have."

I knelt beside them and reached for the young boy, unbuttoning his pajama top to expose the full extent of the injury. It was deep; maybe an inch or two wide and about seven inches long, running from the top of his ribs to his belly button. Things I didn't want to make sense of bulged from his stomach. He looked about eight years old and he watched me warily as I eyed the wound, swallowing back bile and sternly ordering myself not to throw up. I forced a smile. "Hey, Caleb. I'm Charlotte." I held my palm open and let him see the Hjördis. "See this? It's a magic pen and I'm going to draw a special picture on your stomach, right next to that nasty cut. It's going to make it better."

He nodded imperceptibly, his black eyes saucer-like as he watched. My hand shook as I approached him – I knew how much the sigils hurt Conal. I couldn't recall him complaining when I'd healed him though, so I took a deep breath and began to draw a blood sigil on Caleb's flat stomach. When I'd finished I sat back on my heels, watching anxiously to see if it would be enough to help him. The injury he'd sustained was far more serious than what Conal and I had dealt with earlier.

Caleb's parents gasped when the wound began to glow and bind, the skin knitting itself together over the bulging organs. The bloodstain and the bright red scar were the only sign of the injury he'd received. The sigil faded slowly and I turned to his parents with a relieved smile. "He's going to be fine."

Quinn led me to the next victim, then another. We worked as a team, Quinn picking through the injured like a one-man triage unit, making split-second decisions as to whom we could help and ensuring the worst injuries were seen first.

Word of what we were doing spread swiftly, and more and more people stood around watching us work. I was oblivious to them all, focused only on healing as many as I could.

"*You!*" I lifted my head to see Phelan Walker storming towards us, anger in his eyes and rage mottling his skin. "This... all of this... is *your fault!*" he shouted. "I warned them about you, I told Lyell you couldn't be trusted! Now you've caused the deaths of dozens of our people!"

Kenyon ran up, holding his hands out in warning towards Phelan. "Phelan! That's enough!"

"She's a demon witch! She's no fucking Angel!" Phelan shouted. Kenyon motioned to two men who captured Phelan's arms, dragging him away as he continued to rant. Shaken and upset by his outburst, tears streamed down my cheeks.

Kenyon knelt beside me, resting his hand on my shoulder. "Please forgive Phelan. He lost both a son and daughter tonight," he stated quietly.

I gripped the Hjördis fiercely, my fingers trembling as I tried to control my tears. "What about you, Kenyon? Your family, are they safe?" There were so many new voices swirling in my head, I couldn't work out who was who yet.

Kenyon glanced away and when he turned back; his eyes glistened with tears. "Javier is dead. My son." He shook his head as if to shake the memory away and patted my shoulder. "I believe in you, Nememiah's Child." He motioned towards the elderly woman lying beside me. "Continue your work, Charlotte."

Hours later, I sat beside the river, watching the sunrise over the tree line. Exhaustion was swamping me and I rubbed my fists against my eyes, yawning as the sky lightened through a maelstrom of blues before the sun crept over the horizon. My mind was still a swirling pool of nightmarish images and sounds, and I wanted to scream out the frustration, kick something, or punch someone – anything to reduce the rage in my soul. This was all so unfair, innocent people targeted through no fault of their own.

My cell phone lay discarded on the grass and when it rang, I picked it up with a sigh, wishing I could avoid this conversation. "Hello."

"It's Nick."

"I know."

"Consiliului Suprem de Drâghici Vampiri."

His attempt at the foreign words was terrible but I recognized what he was trying to say. I dropped my head against my knees, curled around the phone as I struggled to think.

"Charlotte?"

"I'm here."

"Say something," he growled.

"What do you want me to say?"

"Tell me we're going after them."

"I don't know, Nick. I don't know anything right now."

He swore. "You're the cause of this."

"I know."

"But you're not going to do *anything*? You're not going to try and rescue them?" He sounded incredulous.

"I didn't say that," I muttered, my fragile temper rising another notch as he continued to harass me. I was tired and emotionally overwhelmed – having an angry shape shifter in my face was not helping.

"What are you saying?" he growled.

"I'm going after them, Nick. Not you, not Conal's wolves. Just me."

It was his turn to lapse into silence and I let the stunned silence stretch and lengthen, too tired to do anything else. "What aren't you telling me, Charlotte? What's been going on, since you dumped Lucas?"

I breathed deeply, expanding my lungs and then letting the air release through my mouth slowly. "A lot has gone on, Nick. More than I can explain right now. Do you know the origin of those words?"

"It's Romanian. Means the 'Supreme Council of Drâghici Vampires'."

"They've got them?" I didn't really doubt it; I was only seeking confirmation of what the spirits had said.

"Seems so. I need to make some more inquiries before I can guarantee it, but my gut tells me it's them."

I scratched my fingers absently through my hair. "I guess Romanian words means that's where they're taking them? To Romania?"

"I think so. I can't confirm anything yet."

"How do you know all this?"

"I have my sources."

It was obvious he wasn't going to share any more information and I lapsed into silence again, thinking furiously.

"Charlotte," he snarled angrily. "What the hell's going on?"

"I'll explain it all, but not now right now. Give me until tonight and I'll call you, give you the whole story."

"You're pissing me off."

"I don't mean to, Nick. Just give me a little more time."

"I want in on rescuing them, Charlotte. They're my friends."

The words were stated benignly enough, but the underlying message was clear. He thought they meant more to him than they did to me and he had a right to that opinion. It didn't matter what he thought of me. What mattered was rescuing Lucas and my friends. They were being held because of me and I would rescue them. I refused to consider any alternative outcomes to this mess. "Okay," I finally said.

"Tell me what's going on, Charlotte."

I couldn't blame him for the suspicion in his voice. As far as Nick was concerned, I'd let Lucas and the others down, I'd put them in danger without warning them. I regretted my decision not to tell them what was happening, but tamped the regret down to be dealt with later.

"Nick, I'm exhausted. Conal's pack was slaughtered last night, more than half of them died. Please, believe me when I tell you I will explain it all, just— just not right now."

He sighed heavily. "Alright. But I want to hear everything when you call tonight."

"Okay."

"And I'll be meeting you to make a plan. I don't trust you to do this on your own."

"Alright."

"And I'll be bringing backup."

"I wouldn't expect anything else."

Chapter 33

Pain, Hurt & Agony

I was unaware of the passing of time, what was happening around me until the scent of burning reached my nose. The Tremaine Pack had begun cremating their dead. I'd realized as the long night continued that the pack kept everything in-house; the fires, the deaths, the destruction - despite everything that happened, it was kept within the pack. They were far enough away from civilization that nosy neighbors hadn't called the police. They didn't want outsiders involved in their business. It was a subject I wanted to discuss with Conal; but not now – not yet.

I hadn't seen Conal since we'd arrived and I didn't want to see anyone right now. My clothes and arms were covered in dried blood from the people I'd tried to save. There was no satisfaction in knowing I'd saved some people last night – there had been so many more I hadn't.

I needed to talk to Conal, wanted so badly to hold him and feel safe, but for now, he needed time to grieve. After speaking to Nick, I'd called Epi about the horrific events of this long night. Epi had been unruffled, as if he expected some event to mark the beginning of the conflict.

Logic dictated I needed to sleep. Should eat something. Both necessities of life that I couldn't face right now. I closed my eyes, pressing my fists against them as I pondered the plan formulating in my mind. I had no abilities to help develop a strategy; this situation was new and strange enough that I honestly didn't have a clue. But I had an objective; some rough ideas of how to reach the goal and hoped Epi, Nick and Conal had experience enough to help.

I sensed, rather than heard movement nearby and looked up, apprehension rippling through my spine when I saw Phelan Walker striding towards me. His expression was grim and he looked wound up for another round of verbal abuse— or worse.

When he was within a foot or two of my position, I held a hand out. "Phelan, please. I don't want to fight any more," I begged quietly. "You need to be with your family, not fighting with me."

He stopped walking, his shoulders stiff and his hands gripped into fists. I wasn't certain whether he intended to punch me or yell at me, so I was stunned when he spoke, his voice calm. "May I sit down?"

I nodded and he sat cross-legged on the grass beside me. His actions were graceful and fluid, a sign I now recognized as natural werewolf aptitude. Dressed in faded blue jeans and a grey t-shirt, his clothes were torn and streaked with blood, his face grimy from fighting the fires.

We sat in peaceful silence for a few minutes, while the sun slowly rose further over the horizon, dappled light playing on the water as it swirled past.

"I owe you an apology," Phelan announced abruptly.

I wasn't sure how to respond. Fatigued from everything I'd seen and heard in the long hours I'd been here, my initial reaction was to tell him he did owe me an apology. But the man had lost two of his children – maybe I needed to cut him some slack.

"Phelan, I'm sorry, too. I'm sorry that you lost your children last night."

He squeezed his eyes shut, his hands fisted as he attempted to control his fragile emotions. It was clear he didn't want to show his grief in front of me, but it was so new, so deeply painful, he was struggling to be in control. My heart grieved with him – the memory of losing Mom and my family gave me an insight into his sorrow. We had more in common than I could ever have imagined – both Phelan and I had lost loved ones in a murderous act. I reached out hesitantly, touching his shoulder. Instantly a trickle of voices entered my mind and I realized what I'd suspected was true – Phelan no longer intended me any harm.

I took a deep breath, uncertain how he would react to what I was about to admit. "Phelan, I can hear your son and daughter."

His eyes widened. "You can hear them?"

I bit my lip, nodding hesitantly.

The struggle was apparent in his black eyes – his overwhelming grief for his two children warring with his superstitions regarding me. "What— what are they saying to you?"

"Dolph wants you to know he died quickly, there was very little... pain and he's immensely proud that he managed to kill one of the vampires before he died. He wants you to tell his Mom that he loves her. He thanks you for being such a great father and he says to tell you he loves you." I lowered my gaze, hardly able to bear the pain reflected in his black eyes. The grief was immeasurable, his entire face sharpened and gaunt with it. An image of his son and daughter appeared in my mind, standing with an older woman. Phelan's teenage son was tall and slender, his hair dark and his eyes solemn. He held hands with his sister, a pretty girl with dark curls and chocolate brown eyes, probably about fourteen years old. "Lupita says she doesn't want you to cry for her. She is with Aunt Rica and says their Aunt is looking after them. Lupita is very happy to see Aunt Rica again, because she'd missed her. Lupita wants you to hug her Mom and look after her and Dacia. She wants you to give... Herbert, to Dacia and tell her she has to look after him now."

Phelan was staring at me wordlessly when I opened my eyes, tears streaming down his cheeks. He wrapped both his hands around mine and it took a little while for him to speak. "I've misjudged you, Charlotte, I was wrong. When I'm wrong, I admit I'm wrong." He managed the faintest trace of a smile. "Herbert was Lupita's favorite teddy bear; she got him when she was just a baby. She would never give him up, even though she was nearly fourteen." He swallowed heavily, struggling with his pain. "Our daughter Dacia has— had been nagging Lupita to give Herbert to her. Will you... could you share this with my wife? Faolán will find it a great comfort."

I nodded my agreement and was staggered when Phelan hugged me. I patted his back awkwardly, while he sobbed against my shoulder.

Phelan stayed for a little while longer, as the sun rose higher in the sky and the heat of the day shimmered across the plain on the other side of the river. When he recovered his composure, he restated his desire that I meet his wife and with one last pat on my shoulder, left me to my thoughts.

For the longest time I sat motionless, numbed by the events of the night. When the tears started to flow, I recalled the loss of Phelan's teenage children, along with all the others who'd lost their lives during this long, drawn-out night.

And I cried for the loss of Lucas, Ben, and Rowena – everyone I loved. Terror gripped me as I wondered what would happen to them.

≈†◇◇†◇◇†◇◇†≈

Conal approached me hours later. Despite the heat of the day, I'd remained by the river, preferring the seclusion as I wrestled with bouts of anger and sorrow. The only indication of the passing time had been the sun steadily crossing the sky and I guessed it must be mid-afternoon by now.

Conal sat beside me and wordlessly drew me into his arms. I lay with my head against his chest, sagging with relief. I breathed in deeply, the scent of his skin filling me with peace.

"Thank you doesn't seem like enough. You saved a lot of lives, Charlotte."

I straightened up, guilt bubbling in my chest like a cancer. "If it wasn't for me, none of them would be dead." My voice was bitter, anger vibrating in my throat.

Conal's eyes were red-rimmed, the skin around his eyes shadowed by dark circles. He seemed to have aged overnight; his shoulders, usually so broad and strong had slumped, crushed by the attack on his people. "Charlotte, you know I can't tell you that isn't true. What I can tell you is that the pack— *my* pack stands behind you in this. Kenyon says they were attacked by younglings – vampires with almost no self-control, no ability to contain their savage bloodlust. You didn't do that. Someone else sent them to massacre our people."

"The Drâghici Kiss. The Vampire Council."

"Why would they be interested in you?"

I laughed mirthlessly, startling a few birds who took flight in alarm.

"Because I have something they want. Lucas told me months ago that they collect items of interest. He knew my ability would be of interest to them."

"Do you think they know what you are?"

I shook my head. "I don't know. Epi seems to think so. He's even more convinced all these incidents – including the attack on the Tine Kiss and your pack – are related. They probably thought they'd capture me easily, but whom I choose to hang around with has thwarted their plans, so now they've come out into the open. They attacked your pack, probably thinking I would be here. They've taken Lucas and the others, because they know I'd been with them. I think it's either retribution, or they're trying to draw me out."

"Do you—" He broke off and rubbed my shoulder soothingly for a few seconds, as he composed his question. "Do you think they've killed them?"

I shook my head. "I think they're going to use them as hostages. To force me to come to them."

"How can you be so sure?"

My voice was flat when I answered. "Because I haven't heard any of them in my head. If they were dead – I'd know about it."

Conal sat up a little straighter, tension rolling off him in waves I could physically sense. "Did you know about my father?" he demanded.

I'd walked right into that one. I hadn't even had a chance to reflect on my decision to avoid telling Conal about his father's death. I'd been so consumed with sorrow and worry, the trauma of watching people dead and dying around me, there hadn't been time. Taking a shaky breath, I 'fessed up. "Yes. He spoke to me in the car on the way down here."

Conal's eyes flashed angrily. "Why didn't you tell me?"

I turned to him, knowing I couldn't handle another ounce of guilt, even if I tried. "What possible good would it have done?"

Conal's stare hardened. "Charlotte, he was *my* father. I had a right to know he was dead."

Anger bubbled up, swamping the guilt in seconds. "And you found out he was dead! Would another fifteen minutes have made any difference?" I scrambled to my feet, wrapping my arms around my waist, holding myself together tightly. "Do you think I *like* this? Do you think it's easy to deal with all the people in my head, knowing things other people don't? I don't suppose it occurred to you that it was a shock, hearing your Dad speak to me? I might not have known him well, but he was important to you and you're important to me! Maybe I didn't want to be the one to hurt you so badly! Maybe I was wrong not to tell you what I'd heard! But maybe, just maybe, I thought it was enough of a tragedy, for you to have to hear it at all! Maybe I thought another fifteen minutes of not knowing was better than the finality of what I had to tell you!"

I turned and stumbled along the river's edge, blindsided by his anger. It was the final straw, the last devastating episode in a night of horrifying events, which tipped me over the edge. I ran blindly along the riverbank, sobbing brokenly.

Conal reached my side before I'd gone far and caught my arm, turning me and holding me firmly against his body. I slumped against him, my tears impossible to stop and he waited mutely for me to regain control, his big hands rubbing across my back in a soothing gesture. When my sobbing had reduced to the occasional hiccough, he looked down at me, his black eyes filled with tenderness. "I'm sorry, Sugar. It's been a tough night for everyone, including you."

"I would have told you, if I thought it would have made any difference. But it wouldn't have changed a thing," I said quietly.

"You're right. I know you're right. I'm just pissed about what happened here last night." He rubbed my back thoughtfully. "Charlotte, what are we going to do?"

I met his eyes. "*We* aren't doing anything. I've already caused you and your people more than enough grief. Your father is dead because of me. Dozens of others are dead because of me." With the guilt overpowering me again, I took a firm breath. "I'm going to face the Vampire Council. I've spoken to Nick Lingard and he and his pack are going to help. Lucas and his friends – they've been taken because of me. I have no choice but to try and rescue them."

"The Tremaine pack will join with you. We will avenge ourselves," Conal announced. "And we have a pact with Lucas's Kiss; it's our duty to help them."

It took a minute to remember he was pack leader after Lyell Tremaine's death. The leadership passed from father to son. "I guess that makes us brother and sister," I suggested softly. I wondered what it meant for my relationship with Conal.

"Charlotte," he began huskily, "would you have had sex with me last night, if we hadn't been interrupted?"

I blushed, nodding slowly. I knew without doubt that if events hadn't overtaken us, I would have let him make love to me. Wanted him to make love to me. But everything had changed now.

He sighed and I knew instinctively what was coming. "I love you, Charlotte. I will always love you. But I can't have a relationship with you now. It's my duty to marry a purebloded werewolf. More than ever before, I know that's what I have to do. My responsibility as pack leader is to marry another pureblood and produce a purebloded child. You and I, we can't do that." He turned away, his eyes growing distant and I could sense his pain. It echoed in my own heart.

I put my hand against his cheek, caressing the warmth of his skin for what would probably be the last time. His decision meant we would no longer have the physical relationship we'd had. He could no longer share my bed, platonically or otherwise. That role in his life must be vacated for a woman who could provide what I could not – a purebloded werewolf child. I knew why he had to do this and that the decision wasn't easy for him. But I could make it as painless as possible for him. "Conal, it's okay, I understand. And it would never have worked for us anyway."

"Because you still love the bloodsucker," he grimaced, with something close to distaste crossing his handsome features.

I nodded. "Because I still love the bloodsucker."

Chapter 34

Enchantments

"What I don't understand is why attack the pack? Why take Lucas and his people? Why not just come and snatch me? I couldn't possibly be that difficult to find." I was lying on Epi's couch, hands clasped behind my neck as I voiced my thoughts.

Epi was flitting around the room, doing what he did best – taking numerous books from his expansive library, rifling through them and dropping them haphazardly to the floor when he didn't find what he was looking for.

"As I told you, Charlotte. Your powers are climbing towards their peak now. I believe the Council, for whatever reason, wants you to be as powerful as you can possibly be," Epi responded impatiently.

"But they could have taken me when I was on my own. Or from the apartment... or even from here and let me get powerful while they held me. Why kill innocent people?"

Epi glanced up from the book he was poring over. "You foolish girl. Of course, they can't take you from here. Or from the apartment for that matter."

I sat up, staring at him shrewdly. "And why would that be?"

Epi grinned, his toothless smile only slightly less alarming now than it had been when I first met him. "Because I have placed powerful enchantments over both my home and Conal's apartment." I stared at him blankly and he huffed impatiently. "To protect you, child. Once I realized what you were, I knew I had to keep you as safe as I possibly could. Of course, my home has always had enchantments to keep out unwanted visitors, but when I came to Conal's apartment, I placed similar charms over the structure."

"What exactly do these enchantments do?"

"Stop anyone from breaking in. Nobody will remember the location of the church, or Conal's apartment. Even if they followed you here or there... they would be unable to remember where it was, as soon as they left again. And if by chance they recognized the position of the buildings, they would be struck dumb if they attempted to tell anyone where we are located. Completely unable to vocalize the address." Epi looked immensely pleased with himself over the power of his enchantments.

I had to grin. "Nice one, Epi, but I wish you'd told me before now. You could have used the same enchantments to protect everyone else."

He frowned heavily, his blue eyes sharpening. "I am not a circus performer, young lady. These are powerful enchantments and they take some time to create. They're designed for small areas, not entire suburbs filled with werewolves."

"Then why not try and take me when I was with the pack? They'd been there just a couple of hours beforehand. They could have waited, they must have known Conal would be contacted and surely they would have figured he might take me with him?"

"Perhaps, my dear, they are wanting to see exactly how far you have progressed," Epi stated mildly. "For some reason, unknown to ourselves, they seem to want you as close to the age of twenty one as possible. When your powers will reach their natural peak."

I lapsed into silence again, flopping back onto the couch. It had been a week since the attack and I was holed up with Epi while Conal organized moving the remains of his people to safety. He had taken leadership of his pack and he'd been hard at work ever since, holding endless meetings with the pack elders, supporting the bereaved and reforming his pack into a cohesive unit, albeit with greatly reduced numbers.

His elevation to Alpha had not been without controversy. Whilst he had the support of Lyell's elders, and a right by birth to lead – there was a small group within the pack who'd attempted to stage a coup. Conal had been forced to fight for his right to succession. Some insisted his lack of a spouse and pureblood offspring were enough of a failing to allow the challenge. Conal hadn't divulged the details, but Epi cheerfully explained it involved a physical challenge and ended in the death of the loser – at the hands of the winner. After hearing those details, I didn't press Conal for any more information, but I was relieved beyond belief when he won. If he'd killed the challenger, I didn't want to know about it. Werewolves were not humans and their lifestyle and beliefs weren't human. It was something I'd learned and didn't question.

Conal had been teaching his pack what we'd discovered – that they weren't restricted to transformation during the full moon. More and more of his people were able to transform at will and this would help while they hid from the Drâghici. They were physically stronger and faster in werewolf form and the power to transform if another attack was forthcoming would give them a far better chance of survival.

I hadn't seen Conal since he'd driven back to the city late on Sunday night and deposited me with Epi. He'd told me on the long drive back he only trusted Nonny and Epi after the attack. Conal was convinced there was a spy within his ranks and was doing his best to locate them. He insisted someone had to have tipped off the vampires and organized the simultaneous attack that occurred.

But who could the spy be? Everyone, every single family had lost a member during the attack. Not one person stood out as an obvious suspect.

What Epi said was true; my powers were increasing exponentially. I had cohesive control of the spirits, could summon as many as I needed with barely a thought. Most of my strengths came from the spirits – although I was becoming more adept at physical battle, my strongest weapon was the spirits. Epi continued to train with me each day and I could defeat him with both physical and mental counter-attacks. Epi explained that each of Nememiah's Children had their own particular strengths. Some in the past would have had enhanced physical prowess, or magical abilities. All of Nememiah's Children could converse with the spirits within them, but my unique gift was to be able to summon them corporeally and have them do my bidding.

"Ah! Here it is," Epi announced triumphantly. He marched over to where I was still laying on the couch and handed me a book, pointing to a diagram in it. "This is it."

For the past week, I'd dealt with nightmares, although that was too weak a description for them. They were strange and distressing nighttime terrors. Every time I closed my eyes and slept, I was enmeshed in horrifying images. I'd seen Lucas, Ben and Striker, lying dead at my feet. Acenith and Rowena being murdered by the Council. I'd seen William and Holden being tortured and burnt with holy water, their skin melting away from their bones. Marianne and Gwynn had reached for me, their eyes crazed with agony as they were raped by a faceless monster, screaming for help. Ripley had chased me, driven insane by thirst, fangs dripping blood onto his crisp white shirt as he tore open my throat. I'd seen Katie being murdered by the Drâghici, her tiny body shriveling as they drained her, tiny fingers reaching out in a desperate plea for help. With his eyes glowing blood red, Conal bore down upon me – half man, half werewolf, and his jaws dripping with blood. I'd had nightmares of endless armies of spirits, lined up with lifeless eyes, carrying weapons that gleamed silver, light glinting off their rotting faces. Intermingled through it all, a half-formed sigil kept appearing, something I didn't recognize. Each time I awoke, screaming and terrified, the sigil faded from my memory before I could completely recall it.

There was one other thing about the nightmares. Although it wasn't as terrifying as the other aspects, it was the most disturbing element. I kept seeing a man of similar age to me. His eyes were the same shade of green as mine, his skin coloring and features so identical it seemed as if we could be related. Every time he appeared, he would sprint towards me and his mouth opened in a huge yaw, swallowing me. This part haunted me more than anything else, if only because of the resemblance. Why did this complete stranger keep appearing and what did he have to do with the nightmares? Why did he look like a masculine version of me? I had no answers.

Epi had offered to prepare a sleeping draught, which he insisted would hold the nightmares at bay and allow uninterrupted sleep, but I kept refusing. I was convinced there were answers in the nightmares and I was resolute about analyzing them, no matter how difficult it proved to be.

I'd been trying to remember the sigil since the nightmares began. The spirits had proven less than helpful and when I grumbled, Epi said their purpose wasn't to guide me through this strange new life with any clarity. They could give direction and advice, but wouldn't always give me answers. It was up to me to discover the answers myself. Despite his advice, I needled the spirits, begging for help. How could I fight what I didn't know?

I gazed at the diagram Epi was showing me and I knew it was the same sigil I kept seeing in the nightmares. Where I'd only been able to draw the partial sigil, this one was complete.

"What is it?" I asked, tracing the outlines of the intricate loop and memorizing it.

"Purity," Epi responded. "But I don't understand why you are seeing it in your nightmares. Purity is not a sigil Nememiah's Children have ever used. They were already pure, through the blood running in their veins."

I shrugged unhappily, disappointment clear in the gesture. "I don't know, Epi. I wish I did." It was incredibly disheartening. I'd thought finally knowing the sigil's meaning would give me some insight, some knowledge of what was going on. Yet I was no closer to answers than I'd been before. This sigil meant something; I was convinced it wouldn't appear persistently if there weren't a reason for it. But I didn't have a damn clue as to what it was.

Until I did understand, I knew I couldn't do anything to save my friends. My nerves were on edge, the spirits had been urging me to travel to Romania and attempt a rescue from the very beginning. Epi and Conal were adamantly against any rescue attempt until we had all the information we could acquire. Epi insisted I just wasn't ready, maintaining it was imperative that every minute before I turned twenty-one be used to increase my skills. It was pissing me off, and it was definitely pissing Nick Lingard off. He rang every day, waiting for some news on what was happening, what we were doing. And every day I was fobbing him off. At least now, he knew the whole story, although I wasn't certain he'd believe it until he'd seen my abilities for himself.

Despite my terror about what was happening in Romania, I knew Epi and Conal were right. Whatever I was facing, it was more powerful than I'd faced yet. And I needed to have the full strength of the spirits behind me to fight it. With constant practice, I was growing stronger and more potent every day. Although it was frustrating as hell to be sitting around on our hands, I knew the spirits would tell me if anything happened, would give me warning if they were going to be killed. I knew from the spirits they were being held by the Vampire Council in Romania, at their castle near a city called Sfantu Drâghici. One of the oldest cities in Transylvania, it had been inhabited since 1332. Laying on the Olt River, in a valley between the Barolt and Bodoc Mountains, the Drâghici Vampires, who had merged themselves together as both a Kiss and the Council inhabited a stronghold high in the mountains, overlooking the city. Who would have thought? Vampires actually living in Transylvania. If I hadn't been so horrified, it would've been funny.

I cringed inwardly as I thought again, about what was being done to my friends. The spirits, whilst not exactly helpful in whatever quest I happened to be facing, were unpleasantly vocal about how my friends were being tortured. I knew they were being given no blood, no sustenance and as time went by; their abilities were deteriorating, their strength leaving them. There were ominous warning of what was being done to them, but I knew I had no choice – I had to wait. I needed answers before I could rescue them.

My emotions were being ripped apart. I knew they desperately needed help, but I had to accept what Epi and Conal insisted was true – that we needed more information, before I could march over to Europe and rescue them. Epi assured me he would get me there and I had to trust him. It wasn't as if I could just head out to the airport and book a flight – I had no legal means of travelling. I often wondered if I was putting too much faith in those around me, but what else could I do?

My cell phone rang and I reached into the pocket of my shorts to grab it. "Hello?"

"It's Conal. I'm outside, unlock the door."

I launched off the couch and ran to the heavy doors, throwing off the locks and wrenching them open. Conal stood in the doorway, heavy shadows circling his eyes, but he looked better than when I'd last seen him. I wanted to throw myself into his arms and hug him, but I hesitated uncomfortably. Our relationship had reverted to pleasant cordiality since his father died.

He opened his arms to me, apparently reading the indecision in the expression on my face. "Don't I get a hug?"

I put my arms around him awkwardly and released him just as quickly. "Is everything okay?"

"Yeah, but I haven't found the bastard who's leaking information." He stepped past me and greeted Epi, while I shut and locked the heavy doors. "Everything okay here?"

"We're fine. Epi tells me *now* that he put enchantments on the church and your apartment. Apparently all the worry about whether I was safe or not was for nothing."

"You didn't ask," Epi retorted.

"What sort of enchantments?" Conal slumped onto the couch, resting his arms along the back of the headrest.

I explained what Epi had done and Conal rubbed his chin thoughtfully. "Not bad, old man."

"Thank you for that rousing endorsement," Epi sniffed.

"Are the pack safe?" I questioned. I sat on the floor near Conal, unnerved by the thought of sitting beside him. What was wrong with me? Yes, we had declared anything between us over, but I was wrangling with a discomfort I'd never felt around him before.

"Yeah. We have a place in the mountains; there are caves up there. The pack will hide out for now." He frowned heavily. "Ralph Torres heard we weren't the only ones attacked last week. There were at least two other groups who were hit. Maybe more."

It was my turn to frown. "I don't understand. If they're after me, what use is there in attacking others? They have nothing to do with this."

Conal sighed. "I don't understand it either. But I think I'd feel better if we had more backup down here, to keep an eye on you. Do you think Nick Lingard would come down?"

"He's flying in tomorrow morning," I reported quietly. I hadn't been able to hold him off any longer. He was bringing some of his men with him and little Katie. While she had nothing to offer the vampires in the way of abilities, I wouldn't put it past them to kidnap her, as another way of forcing my hand. I'd told Nick I would feel better if she was here and now that I'd learned of Epi's enchantments, I was certain it had been the right decision.

"Do you think you should contact your dad and warn him?" Conal knew I'd been keeping in contact with my father, using the iPad to send emails back and forth. Our correspondence was regular and we'd been getting to know one another, in fact, he'd been suggesting we meet, something that in light of my current situation, I was trying desperately to avoid.

"And tell him what? That I'm involved with vampires, werewolves, shape shifters and a warlock and oh, by the way, I'm an Angel? I don't think so," I responded with a wry grin.

"Whilst I can see how it would be difficult to explain, he and his family could be in danger," Epi said, surprising me by agreeing with Conal.

"There's no way of explaining," I waved my hand around the room, "all *this* to him and not coming across as a complete lunatic."

"You told me the guy's an ex-marine," Conal said. "He's probably seen some freaky stuff in his time."

"I'm pretty sure he's never met a werewolf. Or a warlock," I stated with certainty. "Look, I'll think about it, okay? Maybe I could talk to Mom, ask her specifically to keep an eye out for him – warn me if anything untoward happens. Is that good enough?"

Conal nodded his agreement. "Okay. For right now though, I'm taking you back to the apartment. You look like hell."

"You'll be back in the morning for more training?" Epi pressed.

Conal groaned as he unlocked the doors. "Naturally. Nothing I like better than starting the morning by getting the crap beaten out of me and smelling as if I've rolled in a corpse. See you, old man."

Chapter 35

A Light Bulb Moment

I lay in Conal's bedroom, the crumpled sheets testimony to the sleeplessness I suffered. I'd been laying here for hours, tossing and turning, unable to quieten my mind enough to doze off.

The drive from Epi's had been painful and I knew it wasn't only affecting me – Conal had been distracted, as awkward as I'd been. We arrived back at the apartment and Conal ordered Chinese take-away for dinner, which we'd eaten in silence.

After dinner, he'd announced he was going to bed, leaving me alone in the living room, staring after him with tears welling in my eyes. I heard the door to the second bedroom shut firmly behind him and dragged myself to the bedroom we'd shared until now. I knew Conal was doing what he needed to do and I'd never given him what he wanted, but I missed him. I missed his closeness, the comfort and security of having him holding me in his arms.

I rolled onto my side, staring at the Hjördis, which was lying by the side of the bed. Maybe I should have stayed at Epi's place. Conal had made it clear he was as uncomfortable having me around, as I was with him. Now he'd decided with certainty what he needed to do, it seemed like a chasm had developed between us. Having me here was a constant reminder of what he couldn't have. A rush of grief swelled in my chest as I realized I'd wanted it too. I loved Lucas, but – and it pained me to admit it - I loved Conal too. Both men were intertwined within my heart and causing me additional pain. Maybe I should swear off men altogether. *Not men, you idiot*, I reminded myself ruefully. *Maybe you should swear off vampires and werewolves.*

Shaking my head, I forced myself to return to more pressing problems. How could we get into the vampires' stronghold, retrieve everyone and get out alive? Nick was inclined towards battling our way in and out, but he was thinking as an enthusiastic fighter. Epi insisted we needed to use stealth and my abilities. I hadn't even tried talking to Conal about what we should do. And I still had that same, unsettling feeling. There was something, which remained elusive – just out of reach in my mind. The vampires had a definite plan, something set in motion months ago. I ran over the events in my life since last October, probing them thoughtfully, trying to pick up a pattern, anything that might give me a clue.

I fell into a restless sleep sometime around 2am, but my mind filled with more horrifyingly graphic imagery. Lucas calling to me, silver chains wrapped around his torso, burning into his skin as his expression filled with agony. Marianne, asking me why I hadn't warned them of the impending danger, her voice melancholy and accusatory. Striker screaming, his mind destroyed by a thirst for blood which wasn't sated. Rowena pleading for the lives of her family, for that's what she considered them, her skin chalk white and almost paper thin, her eyes filled with terror as she watched Ben being tortured. Striker's skin sizzling as holy water was trickled onto his naked torso, burning him like sulfuric acid and the distress in his eyes as he gritted his teeth against insurmountable suffering. The faces of the werewolf pack, their eyes empty sockets as they stepped closer, growling and snarling. Conal being bitten by one of the vampire

Council, his eyes filled with hatred as he watched me standing alone and doing nothing to help – and the sigil, the half-finished purity sigil which I knew wasn't going to help. Interspersed through the nightmare, appearing intermittently, almost as a dream within the nightmare was the man with similarities to myself, with dark curls and fair skin...

"Charlotte. *Charlotte*! Sugar, it's a nightmare. C'mon sweetheart, wake up..." My eyes snapped open and I found Conal crouched over the bed, his arms wrapped around my body and holding me tightly against him as I screamed.

"Conal!" I inhaled a shuddering breath and clung to him as though I'd never let go. I struggled to take back control, taking deep breaths until the nightmare began to fade. Squeezing my eyes shut, I tried to expunge what I'd seen from my memory. It couldn't be real, my mind was playing tricks based on the myths I'd heard about vampires. "I didn't think you'd come," I admitted quietly when I'd calmed enough to speak coherently.

Conal took a moment to speak and when he did, his voice was hushed. "Call me a masochist."

"I'm so sorry."

"For what? For not being a werewolf? For not loving me?" He loosened his hold, settling into the bed with his back against the pillows before he drew me into his arms, nestled me against his chest. "You can't help who you love." He brushed the tears from my cheeks with his thumb. "I can't help loving you. It doesn't matter what I tell myself, how much I try to deny it – that's the truth. I don't want to be with anyone else but you. Hell, I don't want to *think* about anyone else but you."

I needed to be honest with him. "I know it's no consolation, but I do love you, Conal. I wish I could love you enough to forget Lucas. But I *can't*. I don't want to have regrets over this. I don't want you to get the wrong impression, and I don't want to hurt you. I want to have you in my life always. I know that's selfish and I'll understand if you don't want the same thing, when you know I'm still in love with Lucas. I've tried to convince myself that I can forget about him, but it just isn't happening."

Conal's black eyes were solemn, dark pools in the soft glow of the lamp. "You will always be in my life. I'm happy for this not to go any further, if it means I keep you in my life. You need time to sort out your feelings. Don't be sorry, Sugar. Just go to sleep. You need your rest."

I closed my eyes tiredly. "You don't have to stay, Conal. Go back to your bed."

"Yeah, I do need to stay. Because if I'm here with you, the nightmares don't seem to be so bad." He winked. "To be honest, I've kind of gotten used to sleeping beside you." He kissed my forehead softly and burrowed down in the bed, adjusting my position until I was lying against his side. "Go to sleep, Sugar."

Snuggling against him, I listened to his steady breathing and felt the stress dissipating from my body. My eyes drifted shut and I relaxed against him, falling deeply into a sound sleep.

≈†◊◊†◊◊†◊◊†≈

When I woke the following morning, I was still encircled by Conal's strong arms. I rolled over so I could look at him and smiled. His handsome features were softened by sleep and he breathed deeply and evenly.

I yawned and stretched, squirming away from Conal, thinking that some breakfast might be in order. Conal sensed the movement and drew me tighter against him.

"Good morning," he murmured sleepily. "Where are you going?"

"Breakfast. Want some?"

Conal blinked in the bright sunlight. "Yeah. Then I supposed we'd better go and get our butts whipped with Epi again. That should be delightful."

I giggled. "Hopefully the aching muscles, the bruises – they'll all be worth it."

"I guess so, but I'm probably going to get my ass kicked by the leech when he discovers I've been sharing your bed for the past month or so. Platonically or not."

"Lucas will understand," I stated confidently. "He's over one hundred and fifty years old. He's pretty mature about stuff."

Conal looked at me incredulously, one eyebrow raised. "You think so? I'm not so certain. I've seen the way he looks at you. The same way I look at you, in fact. Except somehow, my lustful thoughts seem like they're more impure—"

It felt like one of those cartoon moments, the ones where the light bulb appears over a character's head when they get a brilliant idea. I shook Conal off, sitting up in the bed and staring down at him in astonishment. "What did you say?"

Conal drew himself onto his side, looking at me curiously. "What?"

"Just then – what did you say?"

"I said that I felt like lusting after you was impure—"

"Oh, my, God." I felt like smacking myself over the head and almost did. My mind worked at a dizzying pace and I swiftly realized what I'd been missing. I launched out of bed, hurrying towards the door.

"What's wrong? Charlotte!" Conal pulled the covers from his body and stood up quickly.

"Impurities! Impure thoughts! That's why I keep getting that sigil in my head, over and over again!" I ran from the bedroom and down the hallway, shuffling through the piles of paper Conal had stacked on the breakfast bar.

"What are you looking for?" Conal caught my hand, looking concerned when he caught the flush in my cheeks and the wild look in my eyes. "Calm down, Charlotte."

I took a deep breath. "Where's that list of people who were killed and injured last week?"

Conal rifled through the paperwork, while I grabbed a highlighter from his bureau. "Here it is."

I handed him the highlighter. "Check the list of who was killed. Mark the ones who weren't pure-blooded."

Conal stared down at me for a few seconds; his expression measured, and then shifted his focus to the paper. The highlighter hovered over the paper while he ran down the list. He looked up and I could see what I suspected was true. Anger was evident as the same misgiving occurred to him. "The majority of the dead are half-bloods. Probably more than ninety percent."

"How can you be so sure?"

Conal grimaced, tapping the edge of the bench with the pen. "I know my pack. All pureblood werewolves traditionally receive a name that means wolf. Conal means wolf, Kenyon means wolf. I recognize the names."

I shut my eyes, pressing my forefinger and thumb to the bridge of my nose as I clarified what I'd figured out. "The vampire council is planning an ethnic cleansing," I muttered.

"What?" Conal sounded startled.

My green eyes flashed with anger as the enormity of what I'd began to understand sunk in. "Ethnic cleansing. Lucas told me the Drâghici Kiss; the council, believe themselves to be the equivalent of a vampire government. What if they also think they're superior to other supernatural beings? I'm thinking they know they can't kill all of you, but they can't, or won't accept half-breeds."

"You think they're going to kill anyone who isn't pure-blooded?"

I paced from the bench to the couch and back again, trying to absorb what I'd discovered. I was certain I understood their plan now, what they intended on doing. The purity sigil had been the key. "I'm assuming that like many races in the world, they don't want to tolerate other racial groups, for want of a better word.

For whatever reason, they're culling the people that don't meet their ideals of perfection."

"Like creating a master race?"

"Possibly."

Conal leaned against the bench, crossing his arms over his naked chest, his expression thoughtful. "Mixed blood creates weaknesses in our people."

I lifted my head to stare at him. "How so?"

Conal shrugged. "Some of them can't shift completely; others take a long time to recover when they revert. The mixed blood makes them weaker, not as swift."

"Would the vampires know that?"

Conal thought quietly for a minute. "It's likely," he admitted.

"What percentage of an average pack would have mixed blood heritage?"

"Probably sixty percent." Conal saw my eyebrows rise in surprise and continued. "Charlotte, I've told you how difficult it is to carry a cub to term. Miscarriage rates are high and for werewolf females, the rate is even higher. Most of them can't carry a pregnancy to term."

"Why?"

Conal shrugged. "I know we've discovered that we can shift at will, not just full moon. But we *have* to change at the full moon, there's no option."

I began to understand where he was going with this conversation. "When the females change into their wolf shape..."

"The cub can't survive the shift, Charlotte. We have to sedate the mothers when they're pregnant to try and overcome the need to shift at every full moon during their pregnancy. Sometimes it's successful and they stay in human form. Most of the time it isn't successful and they lose the cub. We have more success with mixed heritage relationships, where both parents have mixed blood. The relationships where the female is human and the male is werewolf are more successful, too."

"So if they kill off all the people who have mixed blood..."

"...they decimate my pack."

"And every other pack that they attack." I tapped my fingers anxiously against the bench top. "I think that's their plan. They're intending to kill everyone who has mixed blood and take control of what's left." I stopped tapping and stared at Conal. "They're going to start a war."

Conal rubbed a hand over his stubbled jaw. "How do Nememiah's Children fit into this?"

"Epi said the Angel children were placed on earth to keep the peace between the supernatural groups."

Conal shook his head. "Sounds great in theory, Charlotte. In case you haven't noticed, there's only one Nememiah's Child and that's you."

Another piece slipped into place. The man I'd been seeing in the nightmares, the one who looked so familiar. Was he something to do with Nememiah's Children? Or was he just a figment of an overwrought imagination?

I paced some more, calling on the spirits as I walked back and forth. I asked questions that I intuitively knew would be answered now. It seemed for each step of headway I made through the puzzle, the spirits would allow a little more information. I'd finally deduced the reasoning behind the vampire council attacking the werewolves, so the spirits were prepared to share a little more of their knowledge.

Conal stood patiently and watched me pace, waves of tension emanating from his body. When I stopped and turned to him, I could see the animal-like stillness in his body as he waited for me to speak.

"We need to go and see Epi."

Chapter 36

Another

Epi threw open the door after I'd banged on it continually for almost five minutes. He peered around the door from behind his round glasses, his eyes appearing much larger than they actually were. "You're late," he muttered mutinously. "And stop banging on my door like that."

I pushed impatiently at the door, nearly knocking Epi off his feet as Conal and I strode into the hushed church. "Epi, tell me about Angel reproduction again," I demanded.

"Pardon me?" Epi took his glasses from his bulbous nose, wiping them carefully on the faded grey tunic he wore. He replaced them, adjusting them on the bridge of his nose and stared at me intently. "You aren't thinking about having a child? Now?"

I shook my head, impatient with him. "Epi, this is important. You said that if I stay as I am until my birthday, I can't be changed – not into a werewolf or vampire."

"That's correct."

"You also said that no matter whom I'm… with, the baby will always take after me, it will have Angel blood. Is that right?"

"Yes, of course." Epi glanced from my face, with my flushed cheeks and bright eyes to Conal, who was looking thunderous. "What is this about?"

I crossed my arms and looked at the tiny old man, wondering if he had the answers I sought. Speculating if I could possibly be right. "How many Nememiah's Children are there?"

"Only you."

"Are you positive?" I stared at him, willing him to think carefully about what he knew.

"Well, yes." He scratched the top of his head thoughtfully. "I should think so. I haven't heard about any others, it took years to discover you and even then, it was completely astounding." He returned my stare, his gaze becoming shrewd. "Where are you headed with this, child?"

"What if there were two?" I questioned. "A girl... and a boy."

Epi rubbed his chin thoughtfully, blue eyes darting back and forth over the stone floor as he considered. "Well, that would only happen if the world faced an apocalyptic event, I should imagine. Nememiah's Children were first created from one male and one female. They mated and produced the first true bloods of the Angels... *oh*... oh dear. I see where you are headed with this line of thought... yes, yes indeed..." He turned and ran towards his bookcases, climbing the tall, rolling ladder he reached towards the uppermost shelves, muttering under his breath and retrieving books before sliding down the ladder in a rush. He dumped the pile of books he'd collected on the table and began to rifle through them, muttering under his breath all the while. "Here! Here it is!" He read an excerpt from one of the books he'd collected. "...and Nememiah created the man Angel and the woman Angel, and they begat a race of powerful Angel progeny, who would protect the earth and rule those upon it, both man and underworlders..."

Dizziness swamped me in a wave and I swayed a little. Conal caught my arm and pulled me against him, wrapping his other arm around my shoulders. "Steady, Sugar."

"Epi." Comprehension and dread filled my mind in equal parts. "I'm not a descendant of Nememiah's Children, am I? I'm the *new* beginning of Nememiah's Children."

"We can't be certain of that," Epi warned. "You may still be a descendant of the originals."

"But to create a new race of Angel children..."

"...you would need a male and a female," Conal finished the sentence.

"But there is only you, child," Epi protested, his eyes wide.

"What if there isn't? What if there is a man and a woman? What would happen if the Drâghici Vampire Council captured two Nememiah's Children – a man and a woman? And created them both as vampires?" I asked shakily.

"Goodness. Goodness gracious. I'm not sure. Let me think." Epi took to pacing across the floor, muttering to himself and using his index finger to make imaginary notes in the air in front of him. "Yes, I think that would be right, though it's hard to be certain... it would be an unprecedented event—" He stopped pacing and turned back to us. "Vampires cannot procreate. Every new vampire is created by the bite of another. But the mixture of Angel blood and vampire blood, whilst it is hard to be entirely certain – I'm only surmising the possibilities – it may be that they could procreate; the Angel blood being the stronger of the two."

"And the children would have Angel blood and vampire blood," I whispered, doing some mental calculations of my own. "Which is technically demon blood."

"So the offspring would be able to call the spirits," Conal added, "because they have Angel blood—"

"Not just any spirits," Epi interrupted, his face considerably paler than it had been a few minutes before. "Charlotte hears and contacts, for lack of a better phrase, the 'good' spirits. The bright spirits. She has no contact with demon spirits because she is human. If she was to be bitten and created into vampire, if there is a second of Nememiah's Children and he was also created..." He grew even paler. "They and any offspring they produce would have the ability to call the demon spirits forth whenever they wanted to. They could amass a force so formidable; nothing like it has been seen in our time."

"That's what the vampires want," I stated with conviction. "To gain absolute control over not only vampires, but warlocks, shape shifters," I glanced at Conal, seeing the tension in his shoulders. "And werewolves."

"And faeries," Epi added.

I gaped at him incredulously. "Faeries?"

"Of course. The Fey folk are part of the earth, too," Epi stated matter-of-factly. "They tend to be secretive and don't mix with others."

Conal squeezed my arm softly. "Guess you hadn't heard about them?"

"Uh, no." In recent weeks, I hadn't thought anything could surprise me. After everything I'd seen and heard, I'd thought I was unshakeable. But faeries? "Are they like the storybooks? Tiny, wings, pointed ears?"

"Nuh. More like our height, nasty temperaments, vicious fighters," Conal responded with a smirk. "They do have pointed ears, though."

I turned back to the matter at hand, pushing the idea of faeries away, to be thought about later. If there was a later, I reminded myself morosely. The more information I gleaned about our situation, the worse it seemed. The thought of what the Drâghici Council intended to do was inconceivable. It made perfect sense though, explaining the attacks on the werewolves, the kidnapping of Lucas and the others. The Drâghici Council was using them as bait. They must be banking on a rescue attempt being made and assumed I would be involved with it. Once I was there— the thought made me tremble and I was chilled all the way to my bones. The thing I feared the most was now a distinct possibility – if they got hold of me, there was no doubt they would create me as vampire. And wanted me to mate with this other Angel. I promised myself that it would never happen. I would rather die first.

"Why do you think there might be a male Angel child?" Epi asked curiously, drawing me from my silent deliberations.

"I'm sure I've seen him," I stated bleakly. "He keeps appearing in my nightmares." I looked from Conal to Epi. "He's already been created as vampire."

Epi walked slowly to the couch and sunk onto it, holding his head in his hands. Conal held me closer to his chest, his hands soothing against my back. "Are you sure?" he began doubtfully. "You've said so yourself, the nightmares contain elements of reality and imagination."

"I can't tell you how I know, but I *know*, Conal," I insisted firmly.

"She may be right," Epi agreed. "The decision of the Drâghici Council to take control of all supernatural creatures would be the type of catastrophic event which could cause the creation of two Angel children." He dragged himself to his feet, returning to the book he'd been reading from and it looked as if he'd aged a thousand years in the past few minutes. "Nememiah's Children were originally created to procreate and produce progeny who would in turn procreate and create other Angel Children to protect the world from danger." He turned the page, reading more before he continued. "It would appear that Charlotte was predestined to meet the man, fall in love, and create Angel children. For some reason, unknown to us, it has not happened. The course of history has been circumvented in some manner, to veer them off on entirely different paths."

"And the bloodsuckers have gotten hold of this male Angel," Conal surmised.

"Yes," Epi agreed worriedly. "It would appear so. This is bad. Very bad."

"Well," I announced with a conviction I didn't feel. "We're just going to have to turn it around."

Chapter 37

Reinforcements

Nick was sitting on the couch, dressed casually in black jeans and a blue t-shirt, the only sign of his emotions was in the coldness of his grey eyes. He'd arrived a couple of hours ago, along with Rafe, Marco and Katie. Nonny had taken the little girl out into the grounds behind the church and was helping her to draw using provisions Epi had magically created.

We'd discussed everything we knew so far, bringing the men up to speed and on Nick's insistence, giving him the opportunity to see how far my powers had progressed since I left Montana. He seemed to have gotten over blaming me for the kidnapping, although certainly he was cooler than he'd been before I left Montana. I couldn't blame him, Lucas was his friend and I'd abandoned Lucas – it was hardly surprising that Nick had taken his side.

"So let me get this straight," Nick announced when I took a break from explanations. "The vamps already have one Angel, who's been created to vampire?"

"Yep." I was sitting cross-legged on the floor, where I'd been perched since we began talking.

"And they want you, to complete their set?"

"Yes."

Nick sat forward on the couch, looking much older than his twenty-five years. "Then we go alone, Charlotte. I'm not taking the risk of you being captured and created. From what Epimetheus says, that would be a disaster."

"I've already told her that," Conal said seriously. He was standing behind the couch, leaning his hands on the back of the frame.

I felt like screaming and controlled the urge with difficulty. Why were men so awkward? Conal, Epi and I had argued this point for days, the two men trying to convince me it would be a bad idea for the only surviving pure Angel child to travel to Romania. I'd argued just as vehemently that I had no choice except to go. I repeated this argument to Nick, but from the stubborn look in his eyes, it was going to be an uphill battle. "If I don't go, they'll kill them. Everything they're planning hinges on me. If you turn up and attempt to rescue the Tines, they'll kill them the second they realize I'm not there."

Nick was shaking his head, even before I'd finished speaking. "You've got no fighting experience, Charlotte. You'll be more of a hindrance than a help and I'd rather not have to worry about protecting your ass."

I bristled angrily. "You've just seen me fight!"

"In controlled conditions, sure. Some of it was even impressive. But I'm not risking myself or my people on you, not when—" he trailed off, rubbing a hand across the scar on his cheek.

"Not when *what*?" I questioned coldly.

"Nothin'," Nick muttered.

I got to my feet and from my peripheral vision; I saw Marco and Rafe exchange a glance. Marco's eyes widened and Rafe shook his head imperceptibly. I didn't know what the look meant, but Rafe stood up. He was six feet five inches tall, powerfully and leanly muscled and moved like a sleek cat, which was a clue to his shape shifted form of lion, the only one in Nick's pack. With startling blue eyes and shaggy dark blonde hair, he was dressed in black – black jeans, a black singlet and wearing a black leather jacket over the top, sunglasses pushed back on his head. He looked every inch the bodyguard, a job he'd worked at since he left home at seventeen.

As Rafe drew himself up, Conal straightened and pushed away from the couch. The air suddenly seemed a little harder to breathe, as they both flexed their supernatural clout at one another and the feeling only increased when Nick growled low in his throat.

"Enough, gentlemen!" Epi announced loudly. "There is no room here for egos or competition."

"Tell that to the Were," Rafe growled.

"You stood up first," Conal retorted.

For a tense moment, the two men glared at one another, but it was Nick who spoke. "Rafe." His voice was quiet, but firm and Rafe glanced at him. As I watched, the tension slipped from Rafe's shoulders and he settled back onto the chair.

Conal's energy dissipated as rapidly as it had appeared and he glanced at me, his expression giving nothing away. This left me still seething, and looking for a fight. I knew Rafe had intended to protect Nick, Conal had intended on protecting me, but I was still angry with Nick. I turned back to him and crossed my arms over my chest. "Say what you mean, Nick. Let's get it out of the way now, before I send you and your men back to Montana."

Nick's gaze was measured as he looked up at me. "I'm not going back without rescuing them."

"Well I don't need you here."

Nick stood up, using his extra height to glare down at me. I stood my ground, giving him just as good a stare as he was giving me. He flickered some of his own considerable power over my skin, making the hairs on my arms stand on end, but I wasn't backing down.

"I have to go, Nick. Whether you like me or hate me, I don't really give a damn, but I'm going to Romania. You either work with me, or you can go to hell."

His lip curled into a snarl which was more wolf than human; his eyes darkening to a stormy gray. "You're a stubborn bitch."

"Thanks."

For a few more tension-filled seconds, he continued to glare at me, but then he inhaled sharply, letting the breath leave his lips in a huff. He inclined his head towards the door. "Let's you and I go for a walk."

"Nick—" Rafe began.

"Stay here," Nick ordered. "Charlotte's right. We need to clear the air and get some things sorted out."

Now it was Conal's turn to protest. "Charlotte, I'm not letting him be with you alone."

I laid a hand on his shoulder. "I'll be fine, Conal."

The muscle in his jaw tightened, his black eyes hard. "Half an hour, Charlotte. Then I'm coming after you."

"I'll look after her, Were."

"That's debatable," Conal muttered.

"Shut up, both of you," I grumbled. I headed towards the door, leaving Nick to follow in my wake. "Are you coming, or not?"

He'd caught up by the time I reached the heavy gate, pushing it open and stepping back to the side. "After you."

I strode through, feeling the heat of the day beating against my back. It was still sultry in Jackson and I wondered how Nick was coping with the difference in temperature and humidity to Montana. Like the werewolves, shape shifters ran at a higher temperature than humans did, but in his jeans and t-shirt, he didn't look hot.

We walked in silence for a few minutes and I took to counting the weeds, which spread up through the cracks in the sidewalk. Fighting for life in such difficult conditions, yet they stood tall and straight in the shimmering heat, seemingly capable of surviving the furnace-like conditions. I wasn't going to be the one to break the silence between us, although I could feel the tension emanating from Nick's body – he'd started this and he could continue it.

"You nearly destroyed Lucas."

Out of all the things I'd expected him to say, his opening volley nearly dropped me to my knees. I was aware, so very aware of how badly Lucas would have been hurting after I left – I had felt a comparable pain. Hearing Nick say it openly just rubbed salt into the still-open wounds.

Nick stopped walking, his eyes flickering over my face and his gray eyes softened, making him look younger. "I'm sorry. That was harsh."

I inhaled heavily, chewing on my upper lip. "But true."

"Why'd you do it, Charlotte?"

I turned on him, abruptly angry and defensive. "Did you *see* what I did to him? To Holden?"

Nick shrugged, hooking his fingers in the pockets of his jeans. "They healed, Charlotte. They've vamps."

I shook my head. "I was frightened, Nick. Frightened of what I'd done and how I'd done it." I turned and kept walking down the sidewalk, not really caring if he followed or not. What was I supposed to say? How could I explain how terrified I'd been of the power, what it might do if I let it loose again?

"So you were frightened, I get that," Nick announced, catching up with me and matching his stride to my own. "But you dumped Lucas like a hot potato, Charlotte. He's my friend. You've gotta understand how pissed that made me, to see him like that."

"Like what?" I didn't want to know, but couldn't help myself but to ask.

"Depressed, lonely. Turning in on himself. Like he wanted to die, but couldn't."

Tears burned in my eyes and I turned to him. "I did what I thought was best, Nick. I know Lucas is your friend, but whether we broke up or not is really none of your business. If you're going to hold it against me, we can't work together."

Nick caught my arm, stopped me from walking away from him. "I blame you for the Drâghici taking them."

"So do I, Nick. So do I." I wrenched my arm out of his grip and started walking again, tears running slowly down my cheeks. What a mess I'd made of things, by being chicken and not wanting to speak to Lucas or the others, I'd put them smack bang in the middle of something which didn't involve them, placed them in danger they couldn't have foreseen. Had Marianne had a vision of the Drâghici coming for them? Or had she been misfiring? Had there been any warning? Did they know why they'd been taken, that it was my fault? I just didn't know and Nick had opened up that can of worms now. Guilt was eating away at me, gnawing at my heart and mind.

Nick caught hold of my arm for a second time and this time I fought him, pushing and punching and clawing at his arms until he caught me up in a bear hug, holding me hard against his chest. I sobbed then, the buildup of emotions too much to deal with. I'd been tense before Nick's arrival – and now with his disapproval obvious, I couldn't hold myself together.

To my surprise, Nick brushed his hand across the back of my head, the action soothing and gentle. "I'm sorry, Charlotte. Shit, I'm sorry. You know I don't trust easily, I told you I'm suspicious of everyone. I was just getting to know you, to trust you, when you ran out on Lucas. It made me doubt you and I blamed you for Lucas's unhappiness. Hell, the whole Kiss's unhappiness. None of them was the same after you left. Marianne told me it was because you'd provided them with light and joy and when you left, those emotions left with you. None of it made much sense to me, but I'm not a vamp."

I drew back from him, brushing the tears away from my cheeks. "It's the Angel blood."

Nick frowned. "What?"

"The angel blood. It makes people care for me, want to protect me. Epi says anyone who doesn't mean me harm will be affected by what I am."

He still had his arms around my waist and for a long moment, his focus was on the distance, further down the street as he thought. "That explains a lot," he finally said.

"Explains what?"

He smirked. "Despite how pissed I am with you, I still want to protect you, Charlotte. Keep you away from danger. All my people who've met you – every one of them wanted to come down here and help you. I've been arguing with Jerome for most of the past week, he nearly attacked me when he heard me on the phone with you that first day. Told me you were like a daughter to him and he would clean my clock if I spoke to you like that again. Not something you generally do to the Pack Leader and survive."

"See? You don't really like me. I knew that. It's the angel blood, messing with your head."

Nick chuckled. "I didn't say I didn't like you, Charlotte. I'm angry with you, sure. But you treated me with respect, didn't put up with my shit and I have to admit, not many people give me a second chance. You did."

"It doesn't change anything. They were taken because I didn't warn them when I should have."

"Why didn't you tell them?"

"Because I'd caused them enough trouble. I honestly didn't know who was after me. Epi had put it all together, knew someone was after me, but we had no idea who. It only came together when the attacks happened."

Nick released my arms and let me stand on my own again. "Didn't the spirits warn you? I thought they talked to you all the time."

"Not necessarily to tell me anything useful. They have some sort of rules governing what and when they can tell me stuff."

"Who controls them? This Nememiah guy?"

I smiled weakly. "I have absolutely no idea."

Nick was thoughtful for a long time, gazing down the street with his hands back in his pockets. He was staring up at the sweet gums that lined the street, casting shade across the houses and road. "So you reckon you have to go with us? To Romania?"

I nodded.

"No choice?"

"That's what the spirits tell me."

Nick turned back to watching the sweet gums and I waited silently, watching him while he wrestled with the idea. Finally, he glanced down at me. "Alright. I'll believe you. But I'm warning you—"

"If I screw up, you'll never forgive me."

Nick shook his head. "Nope. If you screw up, I'll kill you."

"I'll keep that in mind."

Chapter 38

Traitor

There were a line of photographs on the table and I stared at each one, memorizing the faces. Now that Nick and I had come to an agreement, he was sharing what he'd learned through his sources. He had provided photographs of four members of the Drâghici Council but there were others, so secretive that no photos had been available. Even these photographs weren't clear, blurred as if they'd been taken by someone using a hidden camera.

Conal glanced up from staring at the photographs to look at Nick. "Someone took a risk, getting these." It was a statement, not a question and I saw Nick shrug.

"Not me. But I know someone, who knew someone who had them."

I got the impression that Nick had been involved with something illegal or underhanded to get the photos, but I wasn't going to argue about it. We needed them, needed any information we could get on our adversaries. Nick pointed to the first photo of a beautiful woman. "This is Qadesh."

She was a striking woman, petite with hair so blonde it looked white. Perfect makeup framed her beautiful hazel eyes and her lips were artfully made up into a brilliant scarlet pout. The photo was grainy, taken at night, but it was apparent she was a beautiful girl. She looked about my age, although I knew she was probably much, *much* older. The photo showed her face and upper body, dressed provocatively in a black dress which enhanced a buxom chest.

"What do we know about her?"

"Very little," Rafe answered. "She's tiny, less than five feet tall but like all the vampires, she's no doubt powerful. No idea how old she might be."

"What about powers?" Epi questioned.

Nick shrugged again, his gray eyes hard. "Haven't got any info."

"Who's this?" I pointed to the second photograph, which showed a man dressed elegantly in an expensive suit. The shirt, tie and jacket were immaculate, and it was the clearest photo of the four, clear enough to distinguish the gold and diamond tie pin. I wondered vaguely if it was real gold, real diamonds and decided immediately it would be. He looked like the type of man who liked the best of everything. He was classically handsome, his skin a darker pale, the color of milky coffee. There was a deep cleft in his chin and his chestnut brown hair was carefully styled around his features.

"Enlil. He's the youngest of the Council, chosen because his specific power is the ability to create small storms and mini tornadoes, to attack his enemies. He's young to have such power, but the Council loves that sort of thing," Nick explained. "He's Greek."

Rafe pointed to the next picture. "Bellona. She's apparently in charge of military strategy for the Drâghici. She's described as brilliant, bloodthirsty and ruthless."

She didn't look like any of the adjectives Rafe had used. The photo showed a dark skinned woman, with shining black hair pulled into a tight braid. Her lips were a little too full, her nose a little too wide to make her classically pretty, but she was certainly striking. Unlike Qadesh, Bellona appeared to use clothing to hide herself, rather than display her body. The photo was taken from a distance and she was wearing a severe black jacket and trousers, almost masculine in style.

"Do we know what powers she holds?" Epi asked.

"If the rumors are true, she can fly," Nick replied.

I stared at him, my eyes wide. "Excuse me?"

Epi spoke. "She must be very old. Only very few vampires have the ability to fly and it is a power which only appears when they are well over two thousand years old."

"Lucas told me vampires couldn't fly," I stated and cringed when mentioning his name caused the same sharp pain in my chest. I wondered if I would ever be able to voice his name without it hurting, or if it would always be this way.

"Lucas was wrong," Epi announced matter-of-factly. "Of perhaps, he's never met one who could."

Nick turned back to the photos and pointed to the last one. "This is one of the Consiliului, but we don't have any information on him. Not even his name, at this stage."

The photograph showed a man who was muscular and well-built, his hair short and curly, his eyes icy blue. He was wearing a white t-shirt, a well-worn leather jacket over the t-shirt. The photo had been taken in a street somewhere, and even though it wasn't a clear photo, his eyes were frightening. Filled with anger and something else. Although I couldn't tell what it was, it was an emotion which was dark and dangerous. I shivered a little as I stared at the photo then glanced up to Nick. "He looks dangerous."

"Shit, Charlotte, they all look dangerous," Nick responded quietly. "They *are* all dangerous." His eyes searched mine for a long moment. "You still wanna go in there?"

I nodded firmly. "I have to go."

"You should talk to the spirits, child. See if they can give us more information."

I nodded. "I'm going to."

Epi gathered up the photographs into a neat pile on the table. "I think we have learned all we can for now regarding the Consiliului. Nick, I assume if more information comes to light, you will inform us?"

Nick slumped down onto the couch, his long legs spread out before him. "We'll do our best. Information isn't easy to come by, but hopefully we'll have more before we leave for Romania."

"What about this spy?" Rafe asked, looking at Conal. "Charlotte told us you believe someone in your Pack is spying for the Consiliului. Have you gotten any closer to knowing who it is?"

I stole a glance at Conal, his face had hardened at the mention of the spy, his mouth compressed into a thin line. I'd dreaded this subject, but knew it was going to have to come out into the open. "I know who it is," I announced quietly.

Conal's eyes were on me, I could sense them boring into my face. "You know? Why didn't you tell me?" he growled.

I sighed deeply. "Because I needed time to wade through the thought processes. Initially it was only a hunch, but I've been talking to the spirits, trying to confirm what I suspected."

Conal's eyes flashed angrily, a warning sign he was losing control of his temper. "Charlotte, for Christ's sake, if it's someone from my pack, I need to know about it! You should have told me what you knew!"

"This isn't easy, you know," I grumbled mutinously. "Not only do I have my own voice in my head, I have dozens, hundreds of others. I have to be certain before I jump to conclusions. There are lives at risk and I don't want to lose any more than we have to."

"You should have told me who you suspected."

"And what would you have done?" I demanded.

He stopped and thought for only a second. "Interrogated him."

"Using your power?" Conal had the ability to probe a person's mind to discover their thoughts, their history. He'd used it on me, but had worried it could kill me. It was incredibly painful and he'd killed others before when using the gift.

"Yeah," he growled.

"Which is why I didn't want to tell you until I was absolutely certain. I've been on the receiving end of your ability, Conal and I wouldn't wish it on anyone if I wasn't totally sure they were guilty."

"Who is it?" Conal snarled, his voice hard and his expression harder, contorted with barely concealed rage.

"Quinn Saunders."

Conal gaped, looking at me as though I'd lost my mind. "Quinn Saunders," he repeated blankly. "It can't be Quinn Saunders. He was one of my father's closest allies. He's been supportive of you!" He cursed, a flow of expletives flowing from his mouth as he stared at me angrily. "You're wrong. You must be wrong."

I brought my gaze up to meet his, wishing I didn't have to do this and knowing I had no choice. I pulled the list of dead and wounded from my purse and handed it to him. "You gave me the idea. You said that pure-blood werewolves all have names meaning wolf. Look at the list of the wounded. Go through the ones I treated and tell me I'm wrong."

Conal scowled, but snatched the page from me and began running through the list as I'd requested. When he reached the bottom of the page and looked up again, his black eyes were filled with rage. "They're all pure blood. Every last one of them."

"When you were with your mother and Nonny on the night of the attack, Kenyon came to me. I told him I'd try to help the wounded and he introduced me to Quinn Saunders. While I used the Hjördis to treat people's injuries, Quinn worked triage. He's a paramedic, so he was the obvious choice to work amongst the wounded, locate the most badly injured and let me know who to help. Quinn made the decisions that night. It was he who chose who could be helped."

Conal gripped the back of the couch, tearing his fingers through the heavy fabric. He was utterly motionless and I could see the gamut of emotions which crossed his face as he processed what I'd said. He dropped his head and his shoulders slumped dejectedly. "It doesn't make sense."

"I can't be sure, because the spirits don't exactly spell out the answers," I explained, my voice low. "Apparently part of being Nememiah's Child is that I get to stumble around in the dark until I figure out a lot of stuff for myself." I glanced around at the men sitting in the room; saw Rafe, Nick and Marco watching me intently. "I think Quinn Saunders has been working for the vampires. For how long, I can't say. He orchestrated the attack on the Pack on the orders of the Drâghici Council. I think they turned the other Angel much too early. They've known about me for a while, but they needed to give me time to learn as much as I could, before I turn twenty one and can't be created to vampire. I think Quinn's been feeding them information that he's learned from us, through his relationship with your Dad."

"But why attack his own pack?" Conal asked, his voice empty, devastation clear in his hard features.

"Because," I twirled the soda can I'd been drinking from around between my fingers, "he didn't know how powerful I'd become. He's never been here and with Epi's enchantments, he couldn't tell the Drâghici where I was. Who I was with. The attack on the pack was a way of drawing me out, allowing Quinn to see firsthand what I could do. Then he could report back to the Consiliului, allow them to know whether I was as far along as they want me before I'm created."

"But pureblood werewolves were killed," Nick pointed out. "I thought you said the Consiliului want purebloaded werewolves kept alive."

"Nick's right," Conal agreed. "Dad was pure blood."

"I'm not certain Quinn meant for that to happen, and I don't think the Drâghici actually care. They want rid of mixed bloods, but it won't worry them if the pureblood numbers are reduced. The pack was attacked by younglings, vampires who are under a year old. Ben told me during the first year, they're particularly dangerous, with no control over their actions. I don't think Quinn anticipated the Consiliului would send newborns. He probably didn't realize how far out of control it would get."

"I still don't get it," Marco said, shaking his head. He was only eighteen, and his sandy blonde hair hung over his eyes, making him seem even younger. In the months since I left Montana, he'd filled out, his shoulders broadening and it was noticeable he'd been working out. "Why would this Quinn want to align himself with the vamps?"

"A good question, young man," Epi announced and Marco looked delighted with the old man's praise. "Charlotte, while I'm sure you are right, I myself don't see why Quinn would do this."

"That question, I can't answer," I admitted. It was a question I'd asked the spirits any number of times, but on this they were silent. "They may have paid him an exorbitant amount of money. He may have strong feelings about the survival of the pack being reliant on purebloods. He may have something against halfblood werewolves. I don't know. All I do know is that he is the traitor."

"You're certain?" Epi questioned quietly.

I nodded unhappily. "To be positive, I searched amongst the spirits. There's no trace of any of Quinn's ancestors. Not one."

Traces of werewolf were apparent in Conal's features and I knew anger was drawing him close to an uncontrollable rage. "I will kill him, myself. Tonight," he announced through gritted teeth.

This was exactly what I'd been concerned about and I had to act quickly to diffuse Conal's rage before he stormed out and took revenge for his father. "Conal, as much as I understand how angry you are and how much you're hurting, we can't do that."

He looked right through me, his eyes pitch black, his brow furrowed with deep lines. To my intense relief, he didn't storm out, instead drawing a deep breath. "Why?"

"If you kill him now, the Drâghici will know we've discovered him. They'll kill Lucas and everyone else, thinking I won't come." I stood up lithely and slipped around the back of the couch, laying my hand on Conal's arm and trying to soothe him. "We need him, Conal. We need to keep feeding him information until we're ready to make our move. The only difference will be that the vampires hear what we want them to hear."

He stared down at my hand on his muscled forearm, thinking about what I'd said for a long time. I could feel the tendons in his arm, tensed and rock hard beneath the skin. "You're right," he finally said, and the tendons relaxed a little. "But he will die for this. I will have revenge in my father's name."

"You will," I promised.

Nonny appeared from the back of the Church, dressed in a bright yellow peasant skirt and a white boat-necked shirt, her hair plaited and laying against her back. She'd been reading to Katie, helping the young girl settle off to sleep after feeding her macaroni cheese for dinner. Conal had collected her when we knew Nick had brought Katie with him, suggesting she would be good with the little girl. Much to my delight she had been, taking the traumatized little girl under her wing and helping to settle her in this strange place. Nonny was a natural with Katie, helping her to feel comfortable in strange surroundings and making her feel a little more secure being surrounded by virtual strangers. My heart ached for her, knowing she was frightened and worrying about William and Gwynn. Not only them, but everyone else, the people she thought of as family.

Epi had grumbled a little about his home being turned into a refuge, but I'd noticed after Nick and I came back from our walk that the room he'd given Katie had been transformed into a beautiful bedroom for a little girl, with teddies, toys and a pretty coverlet on the bed.

"How is she?" I asked anxiously.

"She's sleeping now. I won't stay out here long, I think I should be with her in case she wakes up," Nonny said cheerfully.

"Thank you, Mrs. Tremaine," Nick said and it was easy to see he was relieved that Nonny had taken on babysitting Katie. He'd taken responsibility for the little girl, but it was obviously far out of his comfort zone to be responsible for a four year old child.

"Call me Nonny," Nonny said firmly. "Everybody does."

"Nonny," Nick repeated, with an uncertain smile. He glanced across at me and I could see the pain in his eyes. "I don't know what the hell I'm going to do if we don't get them back, Charlotte. What in Christ's name can I tell Katie, if her family gets killed?"

I put a reassuring hand on Nick's shoulder. "We'll get them back, Nick. We're going to bring them home."

Chapter 39

Plans

I was sitting on the carpet in Conal's apartment, cross-legged with my hands resting lightly on my knees. This meditative posture helped me to relax and speak to the spirits and as the days passed, I was spending more and more time like this, gleaning what information I could.

There was only a week left; seven days before I would turn twenty one and I was growing increasingly frustrated with our lack of progress. We'd made advancements with regards to fighting - Epi continued to train all of us daily, the demons he produced growing bigger, uglier and stronger. A small smiled flickered against my lips as I recalled the look on Nick, Rafe and Marco's faces when they'd first seen one - I imagined it was remarkably similar to the look on my face the first time Epi had subjected Conal and I to the Valafar. To give the Lingard men their due respect, they attacked with courage and tenacity and their ability to fight off attacks was increasing every day.

My nightmares continued unabated, the Tines were growing weaker and the spirits continued to reinforce my awareness of the fact during my waking hours. I knew they couldn't survive without blood and their ancestors had made it very clear that they were being starved to death by the Consiliului. Although the knowledge of their suffering was enough to encourage me to leave without delay, I knew in my heart that Epi's objections to us leaving immediately were valid.

The warlock insisted I should be as close to my birthday as possible, ensuring I would be stronger psychically than the other Angel child because I'd been allowed to mature. But his creation to vampire meant he would be physically stronger than me and he wouldn't be my only opponent. We had no idea how many vampires were ensconced in the Drâghici's stronghold and didn't know how many more they could marshal.

We were dealing with too many unknowns and it was causing our little group to become edgy and uncooperative with one another. Nick and his men wanted to leave at once, they were spoiling for a fight and wanted to battle the Consiliului head on. Conal was insisting on taking as many of his pack with him as we could, believing that numbers equaled strength. Epi was calling for calm, doing his utmost to stop us from losing focus on the task at hand.

And I was feeling distanced, certain that once again, there was something I was missing. If we arrived in Sfantu Drâghici and launched a full-frontal assault, the Consiliului would have the Tines killed immediately. I was convinced they would have taken precautions against an attack in large numbers and would have enough people in their retinue to defend themselves.

And we couldn't take huge numbers with us, because I didn't know how we were going to get there. Epi assured me he would get us there, but he hadn't divulged how he was going to do it. I didn't imagine it was going to involve a plane. Each time I questioned Epi about our travel plans, he refused to discuss it, insisting we should concentrate on preparation and worry about travel plans later.

While Nick had only brought two pack members with him, Conal's pack was larger and close at hand - Conal had been horrified when I insisted on only three of them training with us. Conal, Ralph Torres and much to Conal's amazement I'd chosen Phelan Walker. Although he and I had suffered a stormy relationship since we met, I knew he was the right one for the group.

Conal had argued vehemently over only allowing three of his pack to train with us, but I'd insisted on three as the maximum. I knew that historically, shifters and werewolves didn't get along together. It seemed wise to keep the numbers of Nick and Conal's men even, to ensure we didn't run into any problems between the two groups. So far it seemed to be working, Conal and Nick were getting along fine and with the constant reliance on one another whilst training with the demons, the other four men were developing a healthy respect for one another. In the past few days though, there'd been increasing issues as everyone became more tense about our foray into Romania.

I knew numbers wasn't the answer to the dilemma. I didn't know why, but it wasn't going to be the amount of people we took with us, it was going to be something else.

We continued to feed Quinn information, albeit incorrect information, to pass on to the Drâghici Consiliului. Conal had an innate ability for allowing Quinn to believe he was important and doing something useful for the pack, when in fact, he was being led in ever-increasing circles.

I heard a key turn in the lock and released my meditative posture, stretching my legs out in front of me as Conal strode in. "Hi."

He was filthy, covered in sweat and demon blood, the putrid combination of excrement and rotting meat wafting around him. "Hi, yourself."

"I take it Epi kept you busy?"

"Yeah. You could say that." He dropped his keys on the bench and came to meet me in the middle of the living room. "How come the boys and I have to keep training and you don't? It hardly seems fair, given you're the Angel," he grumbled, though there was distinct twinkle in his black eyes.

"I think Epi thinks my efforts need to be devoted to a more... spiritual level."

"Well we could have done with you being there," Conal admitted with a grimace.

"Why? What happened?"

Conal pushed his hair back from his face distractedly. "We can't kill the demons."

"What?" I raised my head to look at him sharply, alarmed by the statement. "What do you mean, you *can't* kill the demons?"

Conal's expression was serious, his black eyes filled with concern. "We can damage them, make them bleed, if that black shit can be called blood. Weaken them, I guess. But we can't complete the final blow to send them back to the Otherworld. Epi had to intervene and send them back himself."

I took a minute to process what he was saying, the realization of what it meant hitting like a physical blow. "It's because... oh, *shit*."

Conal finished the thought for me. "Epi believes they can only be killed by the weapons. The weapons that only you can use," he announced.

I breathed deeply, trying to rationalize what he was saying. Knowing it meant we had a massive problem. "Well, there's nothing we can do about it now," I finally announced. "We have to concentrate on rescuing the Tines and then we'll work out a solution." I managed a faint smile, trying to convey confidence I certainly didn't feel.

Conal raised an eyebrow. "The *Tines*?"

I shrugged sheepishly. "I can't figure out what to call them. They feel like family, but they're not really. I'm sick of saying Lucas... and the others. They're the Tine Kiss, so I guess I figure the Tines works on a group level."

Conal grinned and then saw the worry in my eyes. "It'll be okay, Sugar. Epi'll figure something out - he usually does." He leaned forward to kiss me, but I ducked away.

"No way. Go and have a shower, then I'll think about it."

"Chicken." He turned and headed down the hallway, tearing off his ruined shirt as he went. "I'll be glad when all this is over and I can stop stinking like rotting meat."

I watched his retreating form, admiring the muscles flexing in his back and his tight ass as I slipped back into my position on the floor. Uneasiness gripped me when I had to force my eyes away from him. Not good, definitely not good to start considering how I looked at Conal when we were about to rescue Lucas. Nick's disapproval of our living arrangements was already obvious, his body language letting me know he didn't like it. He also didn't like the way Conal and I looked at one another, the way we touch and hugged one another instinctively. Nick hadn't said anything, but I'd seen him watching us and knew he didn't like it. If he didn't like it, how on earth was Lucas going to feel if we managed to rescue him? I pushed the thought away, only to have panic bubble up as I considered the werewolves and shape shifters being unable to kill the demons, further eroding my already fragile confidence. *Okay, don't panic. This is just another couple of problems we need to tackle*, I told myself sternly. I pushed these latest dilemmas to the back of my mind and returned to my more pressing crisis - rescuing the Tines.

Conal was just as frustrated by our lack of action as everybody else, but he believed in me and had more faith than the others. He held an unswerving belief in the fact that I knew what I was doing. A wave of nausea filled my stomach, wondering if he should believe in me with so much conviction. Seven days out from my birthday, I doubted myself. Could I do this? Drops of perspiration broke out across my forehead and I mentally shook myself. I *had* to do this. There was no choice. I was Nememiah's

Child and I had an obligation to rescue the Tines and stop the Drâghici Consiliului from carrying out their plans.

The relationship between Conal and I had settled into a comfortable, easy pattern. He knew what he would do when this was over and I knew what I wanted. We still slept together every night, Conal's arms wrapped around me, but we both accepted it could go no further. I did love Conal, but I loved Lucas more. It was Lucas that I hoped to spend the rest of my life with - if he still wanted me. Conal and I shared a physical relationship of hugs and kisses for now, but that was all it would be. Conal would find someone suitable to marry and I wanted to be with Lucas. *If we were still alive to have a future*, the niggling voice in my head reminded me.

With a sigh, I placed my hands against my knees, deliberately easing the strain out of my muscles and returned to the spirits.

I could converse with numerous voices in unison now. Whereas in months past it had been a confused jumble in my mind, now the spirits worked with me, rather than overwhelming me. I drew Mom, Lady Wadsworth, Galen and Lyell together and they stood side by side. *"Tell me what I need to do,"* I pleaded. *I can't do this on my own."*

Mom looked unhappy, sadness and worry etched in pretty features which were usually so serene. *"We can't tell you, Charlotte. You must work it out for yourself."*

"You have the answer in your heart, Charlotte. It's been there all the time," Galen responded. He was dressed in the religious tunic he always wore, with one hand clasping the opposite wrist. *"You know what you need to do. You have to embrace it."*

"Shouldn't it be easier than this? I'm so close, I've learned everything -done everything you've asked of me. I worked out what the Drâghici are doing. If I'm so good, and they're so evil, why can't you tell me what to do to defeat them?"

"Evil and good. Darkness and light," Mom said. *"There is no true evil, there is no true good. You killed your stepfather, to avenge me."*

"Because he killed you, and my sisters and brother," I yelled back angrily. *"He was evil, because of what he did to you all!"*

"It's not that simple, Charlotte. Yes, he was evil, because of the crimes he committed. But your siblings; were they evil? Because they were spawned by evil, does that make them automatically evil also?" Lady Wadworth asked quietly, fingering the cartwheel ruff at her throat.

I considered her words, studying the concept in my mind. My siblings weren't evil, they had been young and innocent. And yet, they'd been spawned by someone evil. Did that mean they were good, or bad? Good, of course. But would they be good always? Although they'd been fathered by a man whom I'd abhorred, they could have gone either way as they approached adulthood. They could have elected to become solid, respectable member of the community. Or they could have grown into a likeness of their father; vicious, cold-blooded - a murderer. Out of the blue, I realized with clarity what I was being told. Nobody is truly evil, nobody is truly good. It's the choices we make, the paths we choose, that make us who we are. I'd killed my stepfather. Did that make me evil? No. It was the choices I'd made which led me to being the person I was now. I knew in my heart that I was firmly on the side of right, in a war over right and wrong. But how did all this help me?

The spirits were edging forward, their demeanor excited. There was an air of expectation surrounding them, eagerness in their expressions which suggested I was close, very close to the answer I was seeking. *"Charlotte, the answers you seek are right before you. And only you. You must think this through, only with one mind,"* Lady Wadworth implored.

"Others can help you, but you must take the first step alone," Lyell urged. *"All decision, all paths in life are taken with one step, one person alone."*

I snapped my eyes open, knew they were bright as the solution suddenly dawned on me. The spirits evaporated into so much mist and I stood up hastily, pacing back and forth while I thought through their counsel.

I knew the answer.

Chapter 40

Confessions

Conal lay in bed with me, lying on his side, he had one arm in his usual protective stance around my body, the other fisted against his chin. He leaned down to kiss me softly, his eyes warm but troubled. "Are you absolutely sure?"

"Yes." I reached up to touch his face, running my fingers across his cheek. "I know this is what we're meant to do."

"Pray tell - how are we going to do *this*?" he asked. "What you're suggesting, how do we know it's even possible?" His voice had an air of uncertainty in it and I leaned up to kiss him.

"Trust me, there must be a way. Epi will know it." I was uncompromising in my belief that Epi could do what I needed. If anybody could do it, he could. It would involve magic and Epi was a master. At least, that was my fervent wish.

"Alright. We'll talk to him in the morning," Conal stated, putting his trust in me once again. I hugged him close, excited that I'd finally discovered what it was I'd been looking for. I raised my mouth to his and kissed him, with far more enthusiasm than was probably wise.

"Hey, ease up," he grumbled softly, when I dropped back against the pillows. "You'll get me on the wrong track again. A man only has so much self-control."

"Sorry," I made a face.

"It's okay. He rolled onto his back, staring up at the ceiling."It's been a while for me; sometimes I get overwhelmed with those lustful thoughts. Particularly when you throw yourself at me."

"Well, I guess that makes two of us. I've never done it before."

He rolled back to gaze down at me, surprise registering in his eyes. "Never?" he echoed huskily.

I shook my head, the heat of a blush coloring my cheeks. "Lucas had control issues. Passion and biting apparently go hand in hand when you're a vampire."

Conal squeezed his eyes shut. "Too much information. I don't think I want to hear this."

"Okay, I won't tell you then." I settled against his chest and he draped his arm around my back. For a long time, there was silence between us.

"So you've never had someone make love to you?" he queried in a low voice.

"Nope."

He rolled back over, drawing me gently with him so we were face to face. "You know, we could both get killed. If you want to try it once before you die, I'd be honored..."

"Conal," I interrupted gently, "you know that's a really bad idea." I touched his cheek, brushing my fingers across his strong jaw as he gazed at me.

"I know," he replied huskily. "But if I thought you'd be willing, I'd do it in a second." He leaned forward, caught my lips against his and his tongue probed my mouth gently and thoroughly. I kissed him back, couldn't not do it and the kiss was gentle, filled with a world of words and emotions. When he released me, his eyes were filled with tenderness, so much so that it made my chest ache. "I've never wanted anyone as much as I want you."

I bit my lip, fully aware of the desire stirring in my groin as I fought with myself. I loved him. I wanted him, probably as much as he wanted me. And I didn't have a clue what would happen when I saw Lucas again. Despite my firm resolve to rescue him, I wasn't even sure he would want me anymore. I'd left him nearly five months ago. He might have moved on with someone else. Just the thought of him being with another woman filled me with envy and I knew I loved him as much today as I had when I walked out all those months ago. But maybe he'd moved on, found someone else. It would be entirely reasonable after I left and never contacted him again. I guess I could have asked Nick or Rafe and they could have told me, but I hadn't asked. I didn't want to know.

But was all that reason enough to let Conal make love to me? What would Lucas think if he did want me back? Sleeping in the same bed with Conal and kissing him was entirely different to having sex with him. Lucas might be able to forgive me for what I was doing now, but I wasn't certain he could forgive me for having sex with another man.

But Conal was right, we could die in the attempt to rescue the Tines. Did I want to die without ever experiencing a man making love to me?

"You're taking a while to think about this," Conal remarked quietly, rubbing his fingers across my shoulder. "Should I take that as a positive sign?"

I ran my fingers through his hair, treasuring the soft and silky feel against my skin as I struggled with a decision. "I wish I could say yes, Conal. Part of me wants to, so badly, you wouldn't believe it."

He kissed me softly, his lips just a tender sweep against my own. "Oh, I think I would."

"I want you to make love to me, I really do. But it's the wrong place and the wrong time. And I'm not a werewolf," I rcminded him.

"I don't care. I'd give up the pack for you."

"You don't mean that."

I saw the struggle in his eyes, before he squeezed them tightly shut and shook his head. "You're right. I can't give up the pack."

"So making love would be a really bad idea. I'm still in love with another man and you need to marry a werewolf."

"You know, we could make love just for the hell of it," he suggested, rubbing a finger down my arm and making me shiver. "One night, no ties, no recriminations. Nobody needs to know, except you and me."

"No." I punched his chest sharply. "I would know about it, and it might mess up our relationship completely.

He stared at me for a long moment. "You're right, and I know you'll go back to the bloodsucker. It's what you were always going to do. You love him, Charlotte, more than you will ever love anyone else."

I lowered my gaze, battling with my insecurities. "I'm not even sure he'll want me back," I admitted. "We've been separated for months."

Conal looked stunned for a second, then recovered his composure and forced his face to relax into a more neutral expression. "Are you kidding? I saw the way he looked at you, Sugar. He loves you and I don't doubt that he will always love you."

"I'm not so sure," I whispered, tears filling my eyes.

Conal clasped me close to his chest, his fingers brushing through my hair as he spoke. "He still loves you, I'm certain of it." He was silent for a minute, letting me cry before he released me with a gentle pat on the shoulder and slipped from the bed. He strode over to the wooden dresser, opening the bottom drawer and searching for a few minutes before he returned to the bed with an envelope in his hand. "I never got around to getting rid of this. I figured one day, you might want to read it," he admitted gruffly.

It was the letter from Lucas, the one that had been in the packing boxes when I moved to Jackson and Lucas had forwarded my belongings. I stared at it, my hands shaking as I wavered about what to do.

"Read it, Charlotte," Conal stated quietly.

"What if he tells me he never wants to see me again?"

"Then you'll know. One way or the other." He touched my arm softly, leaned over to kiss me. "I'm going to make coffee. Give you some privacy."

He slipped from the room, leaving me alone. I stared down at the envelope, ran my fingers over the elegant copperplate writing on the envelope. It was addressed simply to 'Charlotte'.

Taking a deep breath, I flipped it over and ran my finger under the flap, tearing it open before I pulled the sheet of paper out. Unfolding it with shaking hands, I stared at it for a long moment before I began to read.

Charlotte,

As I write this, I keep my promise to you, although the pain in my chest is never ending and engulfs me constantly. Every day seems to last an eternity as I struggle to exist without you. But I made you a promise, and I will keep my end of the bargain.

My heart may have stopped beating more than a century ago, but whilst I was with you it truly felt as if it had begun to beat again. I've never felt more alive than I did with you.

Rowena and Marianne have packed your belongings, we have accepted your decision to leave, although I myself must admit I will never come to terms with it.

I don't blame you, love. What happened was something I had feared from the first day I met you. You are right to fear me and my friends, we are dangerous and your reaction to Holden's attack was entirely understandable. It reinforced to me that your blood awakens feelings in me that are impos-

sible to ever fully control. It is safer for you to be away from me. And yet I wish with all my being that it was different.

I wish you every happiness in your future, my love. I wish you love and joy, and a life filled with contentment.

You will remain in my heart always, and my love will never fade. How can it fade, when you were my light, my joy, my reason for existence in this world?
Yours eternally,

Lucas

I read and reread the letter a dozen times, tears running down my cheeks and dripping onto the sheets, leaving damp spots.

Conal knocked quietly and slipped into the room. "Do you want to be alone?"

I shook my head, wiping the tears away with the back of my hand.

Conal strode across the room and slipped into the bed, drawing me into his arms. "Was I right?"

I nodded. "But that was a long time ago."

Conal sighed. "For someone who wants to make love to you so badly, I must be a fool for admitting this." He caught my chin against his thumb and drew my face up till I was looking at him. "He loves you, Charlotte. He has always loved you. He *will* always love you."

"You really think so?"

"Absolutely," Conal stated confidently. "Although if we manage to rescue him, there's a good chance the bloodsucker won't even recognize you."

I narrowed my eyes, choosing to ignore the degrading nickname. "Why?"

Conal sighed. "You're a different girl to the one I first met. You were so lost, so alone. Directionless. Now you're full of confidence, some might say overconfident..."

I slapped his arm and in response, he pulled me closer, his arms capturing mine in an iron grip.

"You don't seem to see it, Charlotte," he stated seriously. "I've noticed it, Nick and his men have, and even Epi says you've changed. Everything about you - it's changed. You know who you are, you go after what you want. You have self-control which would be surprising in someone twice your age. And it's not only mental changes, it's physical. You look," he glanced down at my face, his eyes filled with admiration, "... ethereal."

"Guess that's the part of me that's Angel," I whispered.

Conal grinned. "Well, that may be, but the body is definitely all devil. You are absolutely smoking hot."

I blushed, heat rushing up to color my cheeks. I could see the changes in my body, knew the continual activity had made some outstanding changes to my anatomy. Suddenly I was even more worried. "You don't think Lucas will like it?"

Conal growled, deep in his chest and caught my mouth against his for a brief kiss. "Trust me, he's going to love it."

Chapter 41

Sfantu Drâghici

Epi was hovering, watching as I marked sigils on my skin, his small figure a bundle of nervous energy. "That one should go there. Near your heart." He pointed to my chest, above my left breast.

I followed his instructions, feeling amazingly calm for a woman who was about to head into battle. The majority of our plan was in place, the only thing left to do was complete the sigils on my skin and I'd be ready. The men had already prepared and would be standing by when I called for them. The only adverse part of our plan was not knowing exactly what we'd meet at the other end. Nick had been unable to retrieve any further information about the vampires, so we were going in virtually head blind, other than the limited amount of intelligence we had on the four vampires we had photographs for. There was no choice now - we'd run out of time.

The backpack I was taking lay by my side, Katie sitting beside it, watching as I worked. Dressed in a pretty red cotton dress with white polka dots, a matching bow pulled her hair into a ponytail. Her eyes were wide and I knew what she was thinking. "It doesn't hurt, Katie," I reassured her quietly.

"Will they stay there forever?" She ran her small fingers over one of the numerous marks I'd already completed on my right arm.

"No, sweetie. They only stay there while I need them. They give me extra special powers."

"To save Gwynn and William," she announced seriously.

I bit my lip anxiously, glancing away so she wouldn't pick up on the worry in my eyes. "Yeah, sweetie. To save Gwynn and William. I'm going to bring them back for you." I turned back to my arm when I had my expression under control, continuing the sigil I was working on.

"Nonny says you an Angel," Katie stated.

"I am," I agreed.

"Then you'll bring William and Gwynn back. Angels always do good things," she assured me, her little face solemn.

"I'm going to do my best," I promised. I completed the last sigil, high on my shoulder and stowed the Hjördis away in the combat boot I was wearing, making sure it was well hidden below the top of the boot. I stood up, reaching for the jacket that lay on the couch and shrugged it on, zipping it up over the tank top to conceal my skin.

I picked up the backpack and slung it over my shoulder, turning to look at Epi. "Guess this is it, old man."

Nonny ran towards me, tears in her eyes. "Be safe, Charlotte." She caught me around the waist, hugging me hard against her.

I hugged the old woman, just as fiercely. "I'll try."

Epi caught my hand between his own. "I'll have everything ready for you when you get back," he said anxiously. "You remember what you have to do to open the portal from that side?"

I nodded, adjusting the straps on the backpack.

"Whatever you do, don't let the Consiliului members touch you. We don't know enough about their abilities to be confident they couldn't bespell you, or read your mind through touch."

"They could probably do it without touching me," I muttered.

"But I believe touch will be worse. Use the spirits for assistance, as I have taught you."

Again, I nodded. Taking a deep breath, I turned back to Katie, sympathy welling for the little girl when I saw the look of anguish in her grey eyes. "Give me a good luck kiss, Katie?"

The little girl flung herself at me, hugging my waist as if she would never let go. I gently disengaged her hands and knelt in front of her. "Be good for Nonny and Epi, okay? Draw me a picture while I'm gone. Something pretty." She nodded seriously and kissed my cheek.

"We will look after her," Nonny promised.

"I know," I responded simply. There was no doubt in my mind they would care for Katie while we were gone. And beyond, if things went pear-shaped. I walked with Epi towards the wall of the church, where the bookcases had disappeared, replaced by a large pentagram drawn on the wall. Four of the five corners had been marked with sigils, only the last one still waiting to be completed.

"Any last minute advice?" I asked Epi.

"Come back."

I grinned, despite my apprehension. "Thanks for that. Good advice, Epi."

He completed the pentagram with a sigil I didn't recognize and as I watched, the wall shimmered with golden light. Taking a deep breath, I stepped into the light as Epi had described.

It was never going to be my favorite form of travel I decided, as I was thrown head first out of the portal, landing on the rough ground and hitting my shoulder hard against the dirt. I felt faintly nauseous, my head filled with the strange streaks of light which had accompanied my journey.

I got up, checking the backpack was still closed firmly and unzipped my jacket to glance at my shoulder. The jacket had blocked any damage to my skin and I zipped it up firmly again.

The last thing I needed before heading into a vampire stronghold was to be bleeding.

I turned to look at the imposing fortress of Sfantu Drâghici. Situated high on the hills surrounding the town itself, it was both ancient and imposing, with turrets and castellated towers soaring towards the overcast skies.

As Epi predicted, he'd portalled me to exactly where he intended, a few feet from the walls themselves and hidden from view by a lot of tall vegetation. It had amused the heck out of me when he'd resorted to using Google Earth to pinpoint the exact location he wanted. I stepped out from behind the greenery and strode towards the gates. To my right, a cobblestoned road weaved down towards the town of Sfantu Drâghici and I could see tourists milling around, taking photos of the magnificent castle. A horse clip-clopped towards me, pulling a brightly colored wagon which was filled with day trippers come to visit the historical building. I had to remind myself that they didn't know what lay behind those heavy gates was both dangerous and terrifying. People lined up at a booth by the open gates, purchasing tickets for one of the tours advertised on an ornately decorated sign.

I didn't bother lining up for a ticket. Two men approached me as I strode through the gates, dressed in identical dark grey suits, sunglasses covering their eyes. Their faces were impassive, but it was evident they'd been on the lookout. One was tall and heavyset, the other smaller and slender, both fair skinned and dark haired. Silently they took up positions on either side of me. I was expected.

We walked through the crowds of tourists mingling within the castle compound, following a cobblestoned path. Just when I thought I might have to ask them directions, tall and heavyset spoke. "This way."

He took the lead and I followed, passing buildings which held a range of typically tourist-like shops. One sold postcards and souvenirs and I spied a little girl holding a snow globe up to her mother which contained a miniature version of the very stronghold we were in. Next door was a coffee shop, visitors sitting and laughing in the weak sunshine. Smaller and slender followed behind, shadowing my every move.

In the centre of the courtyard, men were performing a re-enactment of a swordfight. Dressed in medieval clothing they were slashing and cutting at one another with very realistic swords. I wondered if they were humans or vampires. Their movements looked too clumsy to be vampire, so I guessed they were human actors. It was disconcerting to know the most powerful vampires in the world were in this castle, where innocent people were milling around and enjoying a day out without a care in the world.

Tall and heavyset motioned towards a heavily reinforced door which was lodged neatly into a stone arch. The sign beside the door said 'Administration', suggesting it was perfectly innocuous. He pushed open the door and waited for me to pass him before following in behind.

We entered into a great hallway, with black and white tiles on the floor which looked aged - like hundreds of years aged. The walls were paneled in oak and covered in tapestries which spread across great expanses of the hall. The tapestries depicted battle scenes - men in body armor sat astride equally protected horses, their arms raised with swords held aloft. Another tapestry showed a scene of a man lying across a boulder, a knife piercing his chest, blood dripping towards the grass below him. A third was of men in medieval clothing, clashing with one another on a vast field with swords drawn and shields raised in battle.

Tall and heavyset silently motioned me towards a second door, holding it open. The contrast was severe, as we left the relatively well-lit great hall and walked down a long hallway, the walls made of the same stone as the outside of the castle. No electric lighting was visible, only flaming torches hung at intervals along the walls to provide pools of flickering light in the darkness. It was ominously quiet, the dark walls cold and dank and my boots echoed sharply on the cobblestoned floor. We reached another door, solid oak with the aged burnish which came from constant use over centuries. Tall and heavy-set pushed it open and I entered another room - which managed to be both elegantly beautiful and garishly ugly. The ceiling was decorated with molded plasterwork, intricately carved ivy leaves draping and coiling around to frame a massive oval centerpiece towering high above the floor. The centerpiece had been exquisitely painted and reminded me of Michelangelo's work in the Sistine Chapel. Along both sides of the room, black marble columns rose skyward, set equal distances apart and I counted twelve to each side. The capital and base of each column was intricately carved, with fretwork decorated with gold. It hovered somewhere between outrageously gaudy and indescribably beautiful.

Between each column, white marble statues stood on plinths of black, their blank eyes staring towards the grey and white granite floor. Each statue wore a crown of laurel leaves around their heads, decorated with copious amounts of gold. The walls behind the columns were still more white marble, intricately carved with a diamond pattern edged with gold. At the far end of the room, furthest from the door we'd come through, seven high-backed thrones stood on a dais. There was a canopy of dark blue velvet over the dais, decorated with elaborate quantities of gold trim and thick braid, gathered and held across the dais by two slender columns.

I blinked rapidly, trying to equate the opulence of this room after the starkness of the hallway we'd just left. The room was beautifully gaudy. Ostentatious to the extreme and I decided there and then it *was* beautiful, but almost to the point of ugliness. It was too much... too much of everything, as if the

Drâghici Consiliului wanted to show off their power, their sense of good taste and had overdone it to the nth degree.

The two men remained silently by the door, closing it as I stepped further into the room.

Facing the dais were ten wooden chairs - separated into two groups of five with a red carpet runner between them. Plain and unadorned, they were the only furniture in the room which was not gilded and polished to within an inch of its lives and each held a person.

My nightmares had burst into stunning, terrifying reality. I walked slowly down the long room along the narrow red carpet, stopping between the chairs. It was bone-chilling to find out my friends looked far worse than they'd appeared in even the worst of my night terrors. It was evident they'd been starved of blood since their arrival and I could see how badly injured they were. They'd been stripped; their torsos, legs, arms and throats draped with multiple chains of silver. I mentally shook myself, trying to control my reactions to the horror I was witnessing, trying to process what I was seeing. Lucas had told me this was a myth. Vampires were impervious to silver, crosses, garlic, holy water. All of those were myths. And yet, the silver chains were embedded deeply into their bodies as if the silver had burnt straight through their skin. They had ghastly, painful looking burns all over their bodies, as though they'd been burnt by acid. The nightmares where I'd seen Striker being tortured with holy water were grimly, disturbingly accurate.

This couldn't be real. I sucked in a deep breath, aware that I couldn't afford to lose focus now. Every one of them looked terrible, their faces haggard and paler than I'd ever seen them, as if the muscle and tendons beneath the skin had wasted away, leaving a paper thin, translucent layer of skin over the bone below. Their eyes were dull and lifeless - the beautiful color of their irises looked washed out, as if the color had been faded by endless hours under a blazing sun. The skin around their eyes looked bruised, and their lips were cracked and blistered.

Lucas was nearest to me on the right and I cringed when I noticed the deep slashes peppering his chest. I'd seen this in a nightmare, seen the damage done to him with a silver knife. There was no blood - only the deep carvings into skin and the muscle beneath. Bone stood out white against the pale pink muscle and flesh and I shuddered. Ben sat on the opposite side of the aisle left between them. He too had been tortured, but his skin was a mass of burn marks, where holy water had been poured over his torso. The skin looked as if it had melted, like rivulets of candle wax running down his chest and shoulders. Bile rushed towards my throat and a tiny groan slipped from my lips unhindered.

Both men lifted their heads and I registered two worrying facts. The first; they were almost out of their minds with hunger. And two; they were both horrified to see me here. I scrutinized the rest of the group, getting an indication of their condition. Gwynn was barely conscious, her copper red hair filthy and knotted, falling over her face where she'd slumped forward listlessly against her bindings. Her left breast was slashed deeply and gaping open. Her panties were ripped down both seams and had been placed back on her body as though they'd been torn away, and then put back in a sick facsimile of giving her some modesty. I hated to think what had caused them to be torn in the first place, but forced the thought to the back of my mind. Deal with it later; deal with the problems at hand right now.

William looked dead, his face a picture of misery, as if he'd taken as much abuse as he could and died, the agony of his suffering still imprinted in his features. He appeared to have shut himself down completely, no animation, no sign of any sort of life came from his body. He looked like a corpse and I worried if that was exactly what he'd become.

Marianne was unconscious and I was grateful for it, for her own sake. The torture she'd been subjected to was clear on her body, every square inch held massive amounts of damage, and her legs looked as though the skin had been removed with a potato peeler, great swathes of skin missing, leaving the pale flesh underneath. I couldn't begin to imagine what it must have felt like; knew I didn't want to.

Acenith's face had been burned with holy water, and I was horrified when I saw her limp hand drooping down the side of the chair. Her fingers had been hacked off. I had to turn away, swallowing deeply to keep the nausea at bay.

Rowena was conscious and her expression held a look which suggested she would be crying if she had tears to do so. Such devastation in such a gentle face, her hazel eyes no longer flashing with life and love. Now they held only unendurable pain and it was easy to see the abuse on her body. Like Gwynn, her underwear had been tampered with and anger flared in my heart, loathing the idea of what might have happened to her. Knowing it may very well be the truth and wondering how she and Gwynn could possibly survive if my worst fears were true.

When I looked at Ripley, he was staring at me, his eyes belying the hunger which was threatening to destroy him. I was certain he wasn't seeing me - all he could see was a food source. Like Ben, he'd been attacked with holy water and there was a burnt image of a cross branded onto his thigh, the skin blackened and blistered.

Holden and Striker sat together, side by side. I'd barely met Holden and yet looking at him, I could only feel sympathy for his plight. Like Lucas, he'd been cut up - one wound was so deep and long, I could see the bone of his ribs protruding through the flesh. Striker looked to be in the best condition of all of them, which wasn't saying much, but he'd always been the strongest. Now he didn't look so strong, he was badly beaten and cut up, but there was more of Striker in his eyes still, more than any of the others.

I straightened my shoulders. I wanted to say something, anything to them that would make this better. But there was nothing I could say. I threw Striker a casual wink and he watched me, misery clearly visible in his blue eyes. They weren't the brilliant blue they had been, faded into a paler version than before, but he seemed to see and recognize me.

"Arawn, I told you she would come!" I glanced up to see three male vampires enter the room from a door behind the dais, each one followed closely by two more men in suits. Judging by the suits and sunglasses, they were guards like the two who'd brought me in here. I only recognized one of the three vampires on the dais - which meant there were at least six on the council. Shit.

I left the Tines behind and strode further into the room, stopping about five feet away from the three vampires. The one who'd spoken was perhaps my height, around five feet six inches with a slender build and a pockmarked, sallow face. His hair was stringy, dark brown and he had a Vandyke goatee and moustache. His body was slender to the point of skinniness, almost effeminate and he wore a long black jacket with a ruffled white shirt and black pants. His feet were encased in black loafers and I could feel his power, even from this distance, as if he was throwing it at me like a grenade.

The second vampire, whom he called Arawn was tall and heavily built, a wall of powerful muscle. I recognized him from the photo Nick had produced, one of the council we didn't have a name for. He had blonde curls which framed a face bordering on pretty, rather than handsome. His eyes were icy blue, like two chips of frozen ocean water and he stared down at me, his expression calculating. His gaze took in every inch of my body, spending an excessive amount of time around my hips and breasts, his eyes lingering as if he could undress me with his gaze. He was wearing blue jeans and a silk t-shirt which strained at the seams to cover the bulging muscles beneath.

The third vampire slumped onto one of the golden thrones, looking utterly unimpressed by the first vampire's excited announcement. His eyes were light green, many shades paler than my own, almost like looking at semi-opaque green glass. Short curly hair, a dark brown, hung almost to his shoulders and his face was long and lean. He was dressed like an ancient Roman, wearing a white tunic with a simple brown belt cinching it at the waist and leather sandals. His legs were bare from the knees down, solidly muscled and dusted with a light smattering of dark hair.

"Well," I said coldly, my green eyes defiant. "If it isn't the Three Stooges. My eyes grazed across the smaller vampire, who'd spoken."Larry, Curly and..." I glanced across at the Roman guy, "Moe."

The vampire who'd spoken eyed me with barely concealed fury, his eyes flashing. "You won't be so insolent when I have created you, child."

"Where are the other salubrious members of the Consiliului Suprem de Drâghici Vampiri?"

"They are not needed for this," the vampire snapped coldly. "I will create you, and then you will be my vampire to control."

"Ah, straight to the point. I like that." I glanced back at the Tines, could see that through the debilitating haze of hunger, Lucas looked distraught, his eyes filled with hopelessness. "What have you done to my friends...Larry?"

His energy blew across me, forcing my hair to shift in the sudden wind he'd created, but he did nothing else, no sign of an attack. "My name is Odin, you rude little bitch." He breathed in sharply, as though he was drawing his anger back in on himself. When he spoke again, he smiled coldly. "We thought we would conduct a few little experiments whilst waiting for your arrival. Starving a vampire to death is such a tiring ordeal for those waiting." He had moved closer, just a foot or two away and his two guards shadowed his every movement. "It was all rather boring. Arawn does get bored so very easily, you see, and he likes to keep his hand in."

I eyed him cautiously. "Keep his hand in?" I repeated, making it into a question.

"Yes. Arawn has a rather sadistic streak, you see. He loves to see others in pain and to keep him from boredom, we must... feed his little foible. Otherwise, he has a tendency of becoming somewhat destructive. Who better to work with your friends here?" He turned to look at Lucas and the others, his eyes moving across them as if he gained great pleasure from their misery. "To amuse ourselves, first we tried to break them, to see how long they could retain use of their powers. We tested Ripley's mind reading abilities with a number of assessments. Sadly, he failed our tests. Rowena - poor thing - her ability as an empath has had her suffer greatly when we insisted she touch our current test subject while they were being brutalized. Such pain, I'm sure you can hardly imagine her suffering. Acenith and Striker attempted to help the others by controlling their agony, but it really did nothing to help their own suffering. It was rather entertaining to see them trying to calm the others, while we were cutting parts of their bodies." He laughed suddenly, a chuckle which was cold and pure evil. "And of course, young Marianne - well, let's just say her future isn't looking very bright. She wasn't much of a challenge anyway, given that she couldn't even predict our arrival at their home. Probably a good thing we have worked with her, to ensure she's aware of how utterly useless she is." He waved his hand towards my friends and I was pleased for the fearless sigil that Epi had shown me, drawn close to my heart. This guy was seriously *creepy*.

He was walking around me in a slow circle, his gaze penetrating as he studied me and spoke again. "As they have begun to starve, Arawn came up with the marvelous idea of testing the validity of some of our myths. Imagine our surprise when we discovered truth in some of them. It appears that weakness allows old foes of the vampire to work. Garlic had no effect, of course, but I never expected it to. But you can't imagine our delight when Arawn discovered that silver could be used to bind them. Not only bind them, but burn into their skin as you see before you. They screamed, Charlotte, they screamed and screamed for days and couldn't move away from it, couldn't free themselves from it. We were interested to discover that it removed any remaining strength from them, which was quite useful because both Holden and Striker have been very naughty boys, trying to escape. That was when Arawn tested the theory of using silver knives on them, knowing the myth suggested a vampire could not heal a silver wound." He chucked again. "It was wonderful to discover truth in that myth too, they now have all these magnificent wounds and not one of them will heal because of the silver used. Arawn has created quite a masterpiece from his work, don't you agree?"

I remained silent, trying to digest what he was telling me, and then stopping myself. I couldn't think about it, didn't dare think about it now, not when I had so much still to do and we were all in such terrible danger. Better to push it to the back of my mind, focus on what I was here to do.

Odin continued to talk, as if I was an enthralled guest and he couldn't wait to boast about his discoveries. "Holy water was remarkable. A few drops here and there on their skin - why, it burns like acid. It's been very entertaining, hasn't it, Hyperion?"

I risked a quick look at Hyperion, who was looking on with bored nonchalance. When I looked back, Odin was staring at me as if mesmerized. "May I touch you?" he asked softly. "You have... an angelic beauty about you, my dear."

I side-stepped away from him, out of reach. "No thanks. I'm not into scrawny ancient bastards."

His eyes hardened until they were like pieces of obsidian, sparking with silver lightning. "You really do need to be taken under control. Hanging around with werewolves and shape shifters, I'm afraid you have developed a rather intolerable rudeness about you, my dear."

"I like it," I retorted. "I'd rather hang with shape shifters and werewolves than you, any day. They're a way better class of people. And I'm not *your dear*, you asshole."

Again with the draught of wind which swirled around me for a second, then dissipated. When he spoke again, his voice was calm, thoughtful. "I'm most surprised you came alone."

"Oh come on, Odin. You knew I was coming alone. Your spy informed you of that fact." I turned my back to him, stepping towards Lucas. "Did you tell my friends why you wanted me so badly?"

"There was no reason to tell them. They have served their purpose and will be destroyed, now that we have you."

When I turned back, Odin was staring at me and my skin prickled. He was practically salivating as he studied my body from top to bottom and his fangs had run out. "That hardly seems fair. They're suffering; they should at least get to know why." I glanced at Lucas, then to Ben and further along to where Striker sat. "You see, the vampire council has been after me for a while. They heard about me from those vampires that came to your house, all those months ago. They knew about my abilities and knew that my talents were unusual, to say the least. They wanted Armstrong to capture me, hand me over to them. What they didn't allow for was that he would try and keep me, take the power for himself. In fact," I turned back to stare at Odin, my green eyes icy cold, "they really screwed up the plan. More than once. You see, the important part of the plan was keeping me human until I was nearly twenty one. So they left me alone for a while and waited, watching from the sidelines to see how much talent I actually had." I looked at Lucas, watching his almost-dead eyes with a sinking heart. "They realized that I'd left your house and traced me to Conal and his pack. But by then, I'd discovered more about my abilities and knew more about what I was facing. So they put this master plan into place. Kidnap you, hold you, torture you - knowing that I would come. What he didn't tell you, was why they wanted me so badly. What it is about me that's so important to them. What he didn't tell you, is I'm one of Nememiah's Children." I looked back down at Lucas, felt my heart breaking a little. "I'm an Angel. Who would have thunk it?"

Chapter 42

In the Devil's Lair

Odin's face was suddenly expressionless, his eyes the only part of him showing any emotion and it was fury which bled out. "Take the backpack from her. She will have the weapons in there."

The pack was wrenched roughly from my shoulders. The guard handed it to Odin and he unzipped the top, peering inside. He put his hand into the bag and drew the contents out. "Rocks? You brought rocks with you?" he stated incredulously.

I was deliberately staring at my fingernails and waited a few seconds before I spoke, making my tone insolent. "I figured you'd take any weapons I had. I was sure one of your goons would frisk me the minute I set foot in the place. Actually, you took longer than I thought you would. Not very security-conscious, is it, to let me wander in here with a backpack and not have someone search it?"

He eyed me suspiciously, throwing the rocks in a fit of temper so they scattered across the floor, the noise echoing throughout the room. "What trickery is this?" he snarled.

I shrugged nonchalantly. "No trickery. Figured if nothing else I could throw a rock at your butt ugly head, see if I could make you bleed. Tell me, Odin, if you're so God-damn special and powerful, if *you* bleed do you want to bite your *own* neck because it'll get your rocks off?"

He stared at me, as if trying to weigh me up and finding he couldn't understand me. It was exactly what I'd hoped for. "I think I will teach you a lesson, see how impertinent you are once you've tasted a little of my special gift."

"No!" Lucas rasped desperately, the sound painful to my ears.

I turned to glance back at Lucas, wanting to reassure him but before I could blink, Arawn was beside him and drawing a blade his pocket. He slashed it down Lucas's face, cutting his cheek open from his eye to his chin. He dropped the knife and smashed his fist into Lucas's stomach and the sound of the impact ricocheted around the room like a thunderclap. Lucas's face convulsed in agony, but his eyes remained on me through the haze of pain which gripped him. There was nothing I could do, except to widen my eyes, hoping he would understand that I was okay, that I had this under control. There was no way of letting him know that clearly, when he didn't understand how much my abilities had increased in recent months, but I would do anything I could to try and get him to realize it was okay.

I turned back to Odin, swallowing deeply as I tried to blank out the sight of Lucas's face, the deep cut in his handsome features. "Do your worst, Odin."

Odin smiled callously, staring directly into my eyes. Again I felt that force of wind around me, and then I could feel something wavering around the perimeters of my mind, although I was uncertain what it was. I stared back coldly, my mind safe from his power and cocooned by the spirits. For a minute, Odin continued, then the smile on his lips faltered and he blinked.

"Sorry, Odin," I said, a deliberately bored tone in my voice. "Your special gift, whatever the hell it is, doesn't work on me. Oh, and by the way - you should ditch the ridiculous beard and moustache. You look like a pathetic wannabe musketeer."

Odin studied me for a minute, maybe two, scrutinizing me carefully. "I grow tired of this. I believe I will just move on to creating you and get it over with. You will learn to treat me with respect."

"I doubt it. I don't treat people with respect if they haven't earned it," I retorted quietly. "Before we move onto the whole 'make me a vampire' plan, how about you let me meet the other one? I'm kind of interested to see him."

Hyperion stood up abruptly, his bored look replaced with startled astonishment. Odin waved his hand and Hyperion sat again, but now he was on the edge of his throne, watching me warily.

"And why would you think there was another?"

I turned back to the Tines, saw Striker watching me with a mixture of emotions clear in his expression. He was definitely in better shape than the others and he managed a faint smile. In his eyes, next to the thirst I recognized another emotion. Hope.

"I don't think there's another one. I know there is." I turned back to Odin, looking from him to Arawn and then on to Hyperion. "Your problem is, you created him a little early, didn't you? Guess that would be called a premature transformation, wouldn't it? Didn't realize it was better to be patient, allow him to reach his full potential before he was taken over to the dark side." I walked towards the Tines, scrutinizing them carefully, seeing if anyone would be capable of helping us when the time came. It was blatantly obvious it would be impossible, they were in such bad shape, I knew it would be all they could do to walk out of here on their own volition. "I guess it would be polite to let my friends here know all the wonderful elements of your cunning plan. See," I said, walking slowly along the row of chairs, catching their eyes with mine, "the Three Stooges here, and the rest of their cronies, had this wonderful idea. They want to take over the world. They think they're superior to every other supernatural being on the planet. Of course, they realize they can't get rid of all the underworld creatures. But they want to do a little tidying up. Rid the world of half breeds, shape shifters, the ones who really aren't up to their high standards. Apparently, you guys don't make the cut, I imagine because you don't drink human blood." I turned back to Odin, who was watching me with a calculating glare and then flicked my attention to my friends, standing between Lucas and Ben. I was almost certain I could see recognition in Ben's eyes as I watched him and it was obvious Lucas knew me. "That's why they need me and the other one. The funny thing about being an Angel is that I reach full maturity at the age of twenty one. My twenty first birthday is tomorrow, so the plan is, I get bitten tonight, before my birthday and wake up in three days with fangs. Then I'm supposed to jump in the sack with this other Angel, produce a passel of brats who will be half vampire, half Angel. And then Odin and his cronies get to take over the world, because they'll be able to summons demon spirits from the Otherworld and they can create an army of the undead to keep all the supernatural in line. Sounds like a hoot, doesn't it?"

I turned away from the Tines, striding back towards Odin. His guards instinctively moved closer to him. "The only problem with their plan is that it *sucks*. For starters, the other one they've got just isn't my type." I stood very close to Odin, staring at him defiantly. "So you've got yourself a problem. Because I don't intend to be transformed, I don't intend to screw this vampire Angel and I certainly don't intend to annihilate half the supernatural beings in your quest for world domination."

Hyperion spoke and his voice was a rough growl, deep and echoing through the marble room. "Let her meet Archangelo."

Odin looked at Hyperion and they conferred with their eyes for a split second. "Yes," Odin announced. "Let's have Archangelo show her exactly how strong his powers have become. Archangelo! Come!"

The door behind the dais was thrust open and the man from my nightmares stepped through it. It was uncanny, the resemblance between he and I, and for a minute we stared at one another, weighing each other up. He was taller than me, but had similar coloring, features which leaned towards being a mirror image of mine in a more masculine face. My first impressions made me think we'd been put on this earth as twins, but been separated all our lives. He was looking intently at me, his expression sinister. "Yes, Master Odin."

"This is Charlotte, Archangelo. She is to be your wife." Odin waved him forward with a little flicker of his fingers and he came to stand beside the older vampire. "It is deeply unfortunate, but we have discovered she has far too much attitude to be a good wife to you. But never fear. I intend to remove that willful nature from her, so she will be the dutiful and submissive wife you deserve. She is also under the impression that you are the weaker Angel and I think we should teach her some lessons, let her see the full strength of your abilities. I want you to summon something for her, something which will make her respect your power for the magnificence it truly is."

I stepped back incrementally, a fraction of an inch at a time. This was what I'd been waiting for, goading them to get a big reaction. I just hadn't expected *this* reaction. Summons something? This guy could do that? Archangelo drew a Hjördis from his pocket and I started to unzip my jacket, worrying about how much more we didn't know. He had the Angel weapons and the ability to summons - both eventualities were things we hadn't allowed for. Tamping those thoughts down, I concentrated on the here and now. The timing had to be perfect, I couldn't dare to show my hand too soon. They were cocky, so very sure of themselves and didn't believe I was as powerful as Archangelo, which made me thankful they'd been receiving the falsified reports from Quinn Saunders. They didn't suspect the true increase in my heightened powers.

Archangelo knelt to the ground and used the Hjördis to mark a pentagram on the marble tiling, which rattled me, even though I knew what summonsing something had meant. I'd expected hand to hand combat between us, a battle of wills and power, which I'd hopefully win. Not for him to draw a pentagram and certainly not to see him drawing the sigils which Epi used to create demons.

I shunted this thought down, as I'd done with others. Not now, don't think about how he could do this at this moment in time. There would be time to think it over later, when we weren't neck deep in shit.

When Archangelo completed the fifth marking, I threw my jacket off, tossing it over towards one of the marble pillars, ensuring I had their attention. Odin's face showed more expression than it had since I arrived and now that expression was stunned, when he saw the mass of indigo blue sigils marking my arms, shoulders and chest like multitudes of bold tattoos.

The floor erupted, billowing red and black smoke through the room, an ominous haze of acrid fumes. I dropped down to one knee, sliding my fingers down the side of my boot and catching the Hjördis in my hand. I drew a rapid sigil on the marble floor by my feet, scorching indigo markings onto the rock. When the demon stepped through the portal I was already back on my feet, watching the rocks that Odin had thrown to the ground so carelessly transforming into my friends in their animal forms.

The vampires were suddenly confronted by four wolves, a coyote and one very impressive lion. As Rafe raised his massive head and roared, the guards hustled Odin back towards the dais, shielding him with their own bodies.

I focused my attention on the demon which was dragging itself out from the pentagram and cursed, a particularly volatile word escaping my lips as I stared incredulously at the size of it. It was huge, bigger than anything Epi had thrown at us. Probably close to fifteen feet tall, in a smaller room it would have needed to crouch, but here it could stand tall and scary. It's head was misshapen and I struggled to comprehend what my eyes were seeing, realizing with trepidation that this was because it had two mouths, one on top of the other, both filled with razor sharp fangs probably three inches long. The top of its head was covered completely with thick black tentacles, glossy in the overhead light as though they'd been dipped in black oil. It had six long arms, three down either side of its enormous body and every one of them terminated with long curving claws. I shut my eyes for the briefest of seconds and when I flicked a glance in their direction, my spirits were encircling the Tines, protecting them. It meant I was more exposed, but that was what Conal and the other men were there to do. Conal was already circling the demon, his black eyes glittering, open jaw displaying a ferocious row of fangs. Ralph and Marco were running interference, keeping the vampires back whilst Rafe, Nick and Phelan launched themselves at the demon. I summonsed the spirits, calling more to my aid and threw my hand forward, watching a wave of pure energy slam into the demon, knocking it off balance momentarily.

Conal took the opportunity to attack, launching himself high into the air, slamming into the demon and tearing at its throat. One of the massive arms caught him, throwing him into the air but Phelan was right there, launching a second attack as Conal picked himself up off the floor and darted back towards the demon.

I caught movement in the corner of my eye, realizing some of the vampires were edging along the sides of the room, using the marble pillars as protection. I threw my hand up and forward, watching with satisfaction as they were hit by a ball of white energy and slammed back against the walls. The marble wall cracked behind them, some of the marble dropping away to reveal the stone wall beneath.

A glance ensured the shield surrounding the Tines was still strong and secure. When I turned back to the demon, it was ambling towards me, its mouths opened and emitting an unearthly roar which shuddered through the air around us. It snapped those heavy jaws at me and I leaped into the air, managing to glide some twenty feet high but the demon's teeth snapped at the wrong time. I dropped back to the floor and rolled neatly onto my feet, aware of the painful stinging in my arm. The arm was still functioning though, so I ignored it and returned to the battle.

Conal was attached to the demon's throat, growling gutturally as he bit deeply into the demon's black skin. Saliva oozed from its mouths, dripping onto Conal's fur where it sizzled and burnt. Conal dropped back to the ground and Nick took his place, worrying at the demon's throat.

I threw another wave of energy towards it, knocking it from its feet, making the huge beast crash onto the floor. My peripheral vision caught movement and I turned in time to see even more vampires coming towards me, their eyes blazing and nostrils flaring as they smelled the blood oozing slowly down my arm.

One was almost close enough to touch me and I launched a high kick, catching his neck with the toe of my boot. He slammed backwards into the wall. A further energy ball threw three of the vampires back and I heard the frustrated scream of fury from Odin.

Archangelo was headed my way and he hurled a burst of energy which knocked me backwards, sliding across the floor until my head slammed against the marble wall.

Shaking my head to clear the pain, I flipped onto my feet, unwilling to wait for the fuzziness to leave my senses. Archangelo was right on top of me, his fangs run out and bloodlust clear in his eyes. He caught my shoulders in a painful grip and we stumbled backwards. I was trying to keep a tight grip on his neck, trying to keep his fangs away from my skin.

He was stronger than me, stronger than I'd expected and I suddenly recalled he was a youngling, at his most bloodthirsty. His mouth moved closer and closer to my throat and I used my left hand to throw energy, at roughly the same time Phelan was coming to my rescue. Both Phelan and Archangelo were blasted backwards across the room, with Phelan hitting the wall and sliding down it to lie in a crumpled heap, yelping softly.

I hastily ascertained the demon was still fighting. I threw another wave of energy, watching the demon collapse to its knees again. Whilst it seemed like an eternity of fighting had passed, we'd come no closer to killing the demon, if anything, we'd managed to aggravate it into a higher level of anger. I groaned when I saw Archangelo coming at me again, the expression on his face dogmatic, holding a Katchet in one hand, a Philaris in the other. He threw the Philaris, his aim strong and true. I ducked hastily but not quickly enough - it caught the side of my cheek as it brushed past, cutting into the skin below my left eye. It sailed around elegantly, spinning back towards Archangelo. Gritting my teeth, I decided he wasn't getting it back and leaped forward, catching it in my palm. It sliced through my hand but I ignored it, intent only on stopping Archangelo from using it again. I hit the ground and rolled, straightening up to throw the Philaris back at Archangelo.

The look in his eyes was pure astonishment as the Philaris slammed into his chest. He dropped to his knees, reaching a hand to his shirt to touch the blood seeping from his heart. He stared at me for a long moment, his eyes filled with surprise; then he keeled over onto the floor, motionless. I ran to where he lay, snatching the Katchet from his hand. I had to flip it into my left hand as the right palm was bleeding uncontrollably.

There was rapid movement up at the dais, where Odin, Hyperion and Arawn were being hustled from the room, the guards pushing them unceremoniously out through the open door. I had no time to do anything about it, my shield around the Tines was failing and the demon was ambling towards them. I launched at it in a flat-out sprint, clambering up its broad back as it screamed. Gripping the massive neck to support myself, I slashed the Katchet into its throat, over and over again while the men continued to bite and worry at its legs and body with their fangs.

Just when I was beginning to think we had no chance of defeating the savage demon it fell, launching me across its head as it hit the ground. I skidded across the floor, covered in a mixture of demon blood and my own sweat pouring from my skin. The demon closed in on itself, shrinking smaller and smaller until all that was left was a small scorch mark on the marble.

Chapter 43

Recovery Operation

I slumped on the floor for a minute, gasping to get air back into my lungs, trying to relearn how to breathe. Adrenaline was coursing through my body, but not enough to keep the pain at bay. Now that the fight was over, pain receptors were operating all over my body and I drew myself up to my feet and sucked in huge amounts of oxygen while I leaned my hands on my knees, waiting for my heart rate to slow before I straightened up.

Conal transformed, eyeing the bodies lying on the floor warily as he padded towards me, gloriously naked and not in the slightest embarrassed. "I'm not sure the fearless sigil is good for you," he announced mildly. "You get pretty crazy. Seriously, Charlotte - 'I'm an Angel, who would have thunk it?' "

I reached for the haversack Nick had carried with him, when he'd been transported into the sigil stone, rummaging through it to find Conal's clothes. "So Epi was right? You could hear everything? Way to go, Epi." I threw his jeans to him. "Put something on, and see if you can lock the doors." I pulled the other clothes from the haversack, laying them in neat piles on the ground.

"That thing was enormous," Nick announced with a broad grin as he transformed back to human. "Biggest damn thing we've fought so far."

I averted my eyes from his body and motioned towards his clothes, before focusing my attention on the Tines. I stepped forward, intent on trying to free them from their bindings but Lucas spoke.

"Charlotte... the chains. Don't... remove the chains," he rasped painfully. "You're bleeding... and our thirst... is too extreme."

"He's right," Ben agreed, his voice sounding as if he'd swallowed shards of glass.

"Good point." I turned back to Nick, who'd slipped on a pair of faded blue denims. The sigil marks on his arms were still strong, but he had a nasty cut across the left side of his chest and purple bruising was blossoming on his face. "Have you got those supplies, Nick?"

Nick pulled another haversack towards him, the one Marco had carried inside his sigil stone. He threw it to me and I tugged it open, pulling the bags of blood we'd brought along with us from inside. I turned back to Ben. "This should help." I held up one of the bags, cutting a corner from it with the Katchet. Nick was doing the same thing, using a small pocket knife. I held the opened bag up, allowing the blood to pour into Ben's open mouth. He swallowed thirstily, desperate, drinking it as rapidly as it fell into his open lips.

"Sugar, we've got a problem. I can't lock this door." Conal was standing at the far end of the room, beside the dais which held the thrones.

I straightened up from Ben's side, throwing the drained blood bag on the floor. "Get out of the way." Conal stepped back from the door and I lifted my hand, summoning a concentrated ball of energy which I threw across the room. It smashed into the wall about the heavy oak door and with a deafening roar, the marble and stone wall smashed, breaking down the door and blocking the entrance. The dais was caught up in the explosion, the velvet canopy falling to the ground and the two marble columns falling, breaking apart into a row of broken pieces.

"You couldn't have just found a way of locking the damn thing?" Conal asked placidly as he strode back towards us.

"Well," I said, pulling a second bag of blood from the rucksack, "now the vamps can only get in here through the one door." I cut the corner of the bag, holding it over Rowena's open mouth. "Check the other door."

"What... was that... thing?" Ben croaked.

"A demon," I responded quietly, watching as Rowena finished the last of the bag and slumped back against the chair, shutting her eyes. I glanced at Ben, alarmed to see he looked no better now that he'd fed. That wasn't a good sign.

"A demon," Ben repeated and I could hear the disbelief in his voice.

"Yeah. Ben, I'll be happy to explain everything, but not now. Right now, I've got to get us out of here. We're not safe yet, not by a long shot."

Nick and I worked our way down the row and when I came to Striker, he managed a weak smile, wincing as the movement stretched some of the wounds on his face. "Squirrel?" he rasped.

"No such luck, Striker. Boring old cow blood. Best I could do on short notice." I grinned at him, relieved to see him still alive and watched as he gulped down the blood swiftly.

"What are we going to do with Marianne and Acenith?" Nick asked worriedly when he'd finished feeding Ripley. "They're both unconscious."

"Try and get their mouths open, pour a little in, see if they swallow. They might, even though they aren't conscious," I suggested. "Ralph, can you give him a hand?" I glanced down at Lucas. "Think we're safe now?"

He looked up and stared at me, as if he was still stunned to find me standing here in this place. "Give us a few minutes," he croaked. "Go help your friends."

Phelan and Rafe, both of whom were back to human, were slumped on the floor beside one another. Rafe's leg lay at an odd angle and Phelan was gripping his own shoulder, the joint between his arm and collarbone swollen and irregular, as though something wasn't in exactly the right place. Conal was dragging Marco across to where they lay and blood was seeping from wounds across his chest. I ran over to them, pulling the Hjördis from where I'd stowed it in my combat pants and knelt down in front of Marco when Conal eased him up against the wall gently. I drew healing sigils near the edge of the gashes and watched them knit together. Marco looked up, his eyes clearing of pain and managed to look slightly abashed at his nudity. "Thanks, Lottie."

"Go put some pants on," I encouraged him, before turning my attention to Phelan.

He grinned weakly. "Nice work, Angel girl." He motioned towards Rafe with his head. "Mine's only a dislocation, Conal'll fix it. Help Rafe, his leg's busted up pretty badly."

"Actually, I think the dislocated shoulder might be my fault. Sorry."

Phelan smiled. "No blood, no foul."

I turned towards Rafe and he lowered his gaze sheepishly. "Charlotte, excuse my..."

"Nakedness? Trust me, I'm getting used to it."

I heard Conal mutter something about the fearless sigil again and I grinned. "You're just jealous because I can say anything, think anything and I don't give a damn." I turned my attention to Rafe's leg, marking his skin near the breaks with sigils. He lay watching, his hands carefully positioned to keep himself decent. He groaned as the bone knitted itself together and after a minute or two, flexed it, testing out the movement.

Conal pulled Phelan's arm back into its socket with a swift movement. Phelan cursed long and loudly, and then glanced at me guiltily. "Sorry, Lottie."

"After what fell out of her mouth? I don't think it's anything she hasn't heard before." Conal winked at me.

"Your turn." He stood up and let me treat him, flexing his arm when the wounds healed. "That demon poison is nasty crap."

I walked back to Nick, who'd finished feeding blood to the Tines. "Give us a look at that wound, Nick."

"Is this going to hurt?" Nick asked with a frown. "Those other sigils burn like hell when you draw them."

It was testament to the strength of his fighting skills that he hadn't needed healing sigils up until now. That didn't stop me from teasing. "Don't be such a baby."

Nick growled softly, his gray eyes darkening. "I am not a baby."

"Ignore her," Conal said, walking back to where we stood. "It's the sigils talking, she's being facetious."

When Nick's arm was healed, I turned my attention back to the Tines, but Conal caught my wrist. "Heal yourself first, Sugar. It would be better for our friends if you weren't still bleeding.

Nick watched as I drew healing sigils on my hand and high on my arm, watching the blood slow and the wounds heal. "I've seen you do that a few times now, but I've got to admit, it still impresses the hell out of me."

"It is pretty cool," I agreed.

Conal stepped in front of me, running his thumb over the cut on my cheek. "That one's stopped bleeding already, it was only a scratch. How's the head?"

I rubbed my fingers over the back of my head, where I'd slammed into the marble wall. "It's okay." There was a fairly sizeable lump but when I lifted my fingers away there was no sign of blood. "Probably going to have a headache, but I'm fine right now."

Turning my attention back to the Tines, I dropped to my haunches in front of Lucas. "Any better?" I kept my tone business-like and although I made eye contact with him, I couldn't overcome the urge to look away. I was uncomfortable now the initial drama was over, but I couldn't afford awkwardness until we were safe. I tamped the emotion down and concentrated on the matters at hand.

"A little," he agreed quietly. "I'm not sure it's enough for us to control the thirst." His nostrils flared at the smell of blood on my skin and with a glance, I confirmed every one of them had their fangs out. "We haven't fed since we were kidnapped."

I glanced at my watch, hyperaware of the time passing. "It's going to have to do. I'm pretty certain the Three Stooges are gathering reinforcements as we speak. We've got to get out of here."

"How do you... do that?" Ben asked, his eyes on the now healed wound on my arm. "How can you heal wounds, mend broken bones?"

I smiled grimly. "Seems there were a few things about my ability that we didn't know. I'll tell you about it once we get you out of here, I promise."

"Hope you've got a plan, Lott," Nick challenged quietly. "These guys don't look like they're capable of moving."

I bit my lip anxiously. Nick was right, none of the Tines were looking well enough to walk and some of them were still not conscious. There were six of us and ten of them and I for one wasn't capable of carrying someone. Not and keep us safe if the shit hit the fan and we were attacked again. I realized with a start that I hadn't allowed for the nightmares being so accurate. I'd thought the silver chains binding them were the result of an overactive imagination because I'd understood vampires were impervious to so many things. Now it seemed I was wrong and that left us with a quandary.

"Can't we create a portal here?" Marco questioned.

I shook my head. "Epi was pretty clear on it. I have to create the portal from where we came in; otherwise he can't seal it when we get back. If we create a portal here, the vamps could trace us back and know our location. That leaves us with a problem."

"Only one?" Conal commented, his voice dry. "We're stuck in the middle of the Consiliului stronghold and you can only see one problem? That fearless sigil is doing your head in, Sugar."

"Shut up," I retorted mildly. "I've got answers to most of our problems, except one."

"Which is?"

"I can get us back to the portal," I scratched my head thoughtfully, "but I'm not entirely certain we can get the Tines there."

"We can carry them," Phelan suggested. "If Conal, Rafe and I transform back, we can carry a couple each on our backs."

"It's not so much getting them to the portal," I explained pensively, still desperately searching for a solution. "I'm more worried that if the silver thing works, so will sunlight."

There was a horrified silence and I took the opportunity to glance at my watch again. It was four o'clock and there would still be sunshine outside. We'd planned this raid during the day because there would be tourists outside and Epi and Conal both agreed tourists would assist because the Consiliului wouldn't want to do anything which would betray their secret. Now though, daylight was a distinct disadvantage.

Ben looked up at me and nodded his head slowly, wincing painfully with the movement. "It's true. The sunlight may burn us in our weakened state."

"It was overcast, not full sunshine," I explained.

He shook his head. "Still… might burn."

"What about the material?" Marco pointed towards the collapsed canopy over the dais. "Could we use that, make some sort of cape?"

"Great idea, Marco," I agreed with a rush of relief. "Gather it up; see if you can get it cut into big enough pieces to cover them. We need ten."

"It won't be enough," Lucas croaked hoarsely. "Any inch of exposed skin... could kill us."

"Lucas is right. There isn't enough material here," Nick confirmed.

I frowned heavily, felt the beginnings of panic stirring. "Okay, let me think." I opened my mind automatically, speaking to the spirits. I hoped they would be helpful now I'd come this far. If they told me it was another quest, I was going to scream. They were remarkably open about what I needed to do, and I cringed as I listened to their instructions.

"Okay, I've got it," I announced. I stepped towards Lucas, grasping the silver chain in my hands and gingerly beginning to pull on it. He closed his eyes and groaned as the chain tore out of his skin, leaving open wounds behind. I shuddered and tried to block out the sound and sight of what I was doing, trying to close my mind to the excruciating pain he was being overwhelmed by. "I'm sorry, God, I'm sorry," I whispered.

"Just do it," Lucas growled. "They won't leave us alone here for long."

"Marco, hurry up with that material."

Rafe hurried over to help Marco while Conal, Phelan, Ralph and Nick worked with me to remove the chains. It was hard to know the best way of doing it, making me think of band-aids. Is it best to ease it off slowly, or just rip it straight off the skin? Even that wasn't a suitable analogy, because a band-aid doesn't eat its way into your skin before you try to remove it. Unfortunately, we didn't have the option of time being on our side, so I worked quickly, praying we weren't doing more damage than had already been done.

Conal was pulling the chains from Striker's body and he was doing it rapidly, obviously having decided fast was better than slow. Striker held his jaw clenched tightly and gritted his teeth, but he was tough enough not to yell out, even though I was certain he must want to.

"How many vampires are in this place?" Conal asked Ben as he worked.

Ben was free of chains and struggling to wrap a piece of material that Marco had given him around his naked body, shuddering as it moved across his badly damaged skin. I wished I could heal their wounds here and now, but time was against us. Conal and Epi had insisted we retrieve them and return home before we treat their injuries and now I wished I'd argued more about their plan, but it was obvious it would take too long, need too much healing to be done here. Ben stopped wrestling with the material and spoke, his voice tense. "At least forty."

Conal and I exchanged a worried look. "We might be better to transform again," he suggested softly.

I glanced at the Tines and shook my head. "Better stay human for now, they're all going to need physical support to get out of here and I think hands and legs will work better than paws."

At last, we had everyone unwrapped from the chains which had bound them. They looked mighty thirsty, but managed to control themselves, and it was obvious to see the intense struggle they were battling. "I promise, it won't be long and we'll get you more blood," I muttered beneath my breath. I caught Ben's arm in my hand and drew a sigil on his wrist. He gasped as the Hjördis burnt the mark onto his arm. When I'd marked all the vampires, I turned to Conal. "Your turn."

Conal frowned. "What?"

"An invisibility sigil."

"Are you kidding?"

"No, this is what Epi was teaching me last night, he thought it might be helpful." I finished drawing and he lifted his arm to look at the marking.

"Do you think I could have a break from these things when we get home?"

"Sure," I agreed easily, turning to Rafe. "If we manage to make it home."

While I finished marking everyone, Conal, Marco and Ralph helped wrap the Tines in the material, covering as much of their skin as possible. One glance and I could see the material wasn't going to be enough. There hadn't been enough to cover each of them completely and various amounts of skin were visible on each of them. I shivered a little, wondering if what I'd been told by the spirits would work, or if we were dooming them to death the minute we took them outside.

"Thank God, the fearless sigil is wearing off," Conal remarked to no-one in particular.

I glanced at my chest, saw the sigil fading away before my eyes. "Do you think I should put another one on?"

"Are you crazy? I never want you to use it again," he retorted dryly. "You are completely out of control with it. I'm going to warn Epi you turned into a complete lunatic when we get back."

I turned back to Ben and Lucas, where they sat huddled with the others. "Okay, there's just one more thing to do before we leave." I reached for the Katchet and ran it across my forearm, wincing as blood welled and rolled down my arm. "You need to drink my blood."

Chapter 44

Blood

Conal was the first to react and he cursed fiercely. "Put the damn sigil back on, you were making more fucking sense with it." He put himself between me and the Tines, who were watching my arm, their eyes mesmerized by the blood dripping to the floor.

"I don't have time to argue with you, Conal. The spirits told me this was the only way," I retorted angrily.

"It's insane, that's what it is! They haven't fed in weeks and the cow blood didn't cut it! They'll suck you dry!"

"Conal, get out of the way!" I pushed past him and strode towards Lucas, saw him cringe away from me. "Lucas, you have to do this. It's the only way to get you out of here alive," I pleaded softly.

"I can't, Charlotte," he whispered, his eyes focused on the blood on my arm. "Conal's right, I won't be able to stop myself."

I held my arm up but he retreated, recoiling in horror. I turned instead to Ben. "Please, Ben. I know you have the strength to do this. Just a little bit, and I can get you out of here."

Ben stared at my arm for a minute, horror and desire mixed equally in his dark brown eyes. "I haven't tasted human blood for so long, Charlotte, almost a century," he said huskily.

"Please, Ben." I became aware of the voices in my head, shouting warnings. We didn't have long. "Please. I know you can stop yourself, you have the willpower. You know it's me, you don't want to hurt me. But you need the blood, it will stop the sunlight burning you. The spirits said this was the only way to get you out of here safely."

He gripped my arm between his hands and stared down at me for a long moment, his eyes blazing with hunger. Suddenly he pressed his mouth against my arm and began to suck strongly. I felt the blood flowing out of my vein, the pressure of his lips sucking and felt weak at the knees. He was being careful to keep his fangs away from my skin and I appreciated the gesture. As quickly as he'd begun, he wrenched himself away, wiping his mouth with his sleeve and looking at me shamefaced.

"It's okay, Ben," I whispered softly.

I turned to Striker, who didn't hesitate. He grasped my arm and went through the same procedure as Ben, sucking powerfully against my arm, his blistered lips cold against my skin. He drew away with a small grin. "Way better than cow."

Rowena was next and she took a few seconds before she touched my arm tentatively.

"Please, Rowena, please do this," I pleaded. Something in my voice forced her into motion and she sucked against my arm, her mouth gentler than the men had been.

I stepped towards Gwynn and she smiled faintly, but there was a haunted look in her pale blue eyes. "I don't think I can," she murmured, her voice low and weak.

"Gwynn, listen to me. You have to drink, you have to drink my blood so I can get you out of here. William is going home and so are you," I coaxed quietly, moving slowly towards where she sat. "Gwynn, you have to do this, you don't need much, just enough to stop you from burning in the sunlight."

"Please, Gwynn, just try," Ben coaxed.

"I don't think I'll stop..." Gwynn began, and I could hear the panic in her words.

"You will, Gwynn. You can stop yourself," I pressed my arm closer to her and she shrunk back, fear and self-loathing appearing in her eyes, but she gripped my arm between her hands, lowering her head. She sucked against the skin for just a moment, and then pulled back.

"You need more, Gwynn, just a little more."

"I can't."

I knelt down in front of her, keeping my voice low, but I knew everyone around us would hear me because their hearing was so much more acute than mine. I was looking for the illusion of privacy though, wanted her to think our words were private. "Gwynn, I've seen the state of your underwear. I can guess what they did to you, and I don't want them to ever do that to you again. Please. Drink a little more, so I can get you out of here safely."

Her eyes widened and she nodded, lowering her mouth to my arm again and sucking for a few more seconds. When she released me, she leaned back against the chair, closing her eyes as though she was too ashamed for me to see her thoughts.

Ripley approached me slowly, his eyes burning, his shoulders set determinedly. "I will go next."

I offered up my arm to him and he captured it between his hands, sucking heavily against the cut in my forearm. I was beginning to feel light-headed, but I knew we had to get through this before I could relax, before I could worry about how much blood I was losing. Ripley forced himself to release my arm, the cost of doing it apparent in the way he stood and shivered. "What about Acenith and Marianne?" he asked quietly.

I glanced at the two women, both lying semi-conscious against the chairs they'd been tied to. Striker was holding Marianne against him, his eyes betraying how worried he was. "I'll try and pour some of my blood directly into their throats. I don't know what else I can do," I responded softly to Ripley.

William stood up and I observed him warily as Rafe and Nick helped him walk towards me. He glanced at them, his features serious. "You'll need to stop me if I lose control," he warned. "Kill me, if you have to." He grabbed my arm and dropped his mouth to my skin, his hands gripping as though he would break the bones. I felt his fangs pierce my flesh and my knees buckled a little. Conal stepped forward.

"No, wait," I cautioned him. I spoke to William, touching my fingers to his filthy hair. "William, that's enough. You need to stop - William, *please*."

With visibly immense effort, William pulled away and the willpower it took for him to do so was evident. He stepped away slowly and Nick and Ralph gripped his arms, stopping him from collapsing.

Six down, four to go. I only hoped my blood supply lasted long enough. Lucas took a pace forward, his eyes on mine. Every emotion he was feeling - the overwhelming craving for my blood, the love he felt for me, the concern he felt in feeding from me - every single one was etched onto his face. He walked resolutely forward, leaning heavily against Marco and I held my arm out, fully aware this could all end in disaster. My blood was different for Lucas, more potent to him than anyone else in the group.

"I trust you, Lucas. You can control this."

He squeezed his eyes shut for a second and sheer terror crossed his handsome features. He gripped my arm and lowered his mouth, his lips forcefully dragging the blood from my veins. The light-headedness worsened as he fed and I was close to passing out. "Lucas, stop. Stop now." He continued to suck strongly and I whimpered, saw Conal moving forward. "Please, Lucas, *stop*!"

With a growl he forced himself to release me, closing his eyes as he swallowed the last of the blood. I breathed raggedly, knowing I'd lost far more blood than was safe but I swayed a little on my feet, determinedly walking towards where Holden sat.

He looked at me, his eyes filled with resolve and waved me away. "Please, try and feed Acenith and Marianne first, before it's too much for you. I terrified you in Montana; I don't deserve to be helped until everyone you love is safe."

I didn't argue, didn't feel well enough to debate the fact that he'd only been trying to protect me because he'd thought I was being attacked. I stumbled towards where Acenith and Marianne were slumped on the chairs. "Ralph, hold Acenith's mouth open for me." He did as I asked and held my arm over her mouth, squeezing at the wound to get as much blood as possible to drop between her lips. She swallowed convulsively, semi-conscious for a few seconds and I continued squeezing until I thought she had enough in her system.

Conal conferred with Ben as I worked, watching me with a worried frown. "How much blood do you think she's lost?"

Ben considered the question for a second or two while he mentally calculated. "At least a couple of pints."

"Is that gonna be too much?" Conal asked roughly.

"I don't know. But it will certainly weaken her."

Marco assisted me with Marianne, holding her mouth open as I squeezed my arm above it and she managed to swallow down some of my blood. She returned to consciousness for a moment or two and tried to smile weakly. "Charlotte... you came for us."

"I did," I agreed quietly. "Marianne, drink a little bit more, please." Obediently, she swallowed some more blood as it spilled from my arm. Conal was busy working with Nick to wrap Acenith in a piece of the blue velvet and when I stood back from Marianne, Ralph and Rafe moved forward to gently pick her up and wrap her in another piece of the material.

I turned to Holden who was leaning back on his chair, the ribs which were revealed through the long slash down his side looked slightly surreal and strongly nauseating. "We haven't been formally introduced," he said in a low voice, gasping as the very act of speaking caused him pain. "I'm Holden Striker."

"Hi, Holden. I'm Charlotte Duncan," I whispered back with a tiny smile. I held my hand out to him and he grasped it, drawing me slowly towards his mouth.

"Hell of a way to do an introduction," he gasped.

"Just drink and we'll have a better introduction later," I promised.

He did as I requested, his mouth firm and relentless against my arm. He released his grip abruptly and held his hands up in front of his face. "No, no more, Charlotte. My need is overwhelming, I don't dare drink more."

I pulled the Hjördis from my pocket and ran it over the skin on my arm, watching the wound close and heal over. I swayed a little, unsteady on my feet and Conal caught me, grasping me against his chest. "Charlotte!"

I shook my head, trying to clear the lightheaded feeling, but I'd lost too much blood. I had to hold it together though, all these people were dependent on me and I couldn't let them down. I straightened up, using sheer force of will to get moving again. "Let's go."

Nick picked Acenith up in his arms and Conal collected Marianne. "Wow, she's light," he commented mildly. The rest assembled into a group, with the werewolves and shape shifters supporting the vampires. I was frightened to death now, worrying how we could possibly make it out of this place when the strong were completely overwhelmed supporting the weak. Besides myself, there wasn't anyone spare to fight if things took a turn for the worst. And I was certain the worst wasn't too far away.

"What now?" Conal asked quietly.

I held the Katchet in my left hand and the Hjördis in my right. "Now, we get out of this place."

I led them back to the door I'd entered through and leaned my ear against it, listening for noises. It appeared the passageway was empty and I unlocked and opened the door. The passage, damp and cold, was vacant and I motioned the others forward.

Nick was striding behind me and he whispered near my ear. "Charlotte, how do you know we are *actually* invisible?"

We'd reached the end of the passage and I listened at the door, heard the soft murmur of voices. "Looks like we're about to find out."

A swift conversation with the spirits confirmed what I suspected. There was only one way out - and the vampires had it covered. They were waiting out in the first large room I'd been brought into, knowing it was the only way we had to escape. "Damn it," I muttered unhappily. "There's a reception party. We need a diversion."

"What would you suggest?" Conal asked softly.

"Shut up, I'm thinking."

"Do you realize how often you've said that to me today?" he muttered.

"That's because you're painfully annoying."

"Always, Sugar. Always."

I closed my eyes, ignoring him as I focused once again on the spirits. When I opened my eyes, I turned back to the group. "Alright, I'm going to create the diversion. When it happens, I want everyone through the door and out into the courtyard." I glanced at my watch, confirmed it was only four thirty, less than half an hour since I'd last checked. It seemed as if much more time should have passed, but I was grateful to discover I was wrong. The castle remained open until five, which meant the courtyard would still be filled with the happy, oblivious-to-danger tourists. "The gates are right opposite the door you'll escape through, don't stop for anything, go as fast as you can and get out of those gates."

"What sort of diversion is this?" Nick whispered.

"A messy one." I turned to the wall and swapped the Katchet for the Hjördis in my right hand. "I need more light," I whispered and Phelan reached for one of the torches on the wall. Passing it back towards me, Nick held it near the wall so I could see. I pushed the Hjördis against the rock and marked a sigil. The others waited patiently whilst I finished, though the tension was tangible in the narrow hallway.

"What now?" Ralph whispered.

The ground began to shake below us, a rumbling noise that penetrated from deep below the ground. Some of the torches sputtered and burnt themselves out, plunging us into semi-darkness. "Think of it as a baby earthquake," I announced quietly. I cracked the door open, watching as the vampires in the room looked around the walls in confusion. One of the massive tapestries was waving backward and forwards, as though it was being whipped by a heavy breeze, before one of the fastenings broke and it fell to the tiled floor. The ground roiled and rumbled beneath our feet and I decided we'd waited as long as we could. I wrenched open the door and hissed to the others. "Go!"

I held back, prepared to attack if it looked like the invisibility sigil wasn't working and the vampires could see our group. It became obvious straight away that the vampires couldn't see anyone, although they lifted their heads as the scents passed them, they were more concerned with the apparent earthquake that shook the room. I caught sight of Odin, standing alongside Hyperion. Arawn was nowhere to be seen. I stumbled a little as a yawning chasm opened in the ground beneath my feet and leaped across it lightly. I ran across the room as the others made it to the door and Ralph Torres threw it open, still supporting Lucas with his left arm. This was the moment of truth, as sunshine filtered through the open doorway. I held my breath as one by one, the Tines were carried or stumbled out into the daylight. It appeared they'd received enough of my blood to keep them safe and my stress levels decreased accordingly. I honestly hadn't been sure they'd taken enough blood, hadn't even been certain what the spirits had advised was correct, but it appeared we'd done it.

Following them through the courtyard, I turned back momentarily and saw Arawn standing beside another vampire at the doorway. Their eyes were searching the courtyard, but Epi and Conal had been right - they wouldn't risk outing themselves to the tourists.

I caught up with the rest of our group and sprinted through the huge entrance gates, dodging and swerving past the tourists. One of the horses which had been pulling a carriage of tourists up from the village below reared, his nostrils flaring and I wondered if he could sense us, even though we were still apparently invisible. I was certain if the invisibility had worn off, the tourists would have reacted and so far, they didn't seem to notice a group of seventeen men and women, most of them semi-naked and wrapped in dark blue velvet, racing down the cobblestoned road. "Follow me."

I sprinted to where the portal had opened, finding the marking on the grass where I'd first appeared. I dropped to my knees and used the Hjördis to mark the ground with the pentagram Epi had taught me. It shimmered for a moment, and then opened in a golden wave of light.

"What is *that*?" Ben asked.

"Our ticket home."

"We can… travel through that?" Lucas asked doubtfully.

"It's a portal. Completely safe, if ever-so-slightly nauseating." I pressed Conal forward, glancing back towards the high parapets of the castle. "Time to go home." Conal stepped into the portal, disappearing in the golden light with Marianne cradled in his arms.

"You did this?" Striker asked incredulously. He was leaning against Rafe, barely able to support himself and Ripley was clinging to Rafe's other arm.

"Yep. It was my only way of getting here. Remember, I'm the girl without a passport." I gave Rafe a gentle push and he stepped through the portal with Striker and Ripley.

In small groups, they all stepped through the golden light, Nick carrying Acenith, Marco supporting Lucas. Ralph was carrying Rowena on his back, his arm around Ben to support his weight. Phelan had Gwynn in his arms and was dragging William along beside him, giving him as much support as he could. Holden came last, struggling along by himself.

When Holden disappeared, I stepped into the portal, turning for one last look at Sfantu Drâghici.

A lone figure stood by the gates, his appearance chilling me to the bone. I tried to turn back, to stop the power of the portal from drawing me back to America, but it was too late and I lost sight of him as the portal drew me away.

To be continued....

Dear reader,

We hope you enjoyed reading *Knowledge* Quickening. Please take a moment to leave a review, even if it's a short one. Your opinion is important to us.

The story continues in *Knowledge Hurts*

Discover more books by D.S. Williams at https://www.nextchapter.pub/authors/ds-williams

Want to know when one of our books is free or discounted? Join the newsletter at http://eepurl.com/bqqB3H

Best regards,

D.S. Williams and the Next Chapter Team

ABOUT THE AUTHOR

Wife and mother to four demanding young adults, D.S. Williams started writing at the age of five, when life was simpler and her stories really didn't need to make sense. When you're five, 'happily ever after' always ends the story and how you got there? Well, that didn't matter so much.

An extreme introvert, D.S. Williams has created her own worlds to exist in, found friends among her characters and traveled the Earth from the safety of her laptop keyboard.

D.S. Williams enjoys writing (obviously), reading (voraciously) and making lists (obsessively). She's enjoyed a lifelong addiction to foods starting with 'ch' - cheesecake, chocolate and chips - and when it comes to books, she loves a multitude of genres and authors.

She shares her life with her beloved husband of twenty nine years, the Gang of Four and the current furry residents, Tuppence the Groodle and Angus the Bull Mastiff.

CPSIA information can be obtained
at www.ICGtesting.com
Printed in the USA
LVHW050502041120
670657LV00004B/496